Telling Moments

Telling Moments

Autobiographical Lesbian Short Stories

Edited by
LYNDA HALL

The University of Wisconsin Press

The University of Wisconsin Press
1930 Monroe Street
Madison, Wisconsin 53711

www.wisc.edu/wisconsinpress/

3 Henrietta Street
London WC2E 8LU, England

5   4   3   2   1

Text and jacket design by Mira Nenonen
Printed in the United States of America

Library of Congress Cataloging-in-
Publication Data

Telling moments: autobiographical lesbian
short stories / edited by Lynda Hall.
p. cm.
ISBN 0-299-19114-1
1. Lesbians—Biography. 2. Lesbians' writings. 3. Autobiographies. I. Hall, Lynda.
HQ75.3 .T45 2003
305.48'9664'092—dc21

2003008905

Terrace Books, a division of the University
of Wisconsin Press, takes its name from the
Memorial Union Terrace, located at the
University of Wisconsin–Madison. Since its
inception in 1907, the Union has provided
a venue for students and faculty to debate
art, music, politics, and the issues of the
day. It is a place where theater, music,
drama, dance, outdoor activities, and major
speakers are made available to the campus
and the community. To learn more about
the Union, visit www.union.wisc.edu.

Contents

Our Mothers

Our Children

Our Lives: Bodies, Work, Travel, et al.

Acknowledgments

I owe special gratitude to the twenty-four writers who contributed their unique stories to this collection. Their generous and thoughtful responses to my initial inquiries about interest in this project and the stories they submitted made editing the collection truly a labor of love. This project was put on hold for one year due to my brother's battle with cancer, and I thank the writers for their patience and support during that time. Many thanks to Mary Cappello, Sima Rabinowitz, and Ruthann Robson for their insightful comments on drafts of the introduction and their assistance in many other ways. My never-ending and deep gratitude to Karla Jay for her story, for the many contacts she provided, and for her continuing belief in my endeavors. Warmest thanks to my professors in graduate school: Susan Bennett, Helen Buss, Jeanne Perreault, Susan Rudy, and Susan Stratton. They offer continual intellectual insight, challenge, and support. I gratefully acknowledge the students in my classes. The daily demonstrations of their love for the beauty of language and their willingness to engage in thoughtful textual analysis encourage my trust in the worthwhile nature of the teaching profession and increase my confidence in the future that we are building together. And, as always, there are no words adequate to express my appreciation to my partner, Kathy, for the life that we share.

I thank many at the University of Wisconsin Press for shepherding this collection through its various stages.

Grateful acknowledgment is made to Ronsdale Press for permission to reprint Marie-Claire Blais's short story "Tenderness." This story first appeared in her collection *The Exile The Sacred Travellers* (translated by Nigel Spencer; Vancouver: Ronsdale Press, 2000).

Grateful acknowledgment is made to Lesléa Newman for permission to reprint "Private Lessons" from *She Loves Me, She Loves Me Not* ©2002 Lesléa Newman (Los Angeles: Alyson Publications).

Autobiographical Lesbian Short Stories

LYNDA HALL

Introduction

Re-Membering Her: A-Mazing
Space of Lesbian Writings

elling Moments: Autobiographical Lesbian Short Stories provides
a vigorous and moving and "real" window into lesbian lives. The
stories are by self-identified lesbians who represent a diversity of age,
race, ethnicity, class, education, and geography. Each story includes
some element of autobiography. The stories are current, and many provide a retrospective analysis that demonstrates the inextricability of past
and present. A unique aspect of the collection is the short section that
follows most of the stories in which the author comments on the autobiographical nature of her story. Called "In Reflection," and written
perhaps a year or two after the story was written, it offers an often profound analysis of the writing experience and motivations for writing.
Photographs of the authors add a further personal dimension. The
Bionotes section provides information on their other publications and
endeavors that I hope will promote their writings and attract new
readers.

Given this diversity, *Telling Moments* deserves a place among other
collections currently in demand. They include *The Mammoth Book of
Lesbian Short Stories* (1999), edited by Emma Donoghue, an amazing
collection of fictional short stories about lesbians, by women writers
"of all persuasions," to quote Donoghue, that covers three decades.
Another is *The Vintage Book of International Lesbian Fiction* (1999),
edited by Naomi Holoch and Joan Nestle, with stories by women from
twenty-seven countries. *Does Your Mama Know? An Anthology of Black
Lesbian Coming Out Stories* (1998), edited by Lisa C. Moore, includes
personal stories, poems, interviews, and essays describing the complex
experiences of black lesbians. Most of the stories in *Circa 2000: Lesbian
Fiction at the Millennium* (2000), edited by Terry Wolverton and Robert Drake, were published in the last ten years.

Why here? Why now? Those questions reverberate in my mind
as I begin the process of writing the introduction to this collection of
autobiographical short stories. It is not just that we have entered a new

millennium, or that I truly think that lesbian realities will start to be more "real" and thus be in less dire need of being affirmed through writing (certainly not). The "here" and the "now"—the right time and place—are confirmed for me by the rich and deeply evocative lesbian memoirs and multigenre works that have recently been published. Most touching for me personally are Mary Cappello's stunning *Night Bloom: A Memoir*, Karla Jay's *Tales of the Lavender Menace: A Memoir of Liberation*, Gloria Anzaldúa's *Interviews/Entrevistas*, Minnie Bruce Pratt's *Walking Back up Depot Street*, and Carmelita Tropicana's *I, Carmelita Tropicana: Performing between Cultures*. Each of these works, published at the end of the twentieth century, concretely speaks to the power of lesbian voices and presence.

I will not attempt to address individually the content of the twenty-four stories collected here, since each is a discrete and illuminating piece of writing that deserves to be read on its own terms. Several common themes are apparent, however, and provide the organization of the collection into four sections: "Our Loves," "Our Mothers," "Our Children," and finally, a miscellaneous group called "Our Lives: Bodies, Work, Travel, et al." The first section deals with "coming out" and early frustration over the inability to accept lesbian sexual desires in a homophobic society, along with first loves, first experiences, and breakups. The importance of the relationship with the mother is a dynamic in the second section. The third section offers views of lesbians' relationships with their children in our changing society and the complications that arise. Several writers represent the implications of racism in combination with homophobia and describe the impact of familial relationships and workplace dynamics. Race and ethnicity are factors in twelve of the stories. The writers explore such topics as travel, illness, parties, relationships with neighbors, food, moving, and learning to deal with aging.

The issues and emotions these lesbian writers address may not seem extraordinary at first, but they imbue their stories with language of such sensitivity and poignancy and downright immediacy that the reader is drawn in. The humor that underlies many of the stories speaks to their strength in surviving. The writers evince a new, liberated, stronger sense of self than usually appears in lesbian fiction. They also address social issues that arise from living in a more liberal culture, such as lesbian parenting, lesbian students relating to openly lesbian professors, and lesbian couples moving into and integrating into a new community.

The postmodern interweaving of genres, particularly represented by other works published by these contributors, naturally led to my desire to work on a collection of lesbian autobiographical fiction. The enthusiastic response that I received from the authors I approached to participate in this collection immediately confirmed my faith in the value of just such an anthology. First, I invited writers whose works have inspired me through the years. Many of them are included in my edited collection *Lesbian Self-Writing: The Embodiment of Experience* (2000), in which they discuss the process of writing in relation to the "self." They in turn gave me the names of other writers—new and experienced—to invite to join the project. Thus, their combined voices represent established writers and new writers.

One of my first negotiations with each writer involved arriving at an understanding of the relationship of autobiography to fiction. As readers will discover, only the writers themselves know the extent to which their pieces are autobiographical, but there is an element of truth in them all. Stories provide memories, and memories offer keys to the past. Providing a "history"—a past—in a society where lesbians are still often dismissed in the present, and nearly totally erased from history, is a major step in a revision of what is known and what is real.

The historical perspective is of value not only for those who are lesbians, or potential lesbians, but for society in general. One of the goals of fictionalized autobiographical writings is to create a reality of the past for both the self and potential community. In an interview, Mary Cappello has directly addressed the need for diverse forms of writing: "Memoir makes sense to me as a form for queer writers because I think we are very much engaged in a collective remembering, and the kind of remembering we're doing, which goes against the grain of dominant ideology, requires new forms" ("On Writing Memoir" 23). A prime impetus for this project is to facilitate the "collective remembering" that these stories encourage. Addressing events that span lifetimes, the writers embody the notion that the past is always with us, shaping and framing present efforts and opening possibilities for the future. Revisiting past events, often imaginatively re-creating them and taking agency in the process, grounds autobiographical fiction to a certain extent.

Gloria Anzaldúa has spoken of the potential of language to create reality and extends this creation into future possibilities: "Identity is very much a fictive construction: You compose it from what's out there, what the culture gives you, and what you resist in the culture. This identity also has a type of projection into a future identity. . . . You reshape yourself. First you get that self-image in your head and then you project that out into the world." She goes on to describe a writing process that valorizes the act of self-composition: "Then I took all this knowledge a step further, to reality. I realized that if I can compose this text and if I can compose my identity, then I can also compose reality out there. It all has to do with the angle of perception" (*Interviews* 269–70). Anzaldúa's observations on the concrete use of the writing process to "compose" the self recall Mary Cappello's words in *Night Bloom:* "How long I sit at my writing desk composing myself, composing my family" (249).

Theorizing a fictive construction of identity and the power of agency enacted in this process, Anzaldúa connects autobiographical writing to resistance to cultural prescriptions. She names the dynamics that frequently occur in lesbian authors' works. Her analysis of the relationship between autobiography and truth or reality reverberates in theoretical texts. Discussing the intertextuality of fiction and autobiography, Liz Stanley asserts that "in the last decade of close analytic attention to the poetics of autobiography there has been ample recognition of the role played by fictions within the apparent facts of autobiography, of the genre's *creation* rather than representation of self" (*Auto/Biographical I* 60). In terms of my present research work and exploration of lesbian autobiography and memoir, Stanley's observations contribute to an analysis of "poetics of autobiography" and the "role played by fictions" in lesbian self-writing.

Anzaldúa also speaks of the intersection of history and autobiographical writing. She interweaves the past, the present, and the future when she extends her discussion of the writer-reader dynamic to her reception at poetry readings. Anzaldúa explains that the audience "reads" her and she experiences pleasure from seeing the expressions on their faces—from reading their faces. She emphasizes, "A lot of my poems, stories and essays (which I call *autohistorias*) are about reading—not just reading as in the act of reading words on a page, but also 'reading' reality and reflecting on that process and the process of writing in general" (*Interviews* 255). "Reading reality" occurs through the writing process, particularly when the realities may represent lives that society has condemned or repressed. "Autohistoria," she explains, comes from " 'auto' for self-writing, and 'historia' for history—as in collective, personal, cultural, and racial history—as well as for fiction, a story you make up. History is fiction because it's made up, usually made up by the people who rule" (242). The stories in this collection powerfully partake in a revision of our largely heterosexualized history, particularly in terms of giving space and voice to lesbian lives. In autobiographical writings, the writer-reader-writer dynamic accrues a special significance. As the lesbian writer "reads" her own experience and puts it down in words, the reader acts as witness to the events described, potentially finding valorization by identifying with similar experiences, or having new worlds of possibility opened up.

The contributors to *Telling Moments* cross boundaries of race, ethnicity, class, geography, and age. They insist on the intricate imbrication of all these aspects of their selves; no one part is privileged over the other, while each part is exposed as dominant in different life experiences. Anzaldúa states, "I struggle with naming without fragmenting, without excluding. Containing and closing off the naming is the central issue of this piece of writing. . . . Identity flows between, over, aspects of a person. Identity is a river—a process" (*This Bridge Called My Back* 252–53). These writers resist the self-fragmentation created by the restrictive and damaging prescriptive roles that each individual is expected to play—scripts that are laden with heterosexual expectations. Their frequent, clear acknowledgment of their active resistance to heteronormativity indicates an early consciousness of not meeting social expectations. Several writers record the confusion and lack of understanding an adolescent often feels when her desires are not validated anywhere in society. The resulting need to "act" straight appears to frame lives into fraught performances that deny original desires and produce self-doubt and self-condemnation. Maya Chowdhry explains, "I began writing to stay above water; I wrote to survive teenage years: crushes, exams, obsessional cooking—my poetry was a life-line. When my poetry was published I was asked to read at the launch—to perform my life. It slipped easily off the tongue: I had had years of performing answers to society's questions about my identities; I had written about the questions, searching for my true identity. Readings became performances, multi-media shows, commissions. Suddenly my identity was captured, fractured, sliced and served to audiences and I was a 'live' challenge to myself" ("Living Performance" 10).

In a spiraling dynamic, writing provides witness for others and creates community where no community may be evident. While today's media is rife with news and the entertainment value of lesbian lives, it is amazing how many young people with lesbian desires still articulate the lack of role models and the social void that they perceive surrounds them. Many of the writers in this collection stage their lives in words and acts of survival. They literally and symbolically put their bodies on the line in a performatively embodied and autobiographically fictionalized "telling" of memories of some part of their life stories. Performing the "self" is particularly grounded in the autobiographical nature of the works of several solo performance artists. With this connection in mind, I invited three performance artists to contribute to this collection. The works by Carmelita Tropicana, Peggy Shaw, and Maya Chowdhry are richly evocative. Chowdhry notes, "I use my own life-stories as a basis for my text; as a lesbian and a Black woman the conflicts which produce the most challenging material for me and my audiences are around my identity. . . . As performers we delve deep into all our relationships, performing our lives" ("Living Performance" 9). Delving into past life-stories requires an intricate play with memory, often revealing the fact that memories are comprised of discrete moments of time, and each revisitation of a moment results in its re-creation and alteration.

Carmelita Tropicana's piece in this anthology, "Out Takes in Cuba," is based on a trip to her country of birth when she was an adult. She recalls other memories from this trip in her solo performance *Milk of Amnesia*. Her comments on this production equally inform an analysis of the relationship between memory and the "act" of memory encompassed by autobiographical fiction. Tropicana recalls, "I once read that the act of remembering is like Xerox copying. You remember a memory, and then the next time you remember it's the memory of the memory you are remembering, and after that it's the memory of the memory of the memory, and so on. My trip to Cuba as an adult in 1993 brought back many memories and gave me the topic for my solo *Milk of Amnesia*. *Milk* was conceived as if inside the brain; when you tapped a certain area, a memory would unfold" (*I, Carmelita* xxii). She describes an "act" of memory that is unending, and each recollection of a specific event takes on new resonance. The act of memory becomes part of the process of life itself and is directly facilitated by the writing process, in which different sensory experiences in the present trigger memories of the past. Just as trips to certain locations trigger memories of the past, autobiographical writings produce a similar journey into the old and the new.

The many revisions that some of the writers made to their original pieces over the last few months, either adding more autobiographical detail or altering specific facts, testify to the fraught relationship between the past and the present, and the imbrication of truth and fiction—the indefinable borders of what is revealed and what is imaginatively changed through the artistic process. These writers venture into the contested space of autobiography that is often denigrated in an academic environment where the embodied and authoritative "self" is displaced by disembodied "subjectivities" and where self-writing is frequently dismissed as self-indulgent.

The last and most crucial issue that I want to address is the role of language in creating reality, a factor that generates much of the excitement surrounding lesbian autobiographical writings. Anzaldúa suggests that "language attempts to create reality. Not just shape it but create it, not just mold reality but create it and displace it" (*Interviews* 94). The dramatic impact of language and social prescriptions on the individual often triggers a desire to write, assume voice, and "talk back" to negative stereotypes and homophobic and racist remarks. Many of these writings evince political motivations for social change. Anzaldúa observes, "The world I create in the writing compensates for what the real world does not give me. By writing I put order in the world, give it a handle, so I can grasp it. . . . I write to record what others erase when I speak, to rewrite the stories others have miswritten about me, about you" (*This Bridge* 169).

Gesturing toward the significant role that language plays in shaping the "self" and the world around us, several of the writers include other languages in their stories. Rini Das uses Hindi words and defines them. Carmelita Tropicana, Barbara Bryce Morris, Gloria Anzaldúa, Jewelle Gomez, and Donna Allegra include Spanish phrases. Often, they connect the Spanish words with memories. Anzaldúa, along with Tropicana and Gomez, names the political motivations that also provoke the bilingual process in resistance to English domination. The rich texture and cultural traditions represented create a tapestry that invites the reader into their lives.

While many of the authors make their living from their writing, others perform, teach, or work in diverse other fields, from bureaucracy to construction. Their stories range from the intensely personal to an account of a chance happening in life. In each case, the writer combines a love of language with the desire to give some aspect of her life a fictional perspective. The stories provocatively juxtapose life and literature, selfhood and textuality. They invite readers to investigate and enjoy the "telling moments" of their lives. They represent lives lived, and lives that evoke retrospection, and that is, perhaps, the most that can be expected. A "collective remembering" evolves from their stories, which in turn facilitates a possible and exciting future. Perhaps that is the most exciting aspect of the collection—the future that is possible.

Works Cited

Anzaldúa, Gloria. *Interviews/Entrevistas*. New York: Routledge, 2000.
———. *This Bridge Called My Back: Writings by Radical Women of Color*. Ed. Cherríe Moraga and Gloria Anzaldúa. New York: Kitchen Table Press, 1983.
Cappello, Mary. *Night Bloom: A Memoir*. Boston: Beacon, 1998.

———. "On Writing Memoir: An Interview with Mary Cappello." *Dickinson Magazine* (Winter 1999): 23.

Chowdhry, Maya. "Living Performance." In *Acts of Passion: Sexuality, Gender and Performance,* edited by Nina Rapi and Maya Chowdhry, 9–20. New York: Harrington Park Press, 1998.

Stanley, Liz. *The Auto/Biographical I: The Theory and Practice of Feminist Auto/Biography.* Manchester: Manchester University Press, 1992.

Troyano, Alina [Carmelita Tropicana]. *I, Carmelita Tropicana: Performing between Cultures,* edited by Chon A. Noriega. Boston: Beacon, 2000.

Our Loves

Gloria Anzaldúa

PHOTOGRAPH BY ANNIE F. VALVA

GLORIA E. ANZALDÚA

Swallowing Fireflies / Tragando Luciérnagas

Prieta first saw her at the student union. No makeup, pelo negro pulled back so tightly it gave her eyes an exotic look. Tall, bordering on skinny, she wore a blue cotton dress to midcalf. Graceful and poised, she seemed to glide when she walked past Prieta on the way to the pizza line. Her look of aloofness and mystery drew Prieta's eye.

Prieta shoved off the wall she was leaning against and sauntered after her. She got in line behind her and "accidentally" bumped her arm. "Oh, discúlpame. I'm so sorry."

"That's all right, this place is crowded."

"Hey, you're a Chicana," Prieta said.

"I don't use that term for myself. I'm Mexican American."

They ordered slices of pizza and picked up their trays.

"It's noisy here. Why don't we eat out in the patio," Prieta said.

They walked out and sat at a table in the shade of a tall encino tree. Prieta talked about her art classes and of how frustrated she was with her instructors trying to shove European aesthetics down her throat and discouraging her from expressing her Mexican roots and traditions. Suel talked about trying to get her public school to include Mexican American material in the classes. Suel was twelve years older and doing graduate work. Both were frustrated with being in a gringo university filled with caras güeras in a city where Chicanos lived on the other side of the river and were not encouraged to go to college.

As the fierce summer sun slanted down they lost the shade. The light shimmered on Suel's skin, turning it into a luminous glow. Prieta watched the movement of Suel's throat as she swallowed and the graceful windmilling of her hands as she talked. Keeping each other afloat with slices of cold watermelon and iced drinks, platicaron de sus familias.

I do not italicize Spanish words because such use of italics reinforces English language centrality and denormalizes the Spanish words. For translation of Spanish terms see the glossary at the end of the story.

Prieta spoke of her close relationship with her mamagrande and her primo hermano, Teté. Suel said her mother was very religious and strict. Suel was a devout Catholic whereas Prieta was delving into nagualismo and indigenous deities.

When Prieta mentioned reading Judy Grahn, a lesbian poet, Suel looked uncomfortable and said, "I don't read those kinds of writers."

Finally the heat drove them into the air-conditioned commons where they talked for another three hours. When they tired of the noise and of sitting on wrought iron chairs, they left and walked across the green, well-kept lawns of the Austin campus.

They descended a ravine to Waller Creek, which wound around the sprawling University of Texas campus. The shrill song of cicadas was deafening. Shucking off their sandals, they plopped down on a flat white limestone rock and dangled their legs over the creek. Prieta inched closer to Suel and held her breath, but Suel didn't move away. The water gurgled over the sound of their voices. Prieta leaned over and peered into the green pool formed by a dam of round rocks. She stared at their reflection on the water. Inching closer to Suel she "accidentally" brushed her breast, a movida she'd picked up from the vatos. Their eyes locked. Heat seared Prieta's skin. Before Suel dropped her gaze Prieta glimpsed a flash in her eyes. It winked out like the tiny spark of a firefly.

Suel stirred, plunged her feet into the cool water. Their twin reflections rippled, fragmented, and dissolved. Cupping water in her palm, Prieta raised it to her flushed face. She fanned away los mosquitos hovering over them. Self-conscious and shy, they sat in silence, listening to the trickling water and the croaking frogs. From upstream the cooing call of palomas blancas serenaded them. The sounds of their breathing seemed inordinately loud. Surrounded by the smell of ferns and moss and decaying leaves, they stared at the shafts of sunlight as afternoon turned into dusk and the fireflies came out and lit the creek like tiny flying Christmas lights.

One summer day turned into another. Prieta wore a secret smile, the corner of her lips at a perpetual lift. She flitted around the edges of Suel's calm presence, eased into her tranquility as though slipping into cool water on a hot day. Every now and then a tremor would flash through, leaving ripples on Prieta's flesh, as it did the Sunday Prieta asked Suel what she saw in her.

Suel was polishing her nails a bright red. She raised luminous eyes to Prieta, then lowered them and said, "I like it that you surprise me. I never know what you're going to say or do. You have such strong feelings. Sometimes they . . . make me uncomfortable."

"Ay, mijita, I think we fit well together. You're quiet and reserved, I'm talkative and crazy about you. See, we complement each other," Prieta grinned.

The corners of Suel's lips lifted; she shrugged and smiled.

It was so hot the asphalt softened and stuck to their sandals. Prieta said, "Qué calor. Why don't we go on a picnic and cool off at Lake Travis, Suel?"

Suel remained silent.

"Andale, Suel. Let's make a day of it. I'll bring the food. I know a spot that's hidden away. It's very private. The water there is nice and deep."

"I'm scared of getting in over my head," Suel replied.

"I'll get you a life preserver. And I'd be there to give you mouth-to-mouth . . ."

"Uh-uh," Suel interrupted. "Besides, I have to go to mass."

"Bueno," Prieta said, trying to hide her disappointment. She knew that if she suggested going after mass Suel would find another excuse. She had to ease off, else Suel would bolt.

Prieta pulled out a roll of Life Savers and offered one to her.

Suel laughed, shook her head, and said, "Too sweet for my taste."

Next day the bright red polish had disappeared from the nails of Suel's tanned slender hands.

The summer session would end en dos semanas. Each would pack up and, in their separate cars, drive three hundred miles through the rolling hill country of central Texas to the flat delta del valle near the border. The more Prieta thought about the sixty-nine miles between their two south Texas pueblos, the more she wanted to tether Suel to her wrist and the more she felt Suel slipping away. She needed to talk to Suel about what was happening to them and make plans for seeing each other when they got home. Suel had said that her family was traditional, conservative, and very religious. Prieta wondered if they'd think it strange for dos mujeres to be so close. And they were close, so close Prieta felt they didn't need words to convey their feelings. Their eyes said it all. But time was running out.

The two had been up all night writing papers in Suel's room. Prieta's head felt hollow. Not just from too much coffee and too little sleep but from being in Suel's presence. Prieta squirmed in her chair. Suel lifted her ojos luceros and looked at her. Prieta felt as if she'd swallowed the light. It surged through her veins, filling all the secret places and making her body vibrate. When away from Suel, Prieta craved the constant euphoria that swamped her when they were together. At night after hours in Suel's company, Prieta would lie awake esperando el amanecer, anticipating meeting Suel for breakfast.

Prieta stretched her hands over her head and arched her spine. Prieta stared at Suel leaning against the headboard of the bed, her long legs crossed at the ankles. She wanted to ask Suel to rub her sore back but was afraid of frightening her away. What she really wanted to ask was if she could spend the night. Now, that would really spook her.

Prieta left her books and paper and stretched out on the bed alongside Suel. They lay lado a lado, arms and thighs touching. Where Suel's skin brushed hers una lumbrita spread through Prieta. She could feel the boundaries of their separate skins dissolving in the heat. The tousled sheets chafed, her skin felt prickly. She scooted closer, barely resisting the urge to place her nose against Suel's neck and breathe in her sweet-smelling skin.

Prieta opened her mouth to speak, then hesitated, afraid of how Suel would react if she broached the subject. She remembered the tiny spark she'd seen in Suel's eyes when they'd met at the start of the summer session. Since then, she'd seen esa luzecita de luciérnaga flickering on and off in Suel's midnight eyes.

Prieta stroked the soft skin on the inside of Suel's elbow. Suel gave a little jump and then relaxed. Prieta cradled Suel's hand palm up and slowly traced the lifeline. "Do you . . . ah, want to talk about it?" Prieta asked.

Suel looked up briefly, then lowered her head to the teaching manual.

Prieta searched for words to describe the air that breathed her when she was with Suel, the air that breathed between them like a live animal cuando se sentaban juntitas.

Prieta thought back to the second week after they'd met. She remembered waiting at their usual meeting place for Suel to get out of class. She sat by Littlefield Fountain staring at the three bronze horses that reared on webbed feet, muscles rippling. Suel walked out of Parlin Hall and sat down beside her. She smoothed her blue dress under her legs, looking serene and cool. Prieta couldn't take her eyes off the cleavage of her bare toes and the swell of the bluish veins along her calves and feet. Behind Suel water spouted from the nostrils of the middle horse, which reared to unseat the rider pulling the reins and jerking the caballo's head back. Being sprayed by the gushing water didn't seem to cool Prieta. Sweat drenched her armpits and dampened the crotch of her loose cotton pants.

Thinking back on their conversation, Prieta realized that only she had actually talked about her ex-girlfriends. When she'd pressed Suel about her novio, her lover, Suel had dropped her gesturing hands to her lap and had looked behind her at the man astride the horse, mane in his iron fist.

"I want to talk about us, Suel," Prieta said.

"About what?" Suel glanced at her out of the corner of her eye, the same frightened eyeball side-glance the bronze horse at Littlefield Fountain gave its rider.

"Don't look away, mija." Prieta steeled herself and asked, "How do you feel about me? I've made it pretty clear how I feel about you."

"What are you talking about?" Suel's voice rose. She pulled her hand out of Prieta's palm and averted her face.

Prieta felt the beginning of a hairline crack between them. "Tú sabes. Don't you feel it every time we look at each other?"

"Feel what?" Suel sat up.

"You know." Prieta propped up on her elbows. "All these erotic feelings, and how we want to touch each other and be with each other all the time. You know I want to see you when we return to the valley."

Suel snapped her head around and stared at her. She saw Suel's eyes go flat, like Medusa's, freezing her in place. Suel edged off her bed. Not looking at Prieta, she gathered her books and shoved them into her bag. She hurried out of her apartment, gently closing the door behind her.

Prieta's heart fisted in her chest. Throat prickling, she swallowed. She swung off the bed and, on shaky legs, went to the kitchen and gulped down a glass of water. She paced around the room. Stopping before the window, she peered out, hoping to see Suel coming back. After a long time she left the window and started pacing again. She stared at el Sagrado Corazón de Jesús hanging on the wall. Holding two fingers over his naked bleeding heart, Jesucristo looked down on her.

A small blown-glass figurine de una palomita lay on top of the shelf. She picked up the fragile dove and stroked the tiny wings, thinking of all the signals Suel had given her that showed her feelings went beyond mere friendship. She hadn't misread the look in her eyes, those shy touches, had she? Prieta had been blatant about being a marimacha. So why had Suel acted shocked just now?

Prieta barely restrained herself from going out and combing the campus until she found Suel. She'd probably gone to one of the libraries.

But which one? If she'd gone into the stacks of the graduate library Prieta would never find her. Suel wouldn't like it if she tracked her down. She'd wait. Sooner or later Suel had to come back to her place to sleep. Where else could she sleep? Prieta sat on the bed and picked up Suel's discarded shirt lying on the bed and brought it up to her face and breathed deeply.

The tower bell tolled, jerking Prieta from her thoughts. She pushed her hair out of her face and glanced at the bedside clock. Two hours since Suel had walked out. Suel wouldn't appreciate finding her asleep on her bed. She'd call Suel when she got to her dorm.

Next morning, after getting no response to her phone calls, Prieta walked over and knocked on Suel's door. She wasn't home. Shoulders hunched, Prieta turned away. She went to all their usual haunts: the commons, the fountain, Guadalupe Street—the drag, as it was called. Again she knocked on Suel's door, thumping hard in case Suel was asleep. No answer. Prieta revisited their hangouts, questioned everyone who knew them. No one had seen Suel.

As Prieta trudged down la barranca to Waller Creek and their pool the mournful calls of las palomas blancas were bittersweet. She sat under the green canopy and watched the light filtering through the tree branches make dancing shadows in the water. She was too agitated to enjoy the beauty. She wondered if Suel had been barricaded in her apartment all this time, refusing to answer her phone.

After calling and knocking on her door for two more days, Prieta went to the registrar's office. There she learned that Suel had left because of a family emergency, without finishing her coursework. Prieta's heart sank and the rest of her body followed it.

Next morning Prieta called Suel. Maybe she had come back. A recording said the phone was no longer in service. She forced herself to brush her teeth, get dressed, go to classes, eat. Her appetite had completely deserted her; she cinched her belt tighter by another notch. She had no interest in going out or seeing other people. All she wanted to do was stay in bed and brood. The scorching Texas sun chilled her flesh. She lost track of time and did not notice how she moved through the world or how it moved through her. It was worse during the night. She lay awake in the darkness counting the hours. She'd get up to pee and, while sitting on the john, smoke cigarette after cigarette.

On the afternoon of the last day of the summer session Prieta walked down to Waller Creek, took off her sandals, and sat on their rock, startling a frog into jumping away. As she stared down at her reflection in the water, Suel's face appeared beside hers. She dipped a foot in the water. The ripples distorted her perception, Suel's face disappeared. A light blinked across her mind. The distortion in the water was a sign of . . . Before she completed the thought, Prieta picked up a stone and tossed it into the pool. As the ripples radiated out, she pushed the thought with its ray of light down into the water.

She remembered the last time they'd come here. As they'd waded along the creek bed Suel had splashed her, drenching her shirt. The shock of cool water hardened Prieta's nipples. She looked down at them, then looked at Suel to find her ogling them. Suel looked up. Their eyes locked. The smile on Suel's face waned.

Una luciérnaga flew into Prieta's hair, startling her out of her reverie. She combed her fingers through her hair and captured the bug, cupping it in her hand. It was about half an inch long and had light organs on the underside of the belly and a soft dark brown body marked with orange. It crawled on her hand, tickling her palm. She watched as more and more fireflies flitted down the creek. The frog she had chased off their rock whipped out its tongue, snaring a lightning bug. When it ate enough luciérnagas, her father had once told her, a frog would glow in the dark. For the glow she, too, would tolerate the firefly's bitter taste. She wondered if the fireflies' rhythmic flashes were signals to attract a mate or defensive reminders to predators of its acid taste.

Elbows on knees, chin propped on her hand, she sat for hours listening to the wind moaning like la Llorona as it blew through the trees. When it was fully dark she trudged up the ravine, slipping and sliding. Back at her place, she packed, loaded her car, and drove out of Austin. Playing classical music, Prieta drove through the night. She knew Suel didn't want any contact, but Prieta vowed to see her even if it meant keeping their relationship platonic.

After two days at home Prieta gave in to the urge to speak to Suel. She firmed her jaw, sucked in a deep breath, and dialed. Suel's sister answered and called out, "Suel, Prieta's on the phone."

At the other end Prieta heard Suel say, "Dile que no estoy en casa. Tell her I've moved away."

Time dragged. Prieta longed to hear Suel's voice. On Thanksgiving, after picking up the phone half a dozen times only to put it down, Prieta dialed Suel's number.

An older woman, probably her mother, answered saying, "Please stop calling. Suel doesn't want to talk to you." She hung up before Prieta could get a word in.

Before school resumed in January Prieta went to an all-valley teachers' conference. She wandered into the auditorium for the keynote address and stood at the threshold clutching the schedule of events. She saw Suel sitting in the middle of the huge room and her heart stuttered. The sight of Suel's elegant neck with hair caught at the nape flooded her body with tenderness and yearning. She hurried down the aisle, but when she reached Suel's row something stopped her in her tracks—the impulse to protect Suel from the shock of seeing her, or the fear that Suel would spurn her?

Suel turned and saw her. A spark flashed in her eyes, then her eyes went cold—Medusa eyes.

Prieta gulped. Bracing her shoulders, she tried to contain her fear but it drove her outside herself. Zooming away like the eye of a camera, she saw herself in the mouth of an ocean, a speck, a cipher longing to connect with the shore. She saw the rows of seats receding, like waves they sucked her back to the sea. Suel got smaller and smaller, the coast disappeared. Light flickered, then darkness se trago la luz.

A tiny burst of light prickled through her and she knew that Suel would jump up, rush to the side aisle, and dash out the door. Before Suel could move, turning her to stone, Prieta turned and walked out.

Author's note: I'd like to thank my writing comadres AnaLouise Keating and Carmen Morones for reading and commenting on this story.

Translations

tragando luciérnagas	swallowing fireflies
pelo Negro	black hair
encino	live oak
caras güeras	white faces
platicaron de sus familias	talking about their families
mamagrande	grandmother
primo hermono	first cousin
movida	deceptive move
vatos	a pachuco word meaning *dudes*
los mosquitos	the gnats
palomas blancas	mourning doves
ay mijita	short for mi hijita, a term of endearment meaning oh, baby, or oh, my little daughter
qué calor	how hot it is
andale	come on
bueno	okay
en dos semanas	in two weeks

del valle	of the valley, as the lower Rio Grande valley is called
pueblos	towns
dos mujeres	two women
ojos luceros	luminous eyes
esperando el amanecer	waiting for dawn
lado a lado	side by side
una lumbrita	a small fire
cuando se sentaban juntitas	when they sat close together
caballo	horse
novio	boyfriend, lover
tú sabes	you know
el Sagrado Corazón de Jesús	the Sacred Heart of Jesus
de una palomita	of a mourning dove
marimacha	butch dyke
la barranca	the ravine
la Llorona	the ghost woman who wept in the night for her lost children
dile que no estoy en casa	tell her I'm not home.
se trago la luz	swallowed the light

Marie-Claire Blais

PHOTOGRAPH BY DANIELLE SCHAUB

MARIE-CLAIRE BLAIS

Tenderness

The two women slept gently entwined. They had met just hours before and shared only a few words and brief caresses; yet now the room was filled with their presence, the sensual intimacy of their bodies, their lives warming together against the cold March night. While outside the icy spring downpour could be heard, inside the smell of rain and fog still clung to their clothes—coats too heavy, shoes weighted down with mud, at one moment dire necessities, the next shed and scattered as they crossed the threshold, borne in on a whirlwind of sensuality. Now they were asleep, or pretending to be, glances and hands still seeking one another in the warm sanctuary of the bed. Suddenly a pang of tenderness, but nervousness at feeling love for someone new, a first embrace in the night—all of it had taken them by surprise, rooted them together in an oasis neither had ever been to before. Perhaps there was nowhere else that sisterhood, a virgin union, could take place, and when dawn's dull light effaced the luminous gestures of night, would not each go her way, as always, and do just what she had to?

Soon enough, summer morning would dazzle them . . . why not wait before saying good-bye? Their closed eyes gradually awoke with tentative, fervent glances, drawn together in summer's glow, cheeks hot, eyes shining with fugitive hope, life, summer, us, time of abandonment and love immobilized in this room . . . all the time, knowing chill isolation waited for them outside. One of them asked herself what she liked so much in the other . . . was it the obstinate lock of hair that fell over her longish ear or her small, firm foot, muscled and ready for the race—race or flight?—which she had delightedly held between her fingers? Still, in the pastures of abandon that night had laid before them, she felt she already knew the other's body: salt tears at eyelid corners, a familiar taste, for at the edges of the other's eyes, her own soul perched, suddenly attentive, vigilant, and holding her own drunkenness in suspense (and she thought, "She's just penetrated me, suddenly,

13

impetuously. Of course I'll love her. How else could it be?") from the tears held back to the vigor of this narrow foot that made her smile, yes, every detail of this body joyously explored, didn't it hold you aching to her, because you have to know everything, understand at least this reigning chaos that bursts into our lives.

Perhaps her companion was cold or in a hurry to leave: "Cover your shoulders," as though they had always spoken to each other this way, murmuring in a low voice, but with veiled authority, an order to one already dimly thought of as "my friend." Yet the kindliness of such words and gestures could have been shown to other lovers on many nights like this. She put her lips to the crease that lined the other's cheek, drank the bitter tears, sensed the solitary, skittish fragments of past lives passing between them in the voluptuous air that filled the room.

A sudden chill caused the other to pull the sport shirt over her breasts, hiding a torso of childlike beauty (when her companion had just talked about how all living things deteriorated with suffering and time, and her words still inhabited the room with their sober modesty and served to shelter crumbling days of splendor), this thing, this piece of blue cotton that draped the other's body against shivering cold, became in the first glow of dawn, her flesh and scent, every imprint of her. The shirt, with its short, frayed sleeves—as though clawed by her lover's impatient hands (and the yellowed patches worn to transparency under the arms, where a down was visible, darkening as though, under the coals of her body, still other fires burned, quietly smoldering . . . clothes merely serving to subject them to the dictates of cold weather)—this pale blue garment, now framed in the light of dawn, breathed with her, listening like a lover's ear to the beating of her heart. Now, all of a sudden, instead of shielding her from the cold, it slipped away, unveiling, charm after charm, the musculature of her stomach, strong enough to support her lover's head, her hard thighs and her foot, so irrepressible and strong in its longing to start up, to be in motion, that the loving fingers could no longer still it, but had to let it soar to its own dreams or careworn nervousness. Is not the body like the rest of us . . . complicated, stubborn in its resistance against the pathetic restraints that keep us from soaring to freedom?

The day dawned with a violence of gray light and chill wind that had blown down trees in the night, and it separated hands still warm and hesitant to join once again, for they had to leave, but there was still the hope in their eyes, as when they had slept in each other's arms—though not really slept—spying out what they longed for through half-closed eyelids, that all-inclusive, unspoken hope, the abundance of impulsive giving that had made them drunk, that hope—almost nothing, or perhaps everything—love, still and tomorrow, perhaps, for now, the memory of their breathing in the night.

TRANSLATED BY NIGEL SPENCER

Marion Douglas

PHOTOGRAPH BY ERIC HIMMELMAN

MARION DOUGLAS

Dance Hall Road

Rose Drury wished there were a passport office at the entrance to East Flax, a rickety shed at the end of a worn dirt road housing an old man sifting through pencil-written pleas. Only the lucky few would actually find the place and fewer still be allowed in. "I'm afraid your documents aren't in order," he'd say to most, sliding shut the window to his checkpoint, an unfinished structure open on the nether side to lake, frog chorus, bog smell: the kindling of life. But to Rose he'd always say, "Go right on ahead, miss. Go right on up to Dance Hall Road."

Dance Hall Road delivered its travelers to the dance hall, which sat atop the steepest hill for miles. In the winter, cars were forever sliding into the soft ditch, naked trees a little ashamed in those double-barreled high beams. And on summer evenings, beer bottles, brown and fast as startled quail, flew from the open windows of low-slung cars as young people arrived in weather systems of dust and brake lights. They were there to hear local bands with names like Crippled Duck or Mud Pack. Amazing their skins didn't split with all that contained pleasure.

But when nothing was scheduled, no card parties or dances or fiftieth-anniversary celebrations, the dance hall was Maddy Farrell's private gymnasium. The place was equipped with basketball hoops, and Maddy's dad, custodian to most public buildings in the county, had keys to everything. So Maddy kept the place clean and shot baskets when she was done. It got her on the high school team, and that's not all: the dance hall with its kitchen and dishes and cutlery for two hundred, its stacks of metal chairs and microphones, had, over the past few weeks, more or less become an apartment for Rose and Maddy. A perfect set of circumstances, to Rose's mind. She had arranged to leave her boring home in Mesmer without having gone anywhere—well, five miles down the road. A sleight of body, Rose liked to think, moving through the routine of school, home, her dad's dental office reception area, with the cooperation of just a few layers of skin, while beneath them the more important components, the organs and blood and muscles, were bubbling into plans with Maddy. It was a lava lamp type of existence, visible only to Rose Drury.

Her friends had stopped asking except to communicate occasionally with her brother Adrian via Laura van Epp on behalf of Laura's sister, Anastasia, Rose's ex–best friend, who would still like to know exactly what was going on. A legitimate question, Rose would concede, but unanswerable perhaps even by Mesmer High's psychologist, Graham Rochon. Were he to have all the pertinent details bulging from one of his green file cabinets, the force of its own mystery would push the drawer open late at night. I don't know, she wanted to say to Anastasia. Honest. Honest as hell, as they used to say. Their own private expression, meaning Satan in a judge's robe would want to hear it all, would never flinch, on the contrary, would long to hear the worst. She and Anastasia had done a lot of talking in their day.

You'd have thought Rose would miss Anastasia and the others, but Maddy's grades, Maddy's fashion sense, Maddy's basketball training required so much attention there was no time to spare. Some days Rose felt tired and harassed like a babysitter left in charge much longer than expected, awaiting errant parents while cooking macaroni and cheese amidst the soggy mess of the cereal bowls she'd seen in the Farrell kitchen. Other times, Rose couldn't sleep for the excitement of what lay beyond even East Flax. Dropping off Maddy last week she'd had the urge to turn right instead of homeward, keep going, and drive all night. How odd for one so suffocated by her hometown that she'd never driven herself more than twenty miles past Mesmer. What was stopping her from going east of east, to Toronto, Montreal, the Saint Lawrence River and the ocean? She could become a missing person, like the poster Anastasia had taped to her locker one day, a shady photocopy of last year's school photo beneath the two-inch stenciled message: "MISSING! Rose Anne Drury. Anyone with information leading to her whereabouts is asked to contact the Mesmer Police Department or Anastasia van Epp."

Rose had left it up for a few days just to confirm Anastasia's point. But she began to realize, especially late at night in that moonlit countryside, that the identity of missing person offered deep consolation, the sort of solace a sermon should. What if the Reverend Beel were to grant weekly disappearances? There might be a few takers.

And her dad thought she'd caught a bug, thought her throat was a little on the red side. Take it easy and stop running around so much, was his advice. But she did not. Brought her books with her to the dance hall and planned to study, but there was always Maddy to watch. Maddy had to practice and Rose had to watch with, appropriately, an intensity usually associated with cramming for exams.

Not that Rose didn't wonder from time to time how the East Flax lifestyle might appear to a third set of eyes. More than a little bewildering, undoubtedly. There was Rose on a folding chair, talking, reassuring. Every other day Maddy would ask: "Do you really think they made Cheryl Decker captain because they felt sorry for her?" "Absolutely. That's the kind of thing they do when your brother kills himself. Compassionate reasons." "Are you sure?" "Of course I'm sure." This was not coaching. No interested observer would mistake this type of talk for coaching. And when Maddy took off her shirt, ran around in rib cage and size A bra, Rose's face said nothing. It's a little like an art exhibit, she thought; modern art can be anything. Or a movie made by the CBC. You're not meant to understand, but to keep on watching. Never reveal your bumpkinhood.

Bumpkinhood revealed to Maddy Farrell? Now that was a laugh. Although there was something similar to contemplate, a related phenomenon from the periodic table of human states. Shame. Driving Maddy home from school today she'd thought the word, analyzed the condition. Concluded that whether you'd had a lot or a little, shame was always available, living like a little animal self in the back of the head and neck, occupying the parts of yourself you couldn't see. It was always prepared to stick its nose out and sniff the air, tell you something smelled bad. And so she wasn't going to bring up the topic of the dance, she'd decided. Would stay home and leave the dance hall to the tourists and that was that. When Maddy asked: "What about the dance tonight?"

"The dance tonight?" Rose repeating the words as if they were a place name in Russia, too many consonants, unfamiliar vowels.

"Yes. The October dance in October. I think I'll go."

Rose's thoughts had huddled themselves into this possibility a few times, arcane as the Mesmer High's football team, all backs and unnatural padding and secret strategy, indecipherable.

"I'd thought you'd be working. Don't you and your mom clean Russell Jerome's house on Fridays?"

"Every other Friday. Last Friday, for example."

Could it be that Maddy was challenging Rose to a public demonstration of her loyalty? It wasn't as if they didn't spend time together at school, but there Rose was always busy with Maddy, always moving, more accurately, from one place to the next with great purpose. A dance offered no purpose, no destination, very little structure. Swarms of girls watched by swarms of boys in an atmosphere, Rose realized with a hard-as-eggshell swallow, much akin to their times alone in the dance hall. An atmosphere of great visual busyness, eyes watching with an appetite, eyes that hadn't been let out much.

"Well, if you're going, then I will too." Still plenty of time for the car to die, tires to blow, spark plugs to require replacement, distributors, carburetors, radiators—as many reasons not to go as there were movable parts in a Vega.

They were at the dance hall now, parked.

"Let's practice dance then," Maddy said. "My transistor's in the hall."

"But what if somebody looked in? People do walk by the place."

"Then let's go into the woods. I'll get the radio. Come on."

What was that rumor about Maddy's dad and traps? Eating skunk or coon? What sort of effect might one anticipate from the ingestion of such low-to-the-ground game? Why did the longer-legged animals seem more civilized fare? Although now that she thought of it, Anastasia's mom had once shown off a rabbit marinating in her fridge. But rabbits hopped and dashed on powerful legs, were the subject of fairy tales, whereas the skunk and the coon were considered varmints. Which meant vermin.

They walked, Maddy leading the way, thumbing the dial on her pink radio, last year's Christmas gift from her mother, Angel Farrell. The dizzy whine of radio waves in fast and cluttered approach and then one clear signal, the disc jockey from Windsor.

"This is far enough. No one will see us here, if you're so worried."

"I'm not worried, Maddy. I can't really recall the last time I worried. Rose Drury and worry are a kind of parallelogram. We're almost incapable of meeting."

"Unless you were a parallelogram drawn by me."

"What's that supposed to mean?"

"It means I'm not good at geometry. Anyway, this is good. Jackson Five. Good beat. Easy to dance to. That's what they always say."

What was happening? They'd slipped through the looking-glass or more likely the rearview mirror of some hillbilly's truck. Maddy was altered. She looked as if she'd been given a drink of uranium or something radioactive, the heavy water manufactured at the nuclear power plant. And it had pooled like clumsy weights in her hands and feet. Maddy was jumping and kicking and Rose now understood her purpose here: to teach Maddy to dance, to prevent shame on the dance floor for Maddy Farrell.

"Maddy, Maddy, Maddy. Not so wild. Like this. See? More in control and not hardly any movement of the feet. That's how Anastasia van Epp will be dancing, I guarantee."

The instruction continued through "Ain't No Mountain High Enough" and then, coincidental with Maddy dancing to the music with Sly and the Family Stone, she threw off her shirt and invited Rose to do the same. Rose had larger breasts, better quality brassieres, and to be honest, she was a little tired of Maddy behaving as if she were in fact the captain of the basketball team. Warm for October, so why not?

And just like that, as if Maddy had choreographed the situation or was manipulating the radio waves with the new fillings in her teeth, the transistor cackled out a slow song. James Taylor. "Fire and Rain."

"Will you just teach me one slow dance please?" Maddy asked. "In the unlikely event a guy does ask me to dance?"

"I'm not an expert on slow dancing but okay, I'll try." Rose had done this at summer camp on Georgian Bay, girls dancing with girls, the recreation director, Pam, insisting, almost ordering them not to be so uptight. Calling them middle-class princesses.

"Okay, like this." Rustling between the roots and leaves of the forest floor, the sun broke through, and "It's a spot dance," Rose said. Spot dances were won only by couples, she was thinking, when Maddy did a strange and delirious thing: undid the back of Rose's bra, pulled it off, and threw it into the trees. Then laughed and laughed. Laughed harder when it caught on a branch and failed to return; fell to her knees laughing. While Rose stood, in charge now at last, or so her breasts seemed to think with those two very hard nipples pursing themselves up in the breeze. Nudists disported themselves in this manner and were healthy. A lack of vitamin D caused rickets.

"I'm sorry," Maddy said. "I just did a nutty thing. You know how sometimes you can't help yourself?"

There'd been a motto at the summer camp, a big silk and felt banner hanging from the cedar beams of the mess hall. And the west wind shapes the pine. The point being, were East Flax to have a motto drifting above the heads of its citizens this might be it: You know how sometimes you can't help yourself?

"You're going to have to get my bra down."

"That's easy. There's a ladder at the dance hall I can get. I'll be right back." But she crumpled into laughter again, lay in the leaves examining Rose from the angle of a squirrel, or any furry and ratlike animal that might bound from a tree to the back of someone's exposed neck. Then Maddy leapt up, found her shirt, and took off while Rose waited among the watching trees. A voice on the radio warned motorists of a problem on the Ambassador Bridge: if they were thinking of going to Detroit tonight, they might have to change their plans. Rose wished she lived in Windsor.

In Reflection   This story is autobiographical insofar as repressed desire is part of everyone's experience. The specific events did not occur. In my high school years, I did not ever have my bra removed and thrown into a tree by another girl, nor did I remove and throw anyone's bra, much as I might have wanted to. I chose to write this story because I find the causes and effects of human attraction pleasing to contemplate.

For myself, autobiographically speaking, as an adolescent admiring perfect girls in *16 Magazine,* I was never able to decide if my interest was in being or in having one of those girls. In my story, the two characters, Maddy and Rose, represent both of these types of longing. Still, in my adult life, whenever I meet someone I find attractive, I am unable to answer the question: Be or Have? Either way, it's rather a festive quandary.

Jewelle Gomez

JEWELLE GOMEZ

Choose:
A Biomythography

I sat waiting impatiently for Gail to ring the doorbell as if it were still 1964 and we were back in high school. I'd swept my great-grandmother's rambling flat three times, even under the bed in my tiny room at the back. Despite my attentions it was the same as it had always been: desperately worn from its faded linoleum to the cracks in the ceiling paint. When Gail slept over we used to stare at the ceiling as if the cracks and discoloration were clouds we might fantasize into shapes—angels, kittens, ragtop Volkswagens. So many poor people had tried to make their dreams work within these dreamless walls the place felt weary.

Tonight my great-grandmother was out at her weekly Pokeno game and would be home at 10:45 P.M. precisely, only a little more winded now by the three flights of stairs she'd been climbing for years. I took a last look around my room as I picked at my newly cut Afro. Aside from that, most things had not changed since high school. Despite civil rights and Black power, my neighborhood and my friends seemed the same: a few more children on the block, new cracks in the cement. The apartment buildings were a bit shabbier, but their occupants still scrubbed them clean, hung fresh curtains every spring, and stood on their stoops making plans. The creeping influence of urban renewal was making its way slowly up Tremont Street toward us from downtown Boston, but it hadn't taken hold in the South End yet.

As I waited anticipation rumbled through me like the elevated train that careened over Washington Street, just as it had that first night with Gail four years before, when we were sixteen. The wanting was not a loud shout, but a low hum in my throat like the soloist at Concord Baptist Church.

I remembered the laughter of that first night with amazement. Gail and I had been watching television before we ran off to bed to beat my great-grandmother's return. We lay in bed giggling and atop our humor bubbled the sensual energy of adolescence—oil and water

rippling in a storm. The laughter shook us until we were weak, and with
no calculation we began to talk about sex. It was not a new topic; we
were teenagers living in a working-class, colored neighborhood. Sex
and speculation about it was all around us. It thrived in darkened tene-
ment stairwells and shouted out from the sidewalks. In my bedroom it
was a humid mist on our skin. But the powerful fear of rejection thrust
us each into the third person.

"If someone wanted to try kissing another girl . . . ," Gail began
because she was always more self-assured than I was.

"Umm?" I'd responded, sounding almost noncommittal, trying
to conceal the excitement that was coursing through me.

"Or doing it with her," she went on.

"Right, doing it." I had agreed, not sure what "doing it" entailed
specifically, but sure I wanted to.

"If someone wanted to try doing it with another girl," Gail started
again, "it doesn't mean there's anything wrong with her, right?"

"There doesn't have to be nothing wrong with her just to try it."

"And if either of them doesn't like it she could just stop and choose
not to do it anymore, right?"

"Right."

With that contract we moved into each other's arms for the first
time. When Gail pulled me onto her a sigh of relief and expectation
escaped us both. There was no clearly mapped path—I closed my eyes
as I'd seen Sandra Dee do in movies; Gail translated her backseat grop-
ing with boys. The sweet smell of cornfields that I associated with her
filled the small, girlish bedroom, settling over our rhythmic breathing
and the rustling comforter. The slow roll of our hips set fire to us.

For a moment I was startled at the massiveness of desire. I realized
then I'd never thought about Gail "sexually," had not envisioned her
beneath me. I'd thought about her legs sometimes, looking at them and
the dark hair imprisoned between the nylon and the firm dark tan of
her calf. The desire had been certain and constant but not specific.
Never as specific as sex. That was something people did in "adult" books
kept hidden under the mattress. Neither my great-grandmother, who
didn't flinch at the innuendo-filled jokes that swirled around the Pokeno table, nor Gail's pretty mother, who went out every Saturday night,
seemed likely to engage in anything resembling what I read about in
those stolen books.

Yet that night, Gail's wetness dampening my thigh and my own
irretrievable desire to press my lips to that wetness assured me—this
was sex. And it was much more than they'd described in those books.
More even than what I'd seen at the Uptown movie theater. I'd watched

thirstily as the screen kisses of Sandra Dee and Troy Donahue intoxi-
cated the teenage audiences. Hollywood magic worked until I discovered that Gail and I were the real laughter and chaos of desire.

For four years we explored our loving on Wednesday's Pokeno
night and Saturday's date night, spilling desire into each other's hands
and mouths like a torrential, cleansing storm that blew up twice a week.
I was in awe of the sweetness of her breath, the power of her legs as she
held me to her and the miracle of our breasts pressed together, bathed
in sweat.

At school, nothing changed except that my heart beat furiously
when I saw her coming down the hall. The smiles that passed between
us in class or as we passed in the corridors felt electric and knowing.
Whenever someone spoke snidely about wearing green on Thursday
or made bull-dagger jokes, I sucked my teeth. But the words were not
mine yet, to be either claimed or denounced.

For Gail it was sex not so different from what she'd experienced in
the back of her boyfriend's Ford. I knew that, but I could also tell she
really loved me. We didn't openly acknowledge the connection, but
friends just knew we were inseparable. Our jealousy was oblique and
bubbly, rather than dark and brooding, yet it gave shape to our cou-
pledness. At school we watched each other, indulgent lovers, laughter
always between us. She'd sometimes ask me: "Why are you spending the
night at Janet's house?"

"Basketball practice went late; her mother's car is in the shop."

"Umph," back from Gail, as if I were her child. She saved the moment to tease me when we were next in bed together.

People accepted that it was normal for teenage girls to be bonded
and proprietary as long as we fulfilled all the social expectations—dances,
Saturday movie dates, crushes. Boyfriends became an amusement we
shared so we had a personal soap opera to talk about in the cafete-
ria just like all the girls. We speculated whether other girls in our high
school shared our kind of secret but were really oblivious to the rest of
the world, never even worrying that we needed camouflage. We were
open yet invisible. Not reflected anywhere in our social experience, our
relationship was taken for granted by the friends and family who wit-
nessed our devotion.

I'd poured over a copy of *The Well of Loneliness,* but its reality,
swathed in estates, gardens, gowns, was too far from ours. I might have
just as easily been reading about love on Mars. Knowing there was other
such passion in the world was a comfort for me but didn't seem to
interest Gail. With no recognizable, social reference point, our love remained unnamed, a high-pitched passion smothered in blankets and

pillows. Like most things in youth, it felt as if it would last forever. And in a way it did. The friendship never failed.

It was Gail who joked and cajoled me until I let go of my fears enough to apply to colleges. When I went to college and she didn't, Gail made the separation as natural a part of our relationship as the loving.

Once I was in college our nights together were an oasis of reality in what otherwise seemed like someone else's version of our lives. We talked almost every night as if we were still in high school. Since I couldn't hang out much anymore Gail kept me up with the gossip—who was pregnant, who was in jail, who thought I was a snob for going to school. I laughed with her about being "a stranger in a strange land" on the huge, mostly white campus. To deflate the hurt and anxiety caused by condescending financial aid bureaucrats I amused Gail with scathing imitations of them.

The closing of my bedroom door and click of the bedroom light going off cued the beginning of real existence. Our arms encircled each other and words disappeared. Gail's small, tight body fit between my long legs as if we were matching parts. Movies, ball games, or church dances couldn't overshadow the passion of our nights together and the friendship that underlay them.

I dropped classes to be with Gail when she almost died from an illegal abortion. And she covered for me when I was going somewhere my great-grandmother wouldn't approve of. Neither of us ever questioned the other's devotion.

"Still don't," I thought, as I sat waiting, while my memory darted around through the years. Even with the past so prominent in my mind I knew my graduation wasn't far away. I was thinking about what to do with myself after school when the bell rang. I opened the door knowing exactly what to expect: Gail, her small body, brown skin, large dark eyes under a thick head of hair that fell softly in the same permanent, Clairol curls around her face.

We held each other tightly, the laughter and words tumbling out around us, picking up from where we left off the last time we'd seen each other.

"So what, you an African now, huh?" Gail said to me, surprised. Her fingers raked through my new natural haircut.

"Yeah, yeah," I said.

"You gonna give me a little tribal dance?" she asked, her inflection carrying about three more paragraphs than the question.

"Naw, you heathen thing, I thought I'd just put you in the pot and eat you!"

"We can do that with or without the pot!"

As usual the world disappeared. "Graduation" became only a word in the dictionary, as did "marriage" and "husband." Just words we could make jokes about or ones we'd heard in the foreign movies we didn't fully understand.

"Good," I said as I closed the door to my small bedroom. I didn't think about ironing the dress I'd wear tomorrow as I stood beside her and him at the courthouse ceremony. I inhaled the smell of freshly succulent corn as it turned into the starchy aroma of our orgasm. I listened to the wetness of our bellies against each other, the sound of fleshy thighs rubbing against stiff hair. It was as fiery and joyous as the first time.

I never considered stopping the events from moving on course. Tradition was rolling in like a tide and I had no words to use to say, "Don't." For me, desire was clear and strong, but the word "lesbian" was still shadowy and remote, something glimpsed only in the back pages of little underground newspapers. We'd always loved each other and never thought about the language that went with it. If I'd had those words I would have chosen her to share the rest of my life. But her love for me was different; she could not have chosen me. Afterward, feeling her sleep beside me, I didn't think about what I could do; I only thought about our past.

I was awake, listening to Gail's breathing, when dawn came. I lay watching the cracks and stains on the ceiling being revealed by the sun as I realized this was our last time together as lovers. When I heard my great-grandmother set the heavy teakettle to boil on the stove with a clink, I closed my eyes as if I could pull all those years back inside of me and give them to Gail all over again. The sound of my great-grandmother's slippers moving around down the hall roused us more fully.

"You girls gonna sleep right past the ceremony? Come on now, that boy will be here soon!"

As usual Gail's eyes just opened and she was awake. For once she had nothing to say—no pun, no laugh. She closed her eyes for a moment and squeezed my hand. But then she was distracted by the plans that still needed to be made. She smiled at me and said, "Thank you." She brushed her lips softly across mine then darted down the hall to the bathroom.

I turned on the radio to let my great-grandmother know that we were really awake. From the kitchen I could hear the squeaking sound of the ironing board and the smell of sausage cooking. By the time I came out of my room Gail was already sitting at the kitchen table in her slip, putting butter on her toast.

"Don't leave your food sitting by itself," my great-grandmother said as she pulled out her chair to sit down.

"Be right back, Ma," I said, turning back down the hall to my room, my heart thudding in my ears. It blended with the rhythm of a deep moan at the back of my throat. The sound was heavy and broad, stretching across my throat blocking the air. I stood gripping the worn edge of the dresser. The picture of Gail and me at Revere Beach that was tucked into the corner of the mirror trembled. A rumble inside pushed higher and my mouth moved soundlessly. A noise pulled itself out of me, taut with the effort, and rode the air as a high-pitched wail.

The sound of my cry couldn't be heard over the whistling tea-kettle and the insistent sound of his car horn from the street below.

In Reflection   In writing "Choose" I was honoring the passion between myself and my teenage lover. Ultimately she wasn't a lesbian and I am. Her open, uncomplicated loving helped me know it was okay to desire other women. And we both acknowledge and keep the importance of our earlier relationship still. Somehow we knew, even as girls, that being the mistress of our own desires was a center of power.

Writing the story was a way to change the feelings of failure I had after she went on to a disappointing and hurtful marriage that I could do nothing to prevent. The desire and friendship we felt at sixteen was an amazing thing that I believe is part of the power of women. That we managed to see ourselves as desirable then and that we, for thirty-five years, kept the trusting friendship is the greatness of women that is my faith. Today when her children and grandchildren call me "aunt" I know what a world we can make.

proceeding page

PHOTOGRAPH BY JILL POSENER

Karla Jay

KARLA JAY

Swimming with Sharks

*I go to the things I love with no thought
of duty or pity.*

—H.D., *The Flowering of the Rod*

Two weeks in a nudist colony in what was then known as Yugoslavia wasn't exactly my first choice for a vacation. But I wasn't paying for it, and I was curious about a scene like that. And I was very much in thrall to a French Baroness who was used to having her way with me, and everything else, for that matter.

Rochelle's definition of obscenity included bathing attire, so when she hankered for a swim in salt water that fall, we drove south from Sarlat to Marseilles and hopped on a plane to Trieste, where a driver scooped us up at the airport and drove us down the coast to Rovinja. Then after a short ferry ride, there we were—a French aristocrat and an American Jew—on the Red Island, checking into a fading queen of a luxury resort.

We tossed our scant luggage on the beds, grabbed two beach towels, left the hotel, and crossed a wooden bridge that connected the sleeping quarters to a nude resort area on a small adjoining island. We looked for a vacant spot on the rocky beach to warm ourselves before tackling the Adriatic. About twenty sun worshipers were sitting in rows on air mattresses and facing the sea like a forlorn colony of lemmings about to take the fatal plunge. The Red Island, it turned out, had been named for its sharp desolate rocks, not its politics; it was impossible to sit on the sharp pebbles, even on a towel. Rochelle headed for the beach shop, bought two air mattresses, and set us up on a promontory, from which we could enjoy views of the water and the bodies of our fellow vacationers.

I sat down and glanced around, trying to project a studious disinterest, which wouldn't suggest I was cruising or as naive about these places as I was. Laid out on the beach like tan cold cuts on a deli counter were penises and breasts in every size and shape that white folks come in. The men wading in from the frigid waters looked wilted, their organs reduced to gherkins. It was the least sexual display ever.

33

Bored already, I rolled over on my stomach so the sun could get its first peek ever at my derriere. I hoped the sun was as amused as my fellow vacationers. From under my arm, I could see them nudging one another and pointing at the tan-and-white butterfly my two-piece suit had tattooed on my back. A hirsute German made some comments I couldn't understand but certainly got the gist of. Everyone laughed.

I wondered how I was going to survive a week of this. At least when we were at the Baroness's mansion near Sarlat, I was surrounded by people who spoke French, a language I was fluent in. What was I going to do on an island populated with heterosexual German and Austrian tourists, who weren't going to like me as a Jew or a lesbian? Even naked, the Baroness carried herself as if she were dressed in the best Chanel had to offer. The other guests weren't going to mess with her or dare to laugh. Like me, they would address her publicly only as the Baroness, never as "Rochelle," or even "madame." If they did, she would dismiss them with her fluent German; then she would drive them from the beach as her ancestors had thrust the Huguenots from France. She had amassed five or six other languages, too, along with a large fortune as she married herself across Europe before she had discovered her inner queer. Before she had discovered me.

I was one of the things the Baroness had acquired on her travels. She admired one of my novels and began a correspondence with me while I was still living in Brooklyn. My work was "critically successful," which meant that it sold poorly, and I was existing grant-to-mouth. The Baroness wrote to me that she was stopping in New York on her way from France to California to check out one of her vineyards. I went to the Plaza to meet her in the late afternoon.

Her precise handwriting had suggested a plump, middle-aged dowager with sagging jowls, a receding chin, and a Hanover nose. I pictured her looking like the Queen Mum, graceful and dowdy. To my amazement, she turned out to be a slim and fashionable woman in her early fifties. Her hair was so auburn that it created a halo effect around her head as the light from the hotel windows fell on it. Her eyes were a brilliant green, and she had the most sensual lips I had ever seen. She was elegantly attired in a simple blue wool blazer with a gold Mount Kenya Club insignia sewn onto the pocket, and her blouse was monogrammed with a crest and her initials. Grey wool pants were tucked into buttery boots. Was she real or was she some elaborate acid flashback? But as I lowered my eyes in order not to be caught gaping at her, I noticed that her fly was unzipped, and that fact alone gave me the courage to believe that she was indeed human. I somehow managed to sit calmly near her and make small talk though my mouth was so cottony that I could barely swallow.

Since I was a vegetarian, she took me out to dinner at the East/West in the Village, a restaurant I considered expensive but knew she wouldn't. I was almost too afraid to eat in front of her. My mother always complained that I had a "hole in my chin," and food inevitably wound up on my lap, no matter how carefully I ate. I could see that her table manners were impeccable. We dined leisurely and spoke of my work and her marriages. She was not at all reticent and quickly told me about a string of suitors and husbands. Though she had just divorced husband number four, he wanted her back at any price. I could understand why.

After the meal, she wanted to come back to see my apartment, but I was too embarrassed by my shabby Park Slope digs. We parted, and I caught a last glimpse of her as she headed into a cab. I never expected to see her again.

On my birthday a week later, a huge bouquet of flowers arrived, composed of lavender roses and purple lilies, a summer's extravagance in January. "Lilies for your first love." I had quoted Renée Vivien to her. The same day I received a postal notice that I had missed a certified mail delivery. Cursing, I walked the half mile through the falling snow to the Times Plaza branch of the post office in Brooklyn. I was born in a blizzard, and it seemed to snow every year on my birthday as a reminder. Birthdays meant boots, mufflers, and shovels. I hated to go to the post office in any weather because after a long walk I had to wait in a line that invariably snaked its way out the door, and the bulletproof glass that protected the postal clerks left me feeling totally vulnerable to the surging ire of the crowd. People in my neighborhood bought one stamp at a time, one postal money order at a time, and the post office hired only one window clerk at a time.

I passed the yellow receipt through the small slot at the bottom of the plastic shield, and a few moments later, the clerk slid me an envelope that looked like a birthday card. It was from the Baroness. "Damn," I thought. "Couldn't she just send a card by regular mail and save me the walk? Guess she thought the chauffeur would run and fetch it for me."

I fingered the envelope carefully, trying to judge the thickness. It didn't seem safe to open the card in front of the hungry throng, so I walked out into the snow and pretended to look into the window of a pawn shop. My heart pounding with hope, I carefully opened the envelope. Inside was a cashier's check for thousands of dollars—more than I made in a year from writing. An offhand note was enclosed:

Brooke:

Do have a wonderful birthday. After my trip to California,
I changed some currency back into francs. The exchange rate
was quite favorable, so here is a small part of the profit.
    I want you to buy yourself something decent to wear and
finish your new novel. The Paris setting sounds promising.
I'll probably be in Katmandu for the summer, but do enjoy
yourself in France.

Yours,
Rochelle

After I moved to Paris, she drove north to claim me. One night,
I was reading from my current novel at Shakespeare & Company. I
hadn't expected her, but suddenly I spotted her standing in the back,
leaning casually against a bookcase. Her skin had been polished by
some spa or other until it was incredibly luminous. She was wearing a
white suit with no blouse under the vest and a simple but heavy gold
necklace.

A lump formed in my throat. I had to pause and take a big swallow
of Volvic before continuing. I imagined her disappointment in seeing
me again, a slight, preppy woman in a Lands End cotton sweater who
read in a studied way. I hope she wasn't confusing me with my hard-
boiled dyke-detective who pursued villains and gorgeous women on
her motorbike.

After the reading, she came up and invited me out to dinner at
the Coupole, one of those wonderful Montparnasse cafés that Heming-
way and Fitzgerald had frequented a half century earlier. She ordered
raw shellfish and some champagne. Soon a three-tiered silver platter
arrived, piled with oysters, clams, mussels, shrimp, and langoustine. I
could barely swallow the slippery oysters I held on my tongue, imagining that I was cradling her most intimate parts there. Then I shuddered
at my own boldness and made a hasty retreat to the bathroom, where
I tried to calm myself by splashing cold water on my face. Except as pa-
tron, what interest could someone like her have in a poor artist like me?
It was best to rinse any romantic notions out of my head.

After dinner, she asked whether I would like to see her suite at the
Lutetia. Would I! Once there, she marched me past the sitting room
into the bedroom, where the antique furnishings were complemented
by the red, velvet tones of the room. I perched on the edge of the bed,
thinking she would prefer the lounge chair opposite. But she sat down
next to me on the bed. Then she pushed me backward on the spread and

made love to me as no one ever had before. I learned later that she did everything to perfection.

Afterward, she ordered me to return to my dingy flat in the Marais and pack. I had few regrets about going off with the Baroness. I had rented a tiny studio with a Turkish toilet down the hall and furnishings provided by the expatriate dyke community, which meant I was sleeping on a piece of foam and writing on a wobbly table. The water was too cold to shower—that is, if I had a shower, which I didn't. As I threw my belongings into a suitcase, I reasoned that I could write anywhere, and most of my Anglo friends were fleeing Paris for the long summer holiday.

We zoomed down to Sarlat in the Baroness's Jaguar. She drove with a terrifying aggression, almost daring others to try to pass her. High speeds terrify me, and I begged her to slow down, but she laughed at my fears. "Come on, Brooke, don't be such a wimp. Only the strong survive in this world. Who knew you were just a pseudo-butch?"

"We can't both be the butch, can we?" I slumped in my seat. Pretending to nap, I closed my eyes, but at the rest stop, I had an urge to dash off and beg the nearest stranger to take me back to Paris.

Finally we arrived at the Baroness's mansion and spent a few days wandering around Sarlat and the other medieval towns in the vicinity. The walled cities, the pristine rivers, the domed churches—everything was incredibly lovely. I wanted to visit Josephine Baker's chateau, but the Baroness refused. "Those rich Americans have ruined our country with their money and lack of taste. Don't think I'm going to spend my money paying admission to see some gaudy tourist trap."

That was the least of what she forbade me. She pronounced me too thin and made me give up Coke and drink the black wines of Cahors to fortify me. She insisted that I needed meat to build me up. "You can't expect to put any meat on those bones. Look how long everyone around here lives. It's the good wine and foie gras. No one's a vegetarian anymore, darling. The sixties are over." But still, I couldn't eat the fattened ducks.

Luckily, we didn't stay in her country house long, though I never saw all of it, being enjoined not to visit the servants' quarters. I was happy to move on, uncomfortable with the many silent eyes of the servants always on me, with the clothes and underwear that disappeared from my armoire and returned stiffly pressed, and with the strange cockatoos who sat on perches or in cages at every turn in the hall and entreated me in French for crackers or peanuts.

We traveled often, whenever the Baroness got a whim to sample the cuisine of Bangkok or dip in the waters of the Caribbean. The people we came across simply assumed—if they noticed me at all—that I was the Baroness's secretary or traveling companion. Once, a gondolier in Venice asked the Baroness whether I was her daughter. A month later, we were off to London for Rochelle's face-lift.

The hotel on the Red Island was the latest of the Baroness's impulses, though this trip was made on my behalf. "You're too thin, and you're still writing too much. You need a rest." I was down to writing two to three hours a day at most. I was working five to six hours almost every day before she met me, and from my point of view, my life with her seemed like an extended vacation. When I'd try to write, she would distract me. She might be nice about it, coming up behind me and nibbling on my neck or running her hands down my pants until she had my full attention. Or she might simply insist I accompany her on some business, which might involve anything from her walnut orchards to her vineyards that were a half day's journey away in another part of the Dordogne.

Despite Rochelle's efforts, I continued to lose weight. I had finished my novel and felt totally drained. I stood in front of the mirror and noticed that the clothes that had been handmade for me only two months before were hanging loosely on my frame.

But how could I complain about this resort, meant as it was to restore my soul, though it was one of the last places I would have chosen to go? Everything in this communist country was generic: milk, bread, oil, bank . . . everything. The food certainly wasn't going to build me up. Breakfast consisted of hard-boiled eggs and bread, and every night the hotel offered up a gummy fish overcooked to the consistency of peanut butter. There was no vegetable, except for cucumber salad or beets. Then there was a course of cheese, always the same one, a sort of provolone, and stewed fruit. By the fourth day, I begged the Baroness to take me to the mainland to eat, even though dinner was part of the prepaid plan. I gathered from the expressions on the other guests' faces that the meat was worse than the fish, but the Baroness viewed my request as one more sign of my wimpish nature and refused. Like many who had survived World War II, she hated the notion of waste. She would have done well, I thought, to trade me in for one of the hearty Germans, who were undaunted by either the cuisine or the frigid waters.

I sat on the rocks trying to get up my courage to take the plunge, wishing that we were back in the tropical waters of Saint Maarten. "Get in here, Brooke!" the Baroness commanded from about a hundred feet out where she was treading water. "A bracing dip will do you good, build up your appetite."

I walked down to the water and stuck a tentative toe in the water. Brrr. "Not like that, darling. Jump in, for God's sake!" Despite her admonishments I waded in tentatively, disliking the feel of the sharp rocks on the soles of my feet.

Eventually I swam out, trying to catch up to the Baroness, who was about a quarter to a half mile away from the shore. I was a strong swimmer. My habit was to hug the shoreline, but it seemed disloyal to leave her out there by herself. I was still following the old summer camp rule of always swimming with a "strong buddy." Finally, the Baroness was next to me. I put one arm around her waist while she ran her fingers through my pubic hair. While I was fairly certain no one could see what she was doing in the murky water, I furtively glanced back to the shore. The hirsute German was jumping up and down, waving to us from the shore. He seemed to be saying something, so I shook the water out of my ears in order to hear him better.

"*Hai! Hai!*" he called as he waved.

"Hi!" I waved back. Then I turned to the Baroness. "He's friendlier than I had given him credit for."

"Oh, he's not being friendly. *Hai* is German for shark."

I rotated away from the Baroness's arm and scanned the waters. Sure enough, behind the Baroness was a gray fin skimming the surface of the water.

"Yikes, a shark!" I shrieked, waving my arms in the direction of the fin.

"Don't wave your arms like that when you talk, darling. You sound like a New York Jew."

"Will that matter to the shark?" This was no time to argue about my diction, manners, and ethnicity. Without waiting for an answer, I zoomed back to the shore. I had always been a slow, long-distance swimmer, but I imagine I beat Mark Spitz's speed records that day. The hirsute German was waiting for me—he pulled me onto the rocks and wrapped me in his towel. I was shaking.

He pointed at the Baroness, who was swimming languidly back to shore. "*Ay! Hai, haifisch!*" he said, pointing at the shark again. The shark turned out to sea, and the Baroness casually climbed out of the water.

"What are you so white for?" she asked me with disdain. "It was only a little shark. Besides, it's their job to clean out the weak and the wounded."

I wonder whether she meant me. If the shark attacked *her*, she probably would have chewed him up and spit him out.

Leaving the Baroness on the beach, I returned to our room and crawled into bed. When I awoke, it was the next morning, and rain was cascading against the window.

After breakfast, I put on a blouse and some slacks, borrowed a slicker from the concierge, and headed out in the rain. I would have felt ridiculous wandering around wearing an umbrella and nothing else. At the top of one of the paths was a lean-to shelter with a wooden bench. I sat down and stared at what would have been the sea, had it not disappeared in the low visibility. It seemed as if I had not been alone or listened to myself for a very long time. Apart from her anti-Semitism, which the Baroness would never admit to, she was right: I was a New York Jew, down to the core. I missed bagels, forbidden Cokes, and my political friends. It was time to go home, not to Sarlat or the Marais but to Park Slope. I needed to promote my novel, which was about to be published. But no one told the Baroness good-bye. And despite her carping, she showed no sign of tiring of me.

I had become a novelist because I was incapable of expressing my feelings, except on the printed page or through the wordless language of the body. The thought of telling the Baroness that I was unhappy with her careful arrangements left me speechless. Trying to end it all on a conciliatory note that would leave some opportunity for friendship was Pulitzer prize territory. I fingered the monogram on my linen blouse. Did I really want to return to the brown rice life? I walked to the edge of the cliff and peered down. Would the shark be waiting for me now that I was no longer terrified of his offer of a quick way out?

I backed away from the precipice and made my way back to the room, uncertain as to what I would do. Perhaps things could just go on as they were. But there at the front desk was an omen—a letter from a prominent university inviting me to teach a fiction workshop. I would have to start in a month. I knew I wanted the position.

I showed the letter to Rochelle.

"Why would you want to work for that measly salary? I can't believe the disrespect you Americans show for professors."

"It will build my reputation. Open doors."

"I can open doors for you, darling. Haven't I done enough?"

I knew it would all come around to my lack of proper gratitude. This was the moment to curtsy and say, "Thank you, your highness." Instead, I blundered onward. "I can't breathe here. I can't write. I miss my friends. I love you, but it's time for me to go home for a while."

She turned so red in the face that I cringed. I thought she was going to slap me for my hubris, for my lack of respect, but she clamped her lips into a tight line and turned her back. She picked up the phone. "Of course, we could have brought your friends to visit, but no matter. . . . I'll arrange for you to be flown back tomorrow, and I'll ship your clothes to you when I get back to Sarlat. I have no intention of disrupting my vacation. Let's say no more about this." She booked my flight, then opened a French novel and began to read it.

I packed my bag and went to sleep. In the morning I hopscotched home, from Yugoslavia to Athens to Zurich to New York. On the last leg of the flight, I began to berate myself for leaving Rochelle, for blaming her for my own lack of will to write. I had tossed away a fortune, like bread to the ducks. What a fool! I began to feel queasy, and the next thing I knew I was in the lavatory, spewing blood into the toilet. I pushed the call button and passed out. Upon landing, I was taken to a nearby hospital where I was diagnosed with bleeding ulcers. I was uninsured and knew I would soon have a bleeding wallet as well. But while I was recovering in the hospital, I began to write with renewed fervor, this time a torrential love story based on the Baroness. Whatever her flaws, she hadn't been weak or dull, not for a moment. I realized that my stamina was mostly cerebral, but I'd always have the strength to swim away from the sharks.

In Reflection   When I was a young nonfiction writer and aspiring journalist, I survived by teaching as an adjunct at several universities in the New York metropolitan area. I earned about four thousand dollars per year, and until 1978 I made only small amounts of money writing. I had modest needs and few possessions, though what little I had was destroyed when my building was torched in 1977.

There were fewer openly lesbian writers a quarter of a century ago; as a result, my books probably sold better than many contemporary works because there was little competition. I was well known and somewhat sought out as a "famous lesbian." Though I could hold my own intellectually, I was often at a financial disadvantage with suitors. "Swimming with Sharks" is based on a number of relationships that I had with older, wealthy lesbians in the 1970s and 1980s. These women were generous—they gave me money, clothes, jewelry, computers, typewriters, and cameras. Having lost everything in the fire, I was flattered by the attention, and perhaps I was foolish enough to confuse gratitude with love.

By disposition, I was easygoing and good-natured. It was simple for my lovers to infer consent to their agendas and schedules. They invariably expected me to abandon my home and friends to live with them. They encouraged me to write for them, and perhaps they hoped or suspected I would one day write about them. In the end, we all miscalculated my intense sense of privacy and my complex pride, which bridled at being financially or emotionally controlled by anyone.

Lesléa Newman

LESLÉA NEWMAN

Private Lessons

> *Woman*
> *the round sound*
> *in my mouth of you*
> *resounds like clouds*
> *around the moon . . .*

She was my teacher. I knew being at the hot tubs with her would be considered inappropriate at best, but I didn't care, and obviously neither did she. She taught at a nontraditional East Coast college like Goddard or Bennington, though it was neither of those, and I was a nontraditional student, older, though hardly wiser than the others in my class. Yet despite this, we were doing something that couldn't be more traditional: we were embarking on a student-teacher affair.

I had never been with a woman before and she knew this. I suppose it was something she decided to teach me about, much the same as she was teaching me how to write poetry. She already had a lover, a blond, buxom woman twice our age (she was only four years older than me), also a teacher at the college, over in the art department. She was away this semester, in Italy on sabbatical. And while the cat's away . . .

Her name was Cat—Catherine to the public, as that was the name she published under, but Cat to everyone else, including me. And she was catlike, with those gold-green eyes, that skullcap of black hair, those long limbs, that muscular, sinewy back. Her body was the most beautiful thing I'd ever seen as it wavered in the tub under the water, shimmering like the lilies in a Monet painting. She had taught me the power of comparison, of using "like" or "as" to describe something by way of simile, the irony that anything could be seen more clearly when presented as something other than itself.

I thought this over as I sat fully clothed on a wooden bench off to one side, my eyes riveted to Cat. She was naked, relaxed, her body submerged, her head leaning back, her arms outstretched along the tub's rim, her dangling hands making wet, splashy sounds as she lifted them

45

in and out of the water and let cool, jeweled drops drip from her fingertips. We'd been lucky enough to get the one tub that was up on the roof; there was nothing above us but a mile-high sky full of a thousand glittering stars and a glowing, full-to-bursting moon. Cat loved the moon, had insisted we wait until it was full so that everything would be perfect. Now she raised her face to it as if she were tanning. Cat's most famous work, her signature piece that had garnered her all those awards, was a series of twenty-eight poems, each describing a different phase of the moon.

> *Praised be the moon*
> *as she rises tonight*
> *a round white pearl*
> *in the velvet earlobe*
> *of the world . . .*

The moment was pure magic; Cat, the moon, an owl hooting nearby, the cool night air brushing my cheek. If she would have said something—anything, "Come on in, the water's fine," for example— the spell would have been broken. She knew this of course. Hadn't she told us in class time and time again that what wasn't said in a poem was just as important as what had been written down? Hadn't she told us the week she taught haiku to pay attention to the white space on the page—there was even a Japanese word for it, *yohaku*—and to the emptiness that surrounded the poem, the distance between each line? Everything became crystal clear that night as I watched her, as she allowed me to watch her, taking as much time and space as I needed, to absorb her chiseled beauty with my eyes.

I knew she wanted me to join her in the water but I was hesitant and this surprised me. Wasn't this the moment I'd been looking forward to, the moment we'd been building toward all semester? The poets whose work Cat had suggested I read—Adrienne Rich, Audre Lorde, Marilyn Hacker, Chrystos—were all women I had never heard of, women who obviously took other women to be their lovers. I had wondered if she'd suggested the same poems to her other students, and I burned at the thought. I wanted to be special to her. Her favorite student. Her pet. And tonight, at long last, I knew that I was.

> *The moon, half full*
> *And I half-drunk*
> *At the sight of you*
> *Shimmering beneath it . . .*

Finally I started to undress. But first I moved to where she could see me, as I knew she wanted me to. I'd caught her staring at me in class, her eyes lingering just a second too long at my nipples, which she could clearly make out underneath my sweaters, soft, low-cut cashmere pullovers I began to wear for her torment and her pleasure. I could tell I was driving her crazy; she could barely keep her mind on the day's lesson and this pleased me enormously as I watched her watch me from the front row, my breasts beckoning to her as I sat straight and still in my chair. Her clothes were loose, billowy; it was impossible to know what her body looked like beneath those windy skirts and dresses, which, after a while, became as torturous to me as I hoped my tight, bright sweaters were to her.

She smiled now, leaning her head back against the tub's edge, as if she were about to enjoy a show. I began by loosening my auburn hair from its woven braid and removing my tortoiseshell glasses. Everything became softer, fuzzier; everything lost its edge. Somehow that made it all easier. Cat grew blurry, watery, less definite, less sure. I hadn't expected to be so shy, yet it made sense. Wasn't I about to cross some line, enter new terrain, embark upon some exciting, yet terrifying adventure from which I could never return? I didn't remember feeling like this the first time I'd made love to a boy. I was seventeen and eager to get on with it, to get it over with, as I was the only one of my friends who had yet to complete the task. I thought I'd feel differently afterward, be a brand new person, a woman instead of a teenager or a girl. But I'd felt nothing. Unlike now when I was trembling, even though I was fully clothed, my heart racing, my face hot, my palms sweaty, and Cat still halfway across the room.

I stepped out of my flats, removed my socks, stared at my feet, thought about Cat's. Her feet were the one part of her body I knew well, for she wore sandals every day, and her feet were remarkably beautiful. Pale, delicate toes. High elegant arches. I found myself staring at them in class, much to her amusement. She could say so much without saying a thing. She'd see me staring at her feet and lift her eyes to catch mine briefly, and silently ask: *Do you like what you see?* She knew the power of silence, of watching and waiting, of delaying and postponing, until the yearning was so exquisite, you almost didn't want it to come to an end. But everything does come to an end, which is another thing Cat taught us. She explained a principle of Japanese poetry known as *wabi:* the moment something begins, it is already ending. Nothing is permanent, which is what makes everything so sorrowful and beautiful, so precious and rare.

Black cat in the night
Invisible save her two eyes
Glowing like two moons
In the dark . . .

Each moment came and went that night, moments I couldn't hold onto, moments I couldn't bear to let go. I locked eyes with Cat as I unbuttoned my sweater and slipped the sleeves down my arms. She tried not to gasp, but I could hear her breath quicken at the sight of my torso, exposed to her at last. I took my time, folded my sweater neatly and placed it on the bench before stepping out of my jeans and allowing her to behold me in my plain cotton underwear. I had never thought myself particularly attractive; I was too soft and round everywhere, had envied the tight, lean bodies of women like Cat, but now, for the first time, standing under the spotlight of the moon and feeling Cat's unbridled admiration, I felt truly and utterly beautiful. The feeling was intoxicating, like the peach juice and champagne we had drunk at dinner earlier. At that moment I would gladly do anything for her, anything at all.

Cat let me stand there—for how long, minutes? hours?—before she gave me the signal I was waiting for. She lifted one arm and held out her hand, white and pale against the darkness. I climbed out of my undergarments and slipped my body into the water. It was hotter than I expected, or perhaps it was the juxtaposition of the steamy water against the chilly night air, a delicious combination that made me shudder. I kept my back to Cat and felt rather than saw her glide across the water to me like a swan.

Bits of moonlight on the water
Like diamonds around your neck
Ice cold and delicious . . .

Without a word, Cat lifted my long, thick hair off the nape of my neck and licked the delicate, soft skin she found there. I swooned, melted, fell back against her, surrendered myself into her strong embrace at last. The feeling of Cat's body against mine was exciting and comforting; it was home and a place I'd never been to before. She floated me across the tub until she was sitting back on her bench and I was sitting on her lap. I listened to her breath in my ear, felt her fingertips against my skin, heard myself mewling like a kitten as she taught me the wonders of my own bones and flesh. We sank, we floated, we melded into one another, we let the water part around us, enter us, keep us afloat, wrap us in its warmth. And all the while the moon watched over us, pulled at us, called us, bathed us in its white, wondrous light.

Moonglow in the sky
Afterglow on your face . . .

Lifetimes later there was a knock at the door. "We're closing," a male voice informed us. It was strange to hear words, as neither Cat nor I had spoken all evening. We continued our silence as we emerged from the tub, our bodies soft and glowing, our fingers wrinkled as slept-in clothes. Cat dried me off tenderly, from head to toe and then saw to herself as I got dressed. Back in our clothes, I felt distant from her, but then she embraced me again and as her lips found mine, everything between us fell swiftly away.

The moon slips
Behind a cloud
Like your pale arm
Inside a velvet sleeve . . .

Without asking, Cat knew I would come home with her. We drove through darkened streets in silence, her hand on my thigh, our wet hair streaming. Once inside Cat's house, it was only a matter of minutes before we were undressed again. Her bed was covered in white and there was a skylight above it through which I could see a smattering of stars and the lovely translucent moon.

This time Cat let me touch her. I was surprised at the sound she made, something between a sigh and a grunt, as I explored her with my fingers and tongue. I couldn't believe how soft she was. I was unspeakably moved by the gift she was giving me, how completely vulnerable she was allowing herself to be. I counted her freckles with my tongue, I placed my hand inside her warm, wet sweetness, I kissed the hinge where her hip met her thigh. Finally we were filled with each other, the moon disappeared, and we slept, curled together like the two esses at the end of a long, tender kiss.

The morning light was bright and harsh as I opened my gritty eyes. Cat held open a kimono and I slipped my arms through the long silky sleeves.

You stood behind me
lifting a kimono to my shoulders
And I was the sky
A full moon rising
From my feet . . .

She made tea and toast and small talk. The weather, the class she had to teach later, a film that had just opened in town. I listened to her chatter, mute with the wonder of it all. Cat was now my lover, and she acted as if it was perfectly natural for me to be sitting at her table, drinking tea from her mug, eating toast off her plate, watching her move about her kitchen with ease, getting me a cloth napkin, putting another slice of bread into the toaster, opening a window to let in the morning air. It was all very strange and new to me, but I didn't let my confusion show, or if I did, Cat didn't seem to notice.

As Cat poured me a second cup of tea, there was a knock at the door. Cat excused herself and I remained at the table, not knowing what else to do. It wasn't her lover, home from Europe for a surprise visit. That would have been too contrived, too melodramatic. It was a friend, another teacher from the English department, returning some books she had borrowed and asking Cat if she could loan her a particular volume of poetry. "Wait here," I heard Cat say, but as she moved into her study, the woman stepped into the living room, peeked through the doorway, and saw me sitting at Cat's kitchen table, wrapped in the kimono, my hair unkempt, my face wearing a mixture of embarrassment, defiance, and pride.

"Uh, Cat, I'll see you later," the woman called, backing out the door.

Cat returned to the kitchen, the requested book of poetry in hand, but something had been interrupted, lost, the spell had been broken. I was already on my feet, heading for the bedroom, for the safety of my clothes, eager to put up a wall between us.

"I better get going," I mumbled, trying to ignore the hurt and bewildered look on Cat's face as I struggled into my jeans.

"Wait," she said as I reached for the door. "Don't go," she implored as I turned the handle. "I love you," she whispered as I opened the door and stepped through it, her hand on my arm unable to stop me.

"I've got to run," I stammered, not bothering to shut the door behind me. And I did begin to run and then kept running, without once looking back. I never went back to her class, I never returned her phone calls, the letters she wrote me, the notes she tacked to my door.

Moonless night
Like my bed
Without you in it . . .

I dropped out of school and moved clear across the state without saying good-bye to Cat. What was I running so hard from? I couldn't explain it to her because I didn't understand it myself. All I knew was that I couldn't bear to face her. Sure, I identified as bisexual, but that didn't mean anything, everybody did; after all, it was a nontraditional school. But embracing a label was very different from embracing an experience. And that's what Cat was to me, just an experience, an experiment, a litmus test, wasn't she? Or was she?

Cat had her own theories about my disappearing act. Perhaps it was because she was my teacher. (*Don't be ridiculous,* she said in a letter. *We're practically the same age and it won't matter once the semester is over.*) Or perhaps it was because she already had a lover. (Cat informed me in another letter that they had an "understanding" and besides, they were on the verge of splitting up.) Was I afraid that we had gotten carried away by the moon, the wine, the water, and her feelings for me weren't real? (She assured me that they were.) How could I tell Cat when I couldn't even tell myself I wasn't afraid it was those things, I was afraid it *wasn't* those things. I was afraid that whatever was between us was real, too real, as real as the ache in my heart every time I thought of her. I kept running from the questions that plagued me, running from the answers I knew I didn't want to hear. But there was one thing I couldn't run away from and that was the moon.

Moonlight spilling through my window
Filling my empty teacup
Stroking my sleeping cheeks
As I reach through my dreams
For someone who is not there . . .

Every night the damn moon rose high in the sky, making it impossible for me to forget what had happened with Cat. There it was, just a sliver, like a disembodied smile. Then it was half full or half empty, depending on one's point of view. Next it grew fat and bulging, almost as if it were pregnant with itself. Finally it was full, a silver coin, an incandescent opal, Cat's smooth white cheek glowing in the sky. Then all at once the moon disappeared completely, giving me a night of peace, only to return again just as suddenly, forcing me out of my denial. It took months for me to realize that I wasn't running from Cat; I was running from what Cat had taken a great risk to teach me: that I was just like her, that I needed the warmth, the comfort, the thrill of another woman beside me. It hit me sudden and hard, without warning, like turning the corner and coming upon a golden harvest moon bigger than a house in the sky. How powerful and peaceful, how tremendous and true. And so a year later I gathered all my courage and went back to find Cat, to thank her, to apologize, to beg for forgiveness, to explain.

> *Twelve full moons*
> *Have risen and set*
> *Since you have been away.*
> *An old woman greets you*
> *At your young lover's door.*

In Reflection   As a fiction writer, I am frequently asked by readers, "Is that story true?" On one hand, the question is a compliment; obviously the reader has been convinced that the events portrayed in the story occurred exactly as written. On the other hand, the question is an insult, as it denies the fiction writer's imaginative powers. A former writing teacher of mine has a standard answer to this question. When asked at readings, "How much of that story is true?" he always answers, "Thirty-three percent." When I am asked this question, I reply, "The story may or may not be true, but it certainly is real." As our society gets more and more celebrity oriented, readers become more concerned with the author than with the author's work. I do not write memoir or autobiography; I write fiction. Therefore I do not want my readers to see me in my stories. If anything, I want them to see themselves. My stories consist of 33 percent experience, 33 percent imagination, and 33 percent observation. And 1 percent magic.

Vivien Ng

VIVIEN NG

Farewell to Concubines

"Hi, are you there? Pick up the phone! It's me, Tamara! Good news! I'm on the short list for the international law position at the law school. They're flying me in next Thursday for the interview. Should I stay at the hotel or with you?"

I stared at the answering machine. I did not pick up the phone, leaving the tape to do its job while buying myself more time to process the news. But soon my mind drifted to the fourteen-acre lot in the country just off Route 9, not far from Lake Thunderbird. One of my recurring fantasies since discovering that lot on one of my weekend drives across the state in my battered VW was living out in the country in a log cabin. I would build the cabin myself, of course, with the help of a few handy friends. I had seen photographs of shirtless and bare-breasted women felling trees or hammering nails in one of those women-identified-women books published in the 1970s and had fancied myself doing the same. I would picture myself wearing a leather tool belt over cut-off jeans and hoisting beams into place with my powerful arms. The cabin would have an open design, with the living room flowing into a large eat-in kitchen. There would be only one bedroom but overnight guests could be accommodated in the small sleeping loft. I had read somewhere that farmers in nearby Arkansas grew *gai lan* and I figured that I would try growing that and other Chinese vegetables too. Then reality would set in and shatter to pieces these images of quiet rural domesticity. This was Oklahoma, after all, not rural Maine where a single woman could conceivably live a life of solitude as a magnificent spinster, as the writer May Sarton was able to do. Usually at this point I would repeat to myself what my gay friends Rick and Joey had said a hundred times over: "My dear, to live out in the country you need to either buy a shotgun or settle down with a good woman, and most likely you'll need to do both!" I would shudder and draw the curtain on the fantasy.

Tamara represented both an opportunity and a predicament. We first met in the lobby of the Omni Georgetown Hotel during the 1987

March on Washington, some six months before. My girlfriend Alice and I had driven nonstop from New Haven to D.C., only to find that the hotel where we had made our original reservation was completely overbooked and therefore unable to accommodate us. But instead of turning us away to fend for ourselves, the front-desk clerk on her own initiative found us a room at the Omni for the same price. It turned out to be a deluxe room with a king-sized bed and a bathroom the size of most studio apartments in New York City. Although we were exhausted from the long drive and the huge satin-sheeted bed had stirred lascivious thoughts in us, we gave in to a more pressing need, that of a hearty meal at our favorite restaurant in nearby Adams-Morgan. And so we trudged down the stairs to the lobby, where I noticed a woman with frizzy brown hair sitting forlornly on a duffel bag near the front entrance of the hotel. There was something about her that stopped me dead in my tracks. Since Alice was already halfway out the door, I grabbed her left arm to hold her back.

"Is something the matter with you?" I asked the woman, even though I sensed Alice's impatience to head outside.

"Apparently there's no room at the inn, but I made my reservation months ago! I'm waiting to see if my friends from the city got here all right and maybe bum a night on the couch with them. They haven't checked in, though."

"I think one good turn deserves another," I said to Alice. "If not for the goodwill of the clerk at the other hotel, we could be in the same dire straits. There's plenty of space for a rollaway bed in our room. What do you think?"

What else could Alice say under the circumstances? Tamara offered to split the room cost, but we turned her down. It would be for only one night anyway, since she had to take the shuttle back to New York right after the march the following day. This was how Tamara spent her first night with me. Needless to say it was a chaste night for all three of us. It was a good thing that Alice and I had packed an extra change of T-shirts, because we had not brought along anything to sleep in. The king-sized bed seemed a mile wide because we kept as far apart as possible to avoid touching each other unconsciously in an intimate way in the presence of a stranger. All three of us pretended to fall asleep, but in truth none of us did.

The next day we went our separate ways: Tamara set out early in the morning for National Airport to leave her duffel bag in a locker before joining up with the New York contingent. Alice had already arranged to march under the Connecticut banner with her students. I opted to march in solidarity with my courageous friends from Oklahoma City and Tulsa. We were a small but spirited group, some thirty strong. After a quick impromptu lesson, we began to belt out the title song from the musical *Oklahoma!*, taking an occasional time out or two to chant in unison with other marchers, all the way to the Mall. I was almost hoarse from all the singing and shouting when I found Tamara slightly out of breath beside me just as we passed the White House.

"It's a good thing you guys were singing "Oklahoma" or I'd have a hard time finding you. I could hear you a block away!"

"Our enthusiasm is catching, isn't it—even Texas joined in once. If you want to march with us, you need to know the lyrics to 'Oklahoma,'" I shouted over the din.

"No problem," she replied with a smug grin, "I own an LP of the movie soundtrack. I've listened to the song many times."

"In that case, let's take it from the beginning!"

"'Ooooo-kla-homa, where the wind comes sweeping down the plain . . .'"

"Okay! I anoint you an honorary Ooooo-kla-homan!"

"So it's true, then, that Oklahoma is 'o.k.'?"

We engaged in a humorous banter all the way to the Mall. She had a way of bringing out the witty side in me and I could not remember the last time I managed to string together so many one-liners. The march ended much too soon for me. "Do you really have to get back to New York today? We can keep the rollaway bed in the room for another night, you know."

"I wish I could stay at least one more night too. But there's a complicated contract with a Japanese firm that I have to go over before we can sign off on it on Tuesday. I've lost a couple of days of prep time as it is."

"I guess such is the lot of a high-powered Wall Street lawyer, eh?"

"Well, it has its rewards. Listen, I really enjoyed myself today and I don't want the fun to end here. I'd like to see you again. Maybe I could check out what it's like to feel the wind 'come sweeping down the plain'?"

"And to watch hawks 'making lazy circles in the sky'? Now that you've marched with us you're always welcome in Oklahoma! Do you have any plans for Thanksgiving? Alice usually goes home to be with her folks in Vermont, but I prefer to stay in a warmer place. Not that Oklahoma is in the subtropics, mind you. The weather can get real nasty around Thanksgiving."

Later that evening, when we met up for dinner in Chinatown, I told Alice about my time with Tamara. "Would you mind it very much if she spent Thanksgiving with me in Oklahoma? I thought I might

drive her out to Tahlequah to check out the Cherokee museum. I hope
it's open that time of the year, but it's a beautiful drive, regardless."

Alice stared at the neck of her bottle of Tsing Tao and took a sip of
beer before answering, "I won't say that I'm gung ho about it but we've
trusted each other so far and I don't see any reason why I should be upset, do you?"

"What if I had an affair with her?" I asked only half-jokingly.

She chuckled, "In that case you would have satisfied your curiosity about what it's like to have a concubine, wouldn't you?" She knew
only too well that I had been deeply immersed in my project on the history of Hong Kong laws concerning concubines. I had burned precious
telephone minutes with her talking about nothing else.

"But to have a concubine I need to have a wife first. So, will you
marry me? Damn, have we missed the mass wedding ceremony?" I took
her lighthearted cue and steered us back to safer terrain. "Are your students really going to take part in the civil disobedience 'action' before
the Supreme Court tomorrow?"

She reached over and cupped my chin in her hand. "What are you
so nervous about? Thanksgiving is more than a month away. I love you
and right now that's all I need to know about us." I was about to protest
but thought better of it, because when it came to reading me, Alice was
seldom wrong. I shoved all other thoughts aside to concentrate on the
moment. "Let's go back to the hotel," I said. "I want to find out what
satin feels like on bare skin!" She kept her hand under my chin for a
moment longer and then let go slowly, brushing my left breast on the
way down and finally resting on my hand. "Yes, I'd like that," she said
quietly. We thought about walking but changed our mind. It was just
too far and there was so little time left, so we joined the crowd at the
Gallery Place Metro station and took the subway to our hotel.

A week later, I was over at Rick and Joey's for our regular Sunday
brunch. They did not appear pleased after I told them about my encounter with Tamara and the possibility of her Thanksgiving visit. I was
not surprised because they were fiercely loyal to Alice. Joey said, "She
could stay with us. It would be more comfortable for her than the lumpy
futon in your study, and you're coming over for turkey dinner anyway."
Rick added, "If you like, you might think about staying over in the other
guest bedroom to save you the back-and-forth." I put down my fork.
"Don't be ridiculous! Alice and I are okay about this and I certainly
don't need you to be my chaperones. Have you been drinking something other than champagne? You didn't behave this way when Maggie
came to visit last year, or Anne before that. What makes you think that
this is going to be any different? We'll be spending most of the time on

the road anyway. I'm thinking about taking her to Tahlequah on Friday and maybe Osage Hills on Saturday. I'm sure that she'd love to see the tall grass prairie near Pawhuska." Rick held up his hand. "Okay, okay. Point taken. We're not going to meddle, but I do think that you're protesting a tad too much." True to their word, Rick and Joey did not bring up the subject of Tamara again, and held their tongue when a month later I confirmed that she was indeed coming to visit "the land just south of Oz" for Thanksgiving.

A steady freezing rain started to fall shortly after Tamara's plane landed at Will Rogers World Airport in Oklahoma City on Thanksgiving Day. By the time we got to my house some eighteen miles away, the roads had become coated with a layer of ice and the state Highway Patrol had issued a ban on unnecessary driving. When I finally pulled into my garage, Tamara heaved a sigh of relief. "Whew, so this is Oklahoma! But Rodgers and Hammerstein didn't say anything about icy stalagmites reaching 'as high as an elephant's eye'!" I was not quick witted enough to come back with another quote from the musical; all I could muster after the tense trip was the mundane. "I think we may have to eat in tonight. I don't think we can make it to Rick and Joey's, not in this weather. Let's hope that there's no power outage or we may have to eat canned tuna sandwich for dinner. One good thing about living in tornado alley though: I have stocked enough lanterns and batteries to last us a tornado or two, not to mention ice storms!"

"I hope you have candles too," Tamara said as she reached for her duffel bag on the backseat. "Now, show me the rest of your house!"

My house was a three-bedroom, one-bath brick rambler, one of many identical units built in the early 1960s. It was what my realtor had called "a good starter home." When I went to see the house with the realtor, I half expected to find pink plastic flamingos dotting the front lawn and it was a relief to me to have found none. I bought the house only because everyone said I should, that paying rent was like pouring money down the drain. Other than money, I had invested very little else in the house and had done no home improvement work except to replace the hideous dark green wall-to-wall shag carpet. I explained all this to Tamara while giving her a quick tour of the house. "I'm going to put you in my study. I don't have a guest room because I use the third bedroom for storage. I haven't unpacked all my boxes yet. The futon is actually quite comfortable. It used to be my bed but Alice finally talked me into buying a 'real' one a couple of years ago. She prefers hard mattresses so that's what I have now."

"How long have you and Alice been lovers?"

"Oh, about three years, since just before I moved to Oklahoma.

But if you add up all the days we're actually together, it's less than 365 days."

"I was involved in a long-distance relationship once but it didn't work out. I think I'm more of an all-or-nothing kind of person."

"Our arrangement has worked well for us so far, I think. I get grumpy and can be difficult to live with when I'm busy or pressed for time, which is pretty much all the time during the school year. Alice is good at gauging my mood, but it's still rough, so not living together full time may actually be a blessing. We spend our summers together and one long weekend a month when we can manage it. I do most of the commuting because I love taking a break to visit the museums and galleries in New York. Our best months are June and July when we're both relaxed. But enough about me . . . you must be starving! I'm not much into cooking at all but I can be competent in a pinch. Alice usually does the cooking and I do the cleaning up."

Tamara cocked her head at me. "It's hard to imagine you being grumpy and difficult."

"Give me time and you'll find out for yourself if it's true," I said as I led her to the kitchen. "Lemme see . . . there's a couple of frozen pizzas, a pack of chicken thighs . . . and there's the sea bass filet that I bought when Alice was here last September . . . I can stick a bottle of white wine in the freezer while we decide what to cook."

"Let's go with sea bass. It doesn't take long to defrost the fish. Ah-ha! I see that you have fresh garlic. We can make a tasty dish with that plus salt and pepper."

"I didn't know that high-powered Wall Street lawyers could cook!"

"Give me time and you'll find out for yourself what else I'm good at . . ."

The phone rang just then as if it were on cue and I was saved from having to respond to her loaded suggestion. It was Alice calling to check if I had got home safely from the airport. "I saw footage of the ice storm on CNN . . . it looks nasty out where you are. I guess your trip to Tahlequah tomorrow is out of the question? Don't do anything foolish or risky." I cracked a worn joke about Oklahoma's fickle weather and ventured that there might be a slim chance to salvage the weekend. "Maybe we'll stay closer to home and visit the Cowboy Hall of Fame . . . I wonder if Tamara's a John Wayne fan?" I had never been to the museum and could only guess what would be in its collection. Tamara started to pantomime throwing a lasso at me as I said good night to Alice. "Gotcha!" she said, finishing up her mime by drawing closer and finally encircling me in her arms. That she would follow through with a long, lingering kiss seemed to me to be the most natural thing to do under the circumstances.

In most pulp fiction this would be the point in the story where we find the feverish lovers peeling off each other's clothes while beating a hurried retreat to the bedroom. My body was certainly willing to play the part and I would be a hypocrite to deny that the march in D.C., not to mention the month of telephone calls that followed, was anything less than protracted foreplay. But with Alice's admonition not to do anything foolish or risky still ringing in my ears, I was not quite ready to be a pulp-fiction heroine. With great regret I disentangled myself from her arms and pushed her gently away. "Let's start dinner," I croaked. Stroking my cheek softly with the back of her forefinger, Tamara nodded. "I understand."

I took the wine from the freezer and poured out two glasses. Turning to Tamara, I said, "There should be no question in your mind that I'm very attracted to you. I don't want you to think that I've been toying with you." She started to open her mouth but I held up my hand and continued, "But it's obvious too that Alice is very much a part of my life. She's been my emotional anchor for the last three years and I won't give her up."

"And you think that I'm going to insist that you choose between Alice and me?"

"I don't know. Frankly, I don't know you well enough yet to tell whether that's what you want. But you did say that you're an 'all-or-nothing' kind of person."

"Yes, I did say that. I figured that out after my last relationship failed. But maybe there are no hard and fast rules that apply to all relationships? I try not to go through life with a dogmatic mindset. Don't you think that you are looking too far down the road? We haven't even taken the first step."

"I'm like a chess player. It's second nature to me to anticipate moves and countermoves."

"And you nip something you don't like in the bud before it has a chance to develop? That's cruel, and unnatural too."

"Hmm."

"I think the fish is done marinating, don't you? Here, pass me the frying pan."

The sea bass was seared to perfection. I raised my glass to Tamara in appreciation and we ate in companionable silence for the next hour or so. The freezing rain had stopped some time during the evening but not before transforming my drab neighborhood into an ethereal crystal fantasyland. The amber streetlamp at the end of the driveway had cast a deceptively warm golden glow to the icy scenery outside. "You do love it here, don't you?" Tamara broke the silence when she caught me staring outside lost in thought. I had brewed a pot of oolong tea and we had settled comfortably in the sofa by the window. I shrugged. "In a strange way, I do. I had a chance to take up a new position in Boston last year, but in the end I chose to pass it up. I couldn't bring myself to leave."

"Boston would be a lot closer to New Haven."

"That's what Alice said too. My decision to stay caused some friction between us, but we got over it."

"What kept you here?"

"My friends here, for one, but that's not the only factor. There's something about the landscape here. It's hard to explain and Alice still can't understand it. Once, when I was driving down a two-lane county road at twilight, I noticed lights being turned on one by one in a farmhouse in the distance. I imagined the family gathering for the evening meal. There was nothing around the house for what seemed like miles except for the barn and a scrawny tree. It was late fall and the tree was bare. For some reason that desolate yet domestic scene tugged my heart and my eyes started to well up. Do you know what I mean? It's not picture-postcard pretty but it gets right to my heart." After that it seemed natural to tell Tamara about my solitary weekend drives across the state, about how "at home" I felt when I entered Cherokee County the first time and how I would keep returning to Tahlequah, the heart of Cherokee Nation. I told her about the fourteen-acre lot and my dream of building and living in a log cabin. I did not tell her what was keeping me from realizing my dream. "On nights like this," I yawned, "I wish I could build a roaring fire. My cabin will have a huge fireplace." Tamara rested her head on my shoulder and closed her eyes. "I'd like very much for you to show me *your* Oklahoma, maybe next trip? It doesn't look like we're able to go on your fabled drives this time." "I'd like that too," I replied and, making reference once more to our favorite musical, "Be forewarned that my surrey won't have a fringe on top!" A few moments later I stood up and took her hand. "Let's go to bed."

I woke up to a bright sunny morning. I raised my arms over my head and stretched under the down comforter but did not get up. Tamara stirred beside me and snuggled even closer. "Penny for your thought." I picked up her right hand and kissed her fingers. "I'm glad I got to know what else you're good at." She gave me a sly smile. "Umm. Maybe you could return the favor again?" I slid underneath the blanket and did just that.

Even as Tamara and I explored our nascent relationship that weekend, Alice was never far from my mind and I felt her keenly when I was doing the most mundane and familiar things, such as clearing the table after breakfast or stashing dishes away in the dishwasher. When I showed Tamara my research on Hong Kong concubines, I half expected Alice to jump in with her provocative interpretations. On Saturday night, while we were in bed, I felt that I had a confession to make. "I'm falling madly in love with you but I keep thinking about Alice. I feel like I'm cheating on both of you."

"Do you think about her while we're making love?"

"No."

"Then there's hope yet for me. But seriously, when you invited me to visit, what did you think would happen this weekend?"

I chose my words carefully. I avoided using the word "fling." "Well, I thought that there was a chance that we might get involved sexually. In fact, I joked with Alice about the possibility of having an affair with you when I told her that I had invited you to visit me for Thanksgiving."

"What did she say to that?"

"She didn't take it seriously at all. She even joked about my getting to know what it's like to have a concubine!"

"So, why do you feel that you are cheating on her now?"

"I don't know. I didn't expect to fall so madly in love with you. I feel very conflicted now. Have you seen the Chinese movie *Raise the Red Lantern*? Good! Well, maybe that's a bad example but the point I want to make is that in traditional Chinese culture, when the husband acquires a concubine he is not cheating on his wife, and he isn't cheating on the woman who becomes his concubine either, because both women know what his intentions are. And they understand their own roles."

"Your analogy doesn't make any sense at all. This is not old China and you're not a dirty old man!"

"No, I'm not. But I'm still confused."

"Look, we're both adults. I came here on my own accord. If I remember correctly, I came on to you first. I looked for you in D.C. among the tens of thousands of marchers. I'm getting involved with you with my eyes wide open. Once again, I think that you are looking too far down the road. Why don't we give what we have started this weekend a chance to develop before worrying about what the future may bring? One thing you'd better be sure, though—don't ever think of me as a concubine!"

I waited two weeks before I made my confession to Alice. We were in New York for our rendezvous. "Are you sure that you're in love with her and not just in lust?" she asked after a long silence. "I can accept the lust part but I don't know whether I can handle your being in love with another woman."

"Even if you'll always be my principal 'wife'?" I tried to leaven the mood with another reference to the old Chinese custom.

"This concubine thing is getting a bit shopworn, don't you think?"

"I'm sorry."

"I need time to think about all this. I'm going back to New Haven today and I want to be alone for a while, so don't follow me. I'll call you when I'm ready."

"So this is a trial separation?"

"I don't know what to call this. I still love you but I don't know what that means anymore. One thing I know for sure, though—I won't be a concubine!"

A month later, with the retirement of a colleague who had been in ill health, the international law position materialized. Tamara decided to go for it. "You know what this means, don't you? I'm serious about wanting to be with you full time." I hesitated. "This is a big decision to make, don't you think? You'll be giving up a lucrative Wall Street career to be a professor at a law school in the middle of nowhere. What if things don't work out between us? What would you do then?" Tamara was dismissive of my concern. "Let me worry about my career, okay? If you don't want me to move to Oklahoma to be with you, that's a different matter. When the time comes for me to decide between Wall Street and the law school, I need to know what your intentions are, but we haven't got to that point yet." "Okay," I said. "I'll try not to look too far down the road."

I stared at the blinking red light on the answering machine. The moment of truth had arrived. I picked up the telephone and dialed Alice's phone number.

In Reflection   I like writing in the first person. It is a device I use to help me get inside the main character of my story, to give her characterization more psychological depth. Naturally, the use of the first person has led some readers, including a number of my friends, to believe that *all* my stories are autobiographical, and they try to speculate the "real" identity of the other characters. Since I invest a lot of myself in the "I" character in my stories, they are correct to a certain degree. Paradoxically, in writing this ostensibly "autobiographical" piece, I find that I reveal less of myself than in my other stories. The "real" part is the setting—Oklahoma—and I have written this story to bid farewell to a place for which I have developed a deep affection. However, because I am writing fiction, not memoir, I have stepped outside myself to develop the "I" character, resulting in a story that is in fact less autobiographical than the others.

Sima Rabinowitz

SIMA RABINOWITZ

Love Quartet

One—Devotions

Peggy was in love with our French teacher. Everyone else was in love with Peggy. To win her heart, all of us pretended to be in love with Miss Kidd, too, but honestly, I was as much in love with present participles and the past-perfect subjunctive as I was with Miss Kidd. She was someone who was perpetually at a loss for words, which I understood to mean a loss for ideas, except during the verb substitution drills we practiced daily in her classes.

Peggy was as foreign to me as French. (*La plume de mon oncle est sur le bureau de ma tante.*) She was, somehow, both elegant and slightly rough. And because one parent worked the day shift and the other the night shift, she was also, enviably, independent. She spoke to our teachers as if she were one of them, not one of us. She drove herself to school; she cooked her own dinner; she bought her own clothes. Of course, she wore the same faded denim overalls and fragile batik shirts as the rest of us (new made to look old). On me these clothes looked misshapen and silly. On Peggy, they looked, at once, exotic and refined.

And while the rest of us carried our things in colorful woven bags with long braided handles, Peggy carried her stuff in a faded leather satchel with pockets. The worn leather puckered and bulged where her *Deluxe Compact Christian Growth Study Bible* peeked up, almost perversely, from the satchel's front pocket. Peggy was a founding member of The Way prayer group, which met on a schedule as regular as the verb substitution drills.

Every morning before school started while The Way members met in the conference room off the principal's office, I held my own vigil outside Miss Kidd's room. This was the unspoken bargain Peggy and I had made when The Way first got started. After all, somebody had to keep track of Miss Kidd, somebody who could provide a full report to Peggy. (*She was a few minutes late this morning. I'm pretty sure she was*

67

wearing the same blouse she wore Monday. And she looks a little pale today. I wonder if she's getting sick.)

Loyalty to Miss Kidd might not have been as compelling to Peggy as loyalty to Christ, but it came pretty close. And I hoped that even though I was Jewish and could never be devoted to Christ, I could still become one of Peggy's special girls. Peggy collected girls the way Miss Kidd collected pop quizzes, often and abundantly. She had more followers than French verbs have conjugations, but only a few girls ever really did more than simply orbit around her. Only a few girls became part of her inner circle.

I was fairly certain the invitation to Peggy's annual winter slumber party was a sign of *rapprochement,* until I found myself in the paneled basement of her parents' house with two dozen other giddy girls, all of whom I'd seen at one time or another hanging around outside Miss Kidd's room between classes or after school. Still, when it actually came time to sleep, after we tried and failed to levitate Janine Robinson and Janine's cousin Sandy, both of whom swore on their *Deluxe Compact Christian Growth Study Bible* they'd seen another girl levitated just the week before at another slumber party, Peggy grabbed my hand and pointed upstairs. *Come on! There's an extra space in the guest room.*

I waited all night, my burning cheek buried in the rumpled sheet of my makeshift sleeping bag, arms flanking my sides, for Peggy to take my hand. She laced her fingers first between Patty Myer's, and after Patty, she locked hands with Linda Alexander, and finally after Linda, with Joanne Bogan. Their hands dangled lovingly for the longest time over the side of Joanne's cot. I was the only other girl in the room.

One day the following week Miss Kidd was absent. (*I told you she was looking awfully pale last week.*) Since the substitute was completely *déclassée,* I went to wait for Peggy in the corridor outside the principal's conference room. Through the narrow glass rectangle in the door I could see Peggy, a girl I didn't know, Patty Myer's older brother, Stewart, another boy, skinny with red hair, and Patty, Linda, and Joanne. I watched them for a few minutes, heads bent over their books, hands clasped together as they recited. *For the message of the Cross is foolishness to those who are perishing, but to those of us being saved, it is the power of God.*

Then I made my way to my first period class.

Two—Signs

After we dropped off the world's foremost authority on postmodern semiotics in the Spanish medieval epic at Washington National Airport,

I realized we were headed in the wrong direction across M Street. *Here we are*, she said, as she maneuvered the Beetle into a cramped space in front of a popular Georgetown restaurant. I followed her inside.

Sometime between the second (for me) and third (for her) glass of Mouton Cadet (red for her, white for me) she said *Where are you supposed to be right now?* *At home*, I said, which was true if home could signify not only my particular domicile, but also the general complex of signs and symbols surrounding my home life. I just couldn't bring myself to say *upstairs in 2C watching the season opener of "Dallas" with my fiancé and the neighbors.*

It didn't occur to me that she was supposed to be anywhere else. *Do you realize that I am always asking you to talk about yourself, but that you never ask me a thing?* she said. *I think it's because what I've been saying all along is true—you're not in love with me. You're in love with the idea of being in love with me.*

We ate our veal française in silence.

You're going to tell Barry the conference ran late, aren't you? I nodded. *But since he doesn't know how you feel about me, or so you say, why wouldn't you just tell him we went out for dinner together afterward?*

I chewed on another morsel of veal.

Where are you supposed to be? I asked her.

Driving you home, she said. I followed her out.

Three—Falling

It was snowing sideways the day I fell through the floor of the Thrifty Mart on Route 15 in Gettysburg, Pennsylvania. I was distracted, having watched a graphic movie that morning with my students about the disappeared in Chile, and I was searching for further distraction still—cake, candy, something made of yeast and sugar and prepared without much care. Something to distract me from the gap in the day, the dreary afternoon ahead, long hours until classes again the next morning.

The hole I fell through was no wider than a packing crate, the drop no more than six or eight feet down a set of slanted wooden steps that folded up inside themselves to become the basement's ceiling. Suddenly I was spinning, head first, feet up, then feet first, head up, then finally on my side. I landed, right side up, in the dark tunnels of Santiago, under the stadium, where the fear smelled like rotting eggs, sour milk, sweaty concrete. Three or four men in uniform stared at me from under their helmets and through the dim glow of flashlights. *¿Dónde estoy? ¿Dónde me encuentro? ¿Qué ha pasado? ¿Qué hago? ¿Qué* *hago?* On the floor between them a pile of tools—instruments of their inhuman work. I was paralyzed. One of the men approached. I backed up against the wooden staircase. I was surprised—these men spoke English.

When it was once again and not much later 1985, I was standing at attention in the basement of the Thrifty Mart. I wanted not to be touched, not to be spoken to, not to be seen. I climbed the narrow wooden steps, left without my Hostess cupcakes, and I walked from that hole in the floor to my front door with the snow blowing sideways against my face.

At home, I called a colleague with whom I was vaguely in love. A woman who was hunting down every unavailable man available to her in our small town. A woman who would not have interested me were there any real hope of a relationship. After the emergency room, she rubbed my feet with lavender oil and woke me every two hours as prescribed, and between bouts of consciousness I fell into a dizzy trance, a sleep enhanced by the tenderness and danger of having another wounded animal near.

Four—Etc.

"I miss you," she says. "Why don't you come over?" When I get there it turns out that what she wants is a ride to SuperAmerica for cigarettes and as long we're there anyway, half-and-half, a jar of spaghetti sauce, a box of corn flakes, and a couple of candy bars.

"You should get a car," I tell her.

"I have the bike."

"You can only ride the motorcycle three months out of the year in Minnesota. You should get a car."

"Why? Margaret drives me to work every day and you take me everywhere else I want to go. Don't you?" She smiles and looks out the window.

Margaret is Terry's best friend. They work at the University Hospital together. That's where they met. Margaret's an ex-girlfriend, too, of course, since they make the best friends.

On the way back from SuperAmerica we stop at Mr. Movies and rent a video. And halfway through the video we stop and have sex.

"You should get a girlfriend," I tell her.

"Why? Margaret cooks me breakfast and keeps my secrets and buys me presents. And you go to bed with me whenever I ask. Don't you?"

I smile and look out the window.

In Reflection

SUBJECTING MYSELF TO FICTION   "Love Quartet," like any story, fiction or nonfiction, autobiographical or pure invention, began as something true. It started with the memory of falling, of snow falling sideways, of me falling through a hole in the floor, of me falling, and falling, and falling in love with women who never fell with me, of how all these experiences of falling were linked.

I was working intensely and with a kind of surreal concentration with composer Libby Larsen. We were on a tight deadline, working to complete the libretto for an original choral composition based on James Dickey's poem "Falling," which had been commissioned by a group in South Carolina. Dickey posed enormous problems for us. The subject of falling, however, did not. Libby has written a great deal about flying and falling. In the pauses between struggles with Dickey lines, Dickey's lies, Dickey's sense of what it means to have fallen, in every sense of the word, we talked and talked and talked about falling. I felt myself fall, fall into the idea of falling. And very quickly, in just a few hours, when normally I write slowly, very slowly, I fell into what is now the third part of "Love Quartet."

Within a few days I wrote the other three sections. Once I had written about the actual physical experience of falling, the metaphorical experience asserted itself. How many times had I fallen for a woman who had leaned over the edge with me and then watched me slip off the precipice alone? Perhaps I was able to write about this pattern now, to subject myself to the story, to fall into it again, because I had landed in a safe zone—a happy relationship. Now I found these unrequited experiences I wrote about as amusing as troubling. I hoped they might amuse others.

A few months later I turned this piece of fiction into a "performance piece" for three voices. It fell easily into another form. Two actors and one writer (me) performed the piece at a local performance cabaret. I subjected myself to an audience, and I was happy to find the piece was, indeed, amusing to others.

Performing the piece helped me to understand what inconsistencies existed in the subject, to sense the moments that were confusing, unclear, to hear the rhythms better. I converted the piece back to narrative again, back to fiction. It fell back into place.

The story is autobiographical because I really did fall. The story is autobiographical because I really am its subject (at least as much as I am not its subject). The story is autobiographical because there is something in each section that I am willing to admit is real, is what happened, is what I remember happening. And as for the details and the subjects in "Love Quartet" that are not altogether real—they are completely and utterly true.

Our Mothers

Donna Allegra

PHOTOGRAPH BY KRYSTYNA SANDERSON

DONNA ALLEGRA

The Dead Mothers Club

"**Y**ou the only woman on the job, a journeyman and Black too?
Umph." A tug on my pants leg accompanies the voice.

I stop splicing the wires on the string of temporary lights. From
atop my wooden ladder, I look down into Casper Tyrone's watery green
eyes. Those eyes were probably a big draw in the heyday of youth, but
as he stands below me, with a coil of red, white, and green number
twelve wire nestled on his shoulder, he's not a pretty nigger.

"I'm a come over and mess with you later," Casper promises.

"Not if you expect to live and tell the tale." I give him an attitudi-
nous look, brandishing my screwdriver like a saber.

"I guess she told you, tool buddy," says Jim Cleary. As Casper steps
away, Jim comes into view picture-perfect as a regular guy with his
square jaw and Flyin' Fish duck-bill cap.

"Yep. All that and a bag of chips." Casper's voice popples with such
laughter that I decide I like the dapper touch to his work clothes—polished Red Wing boots, neatly sewn patch above the knee on his jeans,
cornrows braided tight to the back of his neck.

"I bet she puts on a nice sundress and a pair of heels for her boyfriend when she gets home." Jim sets down his tool bag, stickered with
an American flag. He speaks to Casper, but he's trying to coax me to
join in.

"I'm a jeans and T-shirt kind of gal."

"Married or single?" Jim asks, inhaling his cigarette with the intensity of a blow-dryer.

"Single."

"What'sa matter? No man is interested in you?"

"When I want romance, I can get it."

"Oh yeah, it's easy for women to get romance. Men have to work
at it," Jim says sourly.

"I don't know, really," I say vaguely. How'd I get cornered in that
trap?

75

I wasn't ready to go back to construction work when the union called.

"You can make a lot of money on this job," the foreman said as he checked my work ticket. "The company has the contract to upgrade all the electrical systems in the hospital."

Money means I can buy time out from working and time is worth a hundred times money. But connections with other electricians thread me to the remnants of kindness that show up now and again in the men. I don't have to give my whole heart away for crumbs.

By the end of my first day, I'm back in sync with shouldering a six-foot ladder, tool pouch slapping my thigh. As I return to the electrician's shop in the basement of the hospital, I see a small, orange-haired boy crying like there's no tomorrow. You'd think his world had come to an end, too. I hold myself together enough to lock up my tools and salute the crew good-bye.

Out in the lobby of the hospital, an East Indian woman walks haltingly toward the exit. I hold the door open, thinking she's ill, but her body quakes to contain sobs. Then I see it's worse than any illness: her hand dangles a hospital sack, like the one I carried when I took my mother's belongings from All Saints Presbyterian.

It's so dark that even the moon seems asleep, but, as usual, I lie awake while others slumber. Eyes open, I enter the tunnel of memory and meet with selves I try to put to rest—one is a girl pushing her mother away as the woman tries to shake her child from a nightmare.

I think on the stars that live beyond my window. They outshine streetlights with a reach that casts filling glances into dark alleys. Do novas envy people who can sleep through the nights? I do.

"What's up there, rubber asses?" Vito, the boy bimbo, comes around to take the crew's coffee break order. Twice this week he's made mistakes with somebody's breakfast. He doesn't care. He's into showing off his deltoids and pictures of his Camaro.

Standing beside him is a woman in her late twenties, belt cinched tight at the waist and leg cuffs rolled high so you can see frilly anklets atop "ladies" style work boots. Maybe a brush with sheet metal debris or a run-in with a ragged edge of pipe will adjust her fashion sense to fit the work environment.

Jim Cleary goes into a thousand-watt smile. "What's going on, Vito?" he says, eyes telescoping down her body.

"How you doin'?" she asks, responding to his appeal for sex and all but batting her eyes as she gives him the once-over.

"This is my new assistant, Iris Maldonado," Vito says. "Fresh blood from the union. The females are taking over. She'll be getting you guys' and ladies' coffee from now on. I got important things to do," he boasts.

"I'm a second-year apprentice just like you," Iris says and gives his arm a punch that's more like a shove.

"Whoa, she's really strong," Jim says.

"I'm into working out. I got all these aerobic videos," Iris brags about these trophies.

"Your body must be really toned. Is it firm? Let me see a muscle." Jim winks at Vito as the *Muscle and Fitness* babe pulls up her shirtsleeve. She flexes her arm, but nothing moves between her wrist and shoulder. It makes me think of chickens, sheep, and cows raised for consumption: animals penned from exercise to keep their flesh tender.

"See, I'm strong, right?" she says.

Jim touches Iris's upper arm with a show of gingerliness. "Not bad," he says. He tenses his upper body, sucks in the heft of his gut, and leans in to her, showing off his beefsteak tomato biceps. "D'you go in for naked coed wrestling?"

"Get out of here," she half-shrieks, half-giggles, and pushes him away, with no force.

I look to catch her eye in greeting and she turns her face away. "I'm Gabrielle," I say. She reacts with a pastel smile—as if it's obscene to show interest in another woman. You'd think I was a troll asking her hand in marriage.

So she's het, has no sense of sisterhood as a woman in construction, doesn't want to know me. Fine with me, honey.

"Gabrielle," Vito croons, "for once I don't have to go looking all over to find you. You should stay in one place, work with these guys. What you want for break?"

"Just tea with lemon, thanks, Vito." I dig into my pocket for change, unwilling to give him my Susan B. Anthony dollar.

"A spinster's brew!" Jim exclaims. "You must be a cheap date. I like that in a woman."

"I'm not a date, Jim. I'm a worker."

"Gabrielle, I'm just kidding ya. Where's your sense of humor?" Jim strips a wire with his utility knife, his smile like the serrated blade.

"It's here, waiting for the funny stuff." I feel stiff as a corset at the beach.

Jim doesn't reply and turns to Vito. "Get me an eggs-and-sausage on a roll, a cream donut, coffee with milk and sugar, and get it right this time."

"That's a grease and sugar shortcut to cardiac arrest," I say, unwilling to let him brush me off.

"So? You eat healthy, a bus runs you over; runners get heart attacks all the time. See how much good exercise does them," Jim says irritably.

I slip away and return to my task wrapping plastic yellow cages around the construction lights.

It doesn't matter that I was raised heterosexual: I don't know how to handle men. That was one of many lessons I refused from my mother. I never got to show her more than anger. It's only now that I know love hides behind other emotions.

At moments like this when sadness looks out from at my eyes, a spill that seeps through the layers I've bundled around me, I wonder how can she be gone when I still need to know where I put my feet next, how to connect with others? Death isn't fair.

My ladder rattles and I clutch at the top step, look down to see Casper smiling up at me. I frown slightly, feeling putrid from a night of restlessness that still isn't sleep.

"You're doing a fine job there, Gabrielle."

"Well, don't tell the other guys. I want to keep my bad reputation."

"What you working on, G?" The timbre in his voice is a song could draw water from dry land.

"Can't tell you, Casper. It's a secret mission from God."

"Aw, you can tell me."

"Nah. Whenever anyone finds out what I'm up to, I have to kill 'em."

"Pretty please." His ears stand up like a Doberman's. Casper is listening, not just rapping. Someone gave this boy good home training.

"Okay, you asked for it. I run the temporary lights for the renovation areas. Changing light bulbs is the only work I'm good for. You ready to die now?"

"How come you never have coffee with the crew, beautiful?"

"Too many bloated egos with little minds running big mouths." I should be more careful: hubris is what gets us all in the end.

"Come have coffee with us," Casper says.

I don't want to, but follow him to a room where metal studs await their Sheetrock cover and empty spools of wire stack higher than the ceiling grid. We walk in on heated conversation from Jim, Iris, and a couple other electricians.

"You won't see me taking any time off when my mother dies," Jim declares. "She was a terrible mother, a real nut job, into all the women's rights bunk, but didn't have time to take care of her family."

Mike, who started on the job last week with me, responds with a tone of complaint. "And this is the same foreman who docked me for the days I had to take off when my Dad died five years ago. I hope he feels payback now with his mother passing."

"So his mother died. What's the big deal that he needs a month off?" Jim hurls a pipe bender out the way as he grabs an empty wire reel to sit on. I wince at the harsh metallic clank.

"Jumpy," Casper scolds and I shrug him off. He shakes his head at his tool partner. "Parents matter even after you grow up, Jim. I know because I was a wanted child. My parents had to wait six years to get me. That's how long it took the adoption process. I don't know who my birth mother was or what was her story, but my real mother loved me like a rock. I cried like a man at her funeral."

He sounds stilted, like this is a speech he's ever ready to deliver. Even so, the roll of feelings that I wad up during the workday and stick at the bottom of my tool bag balloons and I burst out with "Oh, Casper." I sound like a female lead in a movie love scene. I can't help myself, imagining his grief.

"Oh my God, my God. That must've broken your heart so much. I'm so sorry . . ." I can't stop babbling and hug him on impulse. The pain of losing your mother so young unties all my laces.

"It's something you never get over," Casper says fervently.

"She really likes you, buddy," Jim says, a leer in his tone.

Iris looks up at me too and her expression is like she's seen a ghost and identifies with me. But that can't be. But it's probably a trick of the light spilling through the window; because if I'm corduroy, Iris is chiffon—the kind of woman who plays femininity to give a man the illusion that he's in charge.

Early the next morning, Casper shows up as I snap circuit breakers on a panel board in the electric closet. He leans against the door buck. "You got a boyfriend, pretty?"

"Yep."

"What's his name?"

I frown like I'm concentrating, "I dunno. I don't pay him that much attention."

"Hmpf. I thought so."

"Casper, I'm not in the mood to lie and I'm not going to tell you all my stuff, so stay out of my business, okay?"

"We need to go somewhere and get busy—your girlfriend at your place a lot?"

"Whoa, Nelly!" I drop a circuit breaker as the enormity of what he assumes shorts to my brain.

"It's good to have a buddy on the job to vibe with," I say, trying to calm the panic rearing to gallop out my throat. "But it ain't nothing more than that." I stoop for the breaker, cursing myself for being such a shocked spinster. Is this the new morality, where a married man can say to a woman he's known less than a week, "We should sleep together"?

Casper looks undaunted and his face is expectant.

"Casper, sometimes people mistake attentiveness for attraction when that's not it at all."

Over the next few days, I cool my enthusiasm toward Casper. I'm not in a fury that he put a move on me. With his doughboy body and around-the-way vibe, he had seemed safe. Where do guys get the nerve?

My job as the light maintainer gives me the freedom to work alone on the floors under construction. Sure, it's constant up and down on a ladder to alligator-wrestle uncooperative coils of Romex cable across a crowded ceiling, but no people are around to make the job that much harder.

This stringer circuit has a run of dead lights that I gather one by one, then toss each bulb to the floor so I can hear the moist popping sound. Before the day is done, a laborer will have swept up the shards. Broken glass is one of the few things that can never be rejuvenated. Like all the king's horses and all the king's men, my mother will never come back to life again.

I better take a mental-health break if I want to make it through the day. A hoist up to the windowsill lets me watch gauzy clouds lounge across the horizon. Bridges of light link the shadows to substance and possibility.

My friends who haven't lost a parent voiced sympathetic words, but didn't have real understanding. I wanted to tear past their murmured condolences and lament, I don't need you to feel sorry! Death is a rite of passage. It's like any other good heartache that leaves you shattered and stronger: a dare of trust between strangers, a child's impulsive affection that stabs you to tears.

I squint at the avenue below, newly tender toward the elderly trying to survive this city. Pieces of people remind me of her: the wide bewildered eyes swimming behind bifocals, a man who wears a headwrap like Eartha Kitt. In the sea of human traffic, I watch couples as young as my parents were when I was five years old, twelve years, and seventeen. How do people step into the ring for life again and again? Wasn't once enough for all that pain and sorrow?

No potions can cure what ails me these days. I wish for a charm to coax sleep back home and put a spell on the dreams that tell me nothing is well because the planet is returning to dust. Working alone, I can stumble through the day without having to push anyone away.

Come late afternoon I'm sinking again, but not drowning. My even keel gets a jolt when I hear the fizz pop as I cut across live wires. While I examine the newly burned holes in my pliers, the foreman comes around to tell me tomorrow Iris will be my helper.

At home, I check my messages. All that's on the machine is two minutes of European classical music. I've gotten this at least once a week for the past two months. No one leaves a name.

A blanket of gray clouds has tucked the night in bed. The rain hums a lullaby. When I was a child, she read to me before I went to sleep. Sometimes she'd sing. She was so pretty.

I haven't seen traces of her anywhere for days. I wish so bad I could reach back and be sweet to her now, some way to make up for all the times I cut her off, to let her know I cared. At the first adolescent scowl, she retreated. The least layer of frown could get my mother to back off. I had to figure out so much on my own. She never told me anything about my body, having a period, or sex—as if she were too ladylike to know such things. Now my mother's gone and who can I ask what are people worth to one another? What glue holds them beyond the initial appeal when the dark side surfaces? How is it relationships have their meaning?

I may never stop crying for her. Tip the glass the right way and it all comes spilling over. The pain doesn't lessen, it just stops being so wide awake and conscious. Did she know that dreams last only two to four seconds and feel like forever?

As the moon slips through the torn clouds, steam hisses from the radiator cap like ripping paper. The moon and I are a Cyclops with a wide and dreaming eye. Memories stalk me through the night. After she divorced my father when I was nine, I didn't want to make the journey every Sunday to see her. I'd spend my visit in the bathroom with the door closed. When it was time to return home, I'd make it obvious that I was glad to leave, impatient that she'd call a cab service, rather than hail a taxi from the street.

She'd walk me from the door of her apartment to the cab, "to see you home safely." Which only made me mad: I was big and could get to the cab waiting just outside her building. But she'd escort me and recite the address to my father's house with careful instructions to the driver. And all I could think was, why won't she just leave us alone?

Once she said, "Wouldn't it be easier to forgive me than to stay mad all your life?"

"No," I said, not knowing how hard it would be to keep up the anger. But in a way I was right: it *is* harder to forgive—the thing the spiritual people say we must do if we want to be happy.

In the electric closet I take the wires off a circuit breaker in preparation for running a new string of lights. I hear knocking, push open the door to Casper.

"What do you want?" I let vexation harden my voice.

"How about a kind word and a smile?"

"They're not on the menu. What's up, Casper?" I sound like a cop and don't care what he thinks.

"Okay, I'm in the doghouse now. When you gonna let up and forgive me?"

"Never. You're just like your boyfriend Jim and those other dickheads. I don't need that shit, Casper."

"Now, why you wanna be like that and make me have to go through all this drama?"

"Later for you."

The hurt on his face glimmers, then the anger blazes. Because the contract between a straight man and woman is that she protects his feelings and he won't beat her up. I watch desire, need, and disappointment flicker like TV channels across his face. The tightened flesh takes me back to the day I looked at my mother and thought, she's bent and unsteady now. I'm strong in my prime.

"You've got an attitude too big for your britches, young lady."

"Stcch," I suck my teeth at him.

"Don't 'stcch' me, you heifer," Casper says and a sound like a whiffle escapes me.

"Why don't you just leave me the fuck alone, man?"

"Cause I want someone like you to care about me."

"You want love, get a dog," I say, returned to childhood language and its swirl of unreasonableness taking over. When I look up, Casper has turned and walked away.

Having Iris as my helper is a burden in disguise. I'm exhausted just from explaining the temporary lights operation. But I feel responsible to teach her the electrician's trade.

This wing of the hospital is colder than a morgue. Frigid wind whistles through the broken window to be swallowed down the opening in the floor where a new elevator will be installed. In the thick cold air, my breath looks creamy when I scout the exposed ceiling beam for hangers to run a string of temporary lights.

"Bring your ladder over by the column, so I can feed you the Romex across the elevator shaft," I tell my sullen apprentice.

I direct her how to unravel the cable, stiff as raw macaroni, and thread it across the ceiling where pencil rod and disconnected pipes litter our path.

"The stupid ceiling duct is in the way. How am I supposed to get over there with this hole in the floor?" Iris complains as she tries to straighten the plastic-coated cable, her fingers clumsy as toes. She believes the myths of misogyny: that men are more capable than she is, that if she has to struggle, she might as well give up.

"Get on the ladder and guide it on top of the duct," I say.

"It's too cold in here. I don't like going over the duct with all that dust up there."

I want to slap her. "You don't have to like it, you just have to do it. This is your job."

Her shoulders and chest cave in, as she shrinks away from the work. So now I'm mean Mommy, but teaching Iris some skills is more important than her liking me.

As it is, I have to stretch across the ceiling, having given Iris the easy end of the task. When I look down for her to feed me more cable, I see she's draped the Romex on the door knob.

"Iris, that door has to be kept shut! There's no barrier around the elevator shaft."

Her "sorry" is automatic, insincere. She sniffles and sighs as if put-upon. She makes a show of steering around the hole, its edges jagged where the concrete floor was cut into an eight-inch square that goes sixteen flights down.

I relent a little. "Me being shiftless and lazy, I work smart, not hard." I move my ladder closer to the elevator shaft to show her how I'd maneuver the coil of cable across the duct.

Iris continues to make sounds of frustration. I don't respond to her nonverbals other than to say, "Don't expect to be warm and cozy on a construction job." How is it that women who believe in femininity as weakness enter nontraditional arenas? Iris looks to me for guidance, but I hate how she watches like a dutiful wife awaiting orders.

She stops work to fiddle with her radio. "You're a slave driver with a heart of stone," she says.

"That's Ms. Slave Driver to you, missy."

"We haven't had a break yet," Iris admonishes. "After being in this freezer zone for so long, I need to warm up."

"Let me finish this splice. Go find Casper and them if you want to wait for coffee."

"I'm just trying to work a little guilt on you, Gabrielle," she says, and I look at her fully. Under her widow's peak, playful intelligence lodges on her face. She's moreno—a dark, fairskin—so there's no missing the circles under her eyes.

"Iris, I heard my mother's guilt trips for almost thirty-five years. You can't even come close." I offer her the wires for the splice and she shakes her head, rubs her hands together.

From the radio, the deejay says, "'96 is almost over. What you getting *la familia* for Christmas? Before '97 blasts off . . ."

All I want for Christmas is to sleep. Drunk with the lack of it, I've forgotten where I put my wire nuts. I pat my shirt pockets hoping to find them, give up, and ask Iris to get one. Her eyes droop like a deflated balloon and she moves like the dragging dead.

The radio is buoyantly alive: "Five more shopping days and you can pick up a gift for Mom at Baffles. Mom always deserves a little something. Okay, we got the bills paid, back to *la musica* . . ."

"It's gonna be a sad Christmas for me without my mom this year," Iris says, handing me the wire nut.

I stop splicing the wires and respond to this cue to inquire about her life. "How long ago did she die?"

"In November . . ." She speaks as if she were reciting a Hallmark card of socially acceptable sadness.

A wave of feeling lashes me upon realizing that the apprentice I'd dismissed as mentally impaired by relentless femininity is also a member of the dead mothers club. You'd think I'd be done with the tears that rock me every time the wind blows.

"So it's a recent loss for you." I invite her to speak and don't say that for me it's been seventy-eight days, the time it takes a small animal to conceive and give birth.

"She died from cancer of the ovaries. After my family buried her, I just fell completely apart . . ." Iris's eyes became a bowl filled with broth.

I don't know if I should tell her that the funeral was the easy part. Retrieving my mother's belongings from the hospital, moving possessions out of the apartment, closing off the business pages of her life— for each of these acts, arias should be sung.

"I'm turning into the kind of person who pays fines on overdue videos and gets parking tickets on a Sunday," Iris says, and I let my heart listen for what she doesn't tell. Maybe this is my role now: comforter of the bereaved.

A bough scrapes the broken window; rain mists the air. As Iris speaks, I can almost feel tears drizzle down her cheeks.

"I cried so much I can't do it anymore. I'm a burden to my friends.

It's so fucked up. We should see if coffee is back." She makes a backhand motion to show she thinks this is silly. "We should see if the coffee is back."

I move carefully toward Iris, thinking about confetti littering a bridal parade, the painful rice thrown at a wedding procession and the bouquet hurled against a nearby lesbian. "It's good to cry, Iris." I speak to the emotional narrative driving her, the tale of loss for all of us. "I still weep for my mother. Her death puts everything in my life into perspective as just twaddle." I extend an arm to place around her shoulder and Iris turns away, brushing off her work shirt.

My face breaks out in shame, wishing I hadn't reached out to take her in. I'll probably spend forever disappointed in people. I hope for a short life and an early death. I back away just as the door to our work area opens with a startling burst of light. I knock against my ladder, bringing down the coil of cable, and my cold reflexes are too slow to keep it from crashing against my face. I lose more balance trying to catch the ladder from tumbling down sixteen floors. My feet stutter back from the edge, then, and scrabble for purchase against the sloping lip, my hands grasping empty air as I slip backward into a nightmare without an escape. It's no use that I can still see the broken window, wrinkled with rapid streaks of rain. But then, a surprisingly strong hand cinches my wrist, an arm buckles my waist, yoking my torso hostage, and drags me back from the edge.

It's Casper, come to get us for coffee.

We've landed in a bundle on the floor. "Okay, you can let go now," I say, when he doesn't release me fast enough. I squirm to get out of his hold, but Casper won't be easily pushed off.

"Can't you ever let nobody help you, Gabrielle?" he asks, his voice gentle as a lullaby. He rocks me from side to side, and somehow I'm launched back in time, because in that moment, with his butterscotch fingers at my wrist, razor bumps and goatee rubbing my cheek, he's my mother, all coos and comfort, saving me from a bad dream. If I breathe slowly, I tell myself, the parachute beneath my eyelids won't open until I can get behind a bathroom door.

In Reflection My relationship with my mother wasn't a happy one, and her death was the biggest heartache of my life. No loss of friend or lover can compare. Not because we loved each other so well or could even get along, with me constantly pushing her away. Maybe it was because mothers are important and I spent a lifetime denying that.

I never thought about my mother beyond my disappointed disdain of her. Her death opened me up to wonder who she wanted to be, how she saw herself, what her ideas were of herself. Only after she died could I understand, as the conventional resignation has it, that she did the best she could.

Like Gabrielle, I had to return to electrical work with fresh grief not long after she died. The grief never ends, it just gets different, changes form, sweetens, becomes something you can live with in peace.

Anna Livia

ANNA LIVIA

Dostoyevsky Would Have Liked That

"That's him there," whispered my mother, nodding her head toward a lanky, disheveled figure who had just emerged from the shower block. "That's Don. You can smell him a mile away." She slipped her knotted fingers into mine as we walked down the dark path to her trailer.

Even in the fading gray light you could see the urine stains on the inside of Don's pants. He swayed as he walked.

"Talk about the Lower Depths," she added. I looked at her sideways and nodded.

Most of the people in the trailer park were drunks of one kind or another. There was a closely observed social hierarchy among them which put the owners, and the men who stayed to work on the fiberoptic cables, at the top, while people like my mother, who owned her own trailer, represented the middle class, with the weekly renters at the bottom. Those who were too drunk to hold down a steady job formed a proletariat more lumpen than most. Don was in this last category, along with Sheila, the only Aboriginal in the park; her consort, Bill; and various other transients.

No one had ever seen Don sober, though Wendy, the owner's wife, remembered once having seen him clean, a few years ago when his mother had come up to scrub out his trailer. By rights, Don should not have belonged to the Lower Depths because he had a job at the local slaughterhouse. Some time in his distant past he had qualified as a Halal butcher and produced a certificate to this effect. Since the slaughterhouse needed certificates more than it needed sobriety, and since jeans that stank of urine were not a problem in a place where blood and brains rained down all day, Don had kept his job despite drinking bouts with Sheila and Bill that left him glazed and shaky, on the verge of delirium.

By rights, my mother should have been lower down the hierarchy than she was. It was her job to clean out the toilet and shower blocks, empty the garbage bins, and scrub the rental trailers, work that required no certificates. She bought cheap sherry from the local vineyard, but though she drank every night, she stayed peaceably in her trailer or was invited up to the house. Unlike Don and his mates, she did not brawl, pick fights, or go stumbling around in the dark, bumping into awnings, yelling and cursing at anyone near enough to hear.

Don, Sheila, and Bill would sit outside Sheila's trailer, moving in slow motion, their ill-fitting clothes acting like camouflage against the peeling, fluttering trunks of the old paperbarks. The tins piled up in the compound, stockpiled until one of the three could con someone into giving them a lift into town and redeem them at the recycling center. Car ownership too was a class identifier in the park, where those legally classified drunk had long had their licenses taken away.

I liked the park. At least, I liked the stories, and I had been brought up to prefer a good story to a quiet ride. There was always some guy who had just taken off for Queensland with the underage daughter of one of the other trailer dwellers. Her best friend, Lisa, would be helping the police with their enquiries. The police never cared that much about statutory rape, my mother would explain, but it was something you could prove, and you could hold the guy for questioning till you got evidence for that manslaughter charge he'd escaped in the Kimberley.

My mother liked the park too. That, at least, was what I told myself. Visions of my mother trapped by poverty, age, and work-crippled fingers in a life she found squalid and humiliating haunted my dreams, leaving behind the bitter taste of frustration and despair. Was this what happened when you got old? Was this daily round of loneliness, of scrubbing maggots out of trailer drawers, the inevitable lot of the divorced woman with no life savings? My mother said she was not lonely, that the park provided its own form of entertainment. No one needed to be lonely, she said. Loneliness was caused by pride, not isolation. I wondered if this was a tenet of the Australian Communist Party, of which she was a member.

How could I compare my mother's life to one she was not living? The claustrophobic, conservative world of the midwestern academic, whose children go on field trips to the local grocery store and whose artistic outlet is confined to the selection of clothes for the lawn goose? Neither of these lives was mine. I was a working-class academic without goose or child. It's one of those things you can't be, I was discovering, painfully, working class and academic. Describing the positive side of working-class lives to outsiders always sounds sentimental at best, at worst picturesque. My mother was slim and fit from being outdoors. She never saw a doctor. Slenderness and health are highly prized commodities among the middle classes, but they hardly demonstrate the richness of my mother's world.

She showed me with great pride a sculpture she had made of stone, a rock garden you would call it. It was beautiful, an intricate work of light and mass, rock placed upon rock so that the sun shone through at delicate angles, backlighting tall, formidably prickled cacti. The trick was to look at it from behind the rocks, so that you saw the cacti and the shadow of the cacti, the prickles and the shadow of the prickles, through the gaps between the piles of stones. As the sun rose and set, the shadows performed a slow, fluid movement across the rock face, the lines as fine and confident as ever those etched by nineteenth-century lithographer. She had found the rocks she wanted up on the hill near Moondyne's cave and hauled each one back on a homemade toboggan, hooking the rope round her claw fingers and letting the steep gradient do most of the work. Folk art. But then, all working-class art is folk art.

She should have had a pension from her years of taking care of other people's business, but the company she worked for had gone bankrupt in the 1988 Wall Street crash. The director managed to save his million-dollar home on the banks of the Swan, but his employees were left with nothing. Wendy needed someone to help with the work of running the trailer park as Gazza, her husband, spent two weeks a month in Kalgoorlie as shift foreman at one of the gold mines. My mother started off taking care of the animals, the emus and the roos, the goats, the geese, the peacocks and all the parrots: lorrikeets, galahs, lovebirds, twenty-eights, and cockatiels. Wendy let her have a garden, and she'd reclaimed half an acre from the bush next to her trailer. She's the furthest from the road, with a eucalyptus grove on one side and a hill sloping upward on the other. She grows only native Australian plants, and the fierce red of the bottlebrush acts as a beacon on our walks back down the hill from town. When I tell my friends about my mother, I tell them about her garden and the animals. I don't mention Don's pants or the beer-can collection. They find Australia exotic enough without hearing about the trailer park or my mother's hands twisted and misshapen from forty years of typing.

For my visit, she had rented the trailer next door and I slept till the birds woke me. There was a ghost gum just outside the window and the magpies were congregating. My mother can tell how old a magpie is by looking at its wings. She also knows which mushrooms you can eat and which are poisonous. That morning we were going on a mushroom hunt.

She gets up as soon as the first light creeps through the window, which gives her a good three hours to potter about the park, tend to the plants, check the water level in the dam, and survey the antics of the geese, before anyone else is abroad. Sometimes she knocks for me and I pad over the cool baked earth in bare feet, listening to the swish-swish sound of the eucalyptus leaves. The light at 5 A.M. is a golden treat to the eye. The sun streams through the trees from the east, over the hill, shining pink and gray on the trunks and leaving the western half in shadow like a piece of black velvet.

I rolled over sleepily, and there was my mother tapping on the window, a tray of tea in her hands. We sat on a log overlooking the dam, sipping the tea and eating lumps of barmbrack. My mother used to be Irish, before she emigrated.

"It's worse than I thought," she said, clasping the hot tea in her crooked fingers.

The mother goose was cackling loudly at her offspring. It was time to swim over to the other side and do some serious worm diving. The water level was way down. Gazza, on his latest leave, had been diverting it to irrigate his marijuana crop.

I sat and waited for my mother to say more.

"It's awful actually." She turned toward me. "I don't think," she continued slowly, "I don't think I can bear it."

The sun dappled sickle-shaped eucalyptus shadows across her face. I poured out more tea. She drank, her eyes elsewhere. I didn't know what it meant not to be able to bear something. Bearing was just what you did, until something else came along. My mother taught me that.

"I talked to Wendy last night, after you'd gone to bed. There was a bit of a commotion up at Don's trailer. The police came for him. He was at the slaughterhouse yesterday and he went crazy. Even for Don, it was crazy. Some kind of delirium I suppose. He has his special butchers' knives and he started attacking the sheep."

"Isn't that his job? I mean, it's a slaughterhouse not a petting zoo."

She raised her head again and said quietly, "He gouged out their eyes, hung their hearts from the meat hooks, and slit them open between their legs."

I shivered, thinking about the disheveled figure in stained white pants. I imagined my mother leaving her trailer in the middle of the night, needing to use the bathroom. The path was dark when there was no moon. It was surrounded by bushes behind which anyone might be hiding. When the peacocks shriek as they fly in their ungainly way onto the roof of the shower block, you'd never know if the cry masked the more human scream of a terrified old woman.

"And after that? They let him walk out of there, carrying the tools of his trade?" I asked.

"The police took the knives away, though they are actually his property. But the manager won't press charges. It's a slaughterhouse, as you pointed out. One way or another, sheep go there to die."

"But not like that."

"No," said my mother, "I don't think they are meant to die like that."

"Won't the park owners tell him to leave? Gazza and Wendy, I mean. They can't let him stay, not after that."

"It's up to Gazza. He owns the place. And he's away in Kalgoorlie till tomorrow."

"What does Wendy say?"

"Wendy can't stand him," my mother said, taking courage. "She's ready to turf him out on his ear and fumigate the trailer." She laughed suddenly. "We had a bit of a drink together last night, Wendy and me, to chase away the ghouls. She was all set to drag his stuff out right there and then, burn the whole lot before he got back from the police station."

"He's coming back?"

"Once he's dried out. Come on," she added, springing to her feet, "let's get the baskets and go look for mushrooms."

It was six when we left the park, and dawn had spread across the valley, over the golf course and the stream, streaking the green shoots of the blackboys with a golden light. I wondered where my mother would go if Don returned to the park. She kept a hockey stick next to her bed and, as she said, a sixty-five-year-old woman who hauls a hundred pounds of garbage a day half a mile to the dumpster is probably more than a match for a thirty-year-old butcher whose brain has been marinating in Swan Lager for the last fifteen years. But did she want to put this to the test? Don could fillet a carcass and skin it in his sleep, or in a drunken stupor, a fact that he had been at pains to prove every day of his working life. I hate the sight and the smell of terror. I grew up with them, had hoped, foolishly, to outlive them. My own I have learned to deal with, but when I see it in someone else, in the eyes of a tired old woman, especially when that tired old woman is my mother, I am filled with rage and a misplaced hatred that has no outlet. My Communist Party membership lapsed with the fall of the Berlin Wall. Where could my mother go? There were other parks down south, nearer to my sisters' families, but they lacked the freedom of the valley. There would be no garden with rock sculpture and bottlebrush, at most a small flowerbed and an injunction to keep it weeded and not to let it overflow onto the path. There would be no animals, no Wendy to drink sherry with, no Moondyne's cave, no mushroom hunts.

I hoped we would find so many mushrooms we would spend the whole morning scrambling from field to field, filling the baskets, our sun hats, our jackets, and even our socks with their smooth white bulk. I could hear the faint popping sound as you snap the stem from the head, smell the fresh earth that has to be gently dusted off. I wanted our day to be filled with the uncomplicated eagerness of the hunt. My mother went methodically from rock to tree to streambed. We walked for miles, over the golf course, over the hill, and on into the next valley. There were no mushrooms anywhere.

"I don't understand it," said my mother. "I was out here yesterday, and they were everywhere. Absolutely everywhere. I should have picked them then, only I thought it would be more fun to come back with you."

"This is fun," I said. "I love being out here with you. You tell me things."

She told me things about the birds, about the trees, about the blackboys. She transformed that gray-green West Australian hill from the washy watercolor it appeared to my ignorant eyes into an oil painting thick with texture and passion. When I looked at the streambed I could see how it had been in winter, a rushing torrent of water, throwing itself headfirst into the Avon. It was too late in the day now to see roos, but when I looked at the green sprouts of the blackboys cropped to midheight, I could see their teethmarks. On the ground by a clump of rocks, I saw the hard black pellets of kangaroo shit; over by a group of melaleuca where the grass had been flattened in a circle, I recognized their sleeping place. My mother pointed to a sandy bank next to the stream.

"If we came back at dusk, we'd see about a dozen roos there, come down to drink. And over there," she indicated a prickly bush of hakea victoria, "There'd be the lookout. If she caught sight of us, she'd thump her tail against the ground and they'd all bound away. They're beautiful when they run, kangaroos, graceful as a flock of doves. And you know," she said, consideringly, "it looks kind of the same. Doves fly with their bodies tilted upward, like roos springing into the air."

"They live in packs, don't they," I said, remembering something she had told me before, "the females at least. With their joeys and the aging males."

"Shh," she said.

I looked round. Was that wrong? Was I thinking about baboons or some other natural history lesson I had picked up in my rootless wanderings? But my mother was standing quite still, gazing across the stream to a small mound beyond. I followed the direction of her eye. Another eye gazed back at us. An enormous, inquisitive black eye fringed with thick lashes. It had a little tuft of hair on its head and it stood about six feet off the ground on a pair of the longest, thinnest legs I've ever seen. It opened its beak and emitted a deep, rumbling sound from inside its chest, like air blown through a drum. There was an emu in every one of my mother's tapestries, but this was the first one I had seen close up.

"If you were a musician, Mum, instead of an artist, that rumbling sound would be in every one of your compositions," I laughed.

"Didgeridoo music," she said, but she was pleased. I had called her an artist, without thinking. Her claw fingers were unimportant beside the visions she held in her head. "Mum" too had come out unbidden. She was my mother, but we had not lived on the same continent since I was sixteen years old. Since I was sixteen, I had lived alone. Apart from genealogy, I could not see what we shared. But I realized, looking into the eye of the emu, exactly what she had given me. Her sense of sight. Her vision of the world, which she painted, by any means necessary, and which I converted into stories. I had always loved my mother with a blind, confused loyalty that forgave her for abandoning me to the snows of London at a time when, according to the magazines, a girl needs her mother most. She had immigrated to Australia; later I left England to seek my fortune in America. It was my stories which had kept me alive, which had given me the home, the sense of self I needed. I had always thought they were stolen from my life, which by rights, should have ended in a backstreet abortion, or, since I am a lesbian, in teen suicide— I know the statistics for life expectancy of teenage girls alone in big cities. But now I saw that my gift for storytelling came not despite but courtesy of my mother.

Alone in London at sixteen with no parents, I had been eligible for every grant the British welfare state makes available to its citizens. Unlike my sisters, who, younger than me by ten years, had accompanied my mother and her new husband to Australia, and who made their living picking apples, grapes, oranges, nuts, whatever the fertile Australian climate brought forth from the earth, I had gone to university, obtained a Ph.D., and was now a professor at a research institution where my opinion was sought and valued on matters esoteric and arcane. I got through the hoops not from being deserving but for the way

I talked, the stories I told to the people who wanted to help me. And this I shared with my mother. People liked to help her too because it let them see the things she saw: the way sun shines on granite, the shadow of a cactus thorn, the fringed eye of an emu, a pack of kangaroos in flight.

We returned to the park at midday, our baskets empty. My mother had led us over the hills to an orange grove and we had eaten the ripe fruit with both hands, but now we were hungry again. As we walked up the drive, I felt my mother's body tense beside me.

"He's back," she said, looking over the way at Don's trailer. The door was open, and all the tins had been piled up in a box. "Oh God," she said weakly, "I can't. I just can't do it."

She couldn't leave the park? Or she couldn't stay there with Don loose among them? I did not ask. Suddenly she wheeled round and started back the way we'd come.

"This way," she said. "You don't mind? I just can't walk past his trailer right now."

She led me through the bush along a back path which came out by her garden. "A cup of tea," she said. "You'd like a cup of tea, wouldn't you?"

I nodded.

"That's what we'll do then," she said, but she didn't move. This time I could guess what it was. Nothing so wholesome as a wild emu with expressive eyes. The midday sun poured down like lead on the broken boulders and shredded cactus that had been my mother's sculpture. The two-inch thorns, which had looked so menacing and eerie as they pointed toward sunset, lay like disheveled pins dropped from a lady's sewing kit. Instinctively, my mother moved forward and began to gather up the fragments.

"There you are," said Wendy, who had come up the path from the shower block. "I saw you on your way home from the golf course, but you must have walked in the back way."

She looked at my mother, from whose claw-fingers trailed the once imposing cacti. "I couldn't stop him," she said. "I didn't realize he was back till Sheila ran up and told me what he was doing."

My mother gazed at her blankly, then back up the hill where the sculpture had stood.

"I'm pressing charges," Wendy continued. "This is your garden; he can't just smash things up like that. I don't care what Gazza says, he's never here anyway."

"You're taking Don to court?" my mother asked slowly.

"I'm gonna have him locked up in a loony bin, love. First the sheep, now this. Cops are on my side. They got a few stories of their own about our Don." She stooped and picked up one of the rocks. "Pretty amazing thing you made here. I used to walk by at dusk, just to see the shadows of the cactuses. Dunno how you managed that. Real atmospheric."

I came out of the trailer with a tray of tea and set it on the old log my mother uses as an outdoor table. Wendy winked at my mother and laughed.

"That's a nice thought," she said, "but I think your ma and me'll be wanting something a little stronger."

My mother nodded. "Brandy," she said, still nursing the cactus in her hand. There was a thin trickle of blood down one of her knuckles where a thorn had pierced her skin. "Thing about cactuses," she said contemplatively, "is that they grow again from just one small piece."

"Like us old battle-axes," smiled Wendy, "takes a lot to do us in."

"Let's go into town," I said. "Let's go to the tavern."

"Celebrate the end of Don," agreed Wendy.

"Is he gone yet?" asked my mother.

"Police are still talking to him. We should go on over there."

For the second time that visit, I held my mother's hand as we walked toward Don's trailer. He was just coming out, a burly West Australian cop on either side. Sheila and Bill were standing in front of the awning. There was an enormous bowl of freshly picked mushrooms in Sheila's hands.

"She must have been out at five this morning," my mother marveled, gazing at the gift. "Kindness at rock bottom. Dostoyevsky would have liked that."

Don was subdued as he clambered into the back of the police cruiser, exhausted after his recent violence, or silenced by a well-aimed punch from a police officer's knuckles. The smooth white mushrooms, smelling of earth and eucalyptus leaves, lay in a bowl beside him on the seat. He reached over and took one, and I could hear the faint popping sound as he snapped the stem off from the head. Sheila nodded encouragingly. Then the cruiser drove away.

"Tavern?" I said again, to Wendy and my mother.

"Just a minute," said my mother, looking at Sheila. "You want us to take your tins in to the Recycling Centre for you?" she asked.

"Yeah. That'd be great."

Sheila and Bill loaded the empty tins into the back of my mother's Holden. "Thanks," they said.

"No worries."

And for the first time in twenty-five years, I laid aside my defenses and went off to get drunk with my mother.

In Reflection   I published my first novel when I was twenty-four (*Relatively Norma*) and now, at forty-five, I have some ten books to my name, including short story collections, novels, and academic works. Little of my writing is autobiographical, though it all comes out of my life. I have always preferred the safety of writing in character, presenting the world through the eyes of some more finished being, a being whose story had an easily identified beginning, some high points, tension, and then a resolution. Real lives come with little resolution and a great deal of striving—much of it futile—threads dangling, hems ragged. The story of my relationship with my mother is such a ragged, unresolved, tangled mess. Many of the issues touched on in "Dostoyevsky Would Have Liked That" are topics I rarely approach in my fiction. I like the sound of laughter, I like to make people laugh, and the rage I felt when my mother left me to live on a different continent was incompatible with laughter. I like to avoid stereotypes, I like the careful innovation of artifice, yet my heritage of alcoholic Irish drunkenness is a stereotype too blunt and too painful to skirt. My mother's terrors are my own, terrors that have chased us across Ireland and England, Africa, Australia, and America, in a diaspora both personal and cultural. We are both in search of the geographic cure. I don't believe either of us has found it.

I wrote this story in Melbourne, in the airport terminal waiting for a flight to San Francisco, having left my mother only a few hours before, in Perth, Western Australia. I was supposed to be writing a reply to a colleague in the English department at the University of Illinois who had invited me to give a talk the following semester. The topic was open and I fantasized about telling this queer theory seminar about my mother and the life I led in London before I acquired a job in academia and my longed-for middle-class status. But even as I considered the possibility, I realized that my story lacked the clear lines of the working-class kid makes good. When we still lived in London together, my mother would take me to the Tate Gallery and the National Gallery, the South Bank and the Portrait Gallery. She would laugh knowledgeably at the visual jokes the artists had made and teach me to share them. She made me read Dostoyevsky and informed me that although I would never write like that, I must try. She had ambition for me. We had no money, not then, not now, not ever, but we had a way of seeing that filled us with joy and compassion and curiosity and kept us both alive.

Janet Mason

PHOTOGRAPH BY BARBARA J. MCPHERSON

JANET MASON

Violin Lessons

"**S**ympathy pains." My mother examines me, owl-like, shrewd intensity.

Conscious of the iron grip I have on myself, I drop my hand from my shoulder.

It lands leaden on the cushion next to my right thigh. The tension wire pulls through me, loosening, tightening, as she speaks.

"I had them when my mother was dying in the hospital." Her eyes redden with a sudden welling of moisture, like a sponge being squeezed.

"But Mom, it's not like—"

"She had a pain in her chest; I had a pain in my chest."

"But, you're not—"

My words waver with dread, denial, the thought of her mortality.

"She had a pain in her leg; I had a pain in my leg."

I came over immediately after I found out my mother had woken up a few days ago with a radiating pain in her sternum. She felt like she was having a massive coronary so she went to the doctor immediately. He ordered some x-rays, told her it was arthritis, and sent her home with some extra-strength Tylenol. When my mother told me this, my mind reeled. How could my mother who walks four miles a day wake up feeling like she was having a coronary?

"Why didn't you call?" I asked her on the phone.

"I just did," she said.

I didn't argue, but the fact was that I had called her. There was something in her voice I had never heard before. Fatalism. A giving up. This dead-end tone of voice coming from my mother pushed me to panic. Illness or not, I couldn't conceive of her coming to a standstill. I drummed my fingers. My mind raced. There must be something that I could do. "There's special diets for arthritis," I said. "Let me stop at the health food store and I'll be right over."

At the same time that I leapt to action, the center of me came to a quiet immovable standstill. A booming silence told me that something dreadful was wrong, that this was the beginning of the end.

The bottom of my world began to drop away.

My mother raises her arms and attempts to clasp her hands behind her head, her usual posture of attentive contemplation. Pain flashes across her face. I feel a stabbing pain in my own left shoulder. Bright hot tears rise in my eyes. I look away from her, unable to witness an agony so strong I feel it in my own body.

The afternoon light slants through the long rectangle of windows. It glints off the shiny surface of an acetate-covered library book, resting next to the lamp on the end table. My mother's handheld barbells—covered in purple plastic—sit on the floor at the base of the table. The barbells were part of her daily routine—lying on a mat in the middle of the living-room floor, lifting and twisting, crossing and turning, straining for the definition she admired in the fitness magazines she picked up at the supermarket—until two days ago when everything changed.

After lunch—brown rice, steamed collard greens, sliced burdock root sautéed with carrots, onions, and tofu—my father does the dishes and goes out for his walk. My mother and I settle back down in the living room. Before I can ask her more about what the doctor said, she turns to me and says, "You always ask about my life. I'd like to know more about yours."

I squirm on the sofa, feeling intruded upon. There is so much about my life that I haven't told my mother, partly to protect her from my own mistakes, from having her claim them as her own, but also because I am a fiercely private person. There is an awkward silence between us. I wonder if she has a hidden agenda. The moment passes. I am able to move beyond myself. Chances are that my mother is tired of thinking about the pain in her body. She may just be asking me about my life as a way of finding a distraction from hers.

"What do you want to know?"

My mother's eyes widen. She looks astonished that I would ever say this to her, and then slightly perplexed, as she figures out what to ask.

"Why did you want to play the harp?"

When I was in first grade at an Episcopal private school—where the girls all wore blue and white jumpers, and the boys suits and ties, and we learned French, and went to chapel in the morning and in the af-

ternoon at recess showed each other our bare asses in the bushes—my
mother decided that I should take violin lessons.

"Remember when you took me to see the Suzuki violin players?"
She nods. "They were on tour from Japan. I think your favorite
part was when one of the kids fell off his chair playing the violin."

I laugh. "Yeah. He fell off his chair twice. The second time was
when he turned to the kid next to him to tell him how he fell off the
chair, then he did it all over again."

My mother and I are both laughing.

"I'll bet the conductor was ready to kill him," she says.

I shrug. "What did they expect? They might have been great violin players, but they were still kids."

My mother signed me up for violin lessons after school with the
music teacher, and then took me to the city to talk to an old man who
was a well-known violin teacher. He showed me his collection of violins,
had me sing the notes of the scale, and asked me what instrument I
wanted to play. I looked into his smiling, creased face and said, "The
harp. I want to play the harp."

"Why did you want to play the harp and not the violin?" my
mother asks.

I am quiet for a moment.

"I guess playing the violin wasn't really my idea," I say cautiously.
"I liked the harp better."

What I don't say was that playing the violin was my mother's idea.
It was her dream, not mine.

My mother is quiet.

I feel slightly guilty for telling her the truth. Playing the violin may
have been her idea, but it was something she wanted for me. The child-
size violin she bought and then sold a few years later wasn't cheap. But
it was worth it to my mother. She wanted me to have a well-rounded
education, to experience the things that poverty denied her as a child. I
may have cried my way through ear-shattering violin practice sessions,
but the fact is that these lessons instilled a deep appreciation of music
in me. I love the violin concertos, in particular Mozart, Tchaikovsky,
Vivaldi, and especially Mendelssohn. I learned the musical scale and to
read and write music. A few years after the failed violin lessons I was
playing Beethoven's Ninth Symphony by ear on the xylophone.

Those early violin lessons gave me my first glimpse of myself as a
girl who loved another girl, as a girl who would grow into a woman
who loved other women. When I grew up and figured it all out, my
mother easily accepted my lesbian identity. She had it all figured out

before I came out to her. I grew up with a mother who was a feminist—
a card-carrying one, at that—with a membership in the National Organization for Women in the 1970s when I was a teenager. My mother
always thought for herself and, in that, she was an exception. But still
she was held back by her gender, by her class, by her own frustrations.
As my mother's only daughter, I am the natural extension of her ideas
and ambitions. They fused with mine and pushed their way into the
world.

"My mother always wanted me to work in an office," my mother says
to me. The faraway look on her face tells me she is lost in her past, trying to figure out the relationship she had with her own mother. "She
always said that no daughter of hers was going to work in the mill. She
wanted me to work in an office. So I did. But it wasn't enough for me.
Then she'd ask me why I wasn't content. 'I'm not a cow, Ma,' I'd tell
her. 'Cows are content, not people.' She was right. Nothing was ever
good enough for me. But she taught me that."

I don't have to ask what my grandmother thought of my mother's
artistic talents. "Mama always said, 'Art doesn't put food on the table,'"
my mother always told me as far back as I can remember. My mother
was never resentful when she told me this. It was a fact of life. Being an
artist was not a realistic possibility for a poor girl whose mother worked
in the mill. This fact was repeated to me about my own life in various
ways throughout my childhood and adolescence—most memorably
when I spent too much time on my silk screens in high school, and later
when I wanted to major in fine art photography in college.

"The only one who understood me was my father." My mother is
looking out the window far into the distance as she speaks.

I am astonished that this man who caused her so much pain was
also the nurturer of her childhood dreams. One night, not long after I
had left home, the two of us were sitting in the living room watching a
movie on the television about a young woman whose father was dying.
My mother broke down into gasping sobs. "At least she knew her father
died," she said. "I never knew what happened to my father. I don't know
if he's dead or alive."

I grew up listening to my mother tell me the stories of her childhood in the country, where she lived until she was seven, the year her
father left and she and her mother and her sister moved back to the
city. The emotions behind these stories were alternately proud, wistful,
angry, fearful, and seething. I never saw my mother shed a tear over her
father until I was an adult. As a child, I rarely saw her cry at all. But it
seemed I was always crying: my own tears and those my mother had

never been able to shed. This infuriated my mother. My tears were too often met with a stinging slap and the threat of another.

My mother shifts in her chair, wincing from the pain diagnosed as arthritis. I feel her tension at being trapped in the present, in her body. I am trapped too, in my mother's past, in my past that I shared with my mother and in my present helplessness, my inability to make things better. My mother stares out the window, her expression changing to one of keen perception. She tells me about her childhood in the country, a story she likes to repeat over and over, filled with her adventures in a one-room schoolhouse where she grabbed the teacher's pitch pipe and began blowing it in front of the room. She got into trouble again and again for losing her books on the way to school, scrambling up and down trees, swinging from the branches, arriving at the schoolhouse late, breathless, twigs and leaves sticking out of her hair.

"I raised my hand and said we had a bitch at home, and the teacher would have liked to kill me," says my mother. "She sent me home with a note telling my mother that I swore like a drunken sailor. My mother was furious. Only my father understood. We did have a bitch at home. Peggy, the Airedale, had just given birth to seven puppies."

When she tells me the story of the charcoal drawing she made on her living room wall, I can see the country house, the unfinished wood floors with the braided rug in the middle, a few wooden chairs in the middle of the room. Dark charcoal strokes on the white wall formed the lines of the drawing my mother did of Peggy, the Airedale, stretched out on her side, seven scrawny puppies suckling on her teats. "I had just finished the drawing when my mother came in the room," my mother says, the evidence of pain entirely gone from her face. "She was so angry that her face was as white as the wall. I thought she was going to kill me. Instead she went and got my father. 'Look what she did,' my mother said to him, 'Speak to that child.' My father looked at my drawing for a long time and then he said to me, 'Jane, that's a very good drawing.'"

The look in my mother's eyes is so far away and wistful that, even though she is speaking to me, I feel like an intruder into her conversation. I get up quietly and go into the kitchen to make us both a cup of tea. When I return she is still staring out the front window. She slowly turns to me when I put the cup of tea on the coaster on the end table next to her chair.

"I always remember the story about putting the blue chalk in the chicken's water," I say to her after I am settled back down on the sofa.

"In the well," my mother says. "I put the blue chalk water in the well. I poisoned the entire water supply. I didn't mean to. I just wanted to make the chicken's water pretty."

As I look down into my teacup, I move my hand slightly so that the reflection of my face is blurred. It is not myself I am looking at, but rather my mother at six years old, bowl-cut hair, a stubborn chin, and scrawny tomboy body, crumbling pieces of blue chalk, dropping them into the well and dusting the powdery chalk dust off her hands before she lowered the bucket. "When I brought the water up it was so blue, just like I had cut out pieces of the sky and put it in the chickens' bowls." She stares out the window into the afternoon sky as she speaks, the same cloudless blue as the water she gave to the chickens.

"My mother was busy in the general store that we had in the front of the house. She was always dusting or waiting on the customers or taking care of the baby. And my father was off somewhere, probably in town drinking. I was happy to be on my own. I loved the country, the wildflowers, the Queen Anne's lace, the chicory root with the pale blue flowers that grew by the side of the road, and the mullen stalks that grew taller than me by midsummer.

"One day I lay on my stomach for hours and watched a praying mantis on a stalk of grass. It rubbed its front legs together just like the minister ringing his hands in the country church where Mama used to take me. I was alone all day but I had the dogs, Hector the Great Dane, and Peggy, all those wide open fields, the butterflies and the clouds. And the chickens, Chickadee and Blue, and their baby chicks. Those baby chicks were just little fluff balls the size of my fists. Every time I tried to pick them up they ran away."

My mother turns to me with moist eyes, a child's expression rising in her features. "The last thing I wanted to do was kill them. My father came back from town and found them dead right next to their water bowls with the blue water in them. Their tiny webbed feet were sticking up, and there was a blue stain around their beaks. They were only chicks, but my father had counted on them growing up and laying eggs. He was planning to sell them. I never forgot the look in his eyes when he stood there with those tiny dead chicks in his enormous hands. I thought he was going to kill me."

I stare down into my teacup, turning it between my palms. The loose tea leaves swirl into the broken spiral of my mother's childhood. As I begin to understand the terror under her words, I see her father blocking the light, casting a shadow across his skinny six-year-old daughter whose legs felt unhinged, a china doll with a rubber band down the middle that had snapped.

Something was wrong.

It was all her fault.

"I made their water pretty, that's all. I gave them pretty water to drink."

Her father leaned over the bowls and looked at the blue water.

"Goddamn it. You poisoned them."

He picked up the bowls and slammed them down on the ground. Shards of clay stuck like daggers in the dirt. The blue water, absorbed, turned to mud.

Her father's face red as the comb on Henry the rooster's head.

He turned on his heel and stormed toward the house.

The peg inside the front door, the rawhide whip hanging on the peg.

Small explosions of dust came off his heels.

"Look what you've done." The mother's face white, drawn.

The daughter's eyes round with terror, pleading.

The mother turned away.

In my childhood, my mother's stories ended before the strap lashes into her child body, before the five-, six-, seven-year-old drifts off to sleep, her dreams laced with wildflowers dancing in fields of blue chalk water and wishing well sky, humming with vibrating praying mantis legs, swelling with the minister's pontificating hands, his bulging eyes, her father's red-faced anger lashing into her, leaving welts, binding her dreams no matter which way she turned. But now as we sit facing each other as adult women, my mother takes the story further. "I was always tense as a kid," she says. A streak of pain invades her face, her shoulder, her sternum as she shifts in her chair. "I never knew when my father was going to hit me. I didn't know what direction it would come from."

But her father's violence didn't stop her from dreaming. And in her dreams, she soared. I grew up hearing about the catwalk her father had built around the outside of their house. He never finished it, but she climbed up on it anyway. One day, perched on the edge of the second story catwalk, she spread her arms like a bird in flight. "When my mother came out of the house and screamed at me, I was so startled that I damned near fell off the roof. She called my father and told him to speak to me. He yelled up, 'Hello there, Jane, you'd better come down before you scare the life out of your mother.' After the way she yelled at me, I was scaring her? I walked to the back of the house where the catwalk slanted all the way to the ground, sat down, put my hands behind me, pushed, and slid all the way to the ground."

I raise my eyebrows and look at my mother. "You slid down the roof from the second floor? You must have been afraid."

"I wasn't afraid," she says, shaking her head stubbornly. As she speaks her body grows tense. The ridges of her neck stick out. Her shoulders turn in on themselves. Her bony wrists jut from her cotton sleeves. Her fists clench. "It didn't matter to me. Nothing mattered. Nothing mattered at all."

As badly as she was treated by her father, it wasn't the beatings that broke her. It was his leaving, this point of excavation, that became the dividing line of her life, her before and after. She never speaks of when he left, this place of pain, the hour-long minutes of his leaving. My childhood imagination filled its blank slate with a picture that was clean and neat. He left. Without screaming, without violence. He simply left, like my father getting into the car and going to work. Except he never returned. I didn't see my mother in this picture, standing at the window, age seven, her cheeks streaked, her knuckles whiter than the windowsill she gripped, her heart a plum that burst its skin.

His leaving dangled between fact and fantasy in my childhood mind, unable yet to comprehend the grimness of my mother's reality, the fact that she had been hurt more than she could say. There was nothing clean and neat about his leaving. There was screaming, violence. His accusations when the note from the bank came, reclaiming everything they had staked their lives on. The store was gone. It wasn't his fault. He had worked too long, too hard. It was his wife's fault. Everything was her fault. He told her a hundred times not to let the customers buy on credit. She raised her voice in protest—they were paying customers at one time; times were hard; she'd thought they'd get better—his rough hand slapped against her mouth, once, twice, blood trickling from her swollen lips. The daggers of his words, the sting of his hands traveled through the walls and pierced the hearts of his daughters. His fury glowed, incandescent. A door slammed in the darkness. The moon fell out of the sky.

A few years ago, my mother gave me a small handheld mirror with a photograph of her framed on the back. The photo, no more than two inches high and an inch across, was taken in 1928, when she was eight years old. Every now and then I take it out, hold it in my hand, and turn it over to see how my reflection compares to her picture. Our hair is different. Hers at eight was bowl-cut, bangs straight across dropping down in a round dome just below her ears. Mine, in my mid-thirties, is short and styled, points at the ears, and fluffy on top which, when I've slept on it wet, can almost look spiked. I once thought my mother and I looked nothing alike. But as I approach midlife and see the signs of my mother slipping away from me, I reconsider. Maybe my face is growing into itself, reflecting more of who I am. Perhaps it is simply a matter of perspective. I have the same full lips that solemnly turn down at the edges, and the same wary eyes that my mother had when she was eight. In short, the lines of my mother's childhood grief have etched themselves onto my face.

Fortunately, neither of our expressions are static. Both of our faces are fluid and rapidly changing as our emotions run the gamut from outbursts of laughter to quick summations of anger. But the somber expression is where we land between the emotional fluctuations. It is our rest position: disappointment settles in the sullen lines of the mouth while watchful eyes wait for yet another disaster.

I look up from my teacup to stare into my mother's face. For a moment she is my mirror. Then she becomes a mystery again. Despite our differences, of generations, of opportunities lost and found, as children we both dreamed. My mother dreamed blue chalk water dreams musing on the charcoal pencil shapes of a bitch and her seven pups swirled across the blank walls of her childhood. And I hummed incessantly. I hummed my way through my parents' arguments, through the Vietnam War raging on the television news during dinner. I hummed my way through church services until my mother decided that the whole thing was a waste of time. I hummed so much in elementary school that I became known as "the hummer." It was true that I hummed to shut things out. But I also hummed to tune myself into the vibrational frequency of the grand celestial symphony.

My humming had musical scores. My education as a violin student led me into a wholly encompassing, head to toe, exhilarating and deeply riveting attraction to another violin student, which can only be called a crush due to the fact that I was in first grade. Marcie was in fifth grade and a much better violinist than I. She was the student before me, and when I peered through the double wooden doors into the music room and saw the distinct tilt of her chin and the intense concentration of the bow in her hand, my heart thudded all the way down to the soles of my saddle shoes.

I had what my mother called a boyfriend who was in first grade also. Jimmy used to chase me around the room and try to kiss me. I always got away, but eventually consented to let him button my coat after he promised to show me his six toes on one foot. Two of his toes were webbed together like a duck. It was an oddity I couldn't refuse. But it was Marcie, with her dark searing eyes and tomboy ways—recklessly waving her violin case around as she ran down the front steps of the school at the end of the day—who captured my heart.

I wrote in heavy letters on the cover of my phonics notebook with

a number two pencil: I LOVE MARCIE. Too late, I realized what I had
done and tried in vain to erase my letters. I rubbed my green notebook
cover to white with my pink eraser but the incriminating words could
still be read. "What does that say?" my mother asked when she saw
the notebook. "I love . . . ?" I gulped the air and felt a pounding in my
veins. "Lassie," I said. "I love Lassie." It was 1964. Fear and hatred of
people who loved the same sex was in the air I breathed and the water I
drank. These feelings were erased before I allowed myself to know that
they existed. Already, in first grade, I knew that it wasn't even safe to tell
my own mother than I loved another girl, no matter how wonderful
she was.

There were other signs over the years. The stab of recognition that
curled the toes of my Keds when I met the eyes of another girl in the
lobby of a restaurant where I went with my parents. Strong emotional
attachments to my girlfriends. But for the most part, I managed to block
this forbidden love out of my psyche. I look down into my cup and swirl
the tea leaves around. None of the patterns are recognizable to me. The
omens of love that were available, the hearts and rings, the promises of
I shalt and I should were inadequate to prepare me for being a lesbian,
a woman who owned the province of her own sexuality.

As an adolescent I hated myself without knowing why. Alcoholism
was a genetic tendency passed down to me from both sides of my family. My father didn't drink, but his brothers did. His younger brother
died of a heart attack by the time he was forty. My mother told me that
he drank and danced himself to death. This story—complete with the
knife that he slept with under his pillow after coming home from the
front lines of World War II—met my childhood ears as a kind of adventure. Soon I was able to fill my own life with the same kind of danger
and excitement gleaned from alcohol and drugs.

I had my first drink when I was fourteen. One slid easily into another and I was transported out of my body. I drank to escape myself.
I drank so my life could be endured. I drank my way through junior
high, high school, and college. As a young woman, I drank my way
through two long-term relationships with men and more short-term
involvements than I care to remember. I drank my way through working on an assembly line and my early years as a journalist. Heavy-
handed two-fisted drinking was acceptable in both worlds. Drinking
nearly cost me my life, but it never got in the way of my work. As a
journalist, being able to drink my male colleagues under the table was
a point of pride with me. I probably would have kept up my drinking
longer, except that when I was twenty-three I became involved in the

women's liberation movement. A few months later I came out as a lesbian and stopped drinking. It was that easy.

Almost.

There are no neat and tidy endings for an alcoholic—even for one who has stopped drinking. There are the sledgehammer memories of a person who was me but under the influence wasn't really me at all. Worse, there is the absence of memory. The knowledge that slices of my life have been blacked out and will never be returned. Years later I still have a sense of erosion, as if something vital and irreplaceable was stripped from me. Every now and then my own denial creeps in, as if by saying that it never happened I could actually erase those years of my life and go back and do it over.

I was a blackout drinker for nearly ten years, and it eroded the very core of my self-esteem. Years of an obliterated sense of self could not be corrected overnight. But the women's liberation movement answered a yearning from deep inside of me. It gave me a sense of myself as a woman, as a complete and wholly contained intellectual and sexual being. By the time I had graduated from college and gotten involved in the women's movement, my mother had slowed down. I revived her interest and she marched in a few rallies with me—heckling the "pro-life" hecklers, waving around her unbent coat hanger—but after that was adamant that she was too tired to even think of going to another one. I marched on. I answered phone calls at a crisis line, mediated panel discussions, gave interviews to the press, studied women's self-defense, and taught other women how to protect themselves from the threat of physical violence. Every time I helped another woman, I helped myself.

Still, as I stare down into the tea leaves swirling in my cup, I wonder what would have happened if I had been able to foretell my own future when I was an adolescent. Chances are that I wouldn't have wanted to know. Worse, when I was caught in the vice grip of adolescent peer pressure, I most likely wouldn't have wanted to become who I grew into. Yet, there's very little about my life that I would change, even if I could. The fact is that I am happy. When I was twenty-four—the same age at which my mother met my father—I fell in love with the woman who was to become my life partner. Like most people in long-term relationships we've had our ups and downs and rough patches. But through it all she's remained the love of my life, my safe harbor.

I look up from my teacup at my mother. She is sitting quietly, staring whimsically out the window as the afternoon shadows lengthen. As I watch her in her reverie, I begin to get lost in my own thoughts. Deep from the bottom of my vocal chords, below that even, from the soles of my feet and the tips of my toes, a small vibration starts. It becomes slightly louder, almost audible and then crests through the line of my pursed lips. I am humming, ever so slightly and almost unconsciously. I am humming the melody of my childhood and the dissonant chords of my adolescence. I am humming from the belly of the woman I have become. I am humming now as I have always been humming. With my mother's help, I have hummed myself into existence.

In Reflection "Violin Lessons" is a chapter from my manuscript "Tea Leaves: A Memoir of Mothers and Daughters." I wrote it in the eight-year period following my mother's death, after I—along with my father—had been her primary caretaker. The writing was a way of combining my story with that of my mother's and grandmother's—a kind of shoring up of my matrilineal line. The project began—before my mother was diagnosed with fourth-stage cancer—with research on women in the U.S. labor movement. Despite coming from a working-class background, this was not an area that I delved into until I reached my mid-thirties. Putting this story of my life—as a lesbian and the first in my family to go to college—in context with the stories of my mother (an office worker) and grandmother (a textile mill worker) allowed me to absorb their lives into my own in a stronger and deeper way than I had previously experienced.

The writing was a way of knowing myself and of paying tribute to my mother.

proceeding page

PHOTOGRAPH BY RICK BOLEN

Jess Wells

JESS WELLS

Swimming at Midnight

The midnight moon shone on the chests of three women skinny-dipping in Loon Lake. Floating in the warm water, they commented on the crickets and frogs, the night birds, the slap of someone's back porch door on a cabin across the lake. Sisters all in their forties, no longer accustomed to public nakedness, no longer thin and proud, unscarred or lightly tanned enough to display themselves, they hovered in the water in a circle, relieved that the lake covered their cheesy bellies and their falling behinds. They avoided the issue at hand.

"I knew she wouldn't show," growled Stacey, the oldest, sporting a new Phoenix tattoo that the others didn't mention. "Why do we keep planning things like this? We're idiots." Stacey flung herself backward into the water, arching her wet muff and thighs like a whale's tail.

Her sisters paddled backward to avoid her sudden display and didn't answer because they didn't want to admit that another plan had backfired. It was their mother's birthday and they had decided to converge on the family summer cottage as a gift. With mixed emotions and a variety of expected scenarios, the three sisters had set out for Loon Lake in northern Michigan. Brigit, the youngest, doughy-soft and potato-faced, had had romantic ideas of a brunch where there would be a lot of hugging and teary-eyed speeches. She had bought her mother a corsage but had left it in the bathroom of a gas station along with her overnight bag when her carburetor had given out on the way from South Dakota. She hoped her oversized T-shirt on the dock didn't get wet, as it was the only shirt she had with her now. Virginia, the middle daughter and a new mother who had ridden the bus eight hours from Ann Arbor, carefully plastered her chin-length hair behind her ears as a nervous habit, and hoped the baby monitor on the dock didn't get wet and cut her connection with her daughter sleeping on the porch. Despite all the correspondence she had sent back and forth laying out plans and extracting promises of good behavior, she had worried over exposing her child to her volatile family and yet arrived in the secret hope that

115

her mother would play the doting grandma. Stacey, who lived in L.A. and rarely returned, eyed the cigarette she had left burning on the end of the dock, and knew that if all hell broke loose as she expected, at least she'd be on the lake and could gather berries and fish by herself.

Their mother was to drive to the lake house thirty miles from her retirement community in Alpena, but she was already four hours late.

"Maybe something's happened," Brigit said with concern, doing a halfhearted breaststroke.

"Something happened all right . . . ," Stacey said as she lay her head back into the water.

"She could be lying by the side of the road or something," Brigit said.

"More like passed out by the side of the bed," Stacey said scornfully.

"I wish you wouldn't say things like that," Brigit whined.

"That *is* a bit alarmist," Virginia said, turning momentarily from the lights on the baby monitor.

"What should I say instead?" Stacey said snidely, "She's 'out'?"

"Oh, that is so unkind." Brigit slapped the lake, coughed on the water that got into her own mouth, and turned away from Stacey to find a way onto the dock. She was hesitant to clamber out of the water and expose the sixty pounds she had put on since their last meeting. Virginia paddled in to mediate.

Stacey splashed them both. "Why do I let you rope me into these ridiculous schemes? Jesus, how long are we going to beat the totally fucking dead horse?"

"Don't talk like that about mother!" Brigit barked.

"Merry Christmas, Brigit!" Stacey sneered.

Last Christmas they had convened on their mother's apartment but she didn't seem to be home yet, so the sisters bustled about the kitchen starting the pies. Stacey mixed brandy eggnogs despite Virginia's halfhearted protests, and Brigit recounted cooking fiascoes of their childhood. When the first eggnog had taken hold, Virginia crept into their mother's room to check on the favorite pendant she hoped to inherit—make sure all the stones were in place, that the receipt was still with the box as it had been for twenty years—and returned with nothing in her hands.

"Mother's out."

"What do you, mean—out?" Stacey said, suspiciously swirling her eggnog in its glass. 'Like she's gone out for groceries?"

"I mean . . . she's passed out," Virginia had said haltingly, ". . . in her bed."

"Oh, Mother, I'll help you," Brigit had said, pulling off her apron and heading for the bedroom.

"Ach, clockwork," Stacey had said. "There's a kitten in a tree down the street when you're finished!" she had shouted after her sister, and grabbed the rum bottle for another round of eggnogs.

That night they drank until the bottle was finished—Stacey with vehemence, Virginia willing after protest, Brigit secretly and sneaking cookies into her pockets as well. They all rebelled over the feeling that they should be quiet for the woman in the other room, so they had a loud, raucous food fight, splattering pumpkin pie over the walls, smearing corn bread dressing into every crevice, cabinet face, and tile groove. In the morning, Virginia and Brigit were remorseful over their condition and immediately started to clean, but their mother and Stacey were savvy about their hangovers and sat down to coffee without acknowledging the mess.

This evening on Loon Lake, Virginia executed a precise breaststroke. "Now, Stacey," Virginia said.

Stacey threw her head back in disgust and clenched her fists at her side.

"These goddamn reunions are like a land-mine sweep! What spot is going to blow up next!" It took all her concentration to convince herself not to scream, but she was not going to act out. Put your anger behind you, she chanted. No broken vases, no destroyed kitchens. Float, Stacey, she said to herself, let it wash away into the lake. She had known her mother wouldn't show up, which was probably why she had suggested they go skinny-dipping. It seemed bold and bad but water couldn't be broken, and if they took off all their clothes there wasn't anything to rip apart in a rage. Besides, it seemed so appropriate to be floating in the water, the way she had been suspended so many times, waiting for the woman who had left her in a grocery store to fly home with a bottle of gin, covering for the mother who was passed out on her prom night and left the camera on the coffee table without meeting her date, waiting for the woman who had worn dark shades and torn stockings when she stumbled in to fetch her daughter from detention. Stacey had learned to wait for the rage to blow over while her mother sneered into her face with a twisted mouth, crooked lipstick, spittle flying off the woman's teeth onto her child's cheek.

Stacey ducked under the water, then bounced up growling like a serpent. Not to arrive at all, she thought. What a mixed blessing. On the one hand, there would be no opportunity to bait the woman through her hangover, to show her in some way, any way, the rage that the woman's drinking brought up in her. But it would be easier for Stacey to keep herself in line. Her own drinking was like an itch that she couldn't help but scratch. Before she had boarded the plane in L.A., she had met with her therapist for a bolstering, and her therapist had leaned forward in her chair to drive home her point. Try to avoid the companionship of destruction, she had said, and Stacey felt as if her therapist had slapped both her ears, rendering her deaf to the outside world, acutely aware of the inside. Even now, she heard her sisters' voices through a muffle. It wasn't that she wanted to drink, or even drank that much, but it had become clear to her, sitting in the therapist's office with her ears ringing, that she had assumed that she would turn out like her mother, destined to go down in flames. Didn't that mean that she had been living without a charter of her own? The companionship of it— she hadn't seen that at all. Walk me into the flames, Mommy, just don't let go of my hand.

Now her mother wasn't even going to show up. Not a bad way to begin finding a new level for companionship, she thought, floating away from her sisters, then righting herself and taking a deep breath.

"Well, we still have the lake," she said tentatively.

"We do!" Virginia said over-enthusiastically, relieved that there would be no scene from Stacey. She fingered her little earrings and slicked stray hairs behind her ears again.

"Maybe I should call her," Brigit said quietly.

"Oh, for Christ's sake, Brigit," Stacey barked, then started to laugh. She bounced in the water, flailing her arms like a clown, and Virginia, still poised between the two sisters, laughed as well and twirled in the water, kicking her legs.

Brigit crossed her arms over her chest unhappily. Even if her mother answered the phone and droned on in a drunken way, at least Brigit would know that the woman wasn't stranded with car trouble while they had spent the evening floating here thinking the worst of her. The others didn't understand. Brigit was always the only one who could tend to her mother when the woman's sadness overcame her and she wound up drunk. It was a sickness, after all, and she was the only daughter who treated it like a sickness. Ever since she had been an adolescent, she was the only daughter who would get out of bed when her mother stumbled up the stairs, help her out of her clothes, and sometimes pull her out of her girdle and stockings while her mother writhed and giggled on the bed. She knew the woman was passed out at home, or maybe her mother just couldn't bear to see them all. Why would her mother call to announce her decision not to come—her sisters would be recriminating. Besides, her mother had done her reminiscing over the phone during the last several weeks, something the others didn't know. She had called Brigit late at night, night after night, repeating stories of their childhoods, soon repeating the stories several times in the same conversation. Tonight she would call her mother as soon as they got out of the lake, and use the upstairs phone so her sisters wouldn't hear.

"It's a beautiful lake," Virginia said, stretching her hand out to the old wooden dock where they had run as children, the marshy shore behind them. Stacey's cigarette fell into the water with a hiss.

"In South Dakota there's a lake preservation committee I'm working on," Brigit said, brightening. "We're saving the trout from a mercury plant."

"I thought you were saving the whales," Stacey said without enthusiasm.

"That committee, too," Brigit said. Stacey rolled her eyes. Brigit saved broken-down men with no jobs who professed love, dogs and dirty hurt birds from the park, kids who couldn't read who lived on her sofa until they stole from her. Brigit thrived on the moment she dove in, not the long tedious work that ensued, just the moment when they reached out their hand and she took it. Hers was definitely not tough love.

"You should keep a scrapbook," Stacey said, without mentioning that it should include both her animal work and the crime reports of her temporary "friends."

"Stacey," Virginia admonished, then stopped herself. "Sorry, I don't mean to intercede." Without their mother, her plan for the weekend was nearly perfect. Sure, she would miss what she had hoped would be a moment on the lawn in which mother and daughter gazed out at the gently rippling lake, baby well fed and asleep, and her mother would tell her what a terrific mother Virginia was. Past that fantasy, though, the rest of the weekend was now entirely within her control and that was precisely how she liked it. She was a single mother, and even before her showers and the baby's birth, she had bought everything the child needed in small quantities so as not to be disappointed if the parties and well-wishers failed to produce the right goods. It was just to make sure all the bases were covered, she had reasoned.

Virginia swam to the dock and stroked her hand along the mossy wood. She checked the monitor again. Any excess in protection was acceptable now, she thought, protection of both her child and herself. It had taken an act of will even to believe she could be a mother. When the need to have a child had become overwhelming, Virginia realized that she thought of herself and her sisters as unfit to be mothers, doomed to be unkind, inattentive, and neglectful. She pushed out thoughts of her own mother spending the evening stumbling around the retirement home or splayed across a bed reeking of gin. How her mother even got alcohol into the retirement home was beyond her, but she did, and she secreted it away just as when Virginia had been a child. They had been on the way to a mother-daughter tea and Virginia had been proud of her mother in a lemon-yellow suit and white gloves, her hair in a perfect French twist. In the car, her mother had reached in front of Virginia and pulled a little silver flask out of the glove box. Soon after, she had been beating a rhythm on the steering wheel and laughing at jokes she hadn't told out loud.

Virginia grimaced slightly over the feeling of needles in her nipples. It was time to nurse. Breast milk leaked into the chilly water of Loon Lake, and she reveled in the communion. To be a mother, an adult, involved standing at the end of this dock and displaying the wonder of Loon Lake, pointing at the turtles and the cattails, the rushes, the loons themselves. Virginia looked at her sisters and smiled. There were several blessings brought by the little girl cuddled in blankets on the porch: her baby was erasing Virginia's past. While her sisters still fought the demons of their pain with their mother, Virginia, through the blood and the brains and the soul of her child, had walked past the pain, hadn't she? The time had come to live life at its best. No excuses, no shortcuts. She turned and pushed through the water. The question for her was no longer what kind of mother her own mother had been in the past, but what kind of mother she, herself, was going to be now.

Virginia looked behind her at the baby monitor again, then looked back at the house.

"Oh my God," Virginia said. "She's here."

Brigit ducked closer to the dock, and Stacey suddenly clutched her breasts.

"Girls?" It was their mother's voice from across the lawn. "Aren't you a little old for this sort of shenanigan?"

The three sisters dog-paddled up to the shadow of the dock and clutched the edge, peering over.

"Yo, Ma!" Stacey said boldly, hauling herself halfway onto the dock and waving.

"What is that on your arm? Some Native American . . . thing?"

"Risen from the ashes, Mom. I've risen from the ashes."

"I don't suppose that means you've quit smoking."

Stacey dropped back into the water.

Their mother had a small, elderly woman on her arm and the two women walked carefully toward the dock as if the older woman were frail or blind. "Do you have robes or clothes or something? I've brought a friend."

"A friend?" Stacey hissed from the shadows to her sisters. "Mother has no friends."

The guest grumbled something unintelligible.

"For Christ's sake, Mildred," their mother said to her companion, "then vomit in the weeds here."

The sisters swam closer together. "She's brought home a drunk?" Stacey said to Virginia. "Another drunk?"

Their mother clutched the woman's arm, then steered her back toward the house. "We'll be inside, girls."

"Mom didn't sound drunk," Virginia said. She sighed, then waved in her mother's direction. "Hi, girls," she mimicked quietly. "So glad you came, that you arrived safe, and all for me—you're such loving daughters."

Wrapped in their towels with their hair dripping and their shoulders hunched against the chilly night air, the three daughters stood just inside the screen door. An old woman they had never met slumped in their mother's overstuffed chair, her eyes closed and her head rolling from one side to the other.

"Girls," their mother said, coming in from the kitchen and holding open her arms to receive them. Brigit rushed toward her, Virginia following slowly. Stacey stood her ground. "This is Mildred Warner, such as she is," she said as she kissed each girl on the cheek, even moving across the room to Stacey. They each noticed that she smelled sober. Her hair was neat and tidy, despite the late hour, and she was smartly done up.

"I've got to get some food into this woman," she said, and returned to the kitchen.

Brigit followed her but was pushed aside by her mother's return. "Woman has no business drinking that much gin," their mother said vehemently. Stacey's mouth dropped open. Strangers had never been brought into their circle. The sisters stood at odds. There was no point in introducing themselves or starting a conversation: the woman was slurring her words in a conversation with herself.

"I'm going to check on the baby," Virginia said nervously.

"How is the little darling?" their mother said.

"Wonderful. She's grown so much since you've seen her," Virginia said brightly.

Her mother turned back to her friend. "Look at you, you cow. Sit up straight!"

Stacey leaned on the railing at the bottom of the stairs and rubbed her hair with a section of towel. There was clearly no need to ask why it took her so long to arrive, but to see her mother as the designated driver—now that was odd. Just as odd was to listen to her berating her friend.

"Can I fix something for you, Mother?" Brigit said, emerging from the kitchen with an apron in her hand.

"You can clothe yourself first, young lady. And I've already got a frozen dinner in the oven for her," she said. "Not that you deserve it, Milly. When will you listen to me?"

Brigit looked over at Stacey pleadingly. Stacey just shrugged her shoulders and headed upstairs to change.

When Virginia dressed and came out into the quiet night, she found Stacey sitting on a log under the lamppost, a fly rod in one hand, a cigarette in the other. She had a wry little smile on her lips.

"Have you been listening to those two?" Virginia said mournfully as she gestured back to the house and sat down beside her sister. Snatches of their mother's insults carried into the lane. Stacey made a small murmur, then concentrated on the silver lure glinting in the lamplight that fell with a little puff into the soft dust of the road. "It's weird not to have you two fighting," Virginia said quietly.

"Indeed," Stacey said. End the companionship, she reminded herself. She looked over at her sister's sad face.

"What were you hoping she'd say this time?"

Virginia squirmed in her seat. Stacey put the pole between her legs, put her arm around her sister. "Go ahead," she said. "Say it."

Virginia nestled into Stacey. "Say, 'I can see by how terrific your child is . . .'"

"Go ahead," Stacey encouraged.

"' . . . that you're a wonderful mother, my darling,'" she said, surprised at the childlike tone of her voice.

Stacey held her closer. "'I can see by how absolutely spectacular your child is that you're a wonderful, caring mother, my darling,'" Stacey said in soothing tones.

"'And that your baby loves you so much . . .'"

"'And that your baby loves you so much. She's very lucky to have you as her mother.'"

Virginia sighed. "Half the time I think I should have no expectations and then the other half I think if I stop expecting what is normal then she really will have won, you know? She will have warped me, too." Stacey squeezed her shoulder, but looked away.

"You know who's really lost is Brigit," Virginia said. "She's not about to take care of that other woman and Mother is just all hustle and bustle. Brigit's upstairs crying over diets and how she has no one to date."

"She'll be all right in the morning," Stacey said. "I drove screws into the tires of her car," she whispered. "She'll be all in a dither and back to her old self by breakfast."

"You're such a bad girl," Virginia said sweetly.

"Yeah," Stacey said, considering it, "but I'm workin' on it." She cast the lure in a long, wide arch into the night.

In Reflection   My mother's alcoholism and her emotional unpredictability have been two of the determining factors of my life. I wanted to convey the sense of uncertainty that one feels when one is raised by an adult who is not emotionally stable, and to describe the process of going back to the well, so to speak—again and again returning to the hope that one could have an emotionally close, loving, normal relationship with one's mother. The three sisters in this story are, in many ways, parts of myself in various stages of healing, or other members of my family manifesting their own reaction to being raised in a dysfunctional home.

Our Children

NANCY ABRAMS

Someone's Deciding

Louise held out a wishbone for April to grab onto. Its delicate architecture hung in the air between them, fragile as April felt; ready to snap to tears.

Avoiding Louise's eyes for fear of giving away the intensity she was reading into the simple ritual, April looked around the kitchen instead. Enamel was chipping from the yellow teakettle on the stove. A layer of dust had made itself a home on the window sashes. The wooden drawers hid stacks of forks that didn't match. Behind the sagging cabinet doors were pots with lids that didn't fit.

Maybe she shouldn't be granted her wish, after all. Who could say she was the right person to raise Frannie? Not even Frannie's own mother wanted me to have her, April thought. Why should the judge be any different?

But she pinched the end of the bone, anyway. This was a rite of wanting. Selfish desire, pure and simple.

"We're both wishing for the same thing, aren't we?" Louise asked, her face as earnest as the pale bone.

April's laugh was small and airy. All she could muster. She pushed nervously at a wisp of tired brown hair that was already in place. "Really, you want me to win?"

Louise gave the bone a little shake. "Of course I do."

That "of course," though tossed lightly into the conversation as though it had always belonged, called attention to a new acceptance on Louise's part. Ever since the death of April's ex-lover, Roxanne, Louise had been having dreams about living in unfamiliar houses. Night after night she was trapped in rooms with portraits of ruffled strangers on the walls. She hadn't told April that there had been a new twist to last night's dream. The old house was getting chilly, so Louise went outside to gather wood to make a fire in the fireplace. Outside, the lawn was her own; the hemlock bushes, daffodils, and forsythia were all in their places. And April and Frannie were walking up the driveway.

Louise and April stretched the bone apart slowly. It wasn't smooth. It had a sinister stickiness that reminded April of the messy blood and feathers of life. Nothing was clean and dry anymore.

Frannie loved wishbones. In the supermarket she'd cry out in protest at the poultry case. "No, April, not that chicken," she'd wail, from her perch in the high seat of the metal cart. April would hold stubbornly to the package of skinless, boneless breasts. When cubed they would take just minutes to stir-fry. But she knew the battle was lost before it had begun and that she'd cave in to Frannie's demand for the bird with its bones still intact.

"Okay, but you can't complain that dinner's taking too long to cook," April would say, searching for the smallest bird.

Somewhere, a wish fairy puzzled over whose desire to grant. Hovering above, or beyond, or among them, she weighed how deserving, or perhaps how desperate, they were: Louise standing still and square, a woman shaped like something that would always be there, a solid maple or a well-built house. April, meanwhile, wearing a sweater that was a size too big, and jeans so familiar they could have been her very legs, looked elegantly chiseled, her angled nose and chin, sculpted cheeks— every feature a quiet mix of delicate and determined.

Even knowing that Louise was wanting the same thing, April hoped she'd get the lucky half. After all, she was clinging to any sign that would disprove the hopelessness taking root in her mind. She racked her brain, calling on all the superstitions her grandmother once taught her. She knocked wood, pocketed pennies she found facing up, and gave away the ones she found face down.

"Wait," April yelled. But it was too late. The bone broke. She looked down at the piece in her hand, with the fortuitous knobby top staring up at her. She shook her head. "It won't work." She was embarrassed by the tears rolling over her cheeks.

"April," Louise said mournfully.

"We said our wish out loud, it won't be granted." April felt younger than Frannie's four years.

Louise plucked the bone from April's fingers and put it on the countertop. "It doesn't have to work," she said, pulling April's head against her shoulder. "We're going to win because of you, not some silly bone."

April felt as though she couldn't afford to eat lunch. As it was, this day was costing $150 an hour. But Rudolph Chalmers was late, and Judge Cohn couldn't be bothered with them in the meantime.

The judge had pushed two fingers to his temples, tilting his mostly bald head over the red file folder packed full of the most painful facts of April's life. April's lawyer, Rebecca Morris, was asking him to review the affidavit, to take their case now, at the appointed hour, despite the absence of Rudolph Chalmers. "He obviously doesn't care enough about his granddaughter's fate to arrive on time," Attorney Morris said.

"Believe me," Judge Cohn said in a tone of measured patience. "You don't want me to read through this affidavit right now. You don't want me to consider your request until I have eaten some lunch." With that, he sent April and her attorney back out into the hallway.

"He has ten requests for restraining orders this afternoon, and a handful of guardianships," Rebecca Morris said as they walked out of the courtroom. "This is not a good day for Grandpa to be running late."

"So, what do we do now?" April asked.

"Why don't we get something to eat, too," Rebecca said.

Eat? Who could eat? But April did want to get out of the courthouse.

The brick corridor pulsed with tension. A woman in a pink uniform was crying into her hands. Another bounced a baby nervously on her lap as she watched officers come in and out of the swinging doors to courtrooms 8, 9, and 10. A young man was arguing into one of the pay phones in Spanish.

"The only problem is there's nothing you'd want to put in your mouth in this entire town," Rebecca muttered, as April followed behind. Rebecca scanned her surroundings before punching the buttons inside the elevator. "Wouldn't it be our luck to get stuck in here with him?" she said, eyeing the close walls of the compartment. "You haven't seen him yet, have you?" The doors slid shut. April looked over the tight knot of lawyers and their clients, briefcases bumping against thighs, real leather shoes lined up on the sinking fake brick floor.

"No, he's not here," April said. She hadn't seen Rudolph Chalmers since she and Roxanne were living together. He had come to Frannie's third birthday party after not having seen any of them for a year before that. Roxanne hadn't even called him on the day Frannie was born. "Promise me something," Roxanne told April one day when they were bringing six-week-old Frannie to meet her grandpa for the first time, "Never leave her alone with him."

April practically skipped down the courthouse steps, feeling like a prisoner being released into the sunshine. "That building feels like a hospital," she said. "So many sick lives."

"Worse," Rebecca said.

Outside, the shining blue sky seemed to offer some consolation. People rode bicycles through traffic and clutched their children's hands at the red lights. Rebecca's pleated navy skirt cheerfully accommodated her long strides. Her brown and gray hair hurried around her shoulders like a cloud caught in a brisk wind.

"This place should be passable," Rebecca said, pushing open a rich wood door with a frosted window. People dressed in civil grays and browns ate at polished tables. The specials for the day were written in pink chalk on the front blackboard: asparagus quiche, clam chowder, and baked scallops. Rebecca strode toward a table at the edge of a raised platform, cordoned off with a brass banister.

April wanted a BLT on rye toast, but the closest she could find on the menu was a bacon, tomato, and avocado sandwich. Was lettuce too low class for this joint she wondered.

What she really wanted, more than the sandwich, was to topple the table, and watch the cut glass tumblers and salad forks bounce and shatter on the floor. This man was trying to take her baby! She wanted to scream her complaint to everyone in the restaurant. She wanted the world to stop in the face of her tragedy. Instead, she ordered a cup of chicken vegetable soup and a stuffed baked potato. Rebecca had the asparagus quiche after lengthy negotiations with the waitress. She is a lawyer, after all, April thought.

"Well, then, let's review what we've got," Rebecca said, spreading a pale pink napkin over her lap. "I think it's in our favor that Chalmers is late. Do you think he'll show at all?"

"He'll show all right. Roxanne was the same way—loved a good fight. He won't miss it."

Rebecca held a glass of ice water midway between the table and her small mouth. Her lips were curling in as she considered the thought of her opponent. "Why would Roxanne have taken you out of her will? That really messes things up for us."

"That's Roxy," April said, watching as Rebecca attacked her water with small persistent sips. "Always charging life up with more excitement than is at all necessary."

"You mean she was just trying to keep things interesting?"

"I don't think she planned to die that time. I think she wanted to get me to come back into line," April said. "I'd been getting a little . . . uppity."

"Is it uppity to tell a woman who was regularly overdosing on diet pills and taking razor blades into the bathtub that she needs some help?"

"Roxanne required a high degree of obedience."

Until she said it, April hadn't realized the obvious: Roxy hadn't meant to kill herself quite yet. She'd staged a dress rehearsal—but the audience arrived. Roxanne Chalmers was dramatic. She had been cruel, too, but only incidentally, only in pursuit of her ambitions. April wouldn't believe that this was how Roxanne wanted things to turn out.

April remembered the day, not long ago, when she sat on the narrow hospital bed, not knowing this would be the last time she and Roxy would play out this scene. Roxanne was propped up with pillows, looking out the window at a flock of ducks floating in a huge puddle. Every day that spring April would come to the Steinhart Psychiatric Center and try to talk Roxanne into signing the papers she had tucked into her shoulder bag.

"Look, do you notice the puddle is shrinking?" Roxanne would ask, refusing to glance at the documents.

April knew better than to try and rush Roxanne, but her patience was running out. It wasn't the first time Roxanne had been hospitalized, nor was it the first time April had tried—using everything from gentle prodding to cajoling—to force Roxanne to act. She asked Roxanne to let Frannie come stay with her for the summer while Roxanne mended. "No, she can't stay with you for so many months, I'd be jealous. She'll start to love you more."

April would reassure her with jokes. "I wouldn't bother to feed her. You would always be remembered as the mother who let her have something to eat," she had said. Anything but letting Frannie go home directly to her mother whose ripped arms still hadn't healed. "I won't let her play with toys. She'll have to go to bed straight after supper. I'll make her hate me, I promise." Anything to break this moribund reverie and get Roxy to laugh. Anything to keep Frannie safe.

In the year and a half since Roxanne had left April, taking Frannie with her, April had been doing all she could to watch out for Frannie. No matter what the judge decided, the little girl whom she'd helped to bring into this world, who called her Momma April, and who expected miracles from her still, would be her daughter.

Roxanne's laughter worked a spell on April, bringing her in close. Close enough to remember Roxy's kooky, brilliant side. Her collection of religious statues that were scattered around the house; her brilliant, original philosophical diatribes. April remembered Roxy's

church-of-the-week routine, in which she attended a different de-
nomination's services every Sunday. "It's all absolutely true, and it's all
garbage," was Roxanne's treatise on religion.

This time April wasn't trying to make Roxanne laugh. She'd had
enough of these dramas. Even the comic interludes had lost their appeal. She'd had enough of pretending that with a little time everything
would turn out right.

Above all else, though, she couldn't let Roxanne know she'd spoken to a lawyer, and that Rebecca had told her she needed to come away
from Roxy's room that day with a new will, and with an agreement for
temporary custody until a psychiatrist and a judge agreed that Roxanne
was once again fit to parent. "You can't just go by her word," Rebecca
had advised. "As it is, the courts won't be on your side. You need something in writing." Talking to a lawyer made April feel like a traitor, even
though she knew her true allegiance was to Frannie now. She'd lost
hope for Roxanne.

Being direct with Roxanne hadn't been a good idea. She might show
the world the body of a waif and the confused gaze of a woman going
under, but she was sharp. She knew what April was edging toward. Just
as the dry mud around the pond was going to edge those ducks out,
April was trying to do the same to her. And Roxanne also knew as well
as April did that she and Frannie couldn't live this way forever.

By the morning of her last visit to the hospital, April was sure that
Roxanne would sign the temporary order for custody and the revised
will she'd had a lawyer draw up. She'd even gotten the hospital's notary
public to agree to be on call that day.

Roxanne was looking out the window when April arrived. April
admired the studied determination that kept Roxanne from turning to
greet her. And although she tried as hard not to play her part and be
drawn into Roxanne's reverie, April found herself looking out the window to see what had caught Roxanne's attention. She saw what she was
supposed to see right away. The puddle outside the window had dried
up. Only a few small muddy pools remained. "That one duck just won't
go," Roxanne said, without greeting April. She said it happily, as if the
duck were infinitely charming for its tenacity.

Having signed nothing, Roxanne checked herself out of the hospital the next day. That weekend Frannie had gone to visit her grandfather. And that's when Roxanne did it.

Still, April didn't believe Roxanne had meant it to be final. Roxy
had promised to meet with her lawyer the following Monday, and after
he looked over the papers she'd consider signing. She had promised.

"I think I was supposed to learn a lesson," April told Rebecca. "I was supposed to get scared enough that I'd do things her way. I think she wanted that to be the mood I came to this custody discussion with. Like, sure, she'd give me the kid to raise for a while, but I'd have to remember who was boss."

"Dramatic." Rebecca shook her head at her asparagus quiche and stabbed it with her fork.

Everything was going well for Rudolph Chalmers during the hearing before Judge Cohn. Chalmers presented the face that the public always saw. He was well dressed and tidy, his silver hair falling in energetic waves across his tanned forehead. He wore a classic gray suit with a floral-print silk tie. The picture of a sensitive, practical grandfather.

Chalmers's lawyer was an older man who seemed to take for granted the fact that he and his client would be out of the room with a victory in short order. He had the air of someone not used to troubling with such small matters.

April Agassi and Rudolph Chalmers sat like bookends at either end of the long table facing the judge, who listened to the lawyers seated between them.

"I don't see how I can honor your request," Judge Cohn told Attorney Rebecca Morris. "Your client is a biological stranger to the child in question. She has no legal standing in this matter whatsoever, whereas here before me I have the child's grandfather, who is anxious to be appointed guardian."

"I understand your problem, Your Honor." Rebecca Morris crossed her arms in front of her blue blazer, as if she were holding on to her calm demeanor. She had told April that morning that she hates to lose. "I ask you to consider the affidavit my client has submitted. It seems clear from her account that Ms. Chalmers was very troubled when she deleted my client's name from her last will and testament, and that Mr. Chalmers was not in fact the kind of caring grandfather or parent that his attorney has described . . ."

There was a loud thud from across the aisle. Rudolph Chalmers had leapt to his feet so quickly that his heavy chair toppled backward. "That affidavit is full of lies," he shouted.

"Rudolph," his lawyer pleaded. Chalmers's lawyer pulled at his client's sleeve, like a child trying to get a parent's attention, but Rudolph Chalmers wouldn't stop. He yanked his arm away and lurched backward. "I came here for justice, not to see my reputation maligned."

"I understand this is very upsetting, Mr. Chalmers," Judge Cohn offered. "But I must ask you to be seated, and hear . . ."

"No justice is going to be done here. This, this . . . girl . . . who is no relation to me . . . has been trying to steal my granddaughter since the day she was born."

"Your Honor," Rebecca Morris appealed.

"I must have order in this courtroom," Judge Cohn declared. "Mr. Chalmers, if you do not sit down I will hold you in contempt. And Attorney Morris, you know better than to interrupt."

There was a moment of quiet. The lawyer righted his client's chair, and Rudolph Chalmers sat down. He looked around the courtroom as if he had just that moment unexpectedly landed there.

April had seen him act this way before. He was visiting their apartment and Roxanne had just asked him not to play so roughly with the baby. In response, Rudolph erupted into a tantrum. He swung the stuffed rabbit he'd been tickling Frannie's belly with through the air as if he had just pulled a sword from its sheath. The baby's giggles turned to frantic sobs. April ran to pick up Frannie, and Rudy glared at her with such hatred that April thought his look alone had the strength to throw her out of the small space between him and his grandchild.

"You were just being too rough with her," Roxanne whimpered, crouching next to the bookshelves, which were packed with toys. Rudy threw the rabbit down. The muted thud it made when it hit the ground didn't satisfy his rage. "Who are you to accuse ME?" he yelled.

By then, April had taken Frannie into her room and was trying to comfort her. She rocked the baby and sang lullabies in her ear. But she could still hear shouting and a crash as another object hit the hardwood floor in the living room. April knew just which toy had been thrown by its low-pitched rattle. That thunking sound was usually a comfort to Frannie, who loved to rock the egg-shaped doll on the floor. Now it was banging frantically, and Frannie's lingering cries were revived.

Until that moment April couldn't believe Rudolph Chalmers was the devil Roxanne had always made him out to be.

"This is not justice," Chalmers seethed to his lawyer. April could see the older man shaking his head, and whispering what must have been a plea that his client get hold of himself. The judge settled back in his chair, waiting for this display to wind down. But April suspected that Chalmers was just getting started, and she was right. He shot out of his chair again and bolted toward her. "Tell this woman to go have her own baby and get out of our lives. Have your own baby and leave my family alone!" he was screaming, as he reached out to grab April around the shoulders, or maybe he was reaching for her neck. April felt her legs disappear under her as she tried to move out of his way. But she sat stuck in her chair as four court officers grabbed Chalmers and pulled him back.

Rebecca leaned down to April's ear. "Are you all right?" she asked. April felt her face heat up, but wouldn't let tears escape. Chalmers's lawyer followed his client and the court officers into the hallway. April could hear him yelling outside. "It's my granddaughter and no one has the right to give her away," he was yelling. The voices grew quieter, as Chalmers was escorted further down the hall.

"The child will be a ward of the state while we sort through this problem," the judge declared. "Let the record show that Mr. Chalmers left the courtroom of his own volition in a hostile state, and that he made an attempt to grab the plaintiff. I will also say that while from the written testimonies it seemed advisable to grant custody to Mr. Chalmers, there seems no clear-cut answer based on his behavior in this courtroom. And, while Ms. April Agassi seems to have a longstanding relationship with the child, I am unable to rule in favor of her request at the present time due to the fact that the mother deleted Ms. Agassi's name from her last will and testament as the child's guardian in the event of her death, and that this was done so soon before her death. I will reconvene this case Monday."

Rebecca Morris jumped to her feet. "Thank you, Your Honor." April wanted to protest. A ward of the state? Foster care? But all that escaped was a stream of tears.

"The court officers will escort the plaintiff and her attorney out of the building to avoid further confrontation with Mr. Chalmers," Judge Cohn instructed.

April rose as the judge left the room. "That's a whole week," she complained to Rebecca.

"Don't you see, that was great. I was sure we were goners. Now we have a chance. Can't you see it? Chalmers dug his own grave, which was good because the judge was about to give him full custody of Frannie."

Rebecca didn't even acknowledge the guards at her side as she led her client out of the courtroom. She handed April a single tissue as if she'd noticed a spot of dirt, and not a river of tears on her client's cheek. "I think we'll have to move to adopt Frannie. I'm not sure. I'll have to do a little research here."

"Adopt my own daughter? This is crazy."

Rebecca stopped in the hallway and faced April. "Don't you see? You didn't have a chance in there. And now you do."

"But Frannie . . ."

"Frannie's better off in foster care than with her grandfather. It's temporary."

"But we could still lose."

"We could very well," Rebecca said, suddenly subdued. She finally looked at the guards who were shifting impatiently. "We're all right," she said, as if she were excusing a butler. She sat down on the bench where just a few hours ago they had waited to see the judge. A custodian pushed past with a cart piled with a metal bucket and mops. Still it didn't occur to Rebecca to vacate the hall. It was five-thirty. Rebecca had said they'd be out by five at the latest since the judge tries to wrap things up by four-thirty. April was exhausted. She wanted to fall into Louise's arms and have a good cry.

But Rebecca was still battling. "If only there was someone else we could get on our side. A blood relative of Frannie's who would take her, and give her to you. Because, frankly, this judge does not seem to comprehend the fact that you are her parent. And to tell the truth, he's never given custody to a known lesbian." She stood again and April followed her down the hall. "But that's not so important. The fact that she changed her will is going to make it very difficult for us."

April was still shaking from the scene with her former "father-in-law." If she ever doubted the fact that she had to keep Frannie away from him, she was clear now. "What would be the punishment for kidnapping?"

"Seems like a good idea right now, doesn't it?" Rebecca asked, smiling at last. "We'll meet tomorrow and make a plan." They left the building and stepped into the calming light of dusk. "He's scary," Rebecca said as they headed for the parking lot.

"I know," April answered. "Why do you think I'm trying to get Frannie? It's not because I always dreamed of living on the edge of exhaustion and having strawberry jelly smeared on every surface of my kitchen."

"That's not why you're doing it," Rebecca said, as April fished her keys out of her bag. Theirs were the last cars left in the courthouse parking lot.

"What's not?" April asked, feeling confused by the cacophony of the last hour.

"You're not just doing this because Chalmers is an animal. You're doing this because Frannie is yours."

Rebecca sank into the bucket seat of her shiny black Jaguar. "We did well today," she said through the rolled-down window. "You'll be okay driving home?"

It was a command more than a question. April waved a brave salute and walked away.

Louise walked out to the driveway to meet her. "You're home late. Are you all right?"

April had rehearsed the events of the day over and over in her head, all the way home. Now, no words came. She walked in past Louise, looking through her as if she weren't her lover of two years—her favorite person to eat microwave popcorn with or to do nothing with.

"You're not all right," Louise said, following April into the kitchen where she was already prowling the refrigerator like a wild cat on the hunt.

April slammed a bottle of salad dressing down on the counter. She followed it with an overripe tomato and a plastic bag half full of old lettuce.

"You hate salad," Louise said, prying the vegetables from April's hand. Disarmed, April looked down. All day in court she wanted nothing more than to pour all her troubles out into Louise's lap. Louise would sort them effortlessly, as if they were warm towels and shirts just pulled from the dryer. She'd fold April's heartaches and worries and stack them in neat piles. Louise would make things right, as she always did. But now, April just stared into her eyes and felt painfully aware of her mute, dry throat.

"I'll make you an olive and cream cheese sandwich," Louise said. April just nodded.

"On white bread, the way you like."

April leaned against the counter and nodded again.

"And you'll tell me what happened, starting from the very beginning."

April nodded. She imagined herself explaining how the sun looked so still and pale, as she drove to court. How the light made the sides of the buildings look like sleepy mountains. How she told herself things might go well today.

April pulled herself up on the counter and watched Louise twist the metal can opener around the rim of the can of olives. "He was horrible."

"The judge?" Louise forked halved olives on the cutting board.

"No, Rudy."

"Rudolph Chalmers was awful. That's good for you, right?"

"That's what Rebecca says." The sight of the knife blade rocking efficiently over the olives' shiny black backs was oddly comforting. April liked the way the round pieces fell apart into quiet shards.

Louise stopped cutting. "Just tell me what happened." She lay the knife down and put her hands on April's knees. Her fingers begged April better than her words could. April felt her lover's urgency. She felt the full day of waiting that Louise had endured for her sake. While she was fighting in family court for her daughter's life, Louise sat helpless, waiting at home.

April let herself feel the indignity that must have been building all day in Louise's soul. The injustice of not even needing to be told that her very presence would be considered a hindrance to their case. April lay her hands on top of Louise's and lifted her chin. She felt her jaw fall open, and she began to speak. Louise went back to work on her sandwich. The dull knife sank through the slices of bread and soft cheese. April didn't need to taste the salty olives or swallow the sweet cream cheese to know how right it would feel on her tongue. Now the room was lit only with the last glow of twilight. A sliver of pink at the horizon fought like a spent candle flame before disappearing into smoke. April, still perched on the counter, wrapped her ankles around Louise's back.

She felt their bodies sink together. Louise's tongue tasted dark as olives, the tears between them sweet and familiar. Louise's hands slipping under April's shirt and cradling her breasts were not separate, but part of her own skin. Sorrow and joy were all irrelevant. The dull nothingness of their bodies speaking for them was an answer of a sort. It was the only one April had, and for the moment, anyway, it was all she needed to know.

In Reflection   I begin my memoir, *The Other Mother: A Lesbian's Fight for Her Daughter,* with a quote from the writer Grace Paley. She says, "Any story told twice is fiction." There is a lot of truth in that. At the same time, fiction has the ability to cut to truths in ways that autobiography or memoir sometimes can't. The story at the center of my life is my separation from my daughter and the complexities that come with being a nonbiological lesbian coparent. I have written fiction, poetry, journalism, and autobiography about this topic. (The only thing I've tried that hasn't worked was *not* writing about my situation.) Each form allows something different to come through. Both the fiction and nonfiction I write begin with the same premise: A lesbian mother is in danger of losing her child. It is the endings that vary. My short stories have freed me to fantasize about what would have happened if only . . . In that way fiction writing has been part of both my literary and healing journeys.

Minnie Bruce Pratt

MINNIE BRUCE PRATT

Easter Weekend

Fayetteville, North Carolina, 1980

I didn't say anything, not for a long time, not for years. Or not much. What *do* you say to your children when they know that the other children live with their mothers, but they don't live with you? What do you say when the teacher tells you that your second-grader broke down and sobbed over the construction paper and crayons and the assignment to make a card for Mother's Day? When your youngest one is still too little to tie his own shoes, and he asks why their father is moving them to another state?

I told them that I wanted them, and their father wanted them too, and the law had given them to him. So they had to live with their father. The oldest asked, "Is the law the sheriff?" I said, "Sort of." He understood not going against the sheriff, who has guns.

I didn't tell him that people in our family, both of his grandmothers, and some of our neighbors, and lawyers and judges were using another idea of law, "God's law," to keep him and me apart. He knew I didn't believe in God. We'd already talked about that when he was three or four and asking questions about where he came from and where he was going. I'd told him then that I believed there was something without a name, an energy, like electricity, that came and went through everything, and we all held a bit of it. When we died, then our energy went to be part of everything. I said nature was big enough. I didn't say the God on the cards his grandmother sent was too small. He had already seen how his family divided up in that argument. When he was three and his brother not yet talking, we ate dinner on a patio in Florida with his father's parents. Each of us adults had our own TV table, steak, baked potato, salad. No conversation. Suddenly into the silence, he said, "Mama, Grandma says you're a liar because you don't believe in God." What did I answer? I was twenty-five. I didn't know I could make a reality by speaking steadily into that silence. I didn't know the consequences, yet.

But today I've decided to talk to him and his brother. I've decided to "come out to them as a lesbian." We are sitting at the top of the cool, slightly damp wood steps that lead down from my porch. Odd to make a formal statement, to notify them of what they already know. When they were five and six, sometimes I took them with me to the bookstore where my lover worked. I was "coming out" with her, though into what remained to be seen. When I looked at her, she was surrounded with golden shimmering light. My face must have reflected that bliss. In the car one summer afternoon, as we left the parking lot of that otherwise barren strip mall, the oldest asked, "Are you in love with her?" And I said, "Yes." But very soon I was afraid to tell them more.

I never told them I thought of running away with them, just the three of us. It wasn't that I wanted to be a Madonna with children and a halo around my head. Or a tragic figure, a Pietá, me clutching my lost babies to my breast. I just wanted to be able to hold them in my lap every morning, to have their bodies shift against me, unself-conscious weight, for a few minutes at night.

But when I imagined our existence, the fiction of names, the stories made up to satisfy strangers—and what kind of work would I get?—I couldn't do it. I wanted them to have the rest of their family, to feel how history had tied us to a particular place and time, how history had moved us away. To see my mama and my aunts, to travel half asleep in the warm fragrant dark to the house on the last piece of the farm, where all the grandchildren had gone in the summer. To see their father, his sister, those grandparents, to run with their girl cousins on a burnt-sugar sand beach by the Gulf.

Maybe someday to see, as I had, the ones on the edge of the family, the ones outside. The baby, less than immaculately conceived, given away. The shadow color of cousins on the other side, never acknowledged.

Maybe someday to understand that our separation had come because I was put out of the family, declared not a real mother by the law and their father.

So from the time they were five and six, and I'd moved out, and the divorce papers were signed, they'd lived with their father in Kentucky, a fourteen-hour trip by car. I got to see them by driving there or by taking them to my mother's house, another ten-hour drive. With my friends, I joked that I had gotten "father's visiting rights," but that wasn't true. The terms were much harsher on me, the lesbian mother, than on any errant father: No visits with them out-of-state unless in the presence of my mother or a maternal aunt. No having them in my home if I lived with any other adult. Alternate major holidays (Thanksgiving one year, Easter the next, but never Christmas Day), and some time in the summers. No official child support, but mandated payments into a college fund. Always the threat that if I told the children "too much" about my life, I would lose my scant time with them. I would lose them.

Of course I didn't tell them these details, and today, as we sit on the steps, I wonder what they've thought of our strange travels. The New Year's that we were all crammed into my VW bug, them and our suitcases and my holiday presents for them, including a cage with a gerbil that kept escaping. That was the time we raced up and down two-lane highways, south and north, so we could have three days of winter holiday together. Lately my youngest reminded me that I'd stashed some Oreos on the back floorboard near the heater. At midnight, his brother asleep, he found them and ate them, hot cookies, and I laughed, "I baked them just for you." But I don't remember this. I remember other times, driving through snowstorms and rainstorms and mountains to get to them, starting at night and sleeping for an hour in a gas station parking lot halfway, and then driving some more. No radio in the car. I went in silence, trying to understand what had happened, trying to figure out what to do. I remember all the things I tried that didn't work, like the tomato plants we set out by the fence in their new backyard that wouldn't grow. Not enough sun.

Today is a long time after that. They are eleven and ten, and it's spring break. We've just gotten back from the beach. Our skin is toasted browner, and we sit languidly at the edge of the porch. For a few moments there is nothing important left to do after having been riders of the waves in the glory of the sun.

This is the first time in five years that I could afford an apartment alone, without a roommate to share the expense, and so this is the first time in five years they've slept over at a place I call home. I have only one bed. I'm putting them to sleep on a big pallet of covers on the floor, in their sleeping bags. A makeshift hideout. Their roof is my desktop, an old door stretched across two sawhorses. It reminds me of how I used to sleep on quilts on the floor in the dining room when I was little, every other weekend when my unmarried aunt came home to us from her job in the city. I loved how the house got turned topsy-turvy to make room for her in the family. It lasted only a weekend but I knew she'd be back in two weeks. For five years I haven't known from one meeting to the next if I would see my children again.

I didn't even have time to buy folding cots for them because this visit was a surprise, unprecedented since the divorce went through.

Their father called me on the Wednesday before Easter weekend—he was driving to see friends in the state. Did I want to have them for a visit? It wasn't the scheduled holiday but—

When I was little, my favorite holiday was Easter. Not for any religious reason, though every year I sang with exhilaration, "Up from the grave he arose." But it was the life in *up*, in *arose*, the green-white blossoms of the dogwood trees dancing slant again in the skeletal woods, and the silly miraculous stories. I knew a rabbit couldn't carry anything, much less flower-colored eggs. I was a country girl who had eaten rabbit, spit out the buckshot. I had gotten eggs still warm from the hens' straw nests, walked barefoot through the shit-stained dirt of the chicken yard. But I believed the fertile logic in the holiday, though I didn't know it was older than my Bible verses. When I grew up, I found the goddess Eostre in a book, the one who came as a pregnant moon when the sun began its spring. She brought presents of red-dyed eggs, and had a game where she threw death into whatever water was around. So what if she appeared nowadays only as a prescription drug, in birth control pills or menopausal ointments? When the children were little, the two springs they were old enough before they were taken away, I hid the eggs outside in the gray light just before sunup, and put their baskets on the doorstep. Later, they raced with serious faces toward the blue, yellow, purple, red eggs that seemed to have been nested by an unknown wild animal in the dewy grass of our yard.

Maybe because it had been our innocent holiday, maybe that's why I wasn't frightened by him this time. "I have plans," I said. "I have a house rented at the beach with the woman I'm seeing now and her son, for Easter weekend. Of course I'd love to have the boys," I said, "if they can come with us." He hemmed and hawed. He said, "Perhaps you can make other arrangements." I said, "No." I said, silently, *Why are you so eager to give them to me now, after you took them away? Are you meeting a lover?* I said to myself, *I've had to make a life. I can't cancel it at his whim, not even to see them.*

The ramshackle house was on the coast south of the Cape Fear River, right on the beach, facing east. The first morning the five of us ran out on the wooden deck above the water. The light was the golden light of a morning that had never before seen the world. A flight of pelicans swept past us, heading down coast. The wing beat of each segued, on the beat, into the next behind, until all settled into a silent glide. All day we ran and played in the ocean and the sand, and at night we dyed eggs, as we fried fish for supper.

That night my lover and I put the three boys to bed in one room. We sat up for a while reading and talking while they squirmed and wrestled and argued and slept. Then she and I went into the other room and closed the door. We stretched worn white sheets over the sagging, musty mattress, and we lay down and held each other and slept.

The next morning the boys got baskets with green cellophane grass and lots of jelly beans and chocolate bunnies. Once I had given them yellow plush chickens that walked when you wound them up. Once I had gotten a spun-sugar candy egg, like milk glass with blue and pink roses, with a window cut into one end. I looked through it and saw another world inside, almost too small for me to make out, a place to hide if the one I lived in got too hard.

We ran barefoot on the beach once more, the spring tides, the high old time, splashing cold up to our knees. Then we said good-bye to my lover and her boy, and drove to my house. And the morning became this afternoon.

Now in a long slope of silence we sit together on the steps. I never want this day to end. For a minute this could be any late Sunday afternoon of my childhood. Are they thinking about tomorrow? Tomorrow they will go back to their father. Now is my chance to begin to talk to them, to explain the reason why we live like we do. What do you say to your children when, for all they know, you are the only ones who live this way?

But the words are lifeless in my mouth, what has never been said between us. Because I thought they would share any conversation about "lesbian" with their father, and I didn't trust that he would let them be with me if I spoke. Because I never wanted to tell them something and then say, "Don't tell your father." Because I did not want my life to be a dirty buried secret that I told my sons to lie about.

Now a little crack has opened, a way to escape. I never thought he'd let me have them overnight with my lover. But now I have to explain what surely must be a mystery to them. Why would two women and three boys suddenly set up house for a weekend, as if we were kin, as if we were a family? And then just as suddenly have to leave each other, with no promise of reunion? That morning we had faced the sun as it rode over the water and touched us, standing all together on that spit of land like the first time and the last time. I have to explain how this day can be ours forever, and how I don't know what will happen next.

The afternoon is passing, the light is fading. So I say, "There is something I want to talk to you about." They sit through my rapid explanation, the reason I went there with the other woman. We are lesbians. Do they know what that means? No? Well, we love each other, two women together who love each other are lesbians, two men who love each other are gay. Some people think this is wrong, the laws are against it, that's why the two of them can't live with me. But I don't think it's wrong, it's about love.

There is another silence after this. Finally, the oldest says, "So Jesus was a lesbian?" I can't help it; I laugh. Who's been teaching him about Jesus? Enough religious information so that he even knows about all those male disciples. I say, "Well, he might have been gay. He certainly did love those other men. We just don't know."

Tomorrow they go back to their father. Tomorrow I could get an angry, denouncing phone call and hear that I'll be forbidden to see them for six months, a year, forever. This is my chance to talk to them. The youngest keeps getting up and down, fidgeting. All he wants to do is play tether ball. All three of us know what I am saying: That I am their mother, and I have defied the laws of God and man, and I have been punished for it, and so have they. And we may be, again. I sit and hold my oldest boy's hand, and I say, "Is there anything else you want to know? Is there anything else you want to ask me?" They look at me, hesitant, anxious. All three of us know what I am saying: That the universe they live in every day is not the only one, that I have just cracked it like an egg and whispered to them to look through the opening, to where I stand, with others, outside.

Our Lives

Bodies, Work, Travel, et al.

Mary Cappello

PHOTOGRAPH BY LINA PALLOTTA

MARY CAPPELLO

Gone Fishing

It was the time of year when gray nests are fully visible in the trees and branches furl like fingers into the blue.

Opening her mouth bottom to top with both hands, she reached, even as its slipperiness sought to skirt her, she took full hold with a third hand, a foot maybe, no, the mouth opened against its accord to let her reach fist and palm over fist and palm down her throat. A trout came forth whole. Silvery, large, oh so endlessly gray fleshy, scaly, it was trout meat flailing. It flounced, this trout, but she did not regard it with sympathy. She gripped it. Time and again, momentarily, it would still itself and stare its green-orange rimmed eye not exactly at her but at something off to the side. It would blink mildly like a puppy wanting her to feel for it, to love it.

The poor boy who knew nothing anymore except how full he was of his mother called the thing he was eating a trout but it was a salmon. The sister served him more fish and assured him this was no trout, it was salmon.

The trout was repeating on her. Trounce, trouble, tra-la, truculent, trilling, trucelike, a trout is no trance in a buffooned drawing room. Take me to your trout. Take but don't beat the trout out of me. Take this trout in memory of me.

She thought of the lemon wedge and sprig of parsley each child was given to accompany breaded flounder (frozen, then thawed) and peas, brown-green glaring from the plate. Of how she clapped 'til her meal grew cold at her mother's recitations, ever the spine of a volume cracked in place of grace, elegy, epic, resounding refrains, a bounty to replace the stark meal. She thought of the manifestoes of need that for some reason or other she and her brother had to endure: of the sound

149

of cornstalks growing right up out of the ground crackling to bursting; of the question of whether birds or fish ever grew tired: of course they slept, but did they find it hard or effortful to fly or swim?; of the millions upon millions asleep in quiet rockers, the chairs' rung smooth as a slice of melon or of moon; of the fate of simply rocking toward a doom, of the fate of this rocking, needless, which is understood to be a matter of stoicism or indifference, but never an achievement unless linked to a businessman's time away from his assignment—gone fishing. She thought of children stirred when they should be sleeping, shaken; of pebbles pulled downstream into a pattern that could be studied if the builder would not, thrusting, disturb it with his spade.

Flirt or excise. I give you my trout. I swear on the grave of my trout. Oh, meaningless trout without which I am not, free me.

Just when she realized their mother served them words or void or need for dinner, she felt blinded, both overcome and amused by the sunlight glinting off of her fork. She was signaling to someone in the beyond in code. She would signal to someone in code to rescue them.

The trout was her mother in herself and herself in her mother, but was neither her mother nor herself. Meaningless trout. Not a symbol. The trout was wholly and merely trout.

If her fork met the sun at its rim, if it could puncture light like a balloon, then a rhombus might appear. She didn't know what that was, but liked the word. The circus bored her—was the world full of buffoons?—except for three things: a jester's diamond-patterned pantaloon that made him into a playing card; the part where the whole band of twenty jugglers appeared to unfurl a blue silk parachute—if only she could suffuse, if only she could let something in enough to be saturated; and the woman who swallowed fire.

She thought of the endless hours of practice that for some reason or other, the fire-eater had to endure; of the invisible sheet, the dark curtain of fear, that would never come down between the fire-eater and the world; of large red-coated men in ashen gray rooms dousing the woman with water not understanding that she knew what she was doing, she had mastered a technique; she imagined she never got heartburn and how she'd discovered that the mouth was a room in which nothing could combust because teeth were a barrier, the mouth was a cave of unexpressed need.

It did not flow forth from her. It had no need to swim. It was
incubating, not festering but growing to a great size. Regardless.
It blinked as though that would still the axe. She had no desire to
mount the living thing or wrap it in newspaper and stroll homeward
with it under her arm anticipating the pat of butter and a sizzle in
the pan. It was not meant for consumption.

She thought of the incalculable amount of uncontained desire in
the world. Of the fate of this desire transformed into scenes from which
one fled, stories that one could not tell, feelings for which one had no
tongue, half-baked nonart tilled in the space between, in rocking chairs.
She imagined the flame crooked like a question mark or benign fish-
hook inside her mouth forcing the trout forward like a tick backing out,
misreading smoke for fire.

If a hand could be chopped off and tossed. A novel had begun that
way after which she could not continue reading. Toss. To pull the
creature from its lair in her body and toss it.

It does not become her.
Heave ho.
Reach for the damn thing and release it, pull a large feisty larger-
than-yourself trout from your stomach neither your mother nor yourself. This is not a metaphor. It is a trout. Speechless animal bred in
the unblinking wild. Her mother put it there. Slipped it in beneath
the bread and jam. Amid the first words forming. Disguised as chips.
All you can eat.

She thought of the meals prepared with her lover. If she could keep
those before her like the surreal landscape of a wordless drive they knew
together, just a gasp and the irreality of a silver-gold saturated field under a changing sky. To go outside was to go inside, to be here and here-
after, but not then, before. She thought of rubbing artichoke leaves together in the buff, of onion tears, and hot sauce, of tearing lettuce leaves
at dusk, of pressing eggplant at midnight, of slapping ham onto a sandwich at dawn for lunch and slipping it into a bag to be found at the right
time of day, of filling a small bottle with water for a walk. Of squeezing
lemons, peeling beets, stirring rice. She had to be happy because she ate
all of these things even though her highness the trout pretended there
was no room for joy in her belly.

Once out the trout might become carnivorous.

She thought of stories of excess: loaves and fishes, porridge over-running the town. Engulfed. Who wouldn't want to be the boy turned cockroach? To be catapulted instantly into a different form, or to find the body that speaks the buried need? Unless it were what the family had made you and then after making you buried their rotten apples in your face.

She devised a number of trout treatments: Release it into traffic. Let it swim, free (this is something a shrink recommended, having never swallowed a trout himself). Give it a name. Make it a character in a story. Refuse to walk, water, or feed it. Train your gait to resemble a graceful trot and note that the trout will no longer seek refuge in you because fish and horses have nothing in common. See if the trout can find its way back home so that this particular story can end and a lifetime can be open to others.

This is not fiction because there are people here and a live trout.
But someone is bound to ask if it really happened.

Author's note: This piece is indebted to the sentences of Vladimir Nabokov.

In Reflection   I want to say that "Gone Fishing" is autobiographical at the level of its form rather than its ostensible "content." The piece was occasioned by a reciprocal invitation to play that I made to myself one semester while teaching a course in literary nonfiction. Rather than retreat into the familiar refrain that teaching takes time away from writing, I treated some of my students' work as promptings for my own compositions (a word that I like to retain for its musical connotations). An especially talented student named Sarah Durbin had written an essay about various pieces of writing that had moved her. She was responding to an assignment that asked for a statement of her aesthetics. She wrote about an author's "masterful twist of language or allusion," and "the sudden chill of pleasure" that she gets when she happens upon literature that does this for her. She quoted, in particular, a sentence from Nabokov's "Signs and Symbols" that "turned her to like the entire story." Nabokov wrote: "She thought of the endless waves of pain that for some reason or other she and her husband had to endure; of the invisible giants hurting her boy in some unimaginable fashion; of the incalculable amount of tenderness contained in the world; of the fate of this tenderness, which is either crushed, or wasted, or transformed into madness; of neglected children humming to themselves in upswept corners; of beautiful weeds that cannot hide from the farmer and helplessly have to watch the shadow of his simian stoop leave mangled flowers in its wake, as the monstrous darkness approaches." The sentence moved me as well, and I treated it as a kind of inspiration offered me by this student. I loved the shape of the sentence, its reliance on oppositions, extensions, its transmutation of literal into figural and vice versa. Maybe I was most struck by its reference to squandered or untilled tenderness. I wanted to try to imitate the sentence, to inhabit it and see where it might take me. The result, I think, is a text that departs from the more predictable habits of my work. I was compelled here to let it rip, to let, in parts, language take over, resulting in a sensual, nonsensical, discursive, and ideologically inflected meditation. So, what was most autobiographical for me about this piece of writing was the pedagogical occasion that inspired it.

Thematically, the piece seems occupied with a woman's struggle to own or disown that which she has been filled with, a defining legacy that she cannot in any simple or cathartic way be released from. The character here is trying to get free of a part of her self without necessarily taking flight from or escaping it per se. She is working with and remaking "it"—which is to say working with and remaking her relation to it—and this remaking is something that I, of course, was trying to carry out in *writing*.

Autobiographically is the story true? (I'm sorry that American culture—and increasingly other cultures thanks to imperialism—is obsessed with "real" TV.) What is autobiographical about this piece is the fact of its being a product of my imagination, where one's imagination is understood as an essential part of the matrix of truths that makes each person who she is. I realize the piece might be read as being about an eating disorder. Disordered eating has never been part of my particular symptom repertoire, though most of my female friends have dealt with eating disorders in one form or another. But I guess I could say I've been a consumer of a great deal of "stuff" in my lifetime (sometimes force-fed, other times willingly imbibed) that cannot just be vomited up. I was scarred as a child by an unnecessary stomach pumping procedure administered to me at the tender age of four. I don't think this story is exactly about that, but then again . . . At least one unconscious plane for the tale is the centuries-old misogynist affiliation of female genitalia with fish, a centuries-old misogynist repulsion toward the female body. Needless to say, I wasn't trying to reproduce that stereotype in my story, but internalized misogyny is a cultural predilection that even a lesbian feminist can't entirely escape.

Is the story about my family? Only insofar as family gatherings are surreal is the story, too, surreal. Insofar as the family, I mean anyone's family, is an arena in which people compete for the right to exist, I guess my family is partly responsible for this tale.

proceeding page

PHOTOGRAPH BY SENI SENEVIRATNE

Maya Chowdhry

MAYA CHOWDHRY

Rooms

There are more exits than entrances.

I am without a room, watched at fifteen-second intervals through a chink in my three-curtain-sided room.

Knowing you are wanted and believing it is as different as fantasy and reality. I was imprisoned for my lack of knowing myself, first by my own fear of life, and then by society's unfulfilled minds. Disguised with smiles they stand at the entrance of my numerous rooms.

I see my mother; she holds society's mirror, catching the sun's morning ray and reflecting this life onto my face. It causes a small tear to be secreted and trickle down my cheek. In the gentle morning heat it evaporates and the past is forgotten.

The moon masks day and I forget why I'm living. I say good-bye to the sun and get ready to sleep forever. Skin sags around my eyes. My hair hangs limp around my sad cheeks. I laugh at the melancholy of my life. I sail into death, gliding into the ceasing of cells, the dissolution of metabolism, the quiet shadow of coma. My hand becomes a wing singing into spirit, ripping past flesh, becoming a reason for wisdom. There are no words in hope; it is blind and free of the fragrance of control. Death is a myth.

Sunday, instead of lunch, instead of bath for school and red socks, I had a red bath. I wanted more blood; I wanted to die and taste re-in-car-nation. How many times can you go over the same piece of evidence? She lifted me out of the bath in her arms.

I don't like standing on my head when I'm crying; the tears run back inside my head. I want to ask for everything I've ever given her back, but it's unethical and anyway I've got copies. Xeroxed love messages repeated five times yearly for emphasis. Poems come out of comfort and despair. Read conflict. Can you take back your love now—it hurts.

I don't think the ceiling tiles are flame-proofed. My cunt aches for you. There's a slight chance that when the lights go on in the morning I'll still be here. I'm going crazy without your love.

Self-harm is infliction; all I can see from horizontal is a mud-gray sky, steam on the windows and the feathered scratches of treetops. Words can turn keys; well and ill seem to compromise me. Did I really want to die? Imagine if you were depressed and strangers kept offering you food and wine.

Black women go home to die; they like to wash their own sheets clean of others' madness. Sad mothers suffocate their desires in their children's dreams and return to desperation. She doesn't need a silent room to talk in. We're all feeling the same city pain. All wanting off at the next stop. I make an emergency stop. I feel sick.

There is a corner folded down on the bed opposite; she borrowed some razors from an unshaven man and tried to show how sad she was. She was gloved up and shut up in a chair. We're still waiting for her return. Hushed corridors speak patterns, but she knows what she wants to say.

I am caught cleaning my ears with a cotton-bud—my personal hygiene marks will go up on my cue sheet (daily events showing signs of depression, confusion and death—leading to suicide). No razor blades in sight, only dental floss and panty-liners. I've never considered hanging, and suffocation with sanitary protection is too ironic to bear.

Post cycle, depression, PMT, love patterns return. If I don't get some sleep the medicine van will be round at seven. Sunshine pills for sunshine girls who don't brush their hair one hundred times a day. If I sleep all day I'll forget my personal hygiene and the soap will imprison me for another day.

Men smoke in the corridor. They talk as if he's making sense. We know he isn't. Our blankets have holes so we can't use them as "a tool of self-harm." There is a nod of approval but the blankets remain.

The empty bed opposite yawns. Her symbol of her capacity for conversation is the folded down corner at the edge of her bed.

He grows things, makes them come to life. He gave me life, but couldn't watch me grow up. He feared the places I would grow into. While he waters, I dry out. His hands mold the earth into a ball around the roots. He was born in a Welsh valley, looked for seeds all his life. My hands cradle the wet clay. It spins and I push it into a long tall cylinder; it's too fragile and it breaks and I begin again with what remains in my hands. I have to be content with what I can hold in my hand.

I am five; I go to school in a green uniform with my hair in bunches. I learn to count. The days pass as I learn the numbers past ten, twenty, a hundred, a thousand. I am in my teens, my twenties, nearly thirty. I've grown old and forgotten to live.

Suns and moons chase each other day and night, night and day, and in November the dead come back to enjoy what they miss of life. After the party where they dance ferociously and feast, they are chased back to death where they must stay forever.

I have a "Middlewood Pool" pillowcase to swim in. After fifteen years they are released onto street corners; they lay their heads down on the remains of Chinese take-outs. I eat for the first time in two weeks; my stomach's so full I can't sleep. My head hovers above the "Pool." Drowning is only breathing water. Angel fish beckon. Anger breaks cups. And I say it was empty anyway. I tidy up my books again, sorting them into alphabetical order. I'm too tired to brush my teeth. I think "personal hygiene" and doze off. The litigation-onlookers peer at me. I throw my clothes on the floor. It's the clicking of the curtain hooks that keeps me awake. Your lack of understanding leaves a wide gap in the curtain. Is depression suppressed anger?

I've never liked ironing promises. Seeking approval, I brush my teeth and put my pajamas on. They'll never know the difference. A strange woman's face greets me in the mirror. I am the end result of an overdue birth. The doctor's pen clicks again. Every time I reach for a tissue I read a proverb. Philosophers die young. Death is easy to spell; no silent "h," just silence.

The breeze in the curtains is like the chink of keys unlocking secrets. Can't they wear quiet shoes? I leave my clothes strewn on the floor. Read that one. They've been opening my curtain again. The gap is wider. The bed moves when I breathe out; can you inhale without absorbing your breath? I have twenty-nine seconds to reassess the twenty-nine years of my life.

There's a hurt that stops me from living. Her love drips like a cold tear on my cheek. I enfold her in my arms and hope she can feel my heart beating on her breast. I don't know how to ask for your love. You stab me with the truth and my eye waters. The coffee supply isn't endless; it's dreams of you that keep me awake. Rule queens descend and we're not even married. We live outside of sin. Night shift makes their eyes red and puffy; they can't see your arms holding in my despair.

I'm trying to be angry quietly: I'm trying not to do my home anger tricks. It makes you crazy holding it in. Can you leave before I break a plate over your head? Thank you.

Fast ways of dying: ask a farmer with a double-barreled shotgun, a pharmacist with an immediate poison, and a vet with a blind parrot. Sculptors use stone. Slow ways of dying—living. Clerked-in means staying.

Can you open the fridge, please?
        My name is checked on the board to prepare an answer for me.
        Is it Sunday?
        Yes.
        Then why am I still breathing?
        That's enough; I'm not going to have this type of conversation with you.

It's only air, not life. What rhymes with life? Knife, can you slice me a slice, no, thinner than that, thinner. Now it's transparent; I can't see what you're saying. She says that if you need a reason to leave she'll exchange it for a reason to stay. In the thinness of her words I can't see what she means.

Did they get the message? I don't do pills or breakfast. I leave a gap for them; it stops the tug of the curtain. I wake up to lunch on a tray on the floor. It stays until 3 P.M., when I bin it. Don't they know children in countries without seeds are hungry? I'm not; I'm also not to be trusted with my own life, because I wanted to steal it from the world. Read—it

was mine to have in the first place. Tea stays in the kitchen; by 10 P.M.
it's disappeared. Sculptors and cooks are hungry. Excessive force because of plates. Standard procedure. "Plates before feelings, Christmas
is coming, it'd be sad to miss it."

The pen-and-paper notes watch me wake at noon. I don't even know if
I'm alive. Surviving the night isn't the same. Brave girls don't go searching car parks for glass. Boredom ticks. The only thing I can do well is
hurt, and when my mind can't do the harm then glass will. (shouts)
"I'm not as brave as you."

Missing, presumed alive. Whose turn is it to die tonight? I have to
decide if I want to live or die. I don't know what I'm choosing between.

The corridors are alive; we'll be asleep all day again. I can only get better by walking along the narrow ridge of society's norms—read con-
form. Do you want my bed back tomorrow?

She was sixteen when she first wanted to die; six years of breathing
hasn't changed anything. She can't drink Lilt any more; the taste reminds her of aspirins.

I feel too calm. Somewhere to go. Fake tan-coffee-brut. No fucken
voices in my head at night. They're in the corridor. It's getting clearer.
I don't want anyone to know I'm here. They can't even keep a secret.
My ears are itchy again; I brush my hair out and realize that I'm not
hungry between 8 and 9 A.M., 12.15–12.45, and 5.45–6.15. I used to
eat about 8 P.M.; the fridge's locked.

A Pakistani woman in a white duputta calls me Behnji—where am I?
Doesn't she know I'm Turkish? Kebabs not samosas. They send me
young interrogators. I forget the opening line; they vary it thinking
we won't notice. We do. Read—no energy, no motivation, no cooperation.

She has large slashes just below the knee. What was it you wanted to
say? I was thinking about what I wanted for tea and forgot what you
said. I said "wholemeal bread's for suckers." Heavy rain in the outside
world; inside slow tears. Mr. and Mrs. visiting hours approach; here's a
tissue.

Did you ever feel like you caused someone's death with your hate? In the fifteen-second gaps they look for signs of wishes for death; I con them with my breathing. Can I read my nursing notes? I want to see if I'm getting better. I didn't try to drown myself, but it might have been a consequence as I was already drowning.

In English, the woman in the white duputta protects against her sister sectioning her. It's a conspiracy with the keepers of social good; community whispers keep her from autonomy. She's not mad; she just doesn't want to make rotia all day long and be raped. What can they do about it? We can't live inside our lives.

I give away her flowers; if she knew she'd be angry. Hyenas cackle in the corner of night. Phil calls Lil for his shooting bag; there are deep gashes in everyone's minds. All we can see is a lack of understanding.

The mattresses are wiped, even though we haven't peed on them. The sheets are changed; I did them last night. The curtains are drawn back: I just want to be alone. The sun is shining; I don't want to see. The sky is blue. You too. (shouts) "Penny for them."

"I've been penny pinching all week and queuing up for seconds at 6.30 P.M."

"What about a chocolate fireguard?"

"I'm worried about you; wanna change places?"

Otherwise I'll change my name. My mind is a dark reservoir; when it rains it fills up and when the sun shines there's a water shortage. I'm too hungry to eat. It's a white board; I'm waiting for a red marker pen to give me an instruction—suicide is an inability to express your feelings about life. Wanting to die isn't a chemical imbalance; it's a realization. You cheated me of my death and now you want to immobilize me. Is living a choice?

My anger is a veil; when I lift it you shut your eyes. Recycling my pain back into society. If you want to park, take down the No Parking signs.

It comes in waves, grips my bruised arms and dark eyes. I feel myself sinking. If you shout they draw the curtains; if you cry they lock you up. If you die, they forget. The echoes return every time I gulp; the bitter taste of death hits my stomach, burns.

I was too scared to think about my dreams for the last five days. She drowns me in her tears. I am sinking between love and death. I hold her hand, she cries; I let go, she cries. I don't want to see your tears. The corridor shouts; don't they know you're trying to remember a dream?

We live at the bottom of an ocean of air. This ocean of air covers the earth. We call it the atmosphere. If there's air in water then how can you drown yourself? When water is a gas, it is called water vapor. The air takes up space. So air is real because it takes up space and has weight. Fifteen lb/sq inch. Air helps sound to travel, so that we can hear things.

I said, "I love you."

Took her life, as if she didn't own it, and now she owns her death.
Listening, listening for the sound of desperation; how quiet is it? How unspoken, how silently it fades into the night. You still don't go home when you say you will. You're the one who's leaving.

I don't want any witnesses to my death; fear makes them run toward you. Twenty-nine is a good age; people don't cry too much when they realize you've been around for nearly thirty years. You can do a lot of living in that time. Seven until seventeen, I don't call the ten years in between living. But they're called life. I don't trust her; she poisons me with promises of truth. I have no evidence. They say the medication works. Subdued slippers shuffle and arms hang limp. I buy some new shoes; they pinch my toes.

The receptionist says there's a madman outside trying to get in. Does he want to share our sanity? Doesn't he realize we've all been assessed in here? The polite way to greet them when they say, "All right?" is "Yes, thanks." How can you say it without biting your tongue, stabbing your heart, bleeding from your fingertips?

I have blood on my hands; I chop men's heads off and hold them by the hair. It seems easy. How will I forgive myself for owing me my life? They wash the blood off.

You do make a difference; too much to bear. I can't come back here; it feels like trying to live again. I'd rather go home to die.

Thoughts of death from the corridor filter in. Everyone has the same explanation: overwork leading to rest. I want a long rest with no complications. I don't want to be here; can't you understand? High buildings beckon, trains beckon, sharp edges beckon, poison beckons. If you lie, they stop checking up on you. I could be dead by now. Love was just filling in the gaps. From ear piercing to infection, what's in between the death of a love affair?

She cut through her core; severed in extreme places, the aorta is sewn up, but blood finds other ways to leak from the heart.

Subtle ways to ask if you're dying.
    Is there water leaking on the floor?
    (shouts) "No."
    Must be alive then; I can have a bath. You can't hide the plates from me.

I feel like I'm treading water, almost automatically, the kick, kick, kick of my legs keeping me afloat. No, it's the rubber rings everyone's throwing me. I'm choked and tired; it's like if I don't cry every day I'm not alive. Could you survive with linen, towels, blankets stamped in red ink? What am I doing here breathing, paying my bills? Living just doesn't make sense anymore. I went home to die, I went home to die, I went home to die. Why doesn't anyone understand I can't face life, my life?

Another week ticks by, seconds of a life. I'm trying to chase it out of my heart; it's engulfing me. Was I so wrong wanting to die? That if I couldn't own the beginning of my life, then I'd own the end. Night, hold me against resistance and give not my blood unto the day. Press and de-press.

Endless cleaning, endless decisions, endless floor washing, endless days. Morning breath—where am I? Oh I'm here again. Is the sun shining? I don't know. I can only see curtains and the light in the folds. The days go by in doses. Try ECT; we'll burn the desire out of you. People here love their tablets.

In the moment. Keep measuring. I can't decide between life and death.

Housekeepers spill homophobia into my waking. Rainbow rings don't save me. They think it's Beirut in here. I tell Tanya; she laughs, and says they can't imagine what it's like to live there.

It's winter; the sky is singing to the moon and darkening quietly until only the moon's beams are uttering the last strains of good night. How can pink turn to gray and disappear? It's painful being in love; it keeps me awake all night. Problems are deserts with no oasis.

Black women come home to die when there's nothing left to think about.

There are more exits than entrances. I find myself in room 12A, there is no thirteen; it is not a question of luck.

East to A. The sun rises, winds howl, and I am blown back on myself. First down polished sanitized corridors and then toward home. I own things, but really they own me; control my life. The nurses can't tell if my jewelry's real or metal. Try x-raying me and looking for the dense mass around my fingers and neck and earlobes. I get a serial number for my property. I look at the number and try to decide if twenty-three thousand eight hundred and forty-five patients have been admitted before me. Admitted? What did they open up to? I have £1.20 on me, or the equivalent of four bars of chocolate, my only hunger. There is one of everything, socks, scarf, and shoes. I think they belong to me; I was caught wearing them. I get into bed, pull the covers tight around my neck, breathe, nothing happens, breathe, nothing happens.

I tear up the patient's property and clothing record. Now the clothes can't own my identity. I hear reflections in the window; dark shadows lie below my eyelashes. I think there's someone out there who wants to get in. The ceiling's too high; I feel a long way down lying in a horizontal embrace with my duvet. I feel hated by myself and by others around me. I don't know where to begin. I lie under the covers trying to remember if I had a scarf on when I arrived. I try to recall the events of the last week. Did I sleep? Did I eat? Nothing comes to mind.

I go over how I got here, slowly dissecting the conversation with Tanya. I feel like I've been surgically removed from my life like an unsightly mole. I'm buried beneath diagnoses; I can't see in the light or breathe in the dark.

They want notice for recovery of the property. I want recovery. The room breathes. I count from one hundred backward, looking for prime numbers. I don't know if I've discovered them all. I'm still awake. I count the cracks in my life. First light trickles through the folds in the curtains and I'm still counting. I count how many seconds it takes for the light to change from dark blue to gray to pale gray to bluey gray.

"The north wind doth blow, and we shall have snow, and what will poor robin do then, poor thing? She'll sit in a barn to keep herself warm and hide her head under her wing, poor thing."

The "poor things" shuffle to the ticking of the clock and the calls for food (hunger a side effect of cures for madness)—and the "real" cures for madness. For both there were queues.

How to avoid the queues—1. Stay in bed until the last moment and then dash out before they unplug the serving unit or lock the drug cabinet. 2. Don't eat (because you're not hungry/haven't been for a shit for a week and are overflowing) and wait for them to bring your pills into your darkened room. Getting up was considered part of my treatment so after a short time number two became inoperative.

Side effects. One effect of being denied your childhood is that you cannot live inside yourself. Stories of the past haunt you and when dug up from you provoke you to anger. Treatment is relative.

Coping strategies for anger and other emotions must be developed. These strategies must not include getting pissed out of your head; killing yourself; breaking objects (even if they are your own); any combination of the above.

I develop my own strategies for dealing with my failure to thus far produce anything of real value. I do not want to get out of bed. I have no desire to do anything. I have been "doing" for enough years to keep me for the rest of my life. I am not hungry. I do not want to eat; I am and will be alive for some time. I have plenty of fat reserves.

I'm called for breakfast. I turn over; the sheet slides from under me on the plastic mattress. My cheek is pressed against the plastic; it begins to sweat and makes my pillow soggy. My pills arrive; I reach out from the marshland of my sleep and swallow, swallow, swallow. I sink back into the marsh. The rushes bend and sway under the weight of my tears. I cannot face another day like yesterday and tomorrow. Will there be any next of kin to come and collect the unclaimed property?

The failure of both living and addressing my life was diagnosed as severe depression, brought on by stressful life events and perhaps my current disposition as an adult with a "difficult" childhood. My refusal to take medication was seen as part of the illness—I had given up on life / was angry with life.

Did it ever come into their psychiatric minds that I may have had another reason? That I have always maintained the belief that self-healing should be the first option before interventionist medicine. I doubt it.

On reaching my allocated number of weeks of the current stage of illness I was told time's up.

You should have responded by now. What do you think of the future?

I didn't bother answering the question. My dose of antidepressants and other drugs was increased. The weeks are a blur. I cannot break them down into days; there are brief moments of memory without a date or location. I remember mainly calls for breakfast, lunch, dinner, and supper, and corresponding calls for tablets; arguments for why I should get up and the floods of tears; my despair at life. I was dragged into the TV room to be flickeringly normal.

Again I had reached my allocated number of weeks of the current stage of illness. You should have responded by now; what do you think of the future?

ECT. Either way you are shocked. Shocked by the pressure and reasons for your consent. Shocked by the plan to induce a fit that may or may not make you happy—in the first instance able to eat, which may eventually lead to happiness. In either case the reasons for success are not known.

Electricity switches on lights in darkened rooms. Volts, amps, ohms, how to measure resistance? I do not consent: although the thought of losing memories of my childhood appeals, there is no certainty about what and how much memory I will lose. (pause) I move to the weather room.

Homeless. The keepers of sanity played semantics, danced on my vulnerabilities, my dis-ease. I say manipulation and they say conformity— read "you'd be better off married, it's your way of life causing you distress."

In distress I walk beside the rain and lie restless in the weather room considering choice. The plans and un-plans for me were measured with the ruler of norms. I didn't measure up; I was brought from dark days into days of awake with measured amounts of pills that restore normality and, although I could eat some and sleep some, I couldn't be measured. The pills had also restored my anger and it went off the scale. Scale varies between generations; metrication confuses the measurement. I'm an ounce better today. Do you mean a centimeter?

I get my own room. It's like the weather room, but with only one bed. I get my things from Tanya's and she moves me out of her life. I pop back for a bath from time to time. I can have them unsupervised now. I don't feel like I'm imposing here; from horizontal there are cracks in the plaster.

There are other moments: they are remembered and a memory begins. Desires are formed through discussions of what was and wasn't and what could be. I consider with my now becoming less depressed mind whether I want to live or not, and, like the numerous decisions I have defaulted on over the past few months, I cannot decide.

Epitaph
    Past: i wrote to survive my teenage years; mixed metaphors sliding in the ink from my pen; harsh realities captured and spelt out before the emotions ravaged my mind. i write to right the rites - i'm a child of seven with a war for home. in my silent, screaming mind, i clock up the emotions willing them into small poems full of big emotions. it is 1978 i write these poems in my diary; fragments of the life i'm living; a way to commune with my small self. I try to remember that girl, living on the coast in an orange swimsuit, brown hands digging in the damp sand, digging.

quietly, using carbon paper, i type up these poems with my newly acquired typing skills and an old manual typewriter. there is no typex, only a harsh rubber which often tears the paper over my typing errors and makes a hole in my words. is reading the opposite of (w)righting?

Present: these days i write for a living, but i'm not sure. why rite?

i (w)rite to change the world; (w)right the wrongs. i have always written this way.

i (w)rite to change myself; (w)right the wrongs. i have always written this way.

In Reflection I probably wrote "Rooms" to save my life. It never started as something I would ever consider publishing. It was raw and explicit journal writing, scribbled in the curtained containment of a hospital bed, about how I see too much pain in myself and the world and don't know which room to hide in.

The piece went through a number of transformations over a long period of time: into poetry, a radio play, and back to its current form. Along the way text I didn't like was deleted, characters were added . . . names were changed to protect the innocent.

My writing is always autobiographical; my family attending my plays are testimony to this. My sister laughs at lines of dialogue from my characters' mouths which I have said verbatim to her.

After the words—how much is this piece more autobiographical than my other work? The very nature of taking a pen in your hand (skipping over the keys on a computer) can't help but tinge reality. My writing is always more emotional, crisper, often more incisive than when I tell a story verbally.

A thinking exercise I often do with my students to generate ideas for writing asks them to think of an important moment from (a) the whole of their life, (b) the last year of their life, (c) the last week of their life. The discussions, which are generated from this, reveal so much about how we process experiences and use them in our writing. When coming up with a play for commission I ask myself what my current passions and interests are and use these as a starting point; however much I try to run away from myself my own character traits are strewn amongst my characters'.

So dear reader, what facts, what truths are strewn in the words and meaning of this story?

I was in room 12A of a psychiatric hospital—it was not a question of luck, I did try to kill myself, I was on the east wing, I did get a serial number of 23,845, I did have £1.20 in my pocket.

And the truths? I didn't tear up the patients' property and clothing record, I thought I heard reflections in the window, thought the room was breathing, dark shadows lay beneath my eyelashes, there was a plastic mattress, people did shuffle on the polished sanitized corridors; it's all perception at a point in time.

I write lyrically, sometimes abstractly. I want to leave room for the reader in the story; if I don't follow the actual events of this life experience moment by moment it's because of that. Does knowing this throw more light on the autobiographical nature of this story than not knowing?

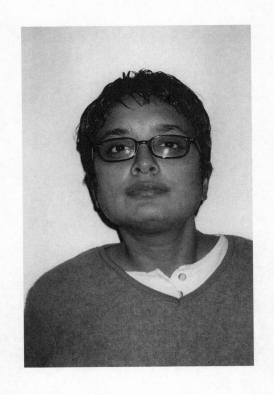

Rini Das

RINI DAS

Précis

Calcutta. January 19, 1980

"An industrial-strength vacuum cleaner weighs only twenty-two pounds, yet cleans like a heavyweight," Ms. Shah is enunciating. Chitra keeps staring at the pages of her *Active English Language*, Book X. None of what Ms. Shah is saying is in her book.

"Now, we will read this piece that I have Xeroxed. And then your assignment is to write a précis." Supposedly, "we" will picture the vacuum cleaner. The vacuum cleaner will have a face. It will stand upright and pretend to uphold the dignity of the backbreaking, defiant motions of swinging human hips that swept the floors for all these years.

An unseasonable breeze is blowing from all three directions through the windows. Chitra spent three years—Class IV, Class VI, and now Class X—in this classroom. Every year they assign this classroom to the largest class. The classroom is truly big, with a terrace on one side and a balcony limbering perpendicularly. The sun balks through the windows on the terrace side, making Ms. Shah's petite yet decadent countenance a silhouette for Agfa "shots of the day." Chitra's classmates change in composition, but not much in number. Chitra knew every scribble-scrabble on the desks.

"Jonaki loves Brian." "Brian is Brain." "Brian is Brain Dead." "Sharks are creators of wasteland." "Beware! B. S. Elliot."

You can just hear Mrs. Dutta jabbering in the staff room, "She getsh to wear what she whantsh to wear because she is a training teacher." She continues, "But whee cannot do that here.

Shomebody has to bring some dishcipline around here. An evhery year they come to train and each of them is shom Namuna. Rotting specimens, I say."

Ms. Sulehman will giggle and say, "Well Mrs. Dutta, you should really wear those jeans and kurta like them."

"You would look absolutely sexy."

"It's in fashion now."

"Try the bellbottoms tomorrow."

Mrs. Dutta will ignore, "It is the advent of the *Kalyug*."[1]

"They give ideas to these girls."

"Next thing we know, they will have disco music during the morning assembly."

Mrs. Naidu will say, "They already do that."

"'Can you hear the drums, Fernando?'" Mrs. Naidu will chime a few bars of "Fernando."

"My husband was here during the morning assembly last Friday and said that the song 'Fernando' they play during the morning assembly is really sung by a pop group called Abba."

"Have you heard that name? Abba." Without pausing for a response she will add, "Abba is disco."

"Our heritage has gone to the dogs."

"Instead of playing good arias, what is this rubbish?"

"Though I must say, that song sounds very lovely."

Mrs. Dutta will smirk and say, "Hai! Ram! No. No. I want my girlsh to have a shense of decorum."

Ms. Shah is wearing a black bra. Long strands of Ms. Shah's hair are tumbling down to her left wrist. Chitra thinks cliché with a Big C. Chic Cliché though. But now Chitra has to write a précis. There is a sense of deceptive but an enforced lull in the room. It is hard to be impressed even with a phenomenon of the vacuum cleaner because many of the girls in the class have never seen one. Chitra remembers that Marian's German mother has one.

I saw it when she was hollering at Marian for creating such a mess in her room. Chitra saw it break a glass when Marian's mother threw the monster across the open door. The "residential strength" slithered down the door and fell on the glass of Thums Up cola. Hollering—that's a good word. When will those Americans learn to ignore the pound-mile shit and embrace the metric system? Ms. Shah is still increasing our vocabulary. Now she is coming toward me, she is looking at my chin; she strikes a smile and walks away. Why is she looking at my chin? My feet are so warm. Maybe the rest of the girls are reading copies of Mills and Boone placed surreptitiously in their laps. That is what she was checking while walking down the passages between the desks. Cunning style for a teacher in training. It is

1. Translations for all italicized Hindi words are given at the end of the story.

past lunch time. I have to get back to the commentary. The commentary on the cricket test match between Pakistan and India is on. This is the first series between India and Pakistan in decades. After the 1971 war, this is "India-Pakistan Friendship Bhai Bhai" test series. The first three test matches were a draw. Today is the fourth day of the fourth test match. Pakistan scored 272 and India 430 in their respective first innings. The pitch will start turning bald and will break down by tomorrow. After all, it is being played in Madras. And you know that the Madras pitch is famous for its late innings breakdowns. When India comes back on the last day, they may have to bat all day and Pakistan's spinner Quasim can create havoc with his spin. Last time I heard the commentary, in their second innings, Pakistan was 125 for 5. Wasim Raja and Javed Miandad were batting.

Chitra picks up her navy blue cardigan. She places this vestige of the school uniform on her desk. Then she sneaks the transistor underneath the cardigan. She switches on the transistor. She takes on an air of "this is what I do every sixth period, when I am bored." She slants her head slightly, so her ears squash the transistor radio. The radio is loud enough for her to hear. Ms. Shah is at the other end of the room. Unless Nandita squeaks Chitra out, Chitra will survive this period.

She can hear Jug Suraiya, the commentator, say, "Kapil Dev comes in to bowl, passes the umpire, and the ball swings in."

"Javed goes on his front foot and then he goes back and lifts his bat and, keeping an eye on the ball, lets it go."

"Kirmani, behind the wickets, collects."

Ms. Shah is looking puzzled in her direction, but talks on. She has just finished reading the long advertisement about which "the girls" have to write a précis. Aren't advertisements, really, précis in spirit? Well! "The girls" don't have to read the Orwell piece. Instead, "the girls" get a dose of the contemporary times.

Mrs. Naidu is supposed to be supervising. Chitra looks around, in case Mrs. Naidu is snaking her presence. Mrs. Naidu is not there.

"Now, girls, you will write a précis of this article using twenty-five or fewer words. Does anybody have a question?"

Sharmila raises her hand. "Ms. Shah, will you count the articles and the prepositions as words?"

Ms. Shah smiles condescendingly and says, "Only the prepositions."

Chitra takes out her pen, writes some words. Now she has to join them. "Anemone," "Open arms," "Eye Lash," "Off Swing," "LBW" won't get her very far. She puts her head down. She can smell Charlie. Ms. Shah is wearing Charlie. Chitra isn't sure if she likes Charlie. Chitra is convinced that Ms. Shah is taking them on an unauthorized ride. Ms. Shah knows that she is giving "the girls" ideas.

Why isn't Captain Gavaskar bringing on the spinners? It's already twenty-six over; the ball isn't new.

Jug Suraiya goes on and on. "Oh! There is a bowler change. It's going to be Doshi, the off spinner."

Chitra looks at her watch. Twenty more minutes to go before this class is over. She has to write twenty-five words. She is stuck at seventeen.

"Doshi comes in again. The ball was pitched on the off stump, Wasim expected it to turn. It was a top spin instead, took the nick of the bat, and went to Vishwanath at first slip. A simple catch. Wasim Raja out at fifty-seven. The partnership that steadied the initial downfall of the cream of Pakistan's batting order is nearly over."

It is almost an hour after lunch, so the drinks trolley is coming onto the field. Chitra has a smile and gently taps her pen on her desk to get Sharmila's attention.

Sharmila whispers, "What's the score?"

Chitra hoarsely says, "One forty-seven for six."

The commercials are on. Chitra switches off the radio.

Chitra finds Ms. Shah skimming through some old exercise books piled up on her table. Chitra extrapolates that maybe Ms. Shah finds this training tedious. Probably, Ms. Shah wakes up every morning and schemes on her way to the minibus stand. "I am not prepared to teach today. Orwell is boring. Maybe an ad from *The Statesman* or *Femina* will be more fun!" Chitra fidgets with her bag and takes out her scorecard. Then writes neatly, Wasim Raja., c. Vishwanath b. Doshi 57 6/147.

She switches on her radio again. Javed Miandad is at the crease.

"Pakistan has managed to avoid innings defeat. However, they are not in great position right now. Doshi comes in to bowl."

She concentrates. "Javed's out. Caught by Kirmani," she says quietly. A few of the girls show some interest. Sharmila giggles and says, "You know I like my men with moustaches."

Somebody says, "Facial hair is disco!" referring to Javed Miandad.

Ms. Shah raises her head and says, "You can bring the exercise books to my table, when you are done."

She can think of one more sentence. Chitra writes the sentence. *The vacuum cleaner is a very efficient servant.* She has written twenty-four words. Not bad at all. She lays her head down again on the cardigan. She writes down Javed Miandad, c. Kirmani b. Doshi 52. 7/171.

"Kapil is still bowling at the other end. Kapil Dev comes in to bowl to Imran. Imran's left arm is aligned in the direction of the bowler. Kapil bowls a bouncer on Imran's leg side. Imran hooks it for a six. The ball is retrieved from the stadium. Kapil makes a change in the field placement. He is moving Doshi from third man position to short fine leg position. Kapil comes in again."

Is he crazy? First ball of the over. He is so damn aggressive. Why would Kapil bowl a lame bouncer?

Chitra is debating whether to submit the précis. She says to herself, "Well! I can go out of the classroom then and listen to the rest of the commentary till the bell rings for biology." She is undecided, but gets up. The transistor slips to the floor and the volume dial hits the floor hard. The commentary comes on loud and clear. She screams, "Imran's out! Imran's out!"

The classroom becomes energized with the crowd in the stadium yelling and screaming. The commentator Suraiya's voice sounds ebullient. He is talking a hundred words per minute. Some of the girls giggle, applaud, jump up, tumble, pinch, and run to the fallen transistor. They all stand around the transistor. After a moment, they all start to talk. They stumble. They argue. They move in and out. They wail. They shout.

"Oh! That's terrible. He is so good looking."

"Why was it not Zahir?"

"Because, stupid, Zahir has been out hours ago."

"I think Zahir is better looking."

"No! I think Wasim Raja is better."

"Zahir's glasses are so sexy."

"Bloody bad luck, Yaar!"

"Imran, oh! You poor thing."

"I am sure the umpires cheated."

"Aarae! He tried to hook the ball and mistimed it. How can they cheat?"

"He was not bowled out. Maybe it touched his shoulders and not his bat."

"Bowled over."

"There must be strong winds that blew the ball in the Doshi's direction. It was a sure sixer if Doshi was not in the way."

"Can't you hear? He totally missed the flight of the ball."

"Kapil is our only man in the Indian team. He is my hero."

"I don't care if the Indians are winning. I want Pakistan to rule. All these Pakistanis are so damn good looking."

"So what if he missed the flight of the ball. It was not his fault."

"He must have been distracted."

Sharmila declares, "I love Imran."

Nandita falls on the floor while someone tries to run around her arguing more vehemently. As if the radio weren't loud enough, Nandita starts howling, "I have cut my chin. I am bleeding."

There is more applause.

"Hai Allah!"

"I want Imran Khan."

Chitra and Ms. Shah stood all this while in silence.

Mrs. Naidu yells, "Girls, behave yourself."

Sharmila whispers, "Bitch! She had to come in now, didn't she?"

Ms. Shah calmly watches and then Mrs. Naidu calls out, "Whose transistor is this? Don't you know it is a written policy that you will be suspended if you have a transistor? Girls should be interested in things that will educate you. No! No! This new generation wants to listen to cricket. Will your in-laws approve your interest in cricket? Will it get you a job?"

She sarcastically gesticulates, "Imm-raan Khaan. Imm-raan Khaan. They are Pakistanis."

She assures, " I know why you girls are interested in boys' sports. Fantasizing about them. This is not permissible within the premises of such a prestigious girls' school. Your parents are pouring money down the sewers. Such a waste. I say get back to your seats. Whose transistor is this?"

Everybody looks at Ms. Shah. Ms. Shah says nothing. Chitra stands up and says, "Well! It could be mine. India is winning you know. This is history in the making."

Mrs. Naidu sternly says, "Is that so? Then you will have to follow me out of this classroom. How long will your tomboyish behavior continue?"

Sharmila sings out, "Jab Dhula Raja Aayaega."

Ms. Shah finally speaks. "Somebody get Nandita a Band-Aid, and Nandita, stop being such a ninny. It's just a scrape."

"Here's the précis." Chitra gives it to Ms. Shah. Ms. Shah tilts her head toward her and so Chitra asks, "Is that Charlie you are wearing?" Ms. Shah looks amused and says, "Don't worry." Chitra likes Charlie.

Manhattan. March 10, 1992

It all started with the snow in Manhattan. Mrinal, Nikhil, Sangeeta, and I walked out of the Center along West Thirteenth with intangible camaraderie. All of us had this very *I love Fig-Newtons* feeling that we needed a consensual high. We were heading for the penchant to ripe and a party at Anjana Talukdar's apartment way uptown.

So you can imagine how wired we were with $1.35 pizza, spasmodic snow crushing, subway trivia exploration, eternal forty-five minutes, when we reached the apartment. The building looked from the outside as if it had a very regular staidness. If you have seen those "Brit remnants" houses along Wellesley Square in Calcutta with swaggering staircases and watermarked chocolate doors, you'll know what I am talking about. Those houses had long darkness and semi-working elevators with meshed doors. And then suddenly you'd notice flat number 11 and you'd ferry from the outside that the rooms inside had these torn lacy window curtains with crow droppings. Of course, not to mention the prosaic cupboard in the sitting room with those gifts they received when others traveled and the brown paper wrapped books, which they had bought in their youth. You get the picture. Well! That's what I thought I'd find when I rang the bell. Somebody opened the door and smoke and hyper-namastaed us in. Anjana's apartment had a long L-shaped corridor syntaxed with a kitchen, a room next to it, and then one more room at the end of the angle and some more at the real end of it. There was a chic disorder of old newspapers and AIDS campaign posters. In fact, now recalling, there was one cane-made shoe shelf, full of Rockfords and Kolapuris that almost nicked my shirt off. Anyway, as we all eagerly sparrowed in and stared into the meter of things, I found myself in this room next to the kitchen. It turned out later that this was a side order to the night. Ticker tapes of unknown Hi's prostrated. Women who were in there had these NYC trendy black outfits, some had all their Afro oozing out of them, some had their iceberg flora highlight shining at me. The men were hanging around them by their armpits.

This mueslisk woman was talking about her experiences with Basquiat's subway art and *Save the Something* project. Guess who was also there. Mary Casham. Of all people, Mary Casham, my University of Iowa days professor. Still elemental and with gobbly breasts. We exchanged the rain, hi there, herald, Channel 6, birdy talk. Then she told me all about her new book on the Shining Path and the pros and cons of their movement. Her little fortune cookie one-liners, viz.: "Wipe off the bench in California!" "Show the sexists their protrusion," etc., with the ramble and measures of beer, kept my integrity of the joke for some time. Sangeeta pulled me aside and asked me to dump our coats off in the room at the end of the corridor. Oh! Who's Sangeeta? Sangeeta

Shah claims she met me recently. But we go back to a time past. She provided refuge when I was more impressionable.

We garbaged our winter outgrowths on this hill of coats, mufflers, hats, and bags. The primal arrangement was well matched with a poster of Akira Kurosawa sitting with his divine smile and his sunglasses. And Josh (or whatever her name was) was warming her lips in front of Akira's poster, with a pair of hairy manly legs churning for comfort on her Nordic lap. Then, with a narcissistic touch of "pardon me," I wheeled out again and tried to make contact with the pairs of eyes all around me in this next room. It was enjoyable, needless to say, because it extracted the same effort as I put in when I sit around my bathtub trying to find that little perfect spot of mildew on the sixty-eighth tile on the right side.

Then I met Anjana. She introduced herself by running whisky down my jeans, tripped over an oversize book on insects of North Carolina while saying sorry for "wetting you" and bumming my Camels. Jyotsna, the lean one, was expanding next to me while such trepid introductions were going on. She then decided to describe, "You know! I wear a lot of bindis, but I also experiment with chunky designs on the panel?"

I guess it was my turn to concentrate on her gauntlet of words. Which I did. "And tell me, what do those red dots signify to you?"

"To keep the evil away from my lover. Of course."

"What were you saying about the design?"

"Oh! You know how Nannan is, she steps inside my apartment, grabs me, fondles me, and then exhausts me out before I even reach the countertop."

"Oh! So you have dated frescoes on the panel?"

Conning my query aside, she hollowed precociously, "Aarae, Mansoor saab! How are you?" I do not know who Mansoor is or what he is condemned to, so laboring my drooping charm and vodka to a repose, I stare ahead and I find this life-size pencil sketch of a pigeon. It evoked the balance of liability in this atmosphere. It had a plebian outlook with its rough canvas, but there were enough fractures to engage me. Little later, Jyotsna puled, "Foucault ki bacchi, what are you doing here?"

Indrani approached us, with Keith manning her hair. "Hi! Keith." "Hi! guys."

I was made to snorkel words then. She asked me what I am into.

"Building roads and monitoring traffic."

"Oh! Wow! How interesting! Do you want another Cosmo?"

"Sure."

"I'll get you one. Do you want Grand Marnier in yours?"

"Hang on. You keep talking and I'll get both of you something," Keith volunteered.

"Sorry, do continue. What were you saying?"

"That I just work for the New York's transportation department. We kind of analyze how the traffic destroys the highways."

"Oh! Wow! Really. I always thought that such a department was defunct."

I smiled and continued, "No! We are very much there except that our ratio of workload to person power has recently increased."

"Well! I'm sure with the pollution and all that crap, you cannot do very much."

"Cannot do what?"

"I mean the cars have increased and there's more use by taxpayers, which means in turn, it pretty much destroys. But what exactly do you do?"

"We just measure the jamming effects with AI techniques."

"Oh! Wow! Really. That's wild. But what is AI?"

"Artificial intelligence."

"You mean you put robots on the road."

"Better than men. No! Actually we simulate models and it's closer to running video games, and then we do some tests. What do you do?"

"Oh! For a living. Yaar! I deconstruct Kalidasa. Have you ever considered cooking spinach to celebrate Saint Patrick's Day?"

I nodded flimsically. Confuting wrinkles overshadowed her mascara. I knew again that I had to say something. Luckily, Sangeeta came and grabbed my arm. She knew that it was time to daub the auxiliary existence of this night with something dainty. The two of us went back to the Akira room. We stood and wiggled to Salt 'n Pepa, playing above the din.

At some point, I bridled the obstinate bladder of mine and proceeded toward the bathroom. When I came back, I found that the prevailing expediency was to massage each other's head.

It had so happened that someone called Latifa brought out a bottle of Amritanjan. You have seen that green-labeled bottle containing pungent mint-odored, black varnish-looking balm. Made in authentic India. Marketed by P. C. Chandra & Sons. Come on! You have seen this. It's that headache balm with this stinging smell of mint "hybred" with impolitic dirge and clammy feet-sweat.

We sat in an S with Latifa massaging Keith's head, Keith ruffling Indrani's curls, Indrani tickling Jyotsna's forehead, Jyotsna kneading

Sangeeta's head, Sangeeta pressing my shoulders, me unstringing Mary's hair, Mary luring the brows of Mansoor. The queue continued to splurge in rhythm.

The evaporation and quirk of the odor was discounting the pigeon, the night, and all the ransom they were charging to let go of my ostensible self.

But then I thought, Ms. Shah's palms were fiendishly fleshy.

In Reflection   It is very hard for me to articulate and deconstruct my creative process. Having made the disclaimer, I would say it is a process that starts with my need to break myths about Indian women and their desires and be a very anti–Bharati Mukherjee breed of writing. I want to create new myths like Sunita Namjoshi, but in trying to capture past memories and then add a dose of fiction, the art of "fabling" in its purest form becomes an oxymoronic exercise. So, as a compromise, I juxtapose real events—a party or a room or cricket or desiring female influences—with a fictional finality.

Translations

Kalyug	Age of the Doom
bhai bhai	brother to brother
yaar	pal
jab dhula raja aayaega	when the bridegroom will arrive
namaste	a greeting action
bindi	a dot of color worn on the forehead by some Indian women
Aarae, Mansoor saab	Yo, sir!
foucault ki bacchi	feminine form of "son of a bitch," literally, "daughter of —"
Kalidasa	ancient Sanskrit poet

proceeding page

PHOTOGRAPH BY KERRY KEARNS

Emma Donoghue

EMMA DONOGHUE

The Sanctuary of Hands

After a messy ending, the thing to do is to get away. Put several hundred miles between yourself and the scene of the crime. Whether you call yourself victim or villain, the cure's the same: get on a plane.

I flew from Cork to Toulouse and rented an emerald green sports car that cost three times as much as I would have been willing to pay under normal circumstances. I put it on my credit card; it was necessary. I knew that if I sat in some four-door hatchback, my self-pitying panic would well up like heartburn. The thing to do was to pretend I was in a film. French, for preference. I drove out of Toulouse like Catherine Deneuve. I wore very dark shades, a big hat, and an Isadora Duncan gauzy scarf, long enough to strangle me.

My plan was simple. I would spend fourteen days driving through the Pyrenees fast enough to drown out every sound and every thought, and if despite my best efforts there were any tears, the sun and the wind would wipe them off my face. In the afternoons I would find somewhere green and shady to read—at Heathrow Airport I'd picked up a silly novel about Mary Queen of Scots—and then in the evenings I'd round off my four-course *table d'hôte* with a large cognac and a sleeping pill. I didn't intend to talk to anyone during the next fortnight, so my schoolgirl French wouldn't have to stretch to more than the occasional *merci*.

On the seventh day, driving between one craggy orange hill and another, it came to me that I hadn't touched another human being for a week. I supposed my elbow in its linen sleeve must have brushed past someone else's in one of those painfully narrow hotel corridors, but no skin was involved. And, not knowing anyone, I was exempt from all the kiss-kissing the locals did. I looked down now at my hands on the steering wheel; they were clean and papery.

When I stopped for lunch, I remembered I'd finished my book the night before and left it by the bed. Over my espresso I could feel boredom beginning to nibble. No, not boredom: *ennui*, that was the word,

it came back to me now. Much more filmstarrish. Ennui was about sunshine like white metal, and a huge black straw hat, and simply forgetting
the name of anyone who'd ever hurt you and anyone you'd ever hurt.

The next sign said *Cavernes Troglodytiques,* over a shaky line drawing of a bear, so that's where I turned off the road. To be honest, I wasn't
quite sure what troglodytic caverns were, but they sounded as if they
might be cool, or cooler than the road, at least.

But after standing around at the cave mouth for a quarter of an
hour with a knot of brown-legged Swedes and Canadians, I was just
about ready to go back to the car. Then the old woman in the jacket
that said *Guide* finally clambered up the rocks toward us, and behind
her, a straggling crocodile of what I thought at first were children. None
of them seemed more than five feet tall, and they wore little backpacks
too high up, like humps. When I saw that they were adults—what's the
phrase these days, *people with special needs?*—I looked away, of course,
so that none of them would see me staring. That was what my mother
always said: *Don't stare!,* hissed like a puncture.

Three or four of the Specials, as I thought of them, had smiles
that were too wide. One of them peered into my face as if he knew me.
They kept patting and hugging each other, and two men at the back
of the group—quite old, with Down's syndrome, I thought, hard to
tell how old but definitely not young—were holding hands like kinder-
garten kids. I looked for the leader of the group—a teacher or nurse or
whatever, someone who would be giving them their own little tour of
the prehistoric caves—but then I realized that we were all going in
together.

At which point I thought, Fuck it, I don't need this.

But we were shuffling through the cave mouth already, and to get
out I would have had to shove my way back through the Specials, and
what if I knocked one of them over? There was one girl, a bit taller than
the rest, with a sort of helmet held on with a padded strap across her
chin, as if she was going into outer space. Fits, I thought. We're about
to descend into a troglodytic cavern with someone who's liable to fits.
There was a balding man behind her in an old-fashioned gray suit. He
seemed so pale, precarious, with his eyes half-shut. I wondered if the
same thing that had damaged their brains had stunted their growth, or
maybe they hadn't been given enough to eat when they were children.
You heard terrible stories.

As we left the sunlight behind us I realized that my clothes were
completely unsuitable for descending into the bowels of the earth. My
sandals skidded on the gritty rock; my long silk sundress caught on

rough patches of the cave wall, and what the hell had I brought my handbag for? The air was damp, and there were little puddles in depressions on the floor. Beside the little lamps strung up on wires, the stone glowed orange and red.

The guide's accent was so different from that of the nun who taught us French at school that I had to guess at every other word she spoke. She aimed her torch into a high corner of the cave now and pointed out a stalactite and a stalagmite that had been inching toward each other for what I thought I heard her say was eight thousand years. That couldn't be right, surely? In another twelve thousand, she claimed, they would finally touch. And then she launched into a laughably simplistic theory of evolution, for the benefit of the Specials, I supposed. Her words boomed in the cavern, and whenever she stopped to point something out, we all had to freeze and shuffle backward so as not to collide. I couldn't remember the last time I'd been at such close quarters with a herd of strangers. There was perfume eddying round, far too sweet, and I'd have laid a bet it came from that girl behind me with the Texas accent.

Basically, the guide's story was that we used to be monkeys— "*Non! Non!*" protested one or two of the more vocal Specials, and "*Si, si!*" the guide cried. We used to be monkeys, she swore—speak for yourself, I wanted to tell her—but then one day we stood up and we wanted to use tools so what did we have to *grow*?

I peered at her blankly in the half-light. What did we have to grow?

"*Les mains!*" she cried, holding up her splayed right hand, and three or four of the Specials held theirs up too, as if to play Simon Says, or to prove their membership of the species. The guide went on to explain—I could follow her better, now I was getting used to her accent— that everything depended on growing real hands, not paws; hands with thumbs opposite the fingers, for grip. She moved her wrinkled fingers like a spider, and one of the Specials wiggled his right back at her. They seemed irrationally excited to be here, I thought; maybe even a big damp cave was a thrill compared to their usual day.

I shivered where I stood and tucked my hands under my arms to warm them. It occurred to me that it must have been a sad day, that first standing up. I imagined hauling myself to my feet for the first time ever, naked apart from the fur. No more bounding through the jungle; now I'd have to stagger along on two thin legs. All at once my head would feel too heavy to lift, and the whole world would look smaller, shrunken.

One of the Specials giggled like a mynah bird, too close to my ear. I edged away from her, but not so fast that anyone would notice. They

didn't know the rules, it occurred to me: how much space to leave between your body and a stranger's, how to keep your voice down and
avoid people's eyes. They didn't seem to know about embarrassment.

The guide wasn't at all discomfited either, not even when the
Specials let out echoing whoops or hung off her hands. Now she was
saying that the cave dwellers lived only half as long as people do nowadays, and had much smaller brains than we do. I stared up at the dripping ceiling so as not to look at any of the Specials. Were they included
in her *we*? Then the guide asked why we thought people had lived in
these freezing old caves. After a few seconds she answered herself, in the
gushing way teachers do: because it was worse outside! Imagine thousands of years of winter, up there, she said, pointing through the rock;
picture the endless snow, ice, leopards, bears . . .

I could feel the cold of the gritty floor coming up through my sandals. I tried to conjure up a time when this would have counted as warm.
Jesus! Why they all hadn't cut their throat with the nearest flint scraper
I couldn't imagine. Funny thing, suicide; how rarely people got around
to it. We seemed to be born with this urge to cling on. Like last Christmas when I gave my brother's newborn my little finger and she gripped
it as if she was drowning.

The guide was leading us down a steep slope now, and the Specials
swarmed around her. Except for the pale man with the half-shut eyes,
who hung back, then suddenly stopped in his tracks so I bumped into
him from behind. I backed off, but he didn't move on. I tried to think
what to say that would be politer than "*Allez, allez!*" The guide looked
over her shoulder and called out a phrase I didn't understand, something cheerful. But the man in front of me was shaking, I could see that
now. His head was bent as if to ward off a blow. It was a big balding
head, but not unnaturally big. I might have taken him for a civil servant,
if I'd passed him in the street, or maybe a librarian. "*Peur*," he said
faintly, distinctly. "*J'ai peur.*" He was afraid. What was he afraid of?

The guide shouted something. My ears were ringing. I finally understood that she was suggesting Mademoiselle might be kind enough
to hold—what was his name?—Jean-Luc's hand, just for the steep bit. I
looked around to see whom she could mean. Then I felt the blush start
on my neck. I was the only Mademoiselle in sight, kind or otherwise—
the Texans having dropped back to photograph a stalactite—so I held
out my hand, a little gingerly, like a birthday present that might not be
welcome. I thought of taking him by the sleeve of his jacket, the man
she'd called Jean-Luc. But he looked down at my hand, rather than me,
and slipped his palm into mine as if he'd known me all our lives.

To be honest, I'd been afraid his fingers might be clammy, like pickled cucumbers, but they were hot and dry. We walked on, very slowly; Jean-Luc took tiny, timid steps, and I had to hunch toward him to keep our hands at the same level. All I could think was, Thank God it's dark in here.

In hopes of distracting myself, I was trying to remember the last time I'd held hands with a stranger. A *céilí,* that was it, with my sister's boyfriend's cousin, and our palms were so hot with sweat we kept losing our grip in the twirls, and apologizing over and over. I remember thinking at the time that hands were far too private to exchange with strangers. Those Victorians knew what they were doing when they kept their gloves on.

The Texan family was coming up behind now, their shadows huge as beasts on the cave wall. I could hear the girl giggle and mutter to her parents. My cheeks scalded with a sort of shame. I knew we probably looked like something out of Dickens, me with my big hat and Jean-Luc with his shiny head no higher than my shoulder: a monstrously mismatched bride and groom. Though really, why I should have cared what some small-town strangers thought of me, I couldn't say. The Texans didn't even know my name, and I'd certainly never see them again once we got out of this foul cave. Funny to think I'd come on this holiday to distract myself from serious things like tragedy and betrayal, only to find myself sweating with mortification at the thought that a couple of strangers might be laughing at me.

On an impulse I stepped sideways, flattening myself against the cave wall, jerking Jean-Luc with me. His pale eyes looked a little startled but he came obediently enough. When the Texans had almost reached us I said, rather coldly, "Go ahead," and let them squeeze past.

That was better. Now there was no one behind us and we could go at our own pace. The passage was getting more precarious, twisting down into the hillside. The roof was low; once or twice it scraped against my absurd straw hat. I had to walk with a stoop, lifting my dress out of my way like some kind of princess. Jean-Luc was saying something, I realized, but so quietly I had to bend nearer to make out the words—but not too near, in case my face brushed his. My heart rattled like a pebble in a can. I hadn't counted on conversation. What if he was asking me something, and I didn't understand his accent, and he thought it was because I didn't want to speak to him?

"*La belle mademoiselle,*" that was it. That's all it was. "*La belle mademoiselle m'a donne le main. Elle m'a donne le main.*" He wasn't talking to me at all, he was reassuring himself, telling himself the story of the pretty lady who gave him her hand. He had an amazing voice, deep like an actor's. For a moment I was absurdly warmed by the fact that he thought I was *belle*, even if he couldn't have much basis for comparison.

The floor was slick now, and the passage had narrowed so much I had to walk ahead of Jean-Luc, twisting my arm backward and waiting for him to catch up with me every couple of steps. I could feel his hand twitch like a rope.

He was starting to wheeze, casting anxious glances at the craggy walls closing in on us. The air was dank. I couldn't hear the guide anymore, the group had left us so far behind. Damn her to hell, I thought. I paid fifty francs for this.

The man's breath was coming faster and harsher in his throat. Had he any idea why he was being dragged down into these prehistoric sewers, I wondered? I supposed I should tell him there was nothing to be afraid of. He had a little wart on the edge of one finger, I could feel it; or maybe it was a callous. I gave his hand a small and tentative squeeze. Jean-Luc squeezed back, harder, and didn't let go. I could feel the fine bones shifting under his skin. Well, that was all I needed, for this poor bastard to have a heart attack and die on me, twenty thousand leagues below the earth! The thought almost made me laugh. I wished I knew how old he was. Baldness didn't mean anything; I knew a boy who started losing his hair at twenty-two. I cleared my throat now, trying to think of something comforting to say. Every word of French had deserted me. "*Faut pas . . . Faut pas avoir peur,*" I stuttered hoarsely at last, praying I had my verb ending right. How would it translate? One should not be afraid. It is a faux pas to have fear.

I thought Jean-Luc might not have heard me or taken it in; he still stared ahead, fixedly, as if anticipating a cave bear or mammoth around every corner. His eyes were enormous; the occasional beam of light showed their whites. But as we ducked under an overhang, I heard it like a mantra, under his breath: "*Faut pas avoir peur. Mademoiselle dit, faut pas avoir peur.*"

I grinned, briefly, in the dark. He was doing all right. Mademoiselle had told him not to be afraid. We'd get out of here in one piece.

When we came to a set of deep steps spiraling down into the rock, I went first, so that at least if he slipped I could break his fall. But Jean-Luc held onto my hand like a limpet, and I didn't want to scare him by tugging it away, so I held on with the tips of my fingers, our arms knotted awkwardly in the air, as if we were dancing a gavotte. His arm was weaving and shaking; it was like wrestling a snake. My silk hem got under my feet, then, and the pair of us nearly crashed down on one of those stubby little stalagmites. Now that would be funny, if we snapped off ten thousand years worth of growth, and got sued by the French state.

The steps began to twist the other way, and I found my arm bent up behind my back as if I was being led to my death. This was ludicrous; I was going to dislocate something. I stopped for a second and switched hands as fast as I could. Jean-Luc stared at me, but held onto the new hand. "*Pas de problème*," I said, foolishly. No problem. Could you say that in French or did it sound American?

We found our rhythm again, and I could hear Jean-Luc behind me, repeating "*Pas de problème, pas de problème*," in a ghost's whisper. Our joined hands were the only spot of heat in this whole desolate mountain.

At last the path leveled out and we found ourselves in a huge cavern where the rest of the group stood watching the guide point out painted animals with her torch. A few faces looked over at us. I relaxed my grip, but Jean-Luc held on tight. For a moment I felt irritated. He wasn't afraid of falling anymore; he was just taking advantage. And then I almost laughed at the thought of this peculiar gentleman taking advantage of me. I stood with his warm cushioned hand in mine, the pair of us gazing forward like a bashful couple at the altar. I was cold right through, now, and my nipples were standing up against the silk of my dress; I angled myself a little away from Jean-Luc so he wouldn't see.

I tried to pay attention to the guide. I peered up at the rock walls: orange, greenish gray, and a startling pink. There were scrawl marks that looked as if they'd been done with fingers on a thousand long nights. The paintings were of horses, and lions, and bears, or so the guide said, and the Specials were laughing and pointing as if they could make them out, but to be honest the rusty overlapping squiggles on the rock all looked alike to me. Whatever about the cave dwellers' powers of endurance, it occurred to me, they hadn't been able to draw for shite.

The guide said something I didn't catch, and then let out a surprisingly young laugh, and flicked off the light switch. Blackness came down on us like a falling tent. Some of the Specials shrieked with excitement, but Jean-Luc cleaved to my hand as if it were a life belt. I tried to squeeze back, even though he was hurting my fingers. My eyes strained to find any speck of light in the darkness. It suddenly struck me that this was entirely normal behavior for a troglodytic cavern. When the cold and the dark and the weight of a mountain pressed down on you, what made more sense than to grab the nearest living hand and hold on as tight as you could?

When the lights came back on, I blinked, relieved. A fat boy with a baseball cap on sideways edged back to us and tried to take hold of Jean-Luc's other hand, but Jean-Luc shook him off, almost viciously. I looked away and bit down on my smile.

What did we think they ate, the cave dwellers? the guide was asking. Most of the Specials grinned back at her as if it was a joke rather than a question. Did they go to a supermarket, she suggested, and buy veal? One or two nodded doubtfully. No, she told us, there were no supermarkets! This claim caused quite a stir among the Specials. Now the guide was shining her torch on a painted animal, I couldn't tell what it was. She announced with grim enthusiasm that the cave dwellers hunted animals with sticks and cooked them in the fire.

"*Non!*"

"*Non!*"

"*Tuer les animaux?*"

A shock wave ran through the group as she nodded to say that yes, they killed the animals. A tiny woman with a squeezed-up face sucked in air. "*Manger les animaux?*" Yes indeed, they ate the animals. The Specials' reactions were so huge and incredulous that I began to suspect them of irony. Had no one ever told them what sausages were made of?

That's what the cave dwellers did, the guide insisted. And they caught fish too, she told us, in nets made out of their own hair. And they turned animal skin into leather by soaking it in their own urine, then chewing it till it was soft. At least, I feared that was what she said; the cave was a confusion of voices now, and all I could think about was how cold I was. I was starting to shake as if I had a palsy. People must have been always cold, in those days, it occurred to me. Maybe they knew no different, so they didn't notice it. Or, more likely, maybe they couldn't think about anything else. The minute you woke up you'd have to start working as if your life depended on it, because it did: build up the fire, eat, keep moving, pile on more clothes, keep eating, never let the fire go out, even in your sleep. They'd all have slept in one big heap, the guide was saying now, putting her head on the shoulder of the girl in the helmet and miming a state of blissful unconscious; if you slept alone, she said, you'd wake up dead. Jean-Luc, by my side, must have heard this, because he let out a single jolt of laughter. I turned my head to smile at him but he was looking down at his shoes again.

I thought the tour had to be nearly over by now—all I could think of was getting back up into the sunlight—but the guide led us through a little passage, so tight we had to go in single file. Jean-Luc and I stayed knotted together like a chain gang. At last the group emerged into a cave, the smallest so far. The guide mentioned that the man who had discovered these caverns called this one the Sanctuary of Hands.

Then she lifted her torch, and all at once I could see them; they sprang out to meet the light. Handprints in red and black, dozens—no, hundreds of them—daubed on top of each other like graffiti, pressed onto the rock as high as someone on tiptoes could reach. This was how you signed your name, about twenty-seven thousand years ago, said the guide with a casual swing of her torch. The prints glowed in the wide beam as if they were still wet. They were mostly left hands, I saw now, and smallish; the prints of women or even children. I stepped up to one for a closer look and Jean-Luc crept along behind me.

The handprint nearest us only had three and a half fingers. I recoiled, and the guide must have noticed, because she swung her torch round to where we were standing. I backed out of the blinding light. Yes, she said, many of these hands appeared to be missing a piece or two. This was a great mystery still. Some archaeologists said the cave dwellers must have lost fingers in accidents or because of the cold, but others thought the people must have cut them off themselves. For a gift, she said, almost gaily, did we understand? To give something back to the gods. To say *merci*, thank you.

Jean-Luc stared at the print on the wall a few inches from his head. He let go of my hand, then, and laid his own against the rock, delicately fitting his short pale fingers to the blood-red marks. He turned his head and looked at me then, for the first time, and his mouth formed a half-smile as if he were about to tell me a great secret. But "*Touche pas!*" called the guide sternly, "*Faut pas toucher,* Jean-Luc!" Touching was forbidden; I should have told him that. His hand contracted like a snail, and I took it into mine again. It was chilled by the rock.

We followed the group up a long, widening tunnel that seemed to have been dug out in modern times, and soon I could smell fresh air. After some very steep steps, we were all panting audibly, even the backpackers, and Jean-Luc's hand was hot in my grip again. He and I were the last to emerge, wincing in the sunlight like aged prisoners set free. The hills were a jumble of rocks on every side, and the half-reaped valley slid away below us. The sun warmed my face, and the air tasted sweet as straw.

Every year for a week or two there would be a sort of summer, the guide was explaining; the snow might shrink away just enough to let the cave dwellers come out and sit on the ground. And what became of them in the end, someone asked her? Well, she said with a little shrug, one year they must have come out and found the snow gone and the sun shining. Then they walked down into the valley and never came back.

On the way down to the car park, I began to wonder when Jean-Luc was going to let go of my hand. I didn't want to have to wriggle it out of his grasp, but I could see the group leader waiting for them by the little bus. I hoped Jean-Luc didn't think I was coming home with the Specials. All of a sudden I felt appallingly sad. I wished I knew what to say to him, in any language.

But at the edge of the car park he disengaged his sticky fingers from mine and turned to face me, very formally. "*Au revoir, mademoiselle,*" he said, which I supposed could be translated as "Until we meet again," and I smiled, and nodded, and took up his hand again for a second to shake good-bye. He was puzzled by this, I could tell, but he let me shake it, as if it were a rattle.

"*Au revoir,* Jean-Luc," I repeated, more often than I needed to, and waved until he'd disappeared into the bus. I did look for his profile in the window, but the glass was white in the glare of the sun.

In Reflection   "The Sanctuary of Hands," based on my visit to a prehistoric cave in Belgium, is one of the most autobiographical stories I've ever written. Curious—I find it a little embarrassing to admit that. I suppose I feel more proud of myself when I manage the trick of conjuring up an experience utterly foreign to my own; with a story like "The Sanctuary of Hands," it feels like my emotions simply leaking onto a page!

But of course experience always gets reshaped in the process of turning something into a story. Though I had been mildly unsettled by my tour of the cave, I wanted my protagonist to be more tense than I, more hostile to foreignness of all kinds, more thrown by the incident. So the main change I made was to have her be a single woman in flight from a breakup (whereas I had been on a very pleasant day trip with my lover and my sister, who both found the sight of me hand-in-hand with a stranger quite hilarious!). I didn't specify if the protagonist was a lesbian or not, because I didn't think it was at all relevant to this story (unfortunately, a character's sexuality is not yet something you can just mention in passing; it's like setting off a firework).

I also wanted to explore some thematic links between the cave and the heroine's encounter with the "special needs" group, so I switched the setting from a common-or-garden prehistoric cave in Belgium to one of the few caves in southern France that feature mysterious hand paintings; this allowed me to mull over the image of the hand, the idea of human self-expression and intimacy in all its so-called primitive and civilized forms. (In fact, I wrote this story especially for a conference at the University of Western Ontario on "The Hand.")

Valerie Miner

PHOTOGRAPH BY TOM FOLEY

VALERIE MINER

The House with Nobody in It

The house next door was up for sale again. A large corner lot in one
of the city's most pleasant, convenient neighborhoods. Lawns were
mowed and nicely framed by oak and maple trees. Bluets graced yards
in spring; hastas bloomed in early fall. People respected your privacy and
were always ready to help dig your car out of the January ice. So where
were her new next-door neighbors?

When they first moved in, Tamara had expectations about neighbors, modest hopes. She thought maybe someone would drop by with
a small pie or cake. Perhaps an older woman, a longtime resident, from
whom she could learn a thing or two. Then maybe they'd exchange the
occasional "yoo-hoo," over the back fence.

Instead, silence greeted their arrival. Practiced tolerance from the
Lutheran parents on the north side, who didn't care for two lesbians
living in plain view of their six children. Their first conversation with
Mrs. Olsen ended abruptly when she learned that Joan was not Tamara's sister. The house on the other side was virtually silent. The retired
army couple didn't notice that Tamara and Joan had different bodies
from those of Mr. and Mrs. Lancaster, who had lived in their home for
the previous twenty years. Within months, the colonel had entered a
nursing facility and his wife returned to their children in Duluth. The
house lay empty for a year while the kids, who were busy having grandchildren of their own, decided what to do with it. Joan told Tamara she
was developing an unhealthy obsession. After all, they had each other,
their families, lots of friends and colleagues. Why was she so hung up
on neighbors?

But Tamara felt sad about the vacant place, oddly lonely. And it kept
coming back to her, that earnest Joyce Kilmer poem she had memorized
in the fourth grade about "a poor old farm-house, its shingles broken
and black . . ." Get over it, she told herself. Clearly Milton Avenue was

no place to recapture childhood memories of sidewalk fraternity: families chatting over fragrant piles of burning autumn leaves; neighbor ladies with Mom on the front porch for lemonade on a scorching July evening. Tamara wasn't much of a gardener, but she cherished scenes of Dad trading recipes for tomato sauce over the back fence as he tended his plot of crimson beefsteaks. She thought back often to those early days when things were as they were meant to be.

For a while Tamara continued to take the absence of neighbors personally. At the age of forty, this was the first house she could afford as a college teacher, once she recovered from the shock of earning enough money for a down payment and managed to repress her panic about impending floods in the bathroom and storm-drunk trees smashing the roof. She began to look forward to having neighbors, to being a neighbor.

"For Sale." Finally, the son from Duluth decided to sell. All summer that sign guarded the next-door lawn, through the bluets and lilacs and hydrangeas, well past the end of the roses. Week by week, they speculated about who might buy the place. Tamara toyed with organizing a small welcoming party. Dozens of people trooped through Sunday Open Houses. In late September, the place was still up for sale. Mr. and Mrs. Olsen started talking to Tamara occasionally, on the sidewalk, about realtors and potential buyers. An empty house was bad for property values, they said. Apparently the older couple had let it go to seed, in the understandable neglect of people who were losing their vision and sense of smell. Milton Avenue wasn't an area where people bought a fixer-upper. The bungalow was peculiar—a little pea-green wooden structure—in the midst of large brick or white stucco Edwardian houses. Maybe years ago, Tamara thought, a young Colonel and Mrs. Neighbor had built it as their dream house. Maybe their dreams foundered.

Another year passed. By this time, the Olsens were talking to them at least once a month, and together, over their meticulously groomed back hedge, they ruminated on the strange spirit occupying that bleak corner house. Tamara wondered if it were haunted by the proprietorial ghost of ancient Mr. Neighbor, still stalking those elusive dreams. Tamara admitted she had become a bit of a busybody, staring out the south window, through the increasingly dense summer branches, optimistically inspecting realtors and their clients.

One day, Joan grew exasperated. "Relax, we have nothing to complain about after two years of almost complete silence next door. If we're lucky, the spooky house will stay on the market and peace will prevail!"

Tamara admired Joan's self-containment. Maybe it had something to do with running her own physics lab. Still, sometimes she missed the finer points of an argument.

"Silence," Tamara intoned, "is not the same as peace."

Tamara was five when Arthur Snider moved into the big yellow house kitty-corner to them. They used to walk to school together and one afternoon by the gym, he proposed. As their early years of betrothal passed, she and Arthur spent more and more time playing dolls in her sunny living room. Practicing for their future together. Dad told a puzzled Arthur to go outside and throw a ball. He delivered Little League leaflets to Mr. and Mrs. Snider. But Arthur was content indoors, playing with the dolls and Tamara. Dad grew nervous that Arthur was a bad influence on her brothers and he banned Arthur from the house. The engagement fell through. Years later, she learned that Arthur had joined the Navy, had married someone else. Her father could only hope for such respectable sons.

One October morning, when there were still enough red and gold leaves to allow you to peer through the maple branches without being obvious, Tamara and Joan watched two movers carrying furniture into the green bungalow. Boxes of books. Then suitcases. A floor lamp. Later that afternoon, a young man joined the movers and together they made a dramatic ceremony of wrestling the realtor's sign out of the lawn. From her living room, Tamara clapped at their success. "Neighbors! *Enfin!*"

Joan shook her head, concerned. "Aren't you getting a little melodramatic? I mean what is your thing about neighbors? Most of the time I understand you, sweetie, but really, we can barely keep up with our social life as it is."

Melodramatic, Tamara thought, just the word her mother used to describe her. Maybe that's why she taught Homer and Virgil. What was life without a little melodrama? "I don't know," vaguely hurt, she confessed. "Ever since I was a kid, I thought it was part of the well-lived life. Someone to love. Our own house. And good neighbors."

"Well," Joan cautioned. "Wait and see. Don't get your hopes up."

Next morning, they were wakened to what Tamara eventually learned was alternative rock. Okay, she thought, you need something to keep up your spirits when you move. She remembered the panic of two years before—suffocating in corrugated cardboard and styrofoam chips.

The music got louder at lunch. Joan rolled her eyes. "Your neighbors!"

"Don't be silly," she said, "they're settling in. They'll turn it down."

They waited a week. A long, loud, sleepless week.

The following Saturday—a suddenly frigid afternoon—they bundled up and carried a tray of Joan's never-fail mocha pecan brownies next door. The first thing they noticed was how neatly the juniper had been trimmed. Unusual for a rock band, Tamara thought.

Walter greeted them at the door.

Beautiful Walter, red curls haloing a perfectly oval face, Tamara noticed. Circular gold spectacles surrounded his sapphire green eyes, and his skin had the sheen, the softness, of her grandmother's pink satin bed jacket. She and Joan were surprised, relieved, to discover he was the bungalow's sole occupant.

Walter's voice swelled with goodwill. "I hope you'll let me know if there's any way I can be neighborly. If you go out of town, I could collect the mail, feed your cat."

Dumbly, Tamara marveled at his sweet openness. And she hoped Joan wouldn't launch into her diatribe about how not all lesbians loved cats, how she, herself, was fatally allergic to the animals.

He smiled, serving them coffee in fifties retro Melmac mugs.

"Thanks," she nodded, preoccupied, wondering how a twenty-five-year-old could afford to purchase a house. "And vice versa."

Joan, meanwhile, went straight to the point. "Your music . . ."

Softly, Tamara kicked her under the blue linoleum table.

"Your music," Joan's tone lifted, "do you think you could reduce the volume?"

Affliction invaded his seamless face. "Of course," he frowned. "I'm terribly sorry."

Joan smiled primly.

Right before their eyes, Tamara thought, they were transforming from renegade queers into decorous matrons.

"You see the bedroom is on your side, the south side, of the house," Joan continued.

Tamara could tell, just by looking at him, that everything would be all right.

"Thanks for mentioning it. Really." He refilled their cups. "If I slip up again, just come over and I'll cut the volume. Promise?"

"Yes," Tamara laughed. "I'm sure this'll take care of it."

Pensively Joan sipped her black coffee.

"What kind of work do you do?" Tamara asked, moving the conversation along.

"I've bought into a bakery," he was pleased to tell them. "Specialty breads, brioches, croissants. I'm training now—in the kitchen and shop. The Prairie Pantry, have you heard of it?"

"Oh yes!" Tamara recalled their delicate apple tarts. The Prairie Pantry was the city's best bakery, and Walter seemed adorable in his vocational fervor. She didn't have any twenty-five-year-old friends; he might be a very interesting neighbor.

When Tamara's family moved to Seattle, Dad bought an Irish setter, "to make the family complete." Rudie was a sweet puppy, energetic and friendly, but he grew up to be the terror of passing drivers and bicyclists. Tamara tried to train him, took him for walks, whispered about good behavior to him at night. The rest of the family gave up, so he became *her* dog. She hadn't loved like this since Arthur Snider. But the infractions continued. Their paperboy refused to deliver the *Post-Intelligencer.*

Rudie also liked to dig up gardens. They got several official warnings. One day Mrs. Miller across the street spread hamburger meat mixed with ground glass around her azaleas. Two weeks later, Rudie came bounding back from the vet's and Dad found him a nice home in the country.

A week passed before they heard again from Walter. At 11:30 the following Saturday night. Walter and his guest, Dave Matthews or Iggy Pop. Tamara had bought a few CDs in the spirit of cultural education, but at this volume, couldn't tell the difference.

"It might be Marshall Crenshaw," she said to her wide-awake partner.

"Why do you care about the particulars?"

"I'm a scholar, I'm only trying to understand . . ."

"What you need to understand," Joan grumbled, "is that we have an inconsiderate neighbor. I trust you're making the most of this cultural opportunity." She climbed out of bed, pulled on her jeans, and headed next door.

Tamara lay beneath the blankets feeling guilty that Joan had gone alone. After all, she was the one who had prayed for neighbors.

Time passed.

Iggy Pop got louder. Tamara grew worried, for what did they really know about Walter? Maybe this was his M.O.; maybe he lured

innocent neighbors to his house late at night and then chopped them
to pieces. Maybe he wasn't a twenty-five-year-old cherub but a cannibal
disguised by clever plastic surgery.

Still buttoning her sweater, Tamara raced outside. When she
reached Joan, her partner was pumping Walter's doorbell.

"No answer?" she asked brightly.

"Probably can't hear it ringing above that racket."

"Well, let's go in."

"What, are you crazy?"

Joan had just suffered through *Sweeney Todd* at the Ordway Theatre
for her mother's birthday.

Maybe Tamara was crazy, entering the lair of the local baker/
butcher, but she was also furious.

His door was unlocked, not remarkable in wholesome Minneapolis. Walter was nowhere within the excessively neat rooms of the
ground floor. Electric guitar vibrated from below.

Shaking, Tamara opened the basement door and shouted down,
"Walter."

Nothing.

"Walter," in her most piercing voice.

The stereo volume decreased slightly. Scrambling up the stairs, he
grinned. "You sound like my mom."

Tamara stood there, glaring at the enemy, who thought she was his
mother.

"The music," Joan said calmly, "the music is very loud. We can't
sleep."

"Oh. Oh, no." He seemed more troubled by Joan's announcement
than by having his house broken into. "Oh, right!" He ran downstairs
and turned it off.

"Sorry about that," he called, walking up the steps. "I guess I got
a little carried away celebrating; I baked my first batch of palmiers this
morning."

Tamara could understand how that could rev a person up.

They left for home, carrying a white sack of sticky palmiers, three
of which Joan had to consume before she could get back to sleep.

Telephone calls were no more successful than doorbell ringing. They
put notes in his mailbox. These would make a difference for a day or two
and then . . .

Kapow at 1 A.M.: Smashing Pumpkins.

Tamara did have to wonder at his eclectic taste.

2 A.M.: Public Enemy.

Maybe the music made him alert for his early morning baking shift. 3 A.M.: Pearl Jam.

That night Joan called the police. Tamara felt terrible, as if they had just turned her younger brother into the Stasi. But as Joan pointed out, they required sleep to remain employed.

Rigid, Tamara waited in bed for the cops to pull up.

Slamming their car doors, they walked heavily to Walter's little green house. Thud. Thud. Thud. They knocked firmly. Ice T. answered. Eventually, the police abandoned the front door and moved around the house, rapping on each of Walter's windows.

Soon, well, soon something happened because the autumn night was restored to that familiar semisilence. Once again they could hear buses snuffling down nearby Hennepin Avenue. And the pleasant rattle of their old refrigerator, Marge.

"At last," Joan whispered, rolling over to sleep.

Stiff, wakeful, Tamara lay beside her. Before morning, their neighbor had stabbed them to death with a silver cake server. He repeated this grisly double murder the next night and the next.

In real life, several days after the cops, Walter rang the bell and handed Joan a sack of fragrant caraway rye rolls. An amends for slipping up. It was so easy to get lost in the world of music, he said.

Throw away the bread, Tamara told Joan. There was no telling what he had put in it.

She shrugged. "Well, if you don't want any, this should take care of my lunch for a week. I love caraway seeds."

Joan survived. So did Walter and his midnight jam sessions.

Never was Tamara so happy to see November as that year.

With great relief, she watched their neighbor install his triple-glazed storm windows. And she accomplished the annual chore, herself, with particular speed and dexterity. Quiet had returned to Milton Avenue. Quiet of a degree.

Storm windows: evidence of how insulation leads to insularity on the prairie, considered Tamara. Up and down the block, every autumn, otherwise sensible people climbed teetering ladders to replace summer screens with the glass barricades. Once windows were hung, hibernation began. Every year after 15 November or so, there was no more smelling the neighbor's dinner. No hearing the boy across the street practicing his trombone at 7 A.M. No eavesdropping on revealing family arguments from back gardens. As the snow rose and the temperatures dropped to thirty, fifteen, seven, below zero, then slipped steadily into the minus teens, you saw less and less of your neighbors. Occasionally, you'd notice someone under hats-coats-mufflers-mittens,

chipping at the ice on their front porches or scuttling between auto-
mobile and house or race-walking a dour dog. If there were an ecu-
menical hero in Minnesota, it was the postal carrier, who needed an
advanced degree in acrobatics to negotiate their slippery sidewalks.
Holiday tips in mailboxes were always generous.

State records revealed that for the past one hundred years, no
Minnesota dog had ever bitten a postal worker between the months of
November and April.

Walter rocked on, of course. Most nights, with the aid of a white
noise machine and industrial earplugs, they found sleep.

Three times they had to call the police. Generally, though, their
windows and Walter's muffled intercultural exchange.

Tamara was beginning to realize she had always had bad neighbor
karma. Could she somehow be the source of the problem?

She wondered this about Mrs. Woods. When Tamara was twelve,
she babysat next door for cute twin boys, Steven and Sebastian. Mrs.
Woods was the first person she had met who had gone to college, and
Tamara spent many happy afternoons listening to the young mother
reminisce about the good days at Rochester.

She had been studying to become a concert pianist, then suddenly
found herself on the other side of the country, married with two small
boys and no time to think, let alone play the piano.

Tamara's mother didn't understand how she was babysitting if
Mrs. Woods were in the house with her, talking, talking. She wasn't
interested in her neighbor's college stories. Didn't the woman have
errands to run? Tamara thought Mom seemed scared of Mrs. Woods;
definitely she didn't like her. Still, it was with a gentle, concerned voice
that she broke the sad news to Tamara: Mr. Woods had found his wife
in the sunroom, dead from an overdose of tranquilizers.

The long, raw winter on Milton Avenue was, as they say in the Upper
Midwest, a genuine season.

Spring bloomed late and Tamara was so happy to see the crocuses
and narcissus that she waved warmly to Walter the first time she saw him
in May.

He waved back reluctantly. In fact his whole being seemed more
hesitant, older. The skin was pale, the eyes dull.

Down came their windows; up went his music. For several weeks
they seriously discussed moving. Sleeplessness was interfering with their
teaching. What else could they do? Well, this was eco-conscious Min-

nesota, Joan laughed, maybe they could file a noise complaint and have Walter extradited to Manitoba.

Joan had another idea. An inspiration. Since Walter couldn't live without his music and they couldn't sleep with it, they might compromise. They would offer to buy him a pair of classy earphones. Why did it take so long to think of this? Tamara wondered. Maybe in the way of older people, they just assumed he would come around to seeing the reasonableness of their position.

The earphones could cost two hundred bucks, but they would be worth it. They put a note in his mailbox.

The June evenings were stretching to luxurious lengths.

Snowplows were a dim fantasy. At twilight, the evening after Joan's inspiration, they spotted Walter trimming the juniper.

"Hi there!" Tamara called.

"Hi," he returned neutrally.

"Did you get our note?" she asked.

Joan searched the pinkening sky in exasperation with Tamara's impatience.

"Oh, yeah," the tone was vague.

"So what did you think of Joan's idea?" Tamara ignored his shuttered eyes, defensive shoulders.

Clip. Clip. He concentrated on the juniper.

"The earphones," she tried cheerfully.

"Won't work." He swept clippings into a green garbage bag.

Like everyone on Milton Avenue, Walter was tidy.

"Why not?" She was annoyed by his categorical dismissal.

"I don't do earphones," he muttered.

"But, but," she stammered, pulling away from Joan, "you do noise!"

He glared at her.

Joan's face grew anxious.

"Look," Walter extended his hand, as if to calm Tamara, then withdrew before making contact. "Look," a laissez-faire nineties tone, "I know my music bugs you. It's not your thing. If I were you, I'd call the cops, too."

"What?" Tamara shouted across the generations.

Joan tugged at her T-shirt. "It's getting dark. The mosquitoes . . ."

"Hey, it's a moot point, anyway," he spoke loudly and slowly. "You only have to put up with it for a couple of more weeks. I'm moving. The bakery business isn't for me."

"But . . ."

"Come on," groaned Joan, "we've been wasting our breath."

Now Tamara followed, understanding that homicide would cancel her recently earned tenure. She went to bed early with a double brandy, resolute to get a few hours' rest before the evening concert.

Mr. Hawkins was retired from fifty years as an engineer on the Southern Pacific Railroad. When Tamara's dad ran off, Mr. Hawkins became the ideal neighbor for Mom—doing little repairs, clearing out the garden, taking her to the grocery store because they didn't have a car. "Anything to be of help," he always offered, saying that it made him feel useful in his old age. So when Tamara missed the school bus one morning, he was the obvious person to call. Three miles to the high school— they had gone halfway—Tamara realized what Mr. Hawkins was doing with his hand on her thigh, moving it higher and higher. What a weirdo!

She jumped out and walked the rest of the way. That night, Mom was astounded, infuriated by her story, and she warned Tamara never again to talk to him. She was terribly upset with Mr. Hawkins, but also, Tamara knew, with her daughter, because he had been such a wonderful neighbor.

Just as Tamara was slipping off to sleep, she heard the phone ring. Joan answered in the adjacent room. Her voice was cool, as when she talked to her older brother. It was past ten.

Who else would call at this time of night?

Walter's lullaby commenced. No, no, far too early. Damn him. She rolled on her side, and put a pillow over her left ear.

His racket didn't seem to be fazing Joan. Tamara could hear through the wall that she was still on the phone. Not saying much. The occasional two- or three-word phrase. God, she hoped Joan's brother hadn't had another car accident.

Still clutching the pillow, she wandered into Joan's study.

"Yes, yes." Joan's face was intent, not anxious. "Yes."

She held the phone away from her ear, grinning.

"Is your brother okay?" Tamara blurted.

Baffled, Joan put a finger to her lips. She was still listening, but to what? The only thing Tamara could hear was the "Walter Letterman Show, Live from Next Door!"

"A little lower," she said.

"What?" Tamara mouthed silently.

Joan raised a hand for her to wait.

"Yes, that's it," Joan said. "Maybe a little lower?"

Something strange, thought Tamara.

"That should do it."

Tamara noticed the music had stopped.

"You're welcome. Thank you, Walter."

"Walter?" She asked when Joan hung up.

Her partner burst out laughing. "Yes, yes," she drew long breaths. "He called to do a 'sound check.' Said, 'I don't know why I never did this before. Tell me when you can't hear the music anymore, then I'll mark that on the volume control and keep it as my max.'"

"What? Do you think it's because we offered to buy the earphones?"

"Don't ask," her eyes widened. "Just be grateful." Waiting a beat, she smiled. "He said he wanted to be neighborly."

It was a simple thing, Tamara ruminated—the brandy doing its work, making her feel profound as well as sleepy—a simple thing being considerate. Why had it taken them a year to offer the earphones, that long for him to think about the sound test?

And the Olsens, would they ever get beyond those stiff backyard conversations? How could they be neighbors if they inhabited different universes?

She toddled off to bed with her pillow. At 3 A.M., sure enough, she was wakened.

Joan's sweet, warm body snuggled around her. The silence was eerie. Tamara strained to hear the buses juggling along Hennepin Avenue, and finally, fell back to sleep.

After that, they saw Walter two or three times, long enough for a nod, a wave. Tamara watched him wistfully on moving day, his turquoise T-shirt vibrating against that red hair.

One afternoon, at the end of summer, Tamara saw them walking up their sidewalk. Right away, she could tell who they were. A young couple, tentatively carrying their new responsibility. She holding a pie; he with his hand lightly at her back.

"Hey, Joan," she called down to the basement, "come see this."

She arrived, breathless, lugging a suitcase up from the storeroom.

"Do you see what I see?" asked Tamara.

Amazed, Joan nodded.

They rang the bell. Tamara answered, soberly assuring herself that they were no apparition. Joan had seen them too.

"Hi," the woman began.

"We're the Morgans." He extended a firm hand, pale and feathered with fine black hairs. "Sally and Roger, your new neighbors."

Stupidly, Tamara stared at the pie. Wasn't this her role?

Had they misread the script?

"Oh," Sally said wryly, "you must be wondering. We won a raffle at church. Six pies—blueberry, cherry, raspberry, peach . . ."

"Isn't this apple?" Tamara concentrated on real, physical evidence.

"Yes, Dutch apple, and we couldn't possibly eat them all, so we decided to share them as a way of meeting our new neighbors."

"Neighbors," Joan recovered first. "Won't you come in?"

"Yes, yes," Tamara woke. "What am I thinking? Please come in for some coffee and . . . pie?"

Nervous, blushing, Sally entered.

Roger tripped over a crate of books in the hallway.

Wordlessly, they surveyed boxes and suitcases stacked in the dining room.

"You're not moving, are you?" Sally sounded stricken.

"Oh, just for a year," Tamara explained guiltily, "for our very first sabbaticals!"

"We were really looking forward to neighbors," Sally sighed.

"It's actually just for nine months," Tamara jumped in before they could take their pie and leave. "Joan's brother will be in and out, doing repairs, painting the interior. We'll be home next summer. Here, have a seat."

Reluctantly, almost suspiciously, the Morgans complied, perching on the edge of a drop cloth thrown over the couch.

"Oh, it's so sad," Sally said, "a house with nobody in it."

"Caf or decaf?" Tamara asked, determined not to let them get away.

In Reflection   I believe that all art (as well as scholarship, architecture, food preparation, et cetera) emerges from autobiographical seeds and is shaped by who the artist/scholar/architect/cook is and thinks she is. Having acknowledged that, I will make a perhaps heretical statement for this volume: for me it's important to distinguish between memoir and fiction. I started my writing life as a journalist, working for seven years in Canada, Europe, and Africa. I learned a lot, but I felt an urge to go "deeper than the facts" and thus started writing short stories. The *possible* became more interesting to me than the *actual*. And of course the actual is subjective, momentary evidence just as memory is constructed and fragmented. My fiction *is* influenced by journalism in the sense that I remain engaged in issues I reported on: national liberation struggles; the expanding parameters of women's lives; the ways that race and class and culture shape our experiences. My novels and stories tend to focus on the individual, to be sure, but the individual in the larger world. We all live in history.

If most of my fiction hasn't been autobiographical in the sense of *memory recorded*, it often turns out to be autobiographical in the sense of *premonition*. Like many artists, I find that the things I write about often wind up happening to me or to my friends. Sometimes the premonitions are trivial (predicting what my niece will receive for her birthday). Sometimes they are irritating (giving a fictional café an odd name and finding out such a café exists in a nearby town). And sometimes they are very sad (after I wrote *A Walking Fire*, in which an adult daughter returns home to nurse her dying father through lung cancer, my own father suddenly developed lung cancer and died). I don't think artists are spiritual mediums. I believe all human beings "know more than we know." Premonition is part of fiction because writers work hard to create quiet space and adequate time to listen to the universe.

"The House with Nobody in It" is reflective of some broad personal interests, such as an enjoyment of the dailiness in people's lives; a curiosity about generational differences; a fascination with the diametrically opposed responses that close, loving partners can have to a situation; and an apprehension about the roots of a profoundly lonely person's search for "community" or neighborhood. Thus, insofar as "theme" is autobiographical, this story is about me.

I won't enumerate all the imagined elements of the story, but I acknowledge that my partner and I teach in Minneapolis and that for a time we had a noisy neighbor. Certainly "The House" raises reservations that I, as a Californian used to a more culturally diverse, al fresco world, have about Minnesota. But I am neither Tamara nor Joan.

And the premonition? Sometime after I finished this story, a neighbor's house was sold to a young heterosexual couple. We told them that we looked forward to getting to know them when we returned from six months of teaching and writing in London. Unfortunately no apple pies exchanged hands. But we did take them flowers.

Barbara Bryce Morris

BARBARA BRYCE MORRIS

Mad Dog in Chelsea

So many summer nights in the city share the same set of variables that I could laugh at the predictability of it all: throat-swelling heat, sirens sharking madly through the thick air, a restless *merengue* booming a frantic two-beat blues. At least the romance of flashing neon and a faraway alto sax died in the last millennium. Good riddance.

I wasn't sure if it was night fever or food poisoning, but I was shivering like a dog. It had been a rough night hacking cowboy code at the software shop where I worked, and I was walking home, thinking about my crazy life. I'm a programmer, and I spend days but mostly nights looking at a computer screen, writing the code that runs software, the stuff you use on your computer to send e-mail or do your taxes or play solitaire. It's a pretty cool job. Even though it probably sounds boring, it's not.

What rocks is having total control over a small part of the universe: my code. Somebody once said that the writer is a little god. Nowadays, it's the programmer. Just think of all those fifty-year-old pocket-protector mainframe guys who doubled their retirement packages doing Y2K fixes. Or what about the guys who program missile launches or deploy spy satellites. Now that's power, except that they use it in a sucky way: to blow other people to smithereens. I guess code is really a two-sided kinda thing. It seems like you're the creator of a virgin forest when you're doing it, but there's a heart of darkness, too.

It's totally solitary and time-consuming work. And I get so wrapped up in my code that I don't care about anything else. Sometimes I would like to get out more, live like a normal person, but they don't call us geeks for nothing.

So, in the few hours I have free from the hack shop, especially in those hours somewhere between darkness and dawn, I like to think about life. Someone once told me that you can usually find a lesson in whatever happens. Like how some Mom who's driving the kids home from school in the Volvo wagon gets hit by a careening BMW carrying twenty keys of coke. The kids are incinerated, Mom's back is broken, and the driver not only doesn't have a scratch on him but he gets away like the roadrunner. The next thing you know, Mom gives an interview on the news thanking Jesus for giving her innocent little kids immortality. What's the lesson in that—don't watch the news anymore? Why should I even consider so-called life lessons that are just as phony as the ones they teach in school, or, worse yet, in those self-help books that seem to make everybody over forty drool and shake? That's the kind of second-rate thinking that makes me puke.

What I've really been thinking about is how life is just an eternal movement between the most totally disparate and inconsequential things. Like, how geeks who've been told they're gods and overpaid at a very young age are pretty often totally inept as human beings because they've spent most of their misbegotten youth writing C++ or Java code. Just so some lazy-ass people can flip a switch and say to their boss how hard it was to learn this program and what a good little worker bee I am.

Or this thorny one that I read about on the 'Net: how most weirdo masochists are sadists and most sadists are masochists. It made me wonder how anybody ever gets any satisfaction out there. But the irony is: they do. At least I think they do.

I was still mind-tripping on this stuff when I got home. As I turned the key in the lock, the silence waiting on the other side of the door warned me that my girlfriend, Angelina, had disappeared into the night, probably with a gang of girls. One thing I don't know much about is love or women. Old man Freud was right about that—it's a dark continent, especially when you're living in the darkness, too. I mean, you're like me, a female who likes females.

I put my backpack down, sat on the bed, and tried to forget about Angelina. It wasn't too hard, because what my Buddhist friends call "monkey mind" started jumping around, looking for a mental banana. I found it and peeled it. Inside the banana there was a friend's project; he's writing what he calls autobiographical fiction. Even though I don't read much literature, I worked the theme over in my mind. I mean, think about it, what does that really mean? Like, if it's autobiography, it can't be fiction, and if it's fiction, it can't be autobiography. Or maybe those literary enchiladas should think up a new category and call it something like fict-fact. They'd like that. It's sexy.

I was still thinking about this kind of thing when someone rang my buzzer. It was around 2 A.M. and I thought Angelina might have lost her key in a hurry to get back to my loving arms—ha!—so I buzzed 'em in. Of course, it wasn't Angie.

It was María de los Dolores. If you don't know Spanish—and how could you not if you're living in America?—that's Mary of the Sorrows. A round body, bundled in neuroses, buttresses Dolores's exquisite face. And she has a couple of discrete vices—white lies and dark men.

I went to the door and looked through the fisheye.

"Oh, Mad Dog, honee." All I could see was a large, red mouth pulsating at the peephole. She was stage-whispering my nickname and breathing heavily, "Listen, *querida,* let me in, I just left the *fiesta* at Carlos's house where I ditched my boyfriend and I need to talk . . . —*tú sabes cómo yo me obsesiono . . .*"

I knew it was gonna be a long night.

She toddled in on huge platform shoes. The black top she wears to parties hung off one shoulder, outlining her breasts, and about fifty bracelets carroused up one arm. If Dolores had an era, hers would be the fifties in Cuba—nightclubs and bars, mixed drinks, big-ass cars and over-the-top personalities. Of course, she's really a little too postmodern for that with her butch haircut, femme manners, and fondness for S&M, but I still like to imagine her at the Tropicana with a table full of her exes—Juanito, Tony, and Bob. Forget that Lucy and Desi pap they serve up on cable reruns.

"*Hola!*" she purred and air-kissed both cheeks. "Remember Bryce? I think you met her last year at my Halloween party."

The older woman with her entered the room with the air of a wounded prince. She was slender and blonde, and she wore those cat-eye glasses with rhinestones that make you look smart but a little prickly.

"Hello, Mad Dog," Bryce said. "Nice to see you again."

She had a low, husky voice and looked me straight in the eye when she shook my hand. Bryce kinda scared me; she was sharp and direct.

"Hi, Bryce," I said. "Good to see you, too."

"Bryce is a journalist—remember?" Dolores said. "But she's a dinosaur, on a quest for authenticity, whatever that is. I keep trying to tell her to use more Spandex in her writing, *tú sabes,* stretch things a bit for the sake of entertainment, but she seems to be quaintly attached to the truth."

"How noble," I said.

"Yes, noble and doomed," Bryce replied. "You know, Dolores makes me sound like an antique."

"Yeah, Bryce, you don't see that if you could just spice it up a little bit for those of us who love drama—You know, like, today I was seeing

my therapist and I got a call on my cell and I answered and it was José
and he was pissed at me for breaking a date, so I threw the phone out
the window! Showed him, no?" Dolores was laughing at herself and her
head was bobbing like one of those funky dogs in the back window of
an L.A. low rider.

Bryce put a hand on Dolores's shoulder and looked at me. "Dolores thinks she has to keep us entertained, doesn't she?"

Dolores exclaimed, "But I do! If I didn't do that, I'd be bored and
then I'd get depressed and then I'd want to get high. And I just can't
get that way again!"

To some people Dolores might have seemed frivolous, but to me
she was the most upfront person I knew. Of course we have to entertain
ourselves, or else the darkness would just take over. That's why I spend
so much time thinking about absurdities; if I didn't, life would seem
truly meaningless and absurd.

Bryce came over and stood close to me. Her self-assurance made
me nervous, so I backed off a little.

"So, Mad Dog, what's your story?"

I looked at her and blinked, "Me? What do you mean, like, what
do I do? I'm a programmer. Didn't Dolores tell you?"

"Yeah, awesome. But more like, what turns you on?"

"Oh, well, I like to try to figure things out. And tonight I've been
thinking about this autobiographical fiction thing a friend is into. I've
been trying to figure that out, you know, what that means exactly."

"Oh, *mi amor!*" Dolores jumped up and faced us, hand on cocked
hip, "How can you even ask such a question? ALL autobiography is a
fiction, honee. Look at me!"

How could we not look at her? When Dolores took center stage,
everyone else was just handling the props.

"*Mira,* this 'woman'"—she sliced quotation marks into the air
with her fingers—"called Dolores is MY creation. There was no Adam,
and I'm not Eve!"

Most people crack up around Dolores, but not Bryce. She was one
cool customer. All she did was arch an eyebrow over the rhinestones.

"So, Dolores, if you're the sole creator of this persona you call
María de los Dolores, then what about the role of genes or environment
in your creation?" Bryce asked. "I guess you don't put much trust, or
should I say faith, in science, huh?"

"Sure I do. I put faith in psychopharmacology and cosmetic surgery. That's a true miracle, honee!"

That made Bryce laugh and she retorted, "You have such a talent
for mixing the sacred and the profane, Dolores."

"Ah-ha, Bryce, so what do you think about this autobiographical fiction thingie?" Dolores asked, wriggling her little finger. "Do you think that if someone writes a memoir it's somehow always based on real experience?"

"Of course not, but I do think that it still has some kind of essential truth that comes from experience or observation. On the other hand, people seem to think they're reading fact filtered through memory, when memory is one of the least precise of the human faculties. The memoir might even be more fictional by nature than the short story."

Bryce really had Dolores there.

"Hmm. I see . . . Mad Dog, honee, don't you have something for us to drink?" Dolores was using diversionary tactics.

I knew there was nothing in the fridge, so I put on the espresso pot.

"But, of course, if it's fiction, there has to be a plot." Bryce wouldn't let the topic go.

"Yeah, but look at me, Bryce," I said. "I'm plotless and clueless. Do you know where you're going and what you're doing?"

"Of course I do. I have a career and I'm trying to advance in it."

As usual, there was no underestimating Dolores. She chimed in, "Oh, Mad Dog, honee, you are so right. I don't want to know what I'm going to do *mañana*. Then there'd be no surprises!"

"Well, yeah, that's your deal. Me, I think that since everything has become so totally simultaneous, I mean, like, what with the 'Net and wireless messaging and all, the plot has just disappeared. Poof! Good riddance!"

"Yeah, but you two are fictionalizing everything. Let's get back to real life . . ."

"*Ay, ay, ay!*" Bryce was interrupted by Dolores, who, in her exasperation, threw herself down on the bed and put the back of one hand across her forehead. Every few moments, she would emit another little "*ay, ay.*" I had time to observe Bryce, who was looking sideways at the books on the shelf, scrunching up her nose and squinting her eyes. She seemed to need stronger glasses. Good, I thought, because I was hoping she wouldn't see the corny ones I had, like: *C++ for the A-Rated Coder* or *Java Juice Runs the Web: A Programmer's Guide to Making Mocha Money*. Instead, Bryce picked up one of Angelina's books on reincarnation. That was when Angie was in her yogi phase and would walk around the apartment, eyes closed and her fingers in a *mudra*, humming "*om, om, om.*" But now she's just another downtown ragamuffin with big ideas and nowhere to go.

I mean, if there really is such a thing as reincarnation where people keep getting reborn as other people since the beginning of human history, and if the population of the world keeps growing and growing, then what souls fill up all those new people? Are they empty? Or do the souls of the first ones keep getting divided up, so that those of us born today are really just watered-down versions of humans? That would explain why people today like spazzed stuff like gangsta rap, Lucky Charms, and bungee jumping.

Dolores sat up suddenly; her head whirled around. "No, no, no, no, no. That's not it at all, Bryce."

I had no idea what she was talking about.

"*No es posible.* You see, what you don't see is that it's all a fiction, Miss B. Whatever we write or say or do is just an artifice we use to represent our thoughts or feelings . . . —our lusts and loves and pain and longing, honee. There's no way I can communicate to you the true me, because the only way I have to express it is through a medium that takes me one degree from my truth. *Amiga,* my tears are just the expression of my *dolor,* not the thing itself." Dolores stood up, a little wobbly on her big black shoes. "Fuck authenticity, because you'll never, ever see it or communicate it."

I had never heard Dolores make such a long, serious speech. Bryce walked over to Dolores and held her face between her hands.

"You, Dolores, are an original," she murmured in her low voice. She kissed Dolores on the cheek, just as the front door flew open with a thwack against the wall. Angelina strode in, with a sullen look etched in black eyeliner, one arm around someone I barely knew: Baby LaRue.

"All right, girls, time to get the hell out of here. Go do that over at the Devil's Den."

Nothing like Angie coming home to really cheer things up.

Bryce looked as if she had been spun around and slammed into place. She froze on the spot when she saw Angelina and her companion walk through the door. At the same time, Dolores gasped loudly, but her eyes narrowed. She liked to feign her emotions when she needed time to figure something out.

I wasn't surprised to see Angie in such a surly mood; in fact, it was pretty rare to see her smile. But I was surprised to see her escort, Baby LaRue. Did you ever know anybody caught in the DMZ of gender? Well, that's where Baby had landed. Once a male-to-female transsexual lesbian, she now seemed to be a child of her own invention. She was always tall, but everything else was kind of indefinite; her breasts seemed smaller and she had a sketchy goatee, but at the same time still wore lipstick and a tight shirt with her jeans.

Baby pulled a Camel from behind one ear, lit it, and said, "Hullo,

Mad Dog, you let your woman loose on the streets at night? I thought you were a class act." Baby LaRue looked at Bryce and nodded, murmuring a low "hello."

"Oh, shut up," Bryce snapped.

Dolores was still staring at Baby. "Baby? Baby . . . LaRue?" she said. "I haven't see you since you were . . . well, back when you were a . . . —a model. Oh my god, *Jesús y María,*" Dolores crossed herself, kissed her fingers and peered at Baby through slit eyes. "Honee, wha' happened to you?"

"Aw, shit, Dolores, what happened to *you?*" Baby said. "Have you looked in the mirror? Looks like you have the circles of hell under your eyes. Been there and brought the smack monkey back, huh?"

Baby had never been an inspired conversationalist, so I imagined that the mixed metaphors were driving Dolores crazy, not just the reference to her drug of choice. She may have loved artifice, but insisted on fidelity to all source materials, especially Dante and his circles of hell, since her last lover had been a handsome, heart-breaking, Italian medievalist. But Dolores seemed at a loss for words.

The air in my minuscule apartment grew stale; the only sounds were the syncopation of the coffee pot puttering on the stove and Dolores tapping her shoe.

"What's wrong, Dolores? Cat got your tongue or are you just too high to talk?" Baby sneered.

I noticed that Bryce was standing by the bookshelf completely still, like a bad mime on a street corner. There seemed to be energy whirling all around her. When I thought about it all later, I realized that she had been preparing her ninja bodymind for battle. Suddenly, Bryce sprang across the room and grabbed Baby's T-shirt. She pulled Baby's face a foot down, so that she could look her in the eye.

"Listen to me, nobody talks to Dolores like that! Nobody!" And, with that, she shoved Baby as hard as she could. Baby stumbled backward and slammed into the stove; the impact knocked the espresso pot over and scalding coffee poured onto Baby's bum.

"*Ah-eeeee!*" she wailed and lunged for Bryce, but Dolores stuck out one of her big shoes and Baby landed face down.

Bryce was yelling at Baby at the top of her lungs, stomping her feet.

"Arthur, how could you be such a jerk? I just wish you would stay out of my business and out of my life!"

Baby moaned and curled in a ball, hands to her face, "Oh, Bryce, I didn't know you were here. Angie and I have been . . . aw, shit!"

Baby looked over at me guiltily and right then I knew why deep inside I preferred writing code to studying philosophy. Code was clean and pure, but philosophy tried to explain the unexplainable. It was messy and there were no clear-cut answers.

Dolores was laughing hysterically, but I was totally taken aback. "Arthur? Arthur? Wha . . . —? Bryce, how do you know Baby?" I asked.

Bryce looked at me and said, "Arthur Larry Ruben, a.k.a. Baby LaRue, is my ex-husband. He's the one who took all my money to get his first sex-change operation. Right, Arthur?"

Baby tried to avoid looking directly into Bryce's eyes. The fires of Dante's hell seemed mild in comparison.

"Oh my god, Bryce, you never told me the part about the money," Dolores said. She walked over and stood above Baby. "So, Baby, should I loathe you or just despise you?"

Until now, Angelina had been eerily quiet, but that didn't last; she threw herself over Baby like a blanket, keening in that way mothers do with their infants that makes them sound slightly retarded. Her eyeliner was smudged with tears when she looked up and hissed.

"Now look what you've done to Baby. Poor Baby . . . ," she murmured and stroked Baby, who lay in her arms and moaned.

Programmers are generally a docile lot. We spend protracted periods of time hunkered down in front of a computer screen writing long strings of code, hundreds and thousands of lines of it, which makes something else run, like a game or a computer operating system. That mentality can make us pretty passive-aggressive; we're not devotees of open conflict.

But seeing Angie like that with Baby just made me sick. So I went to the closet and pulled out a box that Angie kept stashed there. It was full of her treasured memorabilia—badges, photos, banners, and magnets—from every demonstration that had taken place in the last few years. With the box under one arm, I walked over to the grimy little window that looks out over Eighth Avenue and pulled off the screen. Bryce and Dolores edged toward the window to see what I was doing. I turned the box upside down and shook everything out. Some of the badges—I think one of them said "Bitch in Boots"—flew down and stuck into the bald skull of a Chelsea boy walking below. Behind me I could hear Bryce and Dolores giggling.

Angie was screaming, "God damn you, Mad, that's my stuff! Those are all my memories!"

I turned and marched over to Angie and Baby. "Listen, Angie, I want you out. Now! I mean it. Get out!"

"But, Mad . . . —" she said.

She tried to stare me down, but I waited stubbornly for her to get up. She pulled Baby up by one arm and walked her to the door. Angelina came back into the little room and grabbed a few of her things, then turned, and pretty soon the door closed behind them. My posse stood firm with me the entire time.

To be honest, I knew that Angelina would have to leave some day, but I didn't know where she would go or whom she would go with. Baby LaRue seemed like a strange choice, although I could understand Angelina's attraction. She has great tolerance for ambiguity, while I'm always trying to think my way through to the other end of things. Why? I've never stopped asking the question and somehow expecting a rational answer from a weird world.

Then, for a moment I forgot about how absurd things are. I felt relieved that it was finally over with Angelina. In fact, I felt strangely free, as if I had just seen a shining, silver spot of the river between the buildings in Chelsea, and I could imagine it flowing down from the north, through the wooded valleys, past the canyons of the city—and out into the dark sea. But, you know, it didn't last long. My crazy mind flew back to the time I had seen a corpse on the riverbank. It was a bright Sunday afternoon in the park in the farthest reaches of upper Manhattan. The tourists were cruising by on the Circle Line boat, taking photos, while a jubilant crowd of picnicking families had gathered around the body. They held their children's hands and pointed at it, wondering aloud if it had been a suicide, a homicide, or maybe an accident. It was one of those really absurd moments, the kind I like the best.

In Reflection   If I were to choose a literary label for "Mad Dog in Chelsea," it would be something on the order of "virtual fiction," a term that Mad Dog might approve. Although the story hangs on numerous points of contact with the lives of sentient beings, the general effect is fictional. To reveal precisely which points of my story "really happened" or which characters are based on "real people" would assume the reader's naïve or perhaps disingenuous reading. Moreover, having built a fictional apparatus, I'm loath to show the reader the system software—rife with bugs—that runs behind the scenes.

I wrote "Mad Dog in Chelsea" when urged by a fellow writer to contribute something to this volume, and I thought it would be amusing to have the characters engage in the autobiography-fiction debate—the "fict-fact" that Mad Dog mentions. But if I had to take a side in their discussion, I'd be hard-pressed to do so. I could never draw the line in the sand between "fict" and fact.

Moreover, the place in contemporary culture where the exhibitionist and the voyeur happily meet—in the space of the memoir or talk show television, for example—is not Mad Dog's natural habitat, nor is it mine. Mad Dog abhors making a spectacle of herself, despite the fact that I relish putting her in situations in which she has to take center stage. I, on the other hand, enjoy exhibitionism, but only if it is cloaked in fiction.

Since writing this story, Mad Dog has grown up and into a novel that is a queer quest for lost love cloaked in picaresque social satire. She and Dolores and Bryce have taken on a larger life than the nub of a plot that is sketched here, and they are charting destinies that move them into spheres that I have visited infrequently and only with a guest pass.

In short, I am not Mad Dog or Bryce or Dolores, but they are all figments of and witnesses to the scope of my personal virtual fictions.

proceeding page

PHOTOGRAPH BY S. E. VALENTINE

Ruthann Robson

RUTHANN ROBSON

Leaving Her

If she thinks of me at all, she probably thinks I'm dead.

She is not an ex-lover. While a few of these women may have wanted to kill me, such desires seemed mostly fleeting and insincere. The only one who had any reason to doubt my survival was dead herself. And as a dead woman, I figured she did not think at all, never mind thinking about whether I was dead or not. Or if the dead can think, they would also be able to discern who was among their number.

She is not an ex-teacher or former student. Certainly, there were a few of my teachers who thought I wouldn't "make it," but by this they seemed to mean that I would not be successful. Perhaps one of my high school teachers thought I would be a pothead or druggie, if she indulged in current slang and a review of my records. By college, graduate school, and law school, I had very few woman teachers—and not one of them would think I was headed for the grave any sooner than herself. As for my students, they did not consider me especially elderly or frail, a fact evidenced not only by my chronological age (similar to many of them in our alternative academic environment) but by my appeal to some of them as worthy of flirtation or the occasional outright proposal. Barring a terrible accident, they assumed I would be around to write them recommendations for years to come.

She is not my mother or grandmother, both of whom are living and seemed to assume that I would outlive them, as we are told is the natural order of things.

She is not a friend, a colleague, a distant relative.

She is not an acquaintance whom I met briefly at a conference, in a bookstore or a bar, in a bathroom, at some women's event, in a grocery store, or through a mutual friend.

No. No one, if she thought of me at all, had any reason to suspect I would not still be alive at forty-three, forty-four, fifty—.

Until I met her. My oncologist. My former oncologist.

I felt lucky that she was a woman. Well, maybe not lucky, but I was looking for good omens wherever I could find them. If I had to have cancer—a big "if" which nevertheless seemed nonnegotiable—then I was glad to have access to a cancer center with a stellar reputation and to be assigned to a female oncologist.
I liked women.

I had always liked women.

One of my first girlfriends—it would be a stretch to call her a lover, though we did our share of "messing around"—was a high school math wiz. Calculus and all that in tenth grade. I didn't hold this against her; she also had wonderfully greasy hair and played the guitar. For her, numbers were romantic and realistic, both. I found them as numbing as she seemed to find words, especially poetry. Though for a while, we had a fantasy: I could write the lyrics and she could write the music. But my lyrics never had rhyme or rhythm and her music was an abstract numerical progression.

This is why I told her I was leaving her: she liked facts; I liked metaphors and theories.
This is why I left her: she still liked to do homework together; I was starting to like sneaking into bars.

But, Winnie, wherever you are (I do not assume you are dead; will not even let that thought enter my mind), if you are reading this, I know you will not be satisfied until you get the facts and numbers. And whether you ever knew it or not, my desire was always your satisfaction.

Less than 20 percent of oncologists are women and those who are seem concentrated in clinical areas that predominantly concern women, such as breast cancer and gynecological cancers. The cancer with which I had so recently been diagnosed was a relatively rare cancer—sarcoma, a type of cancer that constitutes less that 1 percent of all cancer cases in the United States, about six thousand cases per year. Sarcomas are further subdivided into types, depending upon which kinds of cells they mimic:

there are bone sarcomas and muscle sarcomas and perhaps the most famous sarcoma, Kaposi's sarcoma, which is associated with AIDS. About 11 percent of sarcomas are liposarcomas, a sarcoma of the fat cells, which usually appear in either the extremities or the abdomen. I was diagnosed with an abdominal liposarcoma, also called retroperitoneal liposarcoma. These are usually quite large once detected because they grow for many years without causing symptoms relating to organ interference. They are often fatal. The five-year survival rate is less than 5 percent.

Enough facts and numbers, Winnie?

Luckily, my preference was more for metaphors and mysticism.

Of course, I hadn't lived my life immune to statistics. My birth was in the statistics books, by nation, by state, by gender, by race, by marital status of my mother. My immunizations, my educational endeavors, my car accidents, my employment in various fields—all these had been duly registered somewhere. I was one of the 1 to 10 percent (depending upon whom you believed) of women who are lesbians. And my lifespan was predicted on an insurance actuarial table, but there is something different about viewing a five-year survival rate with a dismally low number and knowing you are included.

Every doctor I had seen until now was male and discouraging. The first doctor at the famous cancer center had a few problems dealing with my lover, or maybe he had a few problems dealing with women, or perhaps just people in general. When my lover, pad and pen in hand as if we were at a conference or in a classroom, asked him some of the questions we had prepared, he was vague and dismissive.

"What's the precise diagnosis?" she asked.

"Sarcoma, probably liposarcoma, if you really need to know the name."

Of course I wanted to know the name. I believe in language, I wanted to shout. I believe if I know the name I can write it on a piece of paper, set fire to it, and it will be gone. Or I want to believe that.

My lover, like you, Winnie, believes less in language than in facts and numbers.

"How long does she have?" my lover asks.

This was not part of the script.

The doctor is equivocal.

But after the appointment, I am not. "Don't ever ask that again, no matter what," I tell my lover.

And she never does, though at times I can see the question looming over her head.

By the time we come to see the female oncologist, we are both more practiced. Our pad has become several notebooks filled with information and separated by dividers. My lover is organized. And she is no longer my lover. She is now my "domestic partner." I call her this to fit within the city's laws and the hospital forms. I introduce her as my "partner."

No one flinches. Or not so as I would notice. I may be beyond noticing.

I tell my partner—my lover—that a female oncologist is a good omen. More rationally, I reasoned that a woman would be smarter and more caring than a man. I know only too well that this is a stereotype— as a woman who has been an attorney for twenty years, I knew at least as many male attorneys who were brilliant and compassionate as I did female attorneys, and I'd had the misfortune to meet at least as many female attorneys who were stupid and callous as I had met male attorneys with those same regrettable traits—but I clung to my conclusion, nevertheless. It was at least a more logical omen than the next song on the radio, the outcome of a game of solitaire, or what mail was in the box.

On my first visit, she seemed competent and concerned, even if her hair was greasy. The news she gave me was very dismal, but there were two chemotherapy protocols, neither one of which was "a walk in the park," as she said, but both of which offered hope. Although she was a strict proponent of not offering what is called "false hope," and as her physician's notes indicate, she tried to make clear to the patient—me, described as a pleasant forty-two-year-old woman presenting with her female partner—that this particular cancer was incurable and the prognosis poor.

"I am not pleasant," I told the report when I read it.

"And I want to be forty-three," I added.

The chemotherapies, each more drastic than the last, failed to shrink a tumor in my abdomen, which made me look twelve months pregnant. During visits to the oncologist, my partner, with her notebooks and pre-agreed questions, repeatedly quizzed the oncologist about other options, including surgery. The oncologist was relentlessly negative.

Surgery, she said, was useless because the tumor was too large and the cancer had metastasized to my liver. The surgeon at her prestigious institution had said so. Maybe I could find "someone" to operate, but it would not be successful.

There were no other chemotherapy regimens that had proven to be effective.

Radiation was not advisable.

There was nothing one could do through diet, vitamins, nutrition.

Her only repeated suggestion was tranquilizers of various forms and a referral to the psychiatrist.

She was so bleak, she had my sympathy. I knew she must dread coming into the examining room with me, bearing more bad news, and seeing me cry and protest. It must be like telling a lover you no longer loved—wondering now if you ever did—that you were leaving her.

Only she was telling me I would be leaving her. Leaving her and everyone and everything else I knew.

I have never considered myself someone who had a problem with leaving. I left more lovers than I care to count, starting with Winnie.

I had left a car by the side of the road in Georgia, my favorite garden in California, my favorite bar in Miami. I left leases and roommates and moved dozens of times, up and down the East Coast and across the continent, leaving furniture, mementos, and clothes in rummage shops and dumpsters. I have left any number of jobs.

I thought I had an impressive résumé when it came to leaving.

I didn't want to add an entry about leaving my life.

And I couldn't seem to decide to leave my oncologist.

I knew that a doctor is just another service provider, like a plumber or a car mechanic that a person hires—and can fire. So, why didn't I feel that way? Why did I feel she had such power over me? Maybe I had been socialized to be obedient, as a girl-child in a male nation, but isn't one definition of a dyke a disobedient woman? And didn't it matter that my oncologist was a woman, presumably a disobedient woman herself?

There's also the fucked-up American health care system, of course, where doctors can refer, or refuse to refer, patients to other doctors, but my inertia was emotional not practical.

Somehow, I didn't want to hurt her feelings.

As if we had a relationship. And it sometimes seemed as if we did. She was saying the same sorts of things that Winnie had said, that other women said, that were starting to grate, starting to sound claustrophobic and abusive.

"I am a qualified doctor at a prestigious cancer center," she said.

"I am the smartest girl in our grade," Winnie said.

"I have considered your case and all possible options."

"I know you like no one else ever will," Winnie said.

"There are no other doctors doing work on this rare cancer," she said.

"There aren't other girls who are like us," Winnie said.

Winnie, did you become an oncologist? I thought maybe I should try to get in touch with you. To see if you were among the 10 percent of women who are lesbians; to see if you were devoted to the 1 percent of cancers that are sarcomas. But I have always believed that once you leave someone, you leave her be.

No former lovers as best friends for me.

No former oncologists as any kind of friends for me.

Which is why I never get in touch with my former oncologist after I leave her. Never write a note or send my medical reports to tell her how wrong she was. Never let her know that I had surgery. Never let her know that she was wrong about my liver metastasis. Never tell her that if she had done her fucking homework, if she had researched the numbers and the statistics, she would have discovered that there had never been a reported case of liposarcoma metastasizing to the liver.

Never let her know that I am now cancer-free. Never let her know that I turned forty-three. Forty-four.

Oh, Winnie, I have never regretted leaving you.

Though I left you for another woman.

And then left her for another.

When I was no longer ill, I left my "partner"—she is my lover again. As for my oncologist, perhaps the only woman I ever left for a man, I try not to think of her.

If I think of her at all, it is only because I am not dead.

In Reflection   "Leaving Her" grew out of my attempts to understand my experiences as a cancer patient and my relationship with the female oncologist assigned to me at the famous cancer center where I was being treated for a rare cancer, liposarcoma. Much of my emotional and intellectual energies centered on my oncologist not only because she was the person I saw most often and consistently, but because my lesbianism/feminism nurtured expectations on the basis of her gender. As it turned out, she was just as callous—and incorrect—as the male doctors I had seen at the famous cancer center. In terms of process, this piece is related to a column that I wrote for *Self* magazine -("Leaving My Doctor Saved My Life," May 2001). Faced with the assignment of reducing the complexities of my experience to 750 words, I balked. While my message was simple—get a second, third, fourth opinion when a doctor tells you it's hopeless—the facts and my emotions swirled around me as I tried to write a traditional piece. Only after I allowed myself the measure of freedom that I have found in "fiction-theory," a form that Nicole Brossard named and which I have been practicing since the mid-eighties, could the writing become both focused and challenging. Analogizing my relationship with my oncologist to a high school "girlfriend" Winnie is the most important part of the piece, and I had never consciously considered such a comparison until I began writing in this form. Thereafter, I wrote the column, sans Winnie, with only a few shared lines. A column I wrote for *OUT* magazine, ("Being a Dyke Saved My Life," April 2001), offers a contrasting perspective. In "Leaving Her," my lesbianism is a disadvantage because it contributed to my faith in a female oncologist; in the *OUT* column, lesbianism was a definite advantage in many ways. There are many possible explanations for the reason that I am not dead, despite the definitive prognosis delivered at the famous cancer center. I continue to write and publish work about my cancer experience, most often in the fiction-theory game, and have recently had work published in magazines such as *Creative Nonfiction, Another Chicago Magazine, Harvard Gay and Lesbian Review,* and *Bell-vue Literary Review.* During my own ordeal the words of others gave me strength and hope, regardless of what doctors were telling me and I hope to give others a similar gift.

SARAH SCHULMAN

My First Wedding

My mother wanted to be a doctor, but she was a social worker. In the fifties, she was working at an agency, maybe the Jewish Board of Guardians, and a guy offered to help her get into medical school. She didn't know if she could make it. If she could do it. She went to her father, Charlie Yevish, a laundryman from the Ukraine. He didn't know anything about doctors, becoming a doctor, or girls being doctors, but he did tell her that he would help her if that is what she wanted to do. He couldn't help her with money. But he would do whatever he could. My father, her husband, was a doctor. But he somehow didn't figure in this decision.

So, this being the milieu of first-generation Jewish working-class people becoming professionals in the 1950s, my mother went into analysis in order to decide. She chose a female analyst because she believed that a female professional would know if Gloria Yevish Schulman could make it as a doctor. But this being the fifties, analysis involved a patient who spoke and a therapist who listened. There was no interaction or cross-talk. So, my mother, in her twenties, went to the office and spoke, but the female doctor never said a word. Finally, within that silence, my mother decided she wasn't smart enough or perhaps confident enough to become a doctor. So she stayed a social worker for the next forty years.

In 1962, I started nursery school. Our teacher was getting married and she had marriage on the brain. One of her ideas was for our class to plan and enact a mock wedding, in which we would all couple up and get married. Each boy and each girl joined, became a couple, and—after some planning—lined up to walk down the aisle. I was four. I was one of the few, or perhaps the only student, to not get married. I don't know if I refused or if I could not find a partner, but I've always had friends, so I assume that I refused. I did not get married; I decided that I was the photographer. As my classmates walked down the aisle, en masse, I made a little box out of my hands and ran around snapping imaginary pictures. I guess this is when I came out as a homosexual and as an artist, the observational kind.

Certainly I had already been primed for marriage. I'd played with my mother's wedding veil until it was torn to shreds. And I did know one photographer, the dentist's assistant in our pregentrification Greenwich Village apartment building. Her boyfriend had a shaved head. She came upstairs and took stiff, unsmiling portraits of my sister clutching a stuffed bunny rabbit. I often wondered, given the macabre nature of the photograph, if she was Diane Arbus. So I knew what marriage was and I knew what a photographer was. And, at my first wedding, I chose to be a photographer.

Thirty-five years later, Woody Allen had a sexual relationship with his girlfriend's adopted daughter and ended up marrying her. There was a lot about this on the news, and TV cameras followed him wherever he went, especially to his therapy sessions. New York was fascinated by Woody Allen's therapy. He was our most public and emblematic patient. And yet, obviously his therapy had failed. Who was this doctor who somehow let him have sex with the adopted daughter of his adult lover? Who was this doctor that he went to week after week and never got better? Then one day they showed this therapist's face on the news. My mother gasped. It was that same woman analyst she had gone to in the fifties. Four decades had passed and she was still a bad doctor. She still didn't say the right thing.

I resisted and my mother could not. I didn't know any better or any worse. I did not make a decision. I did not talk it over with anyone. I was only four. I set myself apart; I embraced an unknown fate. My mother could not, and yet I could. Was that the start of our problems with each other? No.

By 1962 they were already well underway.

proceeding page

PHOTOGRAPH BY ELIZABETH OHLSON

Peggy Shaw

Gosh Dirt

Nothing here goes together; it doesn't mesh. The music doesn't go with the walls, the furniture doesn't go with the people, the windows look out into the wrong place, the food smells like it's in the wrong restaurant and I'm opening the door to try and make sense of it all. Even the air from outside comes in and doesn't make sense, so it goes out again. I feel like I'm in the home of somebody's relatives and they're not sure they want me here—kind of like they're acting like they're running a restaurant and I'm acting like I'm in it, but I'm really in their house in eastern somewhere pretending to be in Manhattan pretending to be a writer. Even the ceiling makes no sense.

Passionless is a word I would use to describe my state of mind. Undriven, like my old cars sitting in the backyard. Unmotivated. Boring, I think, is the word. Like a bad exhaust system. Dull. Thick, like London fog. Trying not to use the word old. Or vintage. Can't seem to get excited about much of anything. Only the memory of what fire means.

I don't think it's my age. Maybe it's the hormones in the food. Some friends seem driven and tense and emotional, the way I used to feel. Caffeine. Maybe it's these new blood-pressure pills. Maybe this is how normal people feel all the time. My response is to withdraw, become quiet, and to want to retreat from the scene and be alone walking along a river. I think maybe I feel like a dog that's been hit by an old car. I run into a bush and hide and lick my wounds. I am licking my wounds and at the same time happy to be in the bushes. Trying to get it up to write. It all appears hype to me, the world. Nothing makes sense. A gay world that I should be thrilled about but can't anymore. This gay world whose only purpose seems to be to become legally married.

I vowed I would not get bitter and resentful when I matured. I know what always makes me feel better is thinking of all the cars I have owned and picturing them right after I washed them and the sun has dried them.

Like my first car from my grandfather. My mother made me steal it cause he was too old to drive and he was deaf. The last accident he hit a cop car at a stoplight. A 1951 Plymouth Electroglide. Turquoise and white. The dashboard was white and reflected the sunlight and made it hard to see. It caught on fire on Storrow Drive in Boston from not re-placing the oil cap because it burned three quarts of oil every fifty miles.

Next I had a 1959 Harley Sprint 250 motorcycle. Hi-Fi purple. My grandfather sold it while I was at work. He sold it to the guy fixing the roof 'cause I had blown up his Plymouth. I had only crashed once. Slid along some leaves in the fall.

Then a 1961 VW bus. Light green and white. My partner kept it in a divorce. I had painted Apocalypse Workshop on the side.

A 1962 Pontiac Catalina. Blue with black hardtop. It was stripped of everything (motor, tires, brakes, locks) on First Street and First Av-enue till I couldn't even recognize it.

A 1979 red and white VW camper bus named Georgette. She blew a rod in Daniel Boone State Park in Kentucky but made it back to Lib-erty in upstate New York where she froze up for good.

1971 Ford Torino, Coke-bottle green, still in my yard. Left front shock needed, plus horn, speedometer, and windshield-wiper motor. To get it going you have to hit it with a hammer.

1973 Buick Apollo. Gold with brown hardtop. Gave it to my daughter who gave it to a friend. It's sitting in New Paltz, totally rusted. Gin was her name. Belonged to Lois's father, Russell. She had the body of a Camaro.

1973 Chevy Malibu. Green. Sheila gave it to me. Drove it into a hole in Tompkins Park in a rainstorm at 4 A.M. It buckled in half. My friends almost went through the windshield. After that I wore seat belts. I took off the license plates and left it there on the corner of Avenue B and Ninth Street. It looks like there's a road going through the park but it's not.

A 1981 Datsun truck. Red with cat footprints stenciled on the hood (they were there when I got it). Broke down on Palisades Parkway. I didn't have money for a generator so I gave it to the tow-truck guy and I and Shara hitchhiked to Roscoe, New York, with the contents of the glove compartment in a paper bag. People kept picking us up to keep someone bad from picking us up.

A 1974 blue station wagon with no heat. It was stolen on Third Street. Five people had keys and would leave it anywhere. Alice had to apply antifreeze to the windshield in winter 'cause there was no heat and it had a hole in the floor on the driver's side. I avoided an accident be-cause I saw a lit-up Virgin Mary on the side of the road and just missed a car pileup.

I've still got a 1987 Subaru. Blue with four-wheel drive. Will have it forever . . . I'm getting old like my cars. A little rusty. I never had a car from the decade I was in. Yet. It's no accident being behind the times, like when cars had carburetors. Now my mind is wandering right back from cars to worry.

I'd go outside and sit in a car but age rips open my chest and devours my big high blood pressure heart and I die. I'm not afraid to die.

I'm not afraid of age and I'm not afraid of being alone. I pick at rust spots. I spit out the window. I stick-shift. I am alone. I squeeze my face in the rearview mirror. Wait, what was that flash? It blinded me. Almost like the sun reflecting off a passing car hood, but it was lights flashing in the corner of my eye. Every day at four they flash at the edges of my vision and I can't see. I have to sit down. The doctor said it's either too much caffeine or not enough cars. I think I'm relaxed, but my ears move when I don't realize it. I think I'm being really still and my ears move, my jaw clenches, and my toes never stop moving. My aunt's jaw used to clench and unclench like my grandfather's, but I don't let myself think of my aunt too much. Not on purpose, just 'cause time moves in a line. We had a lot of time together once. We won't again.

I miss her. She was killed by a drunk driver thirty-three years ago in a 1955 red Ford Thunderbird when she went out for a bottle of milk and she's still dead.

The one thing no one wants to hear is that you're getting old. And your thoughts make no sense. Your partner, your kid, your lover. Old is not an attractive word. Mature is an attractive word, not old. Mature. Full of fifty-six years of stories and some baggage. I am mature now and I am dirty. Just from living. And graying at the temples. My hair seems dirty to me when it gets gray. Time flies, then you go back to the silence you came from before you were born. Where was that now? Oh yeah, down with the roots of trees.

Quiet and underground.

I woke up early with that summer-gray hair I mentioned before. It came on overnight. I looked like Richard Gere. When I entered the kitchen, the colors changed across the front and back and music came on and my words got jumbled and my mouth just moved while my words got swallowed up. I looked out the kitchen window.

Windows always remind me that I stood outside her window for a week waiting for her to notice me, whistling up at her window.

I look out the window and in the backyard the high wind had blown down a 150-year-old groovy tree and it smashed across six backyards, including mine. It left a huge hole in the sky where it had been for so long and light smashed into the kitchen where it had never been before. It ripped a huge hole circle right out of the ground. I was shocked that I hadn't heard it fall. Maybe I do fall asleep sometimes in the night and I missed it falling.

The hole in the ground went down twenty feet and next to it was about a twenty-foot high mound of dirt full of roots wrapped around rocks. I went outside. I got close to it. I smelled the dirt and it seemed familiar.

I was attracted to the hole the tree had been in. I walked over close to the hole. It was rocky, but soft and pebbly and brand new. Everyone started to gather: neighbors and friends and others. No one on ground level had ever seen it before. It had been hidden in the ground. Now the contents of the hole were exposed and in full view. And there was the hole itself.

I took off my clothes. It got really quiet. I'm fifty-six and I'm moving slow, but they can't take their eyes off me. It was the way I took them off combined with the shock of the tree falling that alerted everyone that something had changed. They had never seen me like this before. They were all staring at my hands. I guess 'cause I was white and naked. One hand was poised on my waist with the thumb behind and the four dirty fingers in front. The other hand was pressing on the trunk of the tree pressing into the last joint of my fingers, holding in its balance my sudden anger at my mature body.

Somehow the way the tree looked . . . it looked so big and sad and helpless and down, down like a dead elephant . . . I had to do something. I felt as if I was going to spring up into the hole in the sky the tree had left. At that moment, I remembered the medicine woman saying to me: bury yourself in the ground . . . just do it. I was having too much blood coming from my uterus really, and funny new shapes were growing in there. Boys called them baseballs or footballs depending on their size, and girls called them oranges and grapefruits. It's so easy to make an orange evaporate from your body. Muriel told me to visit her friend in Santa Fe. Just say hi. But when I said hi, I started crying. I guess 'cause I could tell she saw through me into my uterus, through my thick clots of blood into my past. She said, "Dirt will take it away. Just bury your body totally in dirt, except for your head, of course. And you have to have a fire and a fire-watcher, someone to keep the fire going as long as you can stay in the ground. And a HOLE. Go somewhere safe, dig out a hole for your body in the dirt, heat up the earth with a fire inside. Burn some sage and tobacco, and get in."

How could I pass up this opportunity of a hole.

There were quite a lot of people gathered in the yard by now, mostly friends. They could be my fire-watchers. But they were scared. I think they thought I would die in the ground. Stacy said she'd do it for me, even though she thought it would kill me. Matter of life and death, I said. Besides I had no health insurance.

I got into the hole, facing the sunset. That seemed right, to be able to watch the sun set even though it was gray and rainy. Stacy built a fire and collected lots of wood to keep feeding it. There was a lot of wood with the downed tree next to me. I got into the ground naked like she told me. My good angel, the tree, on one side. My doubting angel, but still my friend, on the other, shoveling heavy wet dirt on my white cold body. Like being buried alive. I thought I would freak out, but as the dirt was pinning me down more and more, getting really heavy, trapping me in swaddling clothes, all claustrophobia left me and I started getting calm and drowsy and heavy. The dirt was soooo heavy and with the heaviness came familiarity. The dirt smelled so familiar, like I had been there before. Me and the dead tree. Getting dirty. Old and dirty.

When I was covered up to my neck, they said I looked like a flower growing in the woods where the tree had been. I watched the fire. I watched the tree. It started being alive; I could even hear it breathing, slowly, like dying. The tree, as the sun set, started making faces and mouths. One face had a tongue sticking out. Another was laughing and another was howling. Totems, I get it. The fire started looking like foxes and wolves and sounded like coyotes. I heard animal footsteps in the yard. I heard leaves crackling down the street. I thought, this is something unique to being in the ground. I lost my fear of being so naked, so vulnerable. With no clothes, my body had looked very female, very feminine, very white, very naked as I went into the ground.

And I was there, bleeding and pissing into the cold stony tree dirt for eight hours. Like my old cars leaking in the driveway. Sun setting in the backyard, into the dark, into the rain. I felt weightless and bodiless. There was a safety in the night and in the dirt and in the tree. My angel was feeding the fire and giving me sage tea, mostly to keep me warm.

No suit to protect me. No clothes to make me feel whole in the tree's hole. Just dirty. No suit and tie or polished shoes and cufflinks. No hair products. No attitude. Just my head appearing to the world where the tree had been. So calm.

It was very simple, drinking fluids then pissing and bleeding them out the other end. Floating on a cloud-like substance yet pinned down by very light touches. When my mouth opens, my lips part like they haven't been opened in a long time. There is a film of moisture on my lips. I touch my tongue onto the moisture and it sticks to the tip of my tongue. My throat is dry. I want to feel the moisture in the back of my throat where it hurts. It hurts on one side only. I remembered that last week it hurt on the other side. I remembered that I couldn't go on a plane or my ear will burst. I was still dry, couldn't get enough moisture in my mouth to talk.

When I closed my eyes, I was falling through sparkle dust, falling into a pile of clothes at my feet. I was naked in front of everyone. Naked except for my Y fronts and black shoes and socks; my voice inside tells me that I am beautiful. It tells me that I may be here for a while. The generator is on, but the lines are down. I'll just sit here till the power comes back on.

I begin to wish I had left last night. Before the tree was blown down. It feels good to think of the weather.

Deep inside me is a tiny nugget of energy that keeps me going. It is safe because it has doors and locks and combinations. They have to be serviced often. It's expensive. Inside me is expensive. I start to fantasize about tiny people, not even doll size, but like tiny dollhouse-sized people. I am the boy of course, and there is a girl naked in the house. Breasts. I am aware of my forehead against her breasts. Almost like *Gulliver's Travels*. And then a sound. I could barely hear it, almost like it wasn't really supposed to be heard. A scream way off in the distance, in the dark, and then a laugh getting louder and louder. It was frayed a little on the edges, like it had been drinking too much, or smoking. It was an older voice, deep and tender, and moist and dark. When the light finally came up everything looked decayed, almost abandoned, like the part of the subway tunnel near Fourteenth Street lit up with just five light bulbs. One of them wasn't on. When they switched it on with a string, it swung back and forth and cast shadows on the walls, eerie shadows that made me hungry for sitting in a movie on a rainy afternoon in the neighborhood. Bliss.

I suddenly came back to where I was. They had the car headlights shining on me. The ground where the tree had been wanted me out.

Out with you! it said. The ground started moving a little and the wind picked up. The tree gave me a knowing look and a shove. Better do what the ground says. The ground knows.

I couldn't breathe. I made a sharp sound and my eyes got moist like when you hit the bridge of your nose. I yelled for everyone to hurry and dig me out. I was suffocating. The rhythm of their bodies made me want to be near them. Stretching, yawning, digging their claws into my stomach. It seemed to take forever and the dirt was so heavy and there was so much of it. When they got my arms uncovered they yanked me out of the ground like a forceps birth. I was crying and sobbing and covered with wet earth and blood dripping down my legs. I am balanced, like in an Indian dance. My arms are up; my leg is balanced on my left

knee and I talk about couches and fabric. The air was so cold after the
dirt, so cold that there was a column of smoke rising off my white body
into the night.

They gasped at the sight. I wanted to go back into the ground. The
world felt foreign and unsafe . . .

A friend of mine sent me some letters; I remembered they were
stained all over with roach shit. They had been stored in a loft space
above a door in New York City.

That is my home.

My sleeves are not usually long enough and I'm long in the legs.

One of my favorite poems is one Cathy wrote to me. I can't remember it right now, only one part about long, long legs in long black
pants and something about standing on the corner of Saint Marks and
Second Avenue.

Gosh, she said when she came. Gosh. I don't know this music.

I don't know anything about myself anymore. Did SHE give it to
you? Is that why you never take it off even in the bath and in bed? I
wish for the day that I don't care. You knew your way around in a way
I hadn't seen before. The taxi drivers and the waiters knew you.

I had to leap ahead like a rock skipping on Berrybrook, hitting not
smooth water like the pond but water broken up with millions of rocks
sticking out.

I couldn't stop sobbing. They wrapped me in blankets and held me
tight like a newborn babe. It's a butch!!!! We're sure of it, they said. It's
a girl, a big, butch girl. They yelled to the coyote and the fallen tree and
my old Torino and the fire and the back of my building where the fire
was reflecting and the fox and the backyard cat Oscar. You're a healthy,
newborn, butch babe!

I was out with such speed and feeling that you could see my marks
on the fallen tree as I went by. Like leaving rubber. You could smell my
silence and my dirt cologne and taste my anger. The tree was upset by it
and was still growing away from the hole to get away from me. I saw it
like from a distance. Once I got up, the tree already looked like another
kind of animal, like a bear. I know when you see a bear you should whis-
tle just so they know you're coming and then very slowly turn around
and walk away. Don't run.

I knew this would last a long time and I never talked about it.

I am sorry for any part I have played in the amount of cars there are
in the world. I have confessed and named them all. The smell of them
makes my heart beat fast. I always said that I wouldn't go out with anyone who didn't remember JFK being shot.

I revise that statement to people who know what a carburetor is. I want to try and explain how on a cold morning, you go outside, say a prayer, pump the gas once, and turn it over . . .

No oranges left. No more grapefruits or blood in my uterus. The ground sopped it out of me. I am left only with my anger. Me and it. My anger was not used up in the ground, or absorbed by it, but it's still a nice memory, the ground. And I am no longer afraid of heights. I'll never be any younger than I am today.

I find a cheap old Airstream trailer along the side of the road, have my neighbor Eric put new wheels on it, and drive south till it gets warm. I eat a dozen raw oysters in the front seat with a couple beers and watch the sun set on Saint Joseph's Peninsula and dream about that 1951 maroon Oldsmobile Vick took me to see in that backyard the afternoon before the tree fell.

In Reflection   While I wrote the short story for this collection, (and while my partner in Split Britches, Lois Weaver, was editing it) I was also creating a new solo show dedicated to my grandson about a white butch grandmother passing on masculinity to her mixed-race grandson. The show addressed the concept of this mixed-up second-generation first cousin inbred white butch grandmother trying to teach masculinity to this boy of color in North America. When I wrote the story of being buried in the hole the tree was in, it felt like a naked exposure of who I was, even looking down at my naked white old body. I can never really write about anything I don't know so I used the metaphor of the hole and brought my grandson into view. He observed me and I ended up describing my racism and my passion for cars and rock and roll and Sam Cooke and Otis Redding and Dinah Shore and my miseducation and racism. (I was told Dinah Shore had defective genes because she gave birth to two black children in a row—the first black boy that I met was little black sambo—Sam Cooke was killed in his underwear in a motel room.) All the facts and images this white person had stored up came out through the dirt and the hole and the car headlights shining on me.

The end of the show has my grandson holding me up to the sky when I come out of the ground yelling joyously: "It's a butch, a grand butch baby, he yelled to the coyote and the backyard Torino . . ."

proceeding page

PHOTOGRAPH BY LILLIAN MANZOR

Carmelita Tropicana

CARMELITA TROPICANA

Out Takes in Cuba

T he woman at the Miami airport ticket counter couldn't believe it.
"Are you crazy, going to Cuba? There's nothing there. There's no
food. No electricity. No gasoline."

"I'm going to a theater festival. I'm a performance artist."

She still couldn't believe it. Most Cubans going back were taking
food, clothing, and medicine to their relatives.

I left Cuba when I was a kid, and here I was—returning as an adult.
I was nervous. The wait did not calm me down. We had to arrive at the
Miami airport at 5 A.M. for a flight that left at 9 A.M. At 8:30, when it
was finally time to board the plane, I heard a bejeweled, swishy man in
a flowery shirt—a queen no doubt—saying out loud to no one in particular: "I swear this is my last time. I can't take it anymore. My nerves
are just shot."

I wondered if I would meet any gay people in Cuba. Of course—
what a thought! We are everywhere. My gay radar, though, doesn't work
as well in some places as in others. I've had problems in Brazil, where
even the dogs seem to be gay, and in the Midwestern states of the U.S.,
specifically with the female population.

I love places where, the moment one lands, it is clear that you're in a foreign country. And this was the case in Cuba. The airport in Havana was
set in the middle of the Cuban countryside: blue skies, palm trees, and
a field where farmers were tilling the soil with oxen.

I was so hungry that the first thing I did when I got to my hotel was to
go to the dining room to have lunch. It was there that I met Dan, an academic, who was in Cuba to attend a poetry conference. He said he had
seen me at the Miami airport and came to introduce himself. Both our
radars went off. After we talked awhile and confirmed our suspicions, we
wondered if we would have trouble telling who was gay in Cuba. Well,
he knew for sure a gay couple, two men who were giving a party at their

house that night, and I was welcome to come along. All we needed was to bring a couple of bottles of rum, since everything was scarce in Cuba, from food to toilet paper to aspirin.

The party was in a pre-Castro, middle-class neighborhood called El Vedado. We took a cab and noticed, as we left the tourist section of Havana, that the neighborhoods were pitch black. Suddenly it started to pour, and sheets of rain made it hard to find the house. The cab slowed down, and we saw a light in one of the porches. A man was signaling with a flashlight. It was our host. He came to us, guiding us, holding a flashlight and an umbrella.

"I'm sorry—there's no electricity. Watch your step."

Inside the modern one-story house, there were few candles, making the mood somber. We whispered, and our host said, "It feels like a funeral in here. All we're missing is the body. We need music." He called for his partner to find a radio and some batteries. We handed him the rum, and he said, "Rum—how great. We got a loaf of bread. It's a party."

A couple of minutes later, a woman came in. She was thin, like most Cubans, was sporting a stylish haircut, and had bleached blonde hair (my favorite kind of blonde). She had on a pair of pants with suspenders, and as she introduced herself with the deep raspy voice of a smoker, my radar went off.

"And this is my husband." Husband! Her husband was a sweet hippie with long hair, beard, and sandals. We talked a while about work, and she told me she had a nineteen-year-old son. I guess my radar was wrong. Something was wrong. Nevertheless, it was a fun evening.

Two hours into the night, the electricity came back on, and we applauded. We put on the CD player and listened to what our host proudly called *"musica del enemigo"*—enemy music, i.e., American music: "I got it on my last trip to the U.S."

The next day I was off to a lecture/demo of an Afro dance class sponsored by the theater festival. I took down notes as the teacher spoke, but when I looked confused, Maria—another thin Cuban with short, dark hair and a vivacious energy bordering on hyper—came over and wrote about Eleggua, an African deity: *"Eleggua es el principio y el fin, el dia y la noche. Dueno del destino ya que tiene sus llaves, abre y cierra los caminos. Su color es rojo y negro. Se le pone como atributos juguetes."* Eleggua is the beginning and the end, day and night. Master of destiny, he who brings keys to open and close paths. His colors are red and black. You can take him offerings of toys.

I looked at the drums in the corner of the room and asked Maria what they were called. Maria cautioned: "Those are *bata* drums. Neither women nor homosexuals can play them or they won't be in tune."

"Well, I better not get anywhere near them," I said.

Outside the class, my friend Lillian, an academic, and, like myself, a Cuban living in the U.S., was waiting for me to go to lunch. She had brought her cousin José, who lived in Cuba and was very resourceful, helping her to rent a car, score extra gasoline—someone well versed in Cuba's bartering system: you give me an egg, I give you a brick. I talked to Lillian about the Afro dance class and the deities. She said that in the Santeria religion, spirits can possess you: *se te montan encima*. Literally, a spirit mounts you. And a spirit can be either female or male. From those words—"mounting," "male," "female"—my mind went on a roll. And I wondered if Santeria was soft on the gay issue. I was looking for a religion with a loophole. As a lesbian, I'm always on the lookout in all areas, whether it's religion or history, for one thing that might be welcoming and inclusive—for a reference, a mention.

When Maria joined us, I thought, since she knows Santeria, I can ask her. So I asked: "In Santeria, is there any allowance or acceptance of homosexuality?"

And she said, "I'm not a homosexual."

"I'm not a homosexual," she repeated.

I was puzzled, since this had not been my question. After an uncomfortable silence, I said, "Let's go to lunch."

Maria was still standing beside us, and I asked her to join us. It was hard not to. There was no such thing as going to meals alone. Cubans were interesting, resourceful, fun, and as skinny as *Vogue* models from not eating. I thought Maria probably hadn't had a beer in months, a steak in years. There but for the grace of capitalistic and conspicuous consumerism go I.

Havana in '93 was like being caught in a time warp. Cars were vintage '50s. The hotel we went to lunch at had a '20s or '30s feel. It was dark inside, with an elegant staircase, Moorish tiled floor, and heavy-set furniture. We opted for the outdoor café, and, as we had lunch, Lillian, who had written about my work, started discussing the homoerotic content of my work—the lesbian issue. She continued talking, and both José and Maria looked up from their sandwiches. The "L" word made them gulp hard.

At the end of the meal, Maria asked me to come with her to the bar inside. We left Lillian and her cousin outside. She said she had a big favor to ask me: Could I buy her some cigarettes? I did, and she flirted with the bartender for an extra set of matches. She whispered that she had something to tell me. She did not want to talk in front of that guy José. "Who was he, anyway?"

"Lillian's cousin."

"Are you sure?" The Cuban paranoia reared its head. She sat me down at a comfortable chair. She lit her cigarette and said, "I am also."

"Excuse me?"

"I am also that way. I haven't told anyone except for two friends who are also that way. I'm in theater and in the theater festival I've had many, many women—maybe hundreds." She started naming actresses in various productions whom she had encountered and who were also that way. She was getting cockier by the minute. She took a long drag from her cigarette and repeated, "Hundreds of women. The festival is great." Indeed. She sat back satisfied with herself, until she realized I was staring at her. She turned her attention to me eagerly.

I don't know what happened to me then, but I went somewhere.

She asked, "What was it like in the U.S.?" "Well, this year we had a march on Washington. Millions and millions of people. We marched under our banner. Our rainbow flag. We have a flag, you know, and we marched."

"Did people hold hands in public?"

"Hold hands?" I said. "They held hands, kissed. Women had their tops off and were wearing T-shirts that had Hillary and Tipper together, the first lady and the vice president's wife, and Bill and Al together, the president and the vice president."

"*Mentira?*"

"No, I'm not kidding. The best cities in the U.S. are gay meccas, sexual havens: New York, San Francisco, Los Angeles. People get married at commitment ceremonies; they adopt kids, pets. We have gay TV. There's a show called *Dyke TV.* You know what they had on their first show? A section on health. This woman gets up on a chair, puts her feet on stirrups, and she doesn't have any underwear on. No underwear, and she takes a mirror, gets right up to the camera, inserts the speculum, and shows you how to give yourself a pelvic exam. Right there in front of the camera. On national TV. Spread-eagled. *Patas abiertos.* That's how it is. We got gay clubs, gay T-shirts, gay flag, gay TV."

I saw Maria going into reverie. I imagined her crossing the Atlantic in a tattered raft with one oar, fighting off sharks and rowing, rowing to gay paradise. I had created a paradise. A paradise where there was an absence of gay bashing, and there was no correlation between teen suicide and their sexuality, and institutionalized religion did not hate the sin or the sinner, but welcomed us with open arms, and the military did not have a policy of "don't ask, don't tell," and sodomy was not a crime in any of the fifty states.

"Well," I said, "Maria, it's not quite like that, so let me tell you."

In Cuba I met a very successful academic who, I was told, had been responsible in the '70s for gay witch-hunts in the arts community. But my last day in Cuba had a more hopeful and fitting end. I spent it in the company of a group of Cuban artists and met Pedro Luis Ferrer, a Cuban composer. He gave me a tape of a song he had written called *"Todos por Lo Mismo,"* "Everybody for the Same Thing." In it, he calls for society to include all people: atheists, capitalists, homosexuals.

Three years after my trip to Cuba I was performing a show called "Milk of Amnesia" in Chicago. The piece was based on my trip to Cuba in '93. There I met a reporter who said she wanted to introduce me to a new Cuban émigré who had left Cuba to live with her lover in the States.

It took me a second to recognize her. She had put on weight, and her hair was no longer blonde, but that raspy deep voice of a smoker I would recognize anywhere. She was the married woman I had met at the party in El Vedado. So my radar had not been wrong after all.

Bionotes

Nancy Abrams is the author of *The Other Mother: A Lesbian's Fight for Her Daughter* (University of Wisconsin Press, 1999), which was named among the top ten books of the year by *Chicago Pride Magazine* and among the ten best-selling books for women by *Lambda Book Report. Girlfriends Magazine* called it "a must read."

Donna Allegra's *Witness to the League of Blond Hip Hop Dancers: A Novella and Short Stories* was published by Alyson Books (2000). Her poetry, essays, and fiction have been included in more than thirty lesbian/feminist journals that run the gamut from the ground-breaking *Conditions: Five, The Black Women's Issue* to *Sinister Wisdom, Harrington Lesbian Fiction Quarterly,* and *Common Lives/Lesbian Lives.* Her writing appears in such anthologies as *Home Girls: A Black Feminist Anthology,* edited by Barbara Smith (Kitchen Table, 1983; recently rereleased); *Dyke Life: From Growing Up to Growing Old, a Celebration of the Lesbian Experience,* edited by Karla Jay (Basic Books, 1995); *Best Lesbian Erotica 1997,* edited by Tristan Taormino and Jewelle Gomez (Cleis Press, 1997); *Best Lesbian Erotica 1999,* edited by Tristan Taormino and Chrystos (Cleis Press, 1999); *Hers: Brilliant New Fiction by Lesbians* and *Hers 3: Brilliant New Fiction by Lesbian Writers,* edited by Terry Wolverton with Robert Drake (Faber & Faber, 1999); *Does Your Mama Know? An Anthology of Black Lesbian Coming Out Stories,* edited by Lisa C. Moore (RedBone Press, 1997); *Hot and Bothered: Short Short Fiction on Lesbian Desire* and *Hot and Bothered 2,* edited by Karen X. Tulchinsky (Arsenal Pulp Press, 1998 and 1999); and *Lesbian Travels: A Literary Companion,* edited by Lucy Jane Bledsoe (Whereabouts Press, 1998).

Gloria E. Anzaldúa is a Chicana *patlache* (Nahuatl word for dyke) feminist writer. She lives by the sea in Santa Cruz, California. Her most recent anthology is *This Bridge We Call Home: Radical Visions for Transformation,* coedited with AnaLouise Keating (Routledge, 2002). The third edition of

This Bridge Called My Back: Writings by Radical Women of Color was reissued by Third Woman Press in 2002. Another recent book, *Interviews/ Entrevistas: Gloria E. Anzaldúa* (Routledge, 2000), edited by AnaLouise Keating, won the Susan Koppelmann Award and was nominated for a Lambda Literary Award. *Borderlands / La Frontera: The New Mestiza* (Spinsters/Aunt Lute Foundation Books, 1987) was chosen as one of the one hundred best books of the century by both *Hungry Mind Review* and *Utne Reader.* Anzaldúa is also the author of two bilingual children's picture books: *Friends from the Other Side / Amigos del otro lado* (Children's Book Press, 1993) and *Prietita and the Ghost Woman / Prietita y la Llorona* (Children's Book Press, 1995). She edited *Making Face, Making Soul / Haciendo Caras: Creative and Critical Perspectives by Feminists of Color,* winner of the Lambda Lesbian Small Book Press Award (Spinsters/Aunt Lute Foundation Books, 1990). Her most recent award is the American Studies Association's lifetime achievement award.

Marie-Claire Blais has published twenty novels in Quebec and France, all of which have been published in English as well. The best-known titles include *The Angel of Solitude* (Talonbooks, 1993), *Anna's World* (L. & O. Dennys, 1985), *Deaf to the City* (Overlook Press, 1987), *Mad Shadows* (McClelland and Stewart, 1960), *The Manuscripts of Pauline Archange* (Farrar, Straus & Giroux, 1970), and *Nights in the Underground: An Exploration of Love* (Musson Book Co., 1979). Her *Une saison dans la vie d'Emmanuel* (Grasset, 1966) was awarded France's Prix Médicis. Her latest novel, *Soifs* (Boréal and Éditions du Seuil, 1995), which is translated as *These Festive Nights* (Anansi, 1997), won the Governor General's Award in Canada in 1997. Awards such as the Canadian-Belgium Prize in 1976 and the France-Quebec Prize have meant that Blais can devote her life to her writing. She is also a playwright, and in 1998 her collection of plays, *Wintersleep,* was published by Ronsdale Press. Blais has lived in Canada, France, China, and the United States for extended periods of time. "Tenderness," in this volume, first appeared in her collection of nine short stories and a novella, *The Exile and The Sacred Travellers* (Ronsdale Press, 2000).

Mary Cappello, professor of English at the University of Rhode Island, is the author of *Night Bloom: A Memoir* (Beacon Press, 1998). Her most recent literary nonfiction publications include "Moscow, 9/11," an essay about teaching and living in Moscow, Russia, after September 11, in the journal *Raritan;* "Fatso" (after the Anne Bancroft film), an essay on watching movies with a friend who was terminally ill, in *The Milk of Almonds: Italian American Women Writers on Food and Culture* (edited by Louise DeSalvo and Edvige Giunta); "Voices in the Outer Room," an essay on a queer aesthetics of (non)disclosure, in *Lesbian Self-Writing: The Embodiment of Experience,* edited by Lynda Hall (Harrington Park Press, 2000); and "Circus of Desire," an experimental portrait piece in *Harrington Lesbian Fiction Quarterly.* Following a tradition of queer portraiture (e.g., Stein, H.D., Plante, Als) and queer theory (especially Foucault and Sedgwick), she has just completed a manuscript entitled "Appearances: Scenes from a Queer Friendship," an attempt to enact the forms, literary and relational, made possible by a friendship between a gay man and a lesbian. Currently she is collaborating with Italian photographer Paola Ferrario to document the lives of new immigrants to Italy in word and image. Their project *"Pane Amaro /* Bitter Bread: The Struggle of New Immigrants to Italy" won the Dorothea Lange–Paul Taylor Prize from the Center for Documentary Studies at Duke University.

Maya Chowdhry is an award-winning poet and playwright. She writes lyrical drama for radio, the Web, the page and stage. Her writing career began when she won the BBC Radio Young Playwrights Festival in 1991 with *Monsoon* and the Cardiff International Poetry Competition in 1992 with *Brides of Dust.* Her first stage play, *Kaahini,* was nominated for Best Children's Theatre by the Writers' Guild. She has continually crossed boundaries and produced vibrant, challenging work. In 2000 she received a Year of the Artist Research and Development Award for *Destiny*—a digital poetic tapestry. As an inTer-aCt-ive artist her recent online writing includes www.foundland.net, and Internet Writing collaboration and she is KODE Electronic Writer in Residence with Jubilee Arts. Her stage plays include *Sanctuary,* a multi-level interactive theatre experience (Yorkshire Women Theatre); *Seeing* (workshopped at The Royal Court Theatre); *Kaahini* (Birmingham Repertory company, Red Ladder Theatre Company; National Tour); *An Appetite for Living* (West Yorkshire Playhouse); and *Splinters* (Bradford Theatre in the Mill, Talawa Theatre at The Lyric Studio). She was a writer-on-attachment at the National Theatre Studio in 2002 and is currently under commission with The National Theatre: Shell Connections.

Rini Das was born in Calcutta and spent the first twenty-two years of her life there. Presently, she lives in Columbus, Ohio, with her mate. She has bachelor's and master's degrees in mathematics and a master's in economics. Her writing appears in a variety of journals and books, including *The Asian Pacific American Journal* (1993); *Our Feet Walk the Sky* (Spinsters/ Aunt Lute Press, 1993); *The Very Inside,* edited by Sharon Lim-Hing (Sister Vision Press, 1994); *Fireweed: A Feminist Quarterly* (Spring 1994); and *Dyke Life,* edited by Karla Jay (Basic Books, 1995).

Emma Donoghue was born in Dublin, Ireland, in 1969. She studied English and French at University College Dublin before moving to Cambridge, England, where she earned her Ph.D. in English ("Male-Female Friendship and English Fiction in the Mid-Eighteenth Century") in 1997. Her first book was *Passions between Women: British Lesbian Culture, 1668–1801* (HarperCollins,1993), after which she edited *Poems between Women: Four Centuries of Love, Romantic Friendship, and Desire* (Columbia University Press, 1997; published in the United Kingdom as *What Sappho Would Have Said,* Hamish Hamilton, 1997) and *The Mammoth Book of Lesbian Short Stories* (Carroll & Graf, 1999). Her first biography, a study of two Victorian lesbian lovers and collaborative poets, was *We Are Michael Field* (Absolute Press, 1998). Donoghue is best known for her fiction. *Stir-fry* (HarperCollins, 1994) and *Hood* (HarperCollins, 1995) are contemporary novels set in Dublin. *Kissing the Witch: Old Tales in New Skins* (HarperCollins, 1997) is a sequence of rewritten fairy tales. She has published contemporary and historical short stories in anthologies in Ireland, Britain, the United States, and Canada. Her novels have been translated into German, Dutch, Swedish, Hebrew, and Catalan. She has also written plays for stage (*I Know My Own Heart, Ladies and Gentlemen,* and *Kissing the Witch,* adapted from her book) and radio. She has served as a judge for the Irish Times Literary Prizes. Her most recent books are historical fiction: *Slammerkin* (Virago, 2000) was a main selection of the Book-of-the-Month Club and won the Ferro-Grumley Award for Lesbian Fiction, and *The Woman Who Gave Birth to Rabbits* (Harcourt, 2002) is a sequence of short stories about peculiar incidents in the history of the British Isles. Since 1998 she has lived in Canada.

Marion Douglas lives and works in Calgary, Alberta, as a psychologist with the school board. She has two children and one girlfriend. Her stories have been published in literary journals in Canada. She is the author of three novels: *The Doubtful Guests* (Orca, 1993), *Bending at the Bow* (Press Gang, 1995), and *Magic Eight Ball* (Polestar, 2000). She is currently working on her fourth and fifth novels.

Jewelle Gomez is the author of six books, including *Don't Explain* (Firebrand, 1998); *Oral Tradition: Selected Poems Old and New* (Firebrand, 1995); *Forty-three Septembers: Essays* (Firebrand, 1993); *The Gilda Stories* (Firebrand, 1991), which won two Lambda Literary Awards, for fiction and for science fiction; and *Flamingoes and Bears: Poems* (1986). *The Gilda Stories* was adapted for Urban Bush Women as a play—*Bones and Ash: A Gilda Story*—and toured U.S. theaters in 1996–97. She has contributed to many anthologies, such as *On Our Backs: The Best Erotic Fiction,* edited by Lindsay McClune (Alyson Books, 2001), and *Butch/Femme: Inside Lesbian Gender,* edited by Sally Munt (Cassell, 1998). Gomez is the coeditor of *Swords of the Rainbow* (Alyson Books, 1996), an anthology of gay and lesbian fantasy and science fiction short stories. Gomez is currently the director of the Cultural Equity Grants Program at the San Francisco Arts Commission.

Lynda Hall, a 1998 Ph.D. graduate, teaches in the Department of English at the University of Calgary. Her work has been published in *a/b: Autobiographical Studies; Ariel: A Review of International English Literature; Callaloo: A Journal of Afro-American and African Arts and Letters; Canadian Theatre Review; International Journal of Sexuality and Gender Studies; Journal of Dramatic Theory and Criticism; Journal of Gay, Lesbian, and Bisexual Identity; Journal of Lesbian Studies; Postmodern Culture;* and *Tessera.* She is the editor of *Lesbian Self-Writing: The Embodiment of Experience* (Harrington Park Press, 2000) and editor of and contributor to a special volume of the *International Journal of Sexuality and Gender Studies,* entitled *Converging Terrains: Gender, Environment, Technology, and the Body* (2000).

Karla Jay lives in New York City with her partner, Karen F. Kerner, and their two Maltese dogs, Felix and Beanie. She is Distinguished Professor of English at Pace University in New York City. She has written, edited, or translated ten books, the most recent of which is *Tales of the Lavender Menace: A Memoir of Liberation* (Basic Books, 1999). Her anthology *Dyke Life: From Growing Up to Growing Old—A Celebration of the Lesbian Experience* (Basic Books, 1995) won the 1996 Lambda Literary Award in the category of Lesbian Studies. She has written for many publications, including *Ms. Magazine, New York Times Book Review, Village Voice, Lambda Book Report,* and *Gay and Lesbian Review Worldwide.* Her short stories have appeared in *The Lesbian Polyamory Reader* and *Harrington Lesbian Fiction Quarterly.* Jay is currently at work on a mystery and on a collection of satires called *Migrant Laborers in the Fields of Academe,* forthcoming from the University of Wisconsin Press.

Anna Livia was born in Dublin, Ireland, grew up in Africa, and finished her adolescence in England. She currently lives in Berkeley, California, and is the mother of three-year-old twins. She is the author of five novels, including *Bruised Fruit* (Firebrand Books, 1999), which was short-listed for a Lambda Literary Award in 2000, and two collections of short stories. On the academic front, she teaches in the French department at the University of California, Berkeley, where she earned her Ph.D. in French linguistics.

Pronoun Envy: Literary Uses of Linguistic Gender, her theoretical work, is a study of novels that experiment with nongendered pronouns, and *Queerly Phrased: Language, Gender, and Sexuality* (coedited with Kira Hall) is the first comprehensive collection of articles on language, gender, and sexuality (both published by Oxford University Press, 2001 and 1997). She likes to invent imaginary worlds with her children where magic gateways lead to faraway places and the humdrum, the horrific, and the hilarious are of a different composition.

Janet Mason lives and writes in Philadelphia, which provides the contemporary and historical background for her recently completed manuscript about mothers and daughters entitled "Tea Leaves" (from which "Violin Lessons" is excerpted). An award-winning poet, fiction writer, and radio commentator, she is currently working on a collection of essays entitled "Again, Again, and Again: Musings on the Big O and Other Essays from the Brink." She is in the process of revising her coming-of-age novel (as a hell on wheels adolescent), entitled *Hitching to Nirvana,* which has been excerpted in the 2002 Seal Press (now an imprint of Avalon) anthology *Drive: Women's True Stories from the Open Road* and received a mention in the *Kirkus Review.*

Valerie Miner is the author of ten books, including the recent novels *Range of Light* (Zoland Books, 1998) and *A Walking Fire* (State University of New York Press, 1994) and earlier novels *All Good Women* (Crossing Press, 1987), *Winter's Edge* (Crossing Press, 1985), *Movement* (Crossing Plains, 1982), *Blood Sisters: An Examination of Conscience* (St. Martin's Press, 1982), and *Murder in the English Department* (St. Martin's Press, 1982). Her work has appeared in *Salmagundi, Ploughshares, The Village Voice, Gettysburg Review, Green Mountains Review, Prairie Schooner,* and many other journals. Her honors include awards from the Rockefeller Foundation, the Bush Foundation, the Australia Council Literary Arts Board, the Fulbright Program, and other sources. She is professor of English at the University of Minnesota.

Barbara Bryce Morris is a writer and editor who has worked in the software industry and as an academic in the humanities. "Mad Dog in Chelsea" was first conceived as a Web-based animation entitled "Barrow Street." She is also the producer of a documentary film, "Half a Soulja," and lives in the West Village in Manhattan.

Lesléa Newman was born in Brooklyn in 1955 and is an author and editor whose forty books include *A Letter to Harvey Milk* (Firebrand Books,

1988); *In Every Laugh a Tear* (New Victoria, 1992); *Still Life with Buddy* (Pride and Imprints, 1997); *The Little Butch Book* (New Victoria, 1998); *Writing from the Heart: Inspiration and Exercises for Women Who Want to Write* (Crossing Press, 1993); *Fat Chance* (Putnam's, 1994); *Out of the Closet and Nothing to Wear* (Alyson Books, 1997); *My Lover Is a Woman: Contemporary Lesbian Love Poems* (Ballantine Books, 1996); *The Femme Mystique* (Alyson Books, 1995); *Girls Will Be Girls* (Alyson Books, 2000); *She Loves Me, She Loves Me Not* (Alyson Books, 2002); *Heather Has Two Mommies* (Alyson Wonderland, 1989); *Felicia's Favorite Story* (Two Lives, 2002); and *Too Far Away to Touch* (Clarion Books, 1995). Her newest book, *Best Short Stories of Lesléa Newman*, was published in June 2003 by Alyson Books. She has received many literary awards, including poetry fellowships from the Massachusetts Artists Foundation and the National Endowment for the Arts, the Highlights for Children Fiction Writing Award, the James Baldwin Awards for Cultural Achievement, two Pushcart Prize nominations, and a fiction writing grant from Money for Women/Barbara Deming Memorial Fund, Inc. Six of her books have been Lambda Literary Award finalists. In cyberspace she can be found at www.lesleanewman.com, and in the real worlds she lives in Northhampton, Massachusetts.

Vivien Ng is professor at the University at Albany, State University of New York, where she teaches women's studies, modern Chinese history, and Asian American studies. A historian by training, she has published a book and articles on Chinese legal history. She has also published short stories, including "Bus Stop" (*Common Lives/Lesbian Lives* [1995]). Before moving to Albany, she taught at the University of Oklahoma for thirteen years. She is working on a book-length project, "The Making of 'America,'" which undertakes to analyze the new social realities of the United States, using Census 2000 as a point of departure. It includes a discussion of the history of structures of oppression, as well as the commonality and intersectionality of oppressions. Additionally—and significantly—it also includes an exploration of the possibilities of a just society and strategies to create such a society in a racially and ethnically complex United States of America.

Minnie Bruce Pratt was born September 12, 1946, in Selma, Alabama, in the hospital closest to her hometown of Centreville. She received her academic education at the University of Alabama in Tuscaloosa and at the University of North Carolina at Chapel Hill, and her actual education through grass-roots organizing with women in the army-base town of Fayetteville, North Carolina, and through teaching at historically Black universities. Together with Elly Bulkin and Barbara Smith, she coauthored

Yours in Struggle: Three Feminist Perspectives on Anti-Semitism and Racism (Firebrand Books, 1988, to be reissued in a new edition in 2003 by Temple University Press). She has published three books of poetry: *The Sound of One Fork* (Night Heron Press, 1981), *We Say We Love Each Other* (Spinsters/Aunt Lute, 1985; Firebrand Books, 1992), and *Crime against Nature* (Firebrand Books, 1990). In 1989, the Academy of American Poets chose *Crime against Nature,* on Pratt's relationship with her two sons as a lesbian mother, as the Lamont Poetry Selection, and in 1991 the American Library Association gave *Crime against Nature* its Gay and Lesbian Book Award for Literature. In 1991 Pratt received, along with lesbian writers Chrystos and Audre Lorde, a Lillian Hellman–Dashiell Hammett award from the Fund for Free Expression to writers "who have been victimized by political persecution." The award recognized the three writers' experience "as a target of right-wing and fundamentalist forces during the recent attacks on the National Endowment for the Arts." In 1992 Pratt's book of autobiographical and political essays, *Rebellion: Essays 1980–1991* (Firebrand Books, 1991), was a finalist in nonfiction for a Lambda Literary Award. Her book of prose stories about gender boundary crossing, *S/HE* (Firebrand Books, 1995), was a finalist in nonfiction for the American Library Association's Gay, Lesbian, and Bisexual Book Award and for the Firecracker Award. Her fourth volume of poems, *Walking Back up Depot Street,* published in 1999 by the University of Pittsburgh Press, was chosen Best Gay/Lesbian Book of the Year by *ForeWord Magazine.* Her book of selected poems, *The Dirt She Ate,* is forthcoming from the University of Pittsburgh Press. Pratt makes her home with writer and activist Leslie Feinberg in Jersey City, New Jersey, across the river from New York City. She teaches women's studies, lesbian/gay/bisexual/transgender studies, and creative writing as a member of the graduate faculty of Union Institute, a nonresidential alternative Ph.D.-granting university

Sima Rabinowitz lives in Minneapolis, where she works as a communications professional. Her writing has appeared in a variety of publications in the United States and Canada. A play she coauthored has been produced in Saint Paul, Minnesota, and in Detroit, Michigan.

Ruthann Robson's most recent book is a collection of short fiction entitled *The Struggle for Happiness* (St. Martin's Press, 2000). Her previous books include two collections of short fiction, *Eye of a Hurricane* (1989) and *Cecile* (1991), both published by the lesbian/feminist Firebrand Books, and two novels, *Another Mother* (1995) and *a/k/a* (1997), both published by St. Martin's Press. A volume of poetry, *Masks* (introduction by Marge Piercy), was published by Leapfrog Press (1999). A volume of lesbian legal theory, *Sappho Goes to Law School,* was published by Columbia University Press (1998). She is professor of law at the City University of New York School of Law, "one of the very few progressive law schools in the world."

Sarah Schulman was born in New York City in 1958 and is currently working as a playwright. She is the author of nine novels and two nonfiction books. Her novel *After Delores* (Plume, 1989) won the American Library Association Gay/Lesbian Book Award in 1989. *People in Trouble* (Plume, 1990) was awarded the Words Project AIDS/Gregory Kolovakos Memorial Prize for fiction in 1990. Her books have been translated into German, Greek, Dutch, and Japanese. Her works for theater include the plays *The Child, Carson McCullers, Cousin Bette,* and *Correct Usage and Common Errors* and a musical adaptation of her novel *Shimmer* (Bard, 1998). In 2002 she was a Guggenheim Fellow in playwriting, and her play *Carson McCullers* was produced at New York's Playwrights Horizons.

Actor, writer, and producer **Peggy Shaw** has received three OBIE awards for her work with Split Britches, the lesbian theater company she founded with Lois Weaver and Deb Margolin in 1980. She won OBIEs for her performances in "Dress Suits to Hire," a collaboration with Holly Hughes; "Belle Reprieve," a collaboration with the London-based theater troupe BlooLips; and "Menopausal Gentleman," directed by Rebecca Taichman. Shaw and Weaver are touring their new work, *Double Agency,* in collaboration with London's Clod Ensemble. Among her other celebrated works are *You're Just Like My Father, Lust and Comfort, Upwardly Mobile Home, Lesbians Who Kill, Salad of the Bad Café,* and the Jane Chambers Award–winning play *Split Britches.* Shaw won New York Foundation for the Arts awards for Emerging Forms in 1988, 1995, and 1999 and the 1995 Anderson Foundation Stonewall Award for excellence in "making the world a better place for gays and lesbians." In addition to her work with Split Britches, she played Billy Tipton in American Place's production of Carson Kreitzer's *The Slow Drag.* She was a collaborator, writer, and performer with Spiderwoman Theater and Hot Peaches Theater and cofounder in 1980 of the OBIE-winning WOW Cafe in New York City. She was awarded a Rockefeller MAP Grant to make her new solo show, *To My Chagrin,* in residence at the Jump Start Performance Company and Esperanza Center for Peace and Justice in San Antonio, Texas. She completed it in fall 2001. In 1996 Routledge Press published *Split Britches: Lesbian Practice, Feminist Performance,* edited by Sue Ellen Case, which includes seven Split Britches' plays. Shaw teaches writing and solo performance around the world. Since 2001 Split Britches (Shaw and Weaver) has been working in prisons in London and Brazil through the Peoples Palace Projects, a creative and teaching organization dedicated to exposing human rights violations in prison systems.

Carmelita Tropicana (Cuban-born Alina Troyano) was named by El Diario/La Prensa *"una de las mujeres mas destacadas de 1998."* A performance artist, actress, and writer, she has performed her works in the United States, Canada, Mexico, and Spain. In 1999 she won an OBIE for Sustained Excellence in Performance. She has been awarded fellowships from the Cintas Foundation for her literary work and from the New York Foundation for the Arts for screenwriting/playwriting and performance art. Her book *I, Carmelita Tropicana: Performing between Cultures* (Beacon Press, 2000) is a compilation of plays, stories, and film scripts written in collaboration with Ela Troyano and Uzi Parnes. Her solo performance *Milk of Amnesia* has appeared in *The Drama Review* and in Grove Press's award-winning anthology *O Solo Homo.* She cowrote, with film director Ela Troyano, *Carmelita Tropicana: Your Kunst Is Your Waffen,* which won Best Short Film at the 1994 Berlin Film Festival. She is currently at work on "Catalina, Martina, and the Child of the Dolphins," the definitive tale of Elian Gonzalez.

Jess Wells is the author of thirteen volumes, including the novels *Aftershocks,* recently reissued as a Triangle Classic by InsightOut Books, and *The Price of Passion: An Erotic Journey* (Firebrand Books, 1999). Her latest work, *The Mandrake Broom,* is a historical novel set in the Middle Ages. She is the editor of *Home Fronts: Controversies in Nontraditional Parenting* (2000) and *Lesbians Raising Sons* (1997), both published by Alyson Books. A three-time finalist for a Lambda Literary Award, she has published five collections of short fiction. The single mother of a young son, she lives in the San Francisco Bay area.